W9-ARH-180

Cadderly creeped slowly toward the open door, never taking his gaze from the enticing blackness beyond the meager limits of his torchlight. What wonders remained down there in the oldest rooms of the Edificant Library? He wondered. What secrets long forgotten about the founders and initial scholars?

Despite his consuming curiosity for the mysteries before him, Cadderly kept enough wits about him to relize that he had been betrayed as soon as he felt a boot against his lower back.

* * * * *

The classic adventure series from the *New York Times* best-selling author of *The Dark Elf Trilogy* and *The Demon Wars Trilogy*.

* * * * *

"Bob knows how to fashion a story so that you have to keep reading—even when it's two in the morning and you have to get up a five, even though you still have more than a hundred pages to go, and even if you're so tired you have to keep telling yourself you will read only one more page, just one more, and that's all."

—Terry Brooks

The Cleric Quintet
R. A. Salvatore

Canticle

R. A. Salvatore

The Cleric Quintet – Book One

CANTICLE

Cover art by Daren Bader
First Printing: October 1991
Library of Congress Catalog Card Number: 99-65597

9 8 7 6 5 4 3 2

ISBN: 0-7869-1604-4
T21604-620

U.S., CANADA,	EUROPEAN HEADQUARTERS
ASIA, PACIFIC, & LATIN AMERICA	Wizards of the Coast, Belgium
Wizards of the Coast, Inc.	P.B. 2031
P.O. Box 707	2600 Berchem
Renton, WA 98057-0707	Belgium
+1-800-324-6496	+32-70-23-32-77

Visit our web site at **www.wizards.com**

To anyone who can honestly call himself a friend of the Earth.
And a special thanks to Brian Newton—he knows why.

—RAS

The Dells

Castle Trinity

Daione Dun
(hill of the Stars)

Syldritch Trea

Deny Ridge

Shilmista
(Forest of Shadows)

Snowflake Mountains

The Edificant Library

Impresk Lake

To Riatavin

Carradoon

Shining Stream

The Shining Stream

N

Miles
0   30

Prologue

Aballister Bonaduce looked long and hard at the shimmering image in his mirror. Mountains of wind-driven snow and ice lay endlessly before him, the most forbidding place in all the Realms. All he had to do was step through the mirror, onto the Great Glacier.

"Are you coming, Druzil?" the wizard said to his bat-winged imp.

Druzil folded his leathery wings around him as if to privately consider the question. "I am not so fond of the cold," he said, obviously not wanting to partake of this particular hunt. "Nor am I," Aballister said, slipping onto his finger an enchanted ring that would protect him from the killing cold. "But only on the Great Glacier does the *yote* grow." Aballister looked back to the scene in the magical mirror, one final barrier to the completion of his quest and the beginning of his conquests. The snowy region was quiet now, though dark clouds hung ominously overhead and promised an impending storm that would delay the hunt, perhaps for many days.

"There we must go," Aballister continued, talking more to himself than to the imp. His voice trailed away as he sank within his memories, to the turning point in his life more than two years before, in the Time of Troubles. He had been powerful even then, but directionless.

The avatar of the goddess Talona had shown him the way.

Aballister's grin became an open chuckle as he turned back to regard Druzil, the imp who had delivered to him the method to best please the Lady of Poison. "Come, dear Druzil," Aballister said. "You brought the recipe for the chaos curse. You must come along and help to find its last ingredient."

The imp straightened and unfolded his wings at the mention of the chaos curse. This time he offered no arguments. A lazy flap brought him to Aballister's shoulder and together they walked through the magical mirror and into the blowing wind.

* * * * *

The hunched and hairy creature, resembling a more primitive form of human, grunted and growled and threw its crude spear, though Aballister and Druzil were surely far out of range. It howled again anyway, triumphantly, as though its throw had served some symbolic victory, and scooted back to the large gathering of its shaggy white kin.

"I believe they do not wish to bargain," Druzil said, shuffling about from clawed foot to clawed foot on Aballister's shoulder.

The wizard understood his familiar's excitement. Druzil was a creature of the lower planes, a creature of chaos, and he wanted desperately to see his wizard master deal with the impudent fools—just an added pleasure to this long-awaited, victorious day.

"They are taer," Aballister explained, recognizing the tribe, "crude and fierce. You are quite correct. They'll not bargain."

Aballister's eyes flashed suddenly and Druzil hopped again and clapped his hands together.

"They know not the might before them!" Aballister cried,

his voice rising with his ire. All the terrible trials of two long and brutal years rolled through the wizard's thoughts in the span of a few seconds. A hundred men had died in search of the elusive ingredients for the chaos curse; a hundred men had given their lives so that Talona would be pleased. Aballister, too, had not escaped unscathed. Completing the curse had become his obsession, the driving force in his life, and he had aged with every step, had torn out clumps of his own hair every time the curse seemed to be slipping beyond his reach.

Now he was close, so close that he could see the dark patch of *yote* just beyond the small ridge that held the taer cave complexes. So close, but these wretched, idiotic creatures stood in his way.

Aballister's words had stirred the taer. They grumbled and hopped about in the shadow of the jagged mountain, shoving each other forward as if trying to select a leader to start their charge.

"Do something quickly," Druzil suggested from his perch.

Aballister looked up at him and nearly laughed. "They will attack," Druzil explained, trying to sound unconcerned, "and, worse, this cold stiffens my wings."

Aballister nodded at the imp's rationale. Any delay could cost him, especially if the dark clouds broke into a blinding blizzard, one that would hide both the *yote* and the shimmering doorway back to Aballister's comfortable room. He pulled out a tiny ball, a mixture of bat guano and sulphur, crushed it in his fist, and pointed one finger at the group of taer. His chant echoed off the mountain face and back across the empty glacier ice, and he smiled, thinking it wonderfully ironic that the stupid taer had no idea of what he was doing.

A moment later, they found out.

Just before his spell discharged, Aballister had a cruel thought and lifted the angle of his pointing finger. The fireball exploded above the heads of the startled taer, disintegrating the frozen bindings of the ice mountain. Huge blocks rained down, and a great rush of water swallowed those who had not

been crushed. Several of the band floundered about in the ice
and liquid morass, too stunned and overwhelmed to gain their
footing as the pool quickly solidified around them.

One pitiful creature did manage to struggle free, but
Druzil hopped off Aballister's shoulder and swooped down
upon him.

The imp's claw-tipped tail whipped out as he passed by the
stumbling creature, and Aballister applauded heartily.

The taer clutched at its stung shoulder, looked curiously
at the departing imp, then fell dead to the ice.

"What of the rest?" Druzil asked, landing back on his perch.
Aballister considered the remaining taer, most dead, but some
struggling futilely against the tightening grip of ice.

"Leave them to their slow deaths," he replied, and he
laughed evilly again.

Druzil gave him an incredulous look. "The Lady of Poison
would not approve," the imp said, wagging his wicked tail
before him with one hand.

"Very well," Aballister replied, though he realized that
Druzil was more interested in pleasing himself than Talona.
Still, the reasoning was sound; poison was always the accepted method for completing Talona's work. "Go and finish
the task," Aballister instructed the imp. "I will get the *yote*."

A short while later, Aballister plucked the last gray-brown
mushroom from its stubborn grasp on the glacier and dropped
it into his bag. He called over to Druzil, who was toying with
the last whining taer, snapping his tail back and forth around
the terrified creature's frantically jerking head—the only part
of the taer that was free of the ice trap.

"Enough," Aballister said firmly.

Druzil sighed and looked mournfully at the approaching wizard. Aballister's visage did not soften. "Enough," he
said again.

Druzil bent over and kissed the taer on the nose. The creature stopped whimpering and looked at him curiously, but
Druzil only shrugged and drove his poison-tipped stinger

straight into the taer's weepy eye.

The imp eagerly accepted the offered perch on Aballister's shoulder. Aballister let him hold the bag of *yote*, just to remind the somewhat distracted imp that more important matters awaited them beyond the shimmering door.

One

The White Squirrel's Pet

The green-robed druid issued a series of chit-chits and clucks, but the white-furred squirrel seemed oblivious to it all, sitting on a branch in the towering oak tree high above the three men.

"Well, you seem to have lost your voice," remarked another of the men, a bearded woodland priest with gentle-looking features and thick blond hair hanging well below his shoulders.

"Can you call the beast any better than I?" the green-robed druid asked indignantly. "I fear that this creature is strange in more ways than its coat."

The other two laughed at their companion's attempt to explain his ineptitude.

"I grant you," said the third of the group, the highest ranking initiate, "the squirrel's color is beyond the usual, but speaking to animals is among the easiest of our abilities. Surely by now—"

"With all respect," the frustrated druid interrupted, "I have made contact with the creature. It just refuses to reply.

6

Try yourself, I invite you."

"A squirrel refusing to speak?" asked the second of the group with a chuckle. "Surely they are among the chattiest—"

"Not that one," came a reply from behind. The three druids turned to see a priest coming down the wide dirt road from the ivy-streaked building, the skip of youth evident in his steps.

He was of average height and build, though perhaps more muscular than most, with gray eyes that turned up at their corners when he smiled and curly brown locks that bounced under the wide brim of his hat. His tan-white tunic and trousers showed him to be a priest of Deneir, god of one of the host sects of the Edificant Library. Unlike most within his order, though, this young man also wore a decorative light blue silken cape and a wide-brimmed hat, also blue and banded in red, with a plume on the right-hand side. Set in the band's center was a porcelain-and-gold pendant depicting a candle burning above an eye, the symbol of Deneir.

"That squirrel is tight-lipped, except when he chooses not to be," the young priest went on. The normally unflappable druids' stunned expressions amused him, so he decided to startle them a bit more. "Well met, Arcite, Newander, and Cleo. I congratulate you, Cleo, on your ascension to the status of initiate."

"How do you know of us?" asked Arcite, the druid leader.

"We have not yet reported to the library and have told no one of our coming." Arcite and Newander, the blond-haired priest, exchanged suspicious glances, and Arcite's voice became stern. "Have your masters been scrying, looking for us with magical means?"

"No, no, nothing like that," the young priest replied immediately, knowing the secretive druids' aversion to such tactics. "I remember you, all three, from your last visit to the library."

"Preposterous!" piped in Cleo. "That was fourteen years ago. You could not have been more than . . ."

"A boy," answered the young priest. "So I was, seven years old. You had a fourth to your party, as I recall, an aging lady of great powers. Shannon, I believe was her name!"

"Incredible," muttered Arcite. "You are correct, young priest." Again the druids exchanged concerned looks, suspecting trickery here. Druids were not overly fond of anyone not of their order; they rarely came to the renowned Edificant Library, sitting high in the secluded Snowflake Mountains, and then only when they had word of a discovery of particular interest, a rare tome of herbs or animals, or a new recipe for potions to heal wounds or better grow their gardens. As a group, they began to turn away, rudely, but then Newander, on a sudden impulse, spun back around to face the young priest, who now leaned casually on a fine walking stick, its silver handle sculpted masterfully into the image of a ram's head.

"Cadderly?" Newander asked through a widening grin. Arcite, too, recognized the young man and remembered the unusual story of the most unusual child. Cadderly had come to live at the library before his fifth birthday—rarely were any accepted before the age of ten. His mother had died several months before that, and his father, too immersed in studies of his own, had neglected the child. Thobicus, the dean of the Edificant Library, had heard of the promising boy and had generously taken him in.

"Cadderly," Arcite echoed. "Is that really you?"

"At your service," Cadderly replied, bowing low, "and well met. I am honored that you remember me, good Newander and venerable Arcite."

"Who?" Cleo whispered, looking curiously to Newander.

Cleo's face, too, brightened in recognition a few moments later.

"Yes, you were just a boy," said Newander, "an overly curious little boy, as I recall!"

"Forgive me," said Cadderly, bowing again. "One does not often find the opportunity to converse with a troupe of druids!"

"Few would care to," remarked Arcite, "but you . . . are

among that few, so it would appear."

Cadderly nodded, but his smile suddenly disappeared. "I pray that nothing has happened to Shannon," he said, truly concerned. The druid had treated him well on that long-ago occasion. She had shown him beneficial plants, tasty roots, and had made flowers bloom before his eyes. To Cadderly's astonishment, Shannon had transformed herself, an ability of the most powerful druids, into a graceful swan and had flown high into the morning sky. Cadderly had dearly wished to join her—he remembered that longing most vividly—but the druid had no power to similarly transform him.

"Nothing terrible, if that is what you mean," replied Arcite. "She died several years back, peacefully."

Cadderly nodded. He was about to offer his condolences, but he prudently remembered that druids neither feared nor lamented death, seeing it as the natural conclusion to life and a rather unimportant event in the overall scheme of universal order.

"Do you know this squirrel?" asked Cleo suddenly, determined to restore his reputation.

"Percival," Cadderly replied, "a friend of mine."

"A pet?" Newander asked, his bright eyes narrowing suspiciously. Druids did not approve of people keeping pets.

Cadderly laughed heartily. "If any is the pet in our relationship, I fear it is I," he said honestly. "Percival accepts my strokes—sometimes—and my food—rather eagerly—but as I am more interested in him than he in me, he is the one who decides when and where."

The druids shared Cadderly's laugh. "A most excellent beast," said Arcite, then with a series of clicks and chits, he congratulated Percival.

"Wonderful," came Cadderly's sarcastic response, "encourage him." The druids' laughter increased and Percival, watching it all from his high branch, shot Cadderly a supercilious look.

"Well, come down here and say hello!" Cadderly called, banging the lowest tree branch with his walking stick. "Be polite, at least."

Percival did not look up from the acorn he was munching. "He does not understand, I fear," said Cleo. "Perhaps if I translate . . ."

"He understands," Cadderly insisted, "as well as you or I. He is just a stubborn one, and I can prove it!" He looked back up to the squirrel. "When you find the time, Percival," he said slyly, "I left a plate of cacasa-nut and butter out for you in my room . . ." Before Cadderly even finished, the squirrel whipped off along a branch, hopped to another, and then to the next tree in line along the road. In a few short moments, the squirrel had leaped to a gutter along the library's roof and, not slowing a bit, zipped across a trail of thick ivy and in through an open window on the northern side of the large structure's third floor.

"Percival does have such a weakness for cacasa-nut and butter," Cadderly remarked when the druids' laughter had subsided.

"A most excellent beast!" Arcite said again. "And yourself, Cadderly, it is good to see that you have remained with your studies. Your masters spoke highly of your potential fourteen years ago, but I had no idea that your memory would be so very sharp or, perhaps, that we druids had left such a strong and favorable impression upon you."

"It is," Cadderly replied quietly, "and you did! I am glad that you have returned—for the recently uncovered treatise on woodland mosses, I would assume. I have not seen it yet. The headmasters have kept it secured until those more knowledgeable in such matters could come and appraise its value. You see, a band of druids was not wholly unexpected, though we knew not who, how many, or when you would arrive."

The three druids nodded, admiring the ivy-veiled stone structure. The Edificant Library had stood for six hundred years, and in all that time its doors had never been closed to scholars of any but the evil religions. The building was huge, a self-contained town—it had to be, in the rough and secluded Snowflakes—more than four hundred feet across and half as deep through all four of its above-ground levels. Well staffed and well stocked—rumors spoke of miles of storage tunnels and catacombs beneath—it had survived orc attacks, giant-hurled boulders, and the most brutal mountain winters, and had remained unscathed through the centuries.

The library's collection of books, parchments, and artifacts was considerable, filling nearly the entire first floor, the library proper, and many smaller study chambers on the second floor, and the complex contained many unique and ancient works.

While not as large as the great libraries of the Realms, such as the treasured collections of Silverymoon to the north and the artifact museums of Calimport to the south, the Edificant Library was convenient to the west-central Realms and the Cormyr region and was open to all who wished to learn, on the condition that they did not plan to use their knowledge for baneful purposes.

The building housed other important research tools, such as alchemy and herbalist shops, and was set in an inspiring atmosphere with breathtaking mountain views and manicured grounds that included a small topiary garden. The Edificant Library had been designed as more than a storage house for old books; it was a place for poetry reading, painting, and sculpting, a place for discussions of the profound and often unanswerable questions common to the intelligent races. Indeed, the library was a fitting tribute to Deneir and Oghma, the allied gods of knowledge, literature, and art.

"The treatise is a large work, so I have been told," said Arcite. "Much time will be expended in examining it properly. I pray that the boarding rates are not excessive. We are men of little material means."

"Dean Thobicus will take you in without cost, I would expect," answered Cadderly. "Your service cannot be underestimated in this matter." He shot a wink at Arcite. "If not, come to me. I recently inscribed a tome for a nearby wizard, a spellbook he lost in a fire. The man was generous. You see, I had originally inscribed the spellbook, and the wizard, forgetful as most wizards seem to be, never had made a copy."

"The work was unique?" Cleo asked, shaking his head in disbelief that a wizard could be so foolish with his most prized possession.

"It was," Cadderly replied, tapping his temple, "except for in here."

"You remembered the intricacies of a wizard's spellbook enough to recreate it from memory?" Cleo asked, stunned.

Cadderly shrugged his shoulders. "The wizard was generous."

"Truly you are a remarkable one, young Cadderly," said Arcite.

"A most excellent beast?" the young priest asked hopefully, drawing wide smiles from all three.

"Indeed!" said Arcite. "Do look in on us in the days ahead."

Given the druids' reputation for seclusion, Cadderly understood how great a compliment he had just been paid. He bowed low, and the druids did likewise, then they bid Cadderly farewell and moved up the road to the library.

Cadderly watched them, then looked up to his open window.

Percival sat on the sill, determinedly licking the remains of his cacasa-nut and butter lunch from his tiny paws.

*　*　*　*　*

A tiny drop slipped off the end of the coil, touching a saturated cloth that led down into a small beaker. Cadderly shook his head and put a hand on the spigot controlling the flow.

"Remove your hand from that!" cried the frantic alchemist from a workbench across his shop. He jumped up and stormed over to the too-curious young priest.

"It is terribly slow," Cadderly remarked.

"It has to be," Vicero Belago explained for perhaps the

hundredth time. "You are no fool, Cadderly. You know better than to be impatient. This is *Oil of Impact*, remember? A most volatile substance. A stronger drip could cause a cataclysm in a shop so filled with unstable potions!"

Cadderly sighed and accepted the scolding with a conceding nod. "How much do you have for me?" he asked, reaching into one of the many pouches on his belt and producing a tiny vial.

"You are so very impatient," remarked Belago, but Cadderly knew that he was not really angry. Cadderly was a prime customer and had many times provided important translations of archaic alchemical notes. "Only what is in the beaker, I fear. I had to wait for some ingredients—hill giant fingernails and crushed oxen horn."

Cadderly gently lifted the soaked cloth and tilted the beaker.

It contained just a few drops, enough to fill only one of his tiny vials. "That makes six," he said, using the cloth to coax the liquid into the vial. "Forty-four to go."

"Are you confident that you want that many?" Belago asked him, not for the first time.

"Fifty," Cadderly declared.

"The price . . ."

"Well worth it!" Cadderly laughed as he secured his vial and skipped out of the shop. His spirits did not diminish as he moved down the hall to the southern wing of the third floor and the chambers of Histra, a visiting priestess of Sune, Goddess of Love.

"Dear Cadderly," greeted the priestess, who was twenty years Cadderly's senior but quite alluring. She wore a deep crimson habit, cut low in the front and high on the sides, revealing most of her curvy figure. Cadderly had to remind himself to keep his manners proper and his gaze on her eyes.

"Do come in," Histra purred. She grabbed the front of Cadderly's tunic and yanked him into the room, pointedly shutting the door behind him.

He managed to glance away from Histra long enough to

see a brightly glowing object shining through a heavy blanket.

"Is it finished?" Cadderly asked squeakily. He cleared his throat, embarrassed.

Histra ran a finger lightly down his arm and smiled at his involuntary shudder. "The dweomer is cast," she replied. "All that remains is payment."

"Two hundred . . . gold pieces," Cadderly stammered, "as we agreed." He reached for a pouch, but Histra's hand intercepted his.

"It was a difficult spell," she said, "a variation of the norm." She paused and gave a coy smile. "But I do so love variations," Histra declared teasingly. "The price could be less, you know, for you."

Cadderly did not doubt that his gulp was heard out in the hallway. He was a disciplined scholar and had come here for a specific purpose. He had much work to do, but Histra's allure was undeniable and her fine perfume overpowering. Cadderly reminded himself to breathe.

"We could forget the gold payment altogether," Histra offered, her fingers smoothly tracing the outline of Cadderly's ear. The young scholar wondered if he might fall over.

In the end, though, an image of spirited Danica sitting on Histra's back, casually rubbing the priestess's face across the floor, brought Cadderly under control. Danica's room was not far away, just across the hall and a few doors down. He firmly removed Histra's hand from his ear, handed her the pouch as payment, and scooped up the shrouded, glowing object.

For all his practicality, though, when Cadderly exited the chambers two hundred gold pieces poorer, he feared that his face was shining as brightly as the disk Histra had enchanted for him.

Cadderly had other business—he always did—but, not wanting to arouse suspicions by roaming about the library with an eerily glowing pouch, he made straight for the north wing and his own room. Percival was still on the windowsill when he entered, basking in the late morning sun.

"I have it!" Cadderly said excitedly, taking out the disk. The room immediately brightened, as if in full sunlight, and the startled squirrel darted for the shadows under Cadderly's bed.

Cadderly didn't take time to reassure Percival. He rushed to his desk and, from the jumbled and overfilled side drawer, produced a cylinder a foot long and two inches in diameter.

With a slight twist, Cadderly removed the casing from the back end, revealing a slot just large enough for the disk. He eagerly dropped the disk in and replaced the casing, shielding the light.

"I know you are under there," Cadderly teased, and he popped the metal cap off the front end of the tube, loosing a focused beam of light.

Percival didn't particularly enjoy the spectacle. He darted back and forth under the bed, and Cadderly, laughing that he had finally gotten the best of the sneaky squirrel, followed him diligently with the light. This went on for a few moments, until Percival dashed out from under the bed and hopped out the open window. The squirrel returned a second later, though, just long enough to snatch up the cacasa-nut and butter bowl and chatter a few uncomplimentary remarks to Cadderly.

Still laughing, the young priest capped his new toy and hung it on his belt, then moved to his oaken wardrobe. Most of the library's host priests kept their closets stocked with extra vestments, wanting always to look their best for the continual stream of visiting scholars. In Cadderly's wardrobe, however, the packed clothing took up just a small fraction of the space.

Piles of notes and even larger piles of various inventions cluttered the floor, and custom-designed leather belts and straps took up most of the hanging bar. Also, hanging inside one of the doors was a large mirror, an extravagance far beyond the meager purses of most other priests at the library, particularly the younger, lower-ranking ones such as Cadderly.

Cadderly took out a wide bandoleer and moved to the bed. The leather shoulder harness contained fifty specially made darts and, with the vial he had taken from the alchemist's shop, Cadderly was about to complete the sixth. The darts were small and narrow and made of iron, except for silver tips, and their centers were hollowed to the exact size of the vials.

Cadderly flinched as he eased the vial into the dart, trying to exert enough pressure to snap it into place without breaking it.

"Oil of Impact," he reminded himself, conjuring images of blackened fingertips.

The young scholar breathed easier when the volatile potion was properly set. He removed his silken cape, meaning to put on the bandoleer and go to the mirror to see how it fit, as he always did after completing another dart, but a sharp rap on his door gave him just enough time to place the leather belt behind him before Headmaster Avery Schell, a rotund and redfaced man, burst in.

"What are these calls for payment?" the priest cried, waving a stack of parchments at Cadderly. He began peeling them off and tossing them to the floor as he read their banners. "Leatherworker, silversmith, weaponsmith . . . You are squandering your gold!"

Over Avery's shoulder, Cadderly noticed the toothy smile of Kierkan Rufo and knew where the headmaster had gained his information and the fuel for his ire. The tall and sharp-featured Rufo was only a year older than Cadderly, and the two, while friends, were principal rivals in their ascent through the ranks of their order, and possibly in other pursuits as well, considering a few longing stares Cadderly had seen Rufo toss Danica's way. Getting each other into trouble had become a game between them, a most tiresome game as far as the headmasters, particularly the beleaguered Avery, were concerned.

"The money was well spent, Headmaster," Cadderly began tentatively, well aware that his and Avery's interpretations of "well spent" differed widely. "In pursuit of knowledge."

"In pursuit of toys," Rufo remarked with a snicker from the doorway, and Cadderly noted the tall man's satisfied expression. Cadderly had earned the headmaster's highest praise for his work on the lost spellbook, to his rival's obvious dismay, and Rufo was obviously enjoying bringing Cadderly back down.

"You are too irresponsible to be allowed to keep such sums!" Avery roared, heaving the rest of the parchments into the air. "You have not the wisdom."

"I kept only a portion of the profits," Cadderly reminded him, "and spent that in accord with Deneir's—"

"No!" Avery interrupted. "Do not hide behind a name that you obviously do not understand. Deneir. What do you know of Deneir, young inventor? You have spent all but your earliest years here in the Edificant Library, but you display so little understanding of our tenets and mores. Go south to Lantan with your toys, if that would please you, and play with the priests of Gond!"

"I do not understand."

"Indeed you do not," Avery answered, his tone becoming almost resigned. He paused for a long moment, and Cadderly recognized that he was choosing his words very carefully.

"We are a center of learning," the headmaster began. "We impose few restrictions upon those who wish to come here— even Gondsmen have ventured through our doors. You have seen them, but have you noticed that they were never warmly received?"

Cadderly thought for a moment, then nodded. Indeed, he remembered clearly that Avery had gone out of his way to keep him from meeting the Gondish priests every time they visited the library. "You are correct, and I do not understand," Cadderly replied. "I should think that priests of Deneir and Gond, dedicated to knowledge, would act as partners."

Avery shook his head slowly and very determinedly. "There you err," he said. "We put a condition on knowledge that the Gondsmen do not follow." He paused and shook his head again, a simple action that stung Cadderly more than any wild screaming fit Avery had ever launched at him.

"Why are you here?" Avery asked quietly, in controlled tones. "Have you ever asked yourself that question? You frustrate me, boy. You are perhaps the most intelligent person I have ever known—and I have known quite a few scholars—but you possess the impulses and emotions of a child. I knew it would be like this. When Thobicus said we would take you in . . ." Avery stopped abruptly, as if reconsidering his words, then finished with a sigh.

It seemed to Cadderly that the headmaster always stopped short of finishing this same, beleaguered point about morality, stopped short of preaching, as though he expected Cadderly to come to conclusions of his own. Cadderly was not surprised a moment later when Avery abruptly changed the subject.

"What of your duties while you sit here in your 'pursuit of knowledge'?" the headmaster asked, his voice filling with anger once again. "Did you bother to light the candles in the study chambers this morning?"

Cadderly flinched. He knew he had forgotten something.

"I did not think so," Avery said. "You are a valuable asset to our order, Cadderly, and undeniably gifted as both a scholar and scribe, but, I warn you, your behavior is far from acceptable." Avery's face flushed bright red as Cadderly, still not properly sorting through the headmaster's concerns for him, met his unblinking stare.

Cadderly was almost used to these scoldings; it was Avery who always came rushing to investigate Rufo's claims. Cadderly did not think that a bad thing; Avery, for all his fuming, was surely more lenient than some of the other, older, headmasters.

Avery turned suddenly, nearly knocking Rufo over, and stormed down the hallway, sweeping the angular man up in his wake.

Cadderly shrugged and tried to dismiss the whole incident

as another of Headmaster Avery's misplaced explosions. Avery obviously just didn't understand him. The young priest wasn't overly worried; his scribing skills brought in huge amounts of money, which he split evenly with the library. Admittedly, he was not the most dutiful follower of Deneir. He was lax concerning the rituals of his station and it often got him into trouble. But Cadderly knew that most of the headmasters understood that his indiscretions came not from any disrespect for the order, but simply because he was so busy learning and creating, two very high priorities in the teachings of Deneir—and two often profitable priorities for the expensive-to-maintain library. By Cadderly's figuring, the priests of Deneir, like most religious orders, could find it in their hearts to overlook minor indiscretions, especially considering the greater gain.

"Oh, Rufo," Cadderly called, reaching to his belt.

Rufo's angular face poked back around the jamb of the open door, his little black eyes sparkling with victorious glee.

"Yes?" the tall man purred.

"You won that one."

Rufo's grin widened.

Cadderly shone a beam of light in his face, and the stunned Rufo recoiled in terror, bumping heavily against the wall across the corridor.

"Keep your eyes open," Cadderly said through a wide smile. "The next attack is mine." He gave a wink, but Rufo, realizing the relatively inoffensive nature of Cadderly's newest invention, only sneered back, brushed his matted black hair aside, and rushed away, his hard black boots clomping on the tiled floor as loudly as a shoed horse on cobblestones.

* * * * *

The three druids were granted a room in a remote corner of the fourth floor, far from the bustle of the library, as Arcite had requested. They settled in easily, not having much gear, and Arcite suggested they set off at once to study the newly found moss tome.

"I shall remain behind," Newander replied. "It was a long road, and I am truly weary. I would be no help to you with my eyes falling closed."

"As you wish," Arcite said. "We shall not be gone too long. Perhaps you can go down and pick up on the work when we have ended."

Newander moved to the room's window when his friends had gone and stared out across the majestic Snowflake Mountains. He had been to the Edificant Library only once before, when he had first met Cadderly. Newander had been but a young man then, about the same age as Cadderly was now, and the library, with its bustle of humanity, crafted items, and penned tomes, had affected him deeply. Before he had come, Newander had known only the quiet woodlands, where the animals ruled and men were few.

After he had left, Newander had questioned his calling. He preferred the woodlands, that much he knew, but he could not deny the attraction he felt for civilization, the curiosity about advances in architecture and knowledge.

Newander had remained a druid, though, a servant of Silvanus, the Oak Father, and had done well in his studies. The natural order was of primary importance, by his sincere measure, but still . . .

It was not without concern that Newander had returned to the Edificant Library. He looked out at majestic mountains and wished he were out there, where the world was simple and safe.

Two

Agent of Talona

From a distance, the rocky spur at the northeastern edge of the Snowflake Mountains seemed quite unremarkable: piles of strewn boulders covering tightly packed slopes of smaller stones. But so, too, to those who did not know better, might a wolverine seem an innocuous thing. A dozen separate tunnels led under that rocky slope, and each of them promised only death to wayward adventurers seeking shelter from the night.

This particular mountain spur, which was far from natural, housed Castle Trinity, a castle-in-mountain's-clothing, a fortress for an evil brotherhood determined to gain in power.

Wary must wanderers be in the Realms, for civilization often ends at a city wall.

"Will it work?" Aballister whispered nervously, tentatively fingering the precious parchment. Rationally, he held faith in the recipe—Talona had led him to it—but after so much pain and trouble, and with the moment of victory so close at hand, he could not prevent a bit of apprehension. He looked up from the scroll and out a small window in the fortified complex. The

21

Shining Plains lay flat and dark to the east, and the setting sun lit reflected fires on the Snowflake Mountains' snow-capped peaks to the west.

The small imp folded his leathery wings around in front of himself and crossed his arms over them, impatiently tapping one clawed foot. "*Quiesta bene tellemara*," he mumbled under his breath.

"What was that?" Aballister replied, turning sharply and cocking one thin eyebrow at his often impertinent familiar. "Did you say something, Druzil? "

"It will work, I said. It will work," Druzil lied in his raspy, breathless voice. "Would you doubt the Lady Talona? Would you doubt her wisdom in bringing us together?"

Aballister muttered suspiciously, accepting the suspected insult as an unfortunate but unavoidable consequence of having so wise and wicked a familiar. The lean wizard knew that Druzil's translation was less than accurate, and that "quiesta bene tellemara" was undoubtedly something uncomplimentary. He didn't doubt Druzil's appraisal of the powerful potion, though, and that somehow unnerved him most of all. If Druzil's claims for the chaos curse proved true, Aballister and his evil companions would soon realize more power than even the ambitious wizard had ever hoped for. For many years Castle Trinity had aspired to conquer the Snowflake Mountain region, the elven wood of Shilmista, and the human settlement of Carradoon. Now, with the chaos curse, that process might soon begin.

Aballister looked beside the small window to the golden brazier, supported by a tripod, that always burned in his room. This was his gate to the lower planes, the same gate that had delivered Druzil. The wizard remembered that time vividly, a day of tingling anticipation. The avatar of the goddess Talona had instructed him to use his powers of sorcery and had given him Druzil's name, promising him that the imp would deliver a most delicious recipe for entropy. Little did he know then that the imp's precious scheme would involve two years of painstaking and costly effort, tax the wizard to the limits of his endurance, and destroy so many others in the process.

Druzil's recipe, the chaos curse, was worth it, Aballister decided. He had taken its creation as his personal quest for Talona, as the great task of his life, and as the gift to his goddess that would elevate him above her priests.

The interplanar gate was closed now; Aballister had powders that could open and shut it as readily as if he were turning a knob. The powders sat in small, carefully marked pouches, half for opening, half for closing, lined up alternately on a nearby table. Only Druzil knew about them besides Aballister, and the imp had never gone against the wizard's demands and tampered with the gate. Druzil could be impertinent and was often a tremendous nuisance, but he was reliable enough concerning important matters.

Aballister continued his scan and saw his reflection in a mirror across the room. Once he had been a handsome man, with inquisitive eyes and a bright smile. The change had been dramatic. Aballister was hollowed and worn now, all the dabbling in dark magic, worshiping a demanding goddess, and controlling chaotic creatures such as Druzil having taken their toll.

Many years before, the wizard had given up everything—his family and friends, and all the joys he once had held dear—in his hunger for knowledge and power, and that obsession had only multiplied when he had met Talona.

More than once, though, both before and after that meeting, Aballister had wondered if it had been worth it. Druzil offered him the attainment of his lifelong quest, power beyond his grandest imaginings, but the reality hadn't lived up to Aballister's expectations. At this point in his wretched life, the power seemed as hollow as his own face.

"But these ingredients!" Aballister went on, hoping, that he could find a weakness in the imp's seemingly solid designs. "Eyes of an umber hulk? Blood of a druid? And what is the purpose of this, tentacles of a displacer beast?"

"Chaos curse," Druzil replied, as if the words alone should dispell the wizard's doubts. "It is a mighty potion you plan to brew, my master." Druzil's toothy smile sent a shudder of revulsion along Aballister's backbone. The wizard had never become overly comfortable around the cruel imp.

"*Del quiniera cas ciem-pa*," Druzil said through his long and pointy teeth. "A powerful potion indeed!" he translated falsely. In truth, Druzil had said, "Even considering your limitations," but Aballister didn't need to know that.

"Yes," Aballister muttered again, tapping a bony finger on the end of his hawkish nose. "I really must take the time to learn your language, my dear Druzil."

"Yes," Druzil echoed, wiggling his elongated ears. "*Iye quiesta pas tellemara*," he said, which meant, "If you weren't so stupid." Druzil dropped into a low bow to cover his deceptions, but the act only convinced Aballister further that the imp was making fun of him.

"The expense of these ingredients has been considerable," Aballister said, getting back to the subject.

"And the brewing is not exact," added Druzil with obvious sarcasm. "And we could find, my master, a hundred more problems if we searched, but the gains, I remind you. The gains! Your brotherhood is not so strong, not so. It shan't survive, I say! Not without the brew."

"God-stuff?" mused Aballister.

"Call it so," replied Druzil. "Since it was Talona who led you to it, that her designs be furthered, perhaps it truly is. A fitting title, for the sake of Barjin and his wretched priests. They will be more devout and attentive if they understand that they are fabricating a true agent of Talona, a power in itself to lavish their worship upon, and their devotion will help keep orc-faced Ragnor and his brutish warriors in line."

Aballister laughed aloud as he thought of the three clerics, the second order of the evil triumvirate, kneeling and praying before a simple magical device.

"Name it *Tuanta Miancay*, the Fatal Horror," Druzil

offered, his snickers purely sarcastic. "Barjin will like that."
Druzil contemplated the suggestion for a moment, then
added, "No, not the Fatal Horror. *Tuanta Quiro Miancay*, the
Most Fatal Horror."

Aballister's laughter trebled, with just a hint of uneasiness
in it. "Most Fatal Horror" was a title associated with Talona's
highest-ranking and most devout priests. Barjin, Castle Trinity's clerical leader, had not yet attained that honor, being referred to only as a Most Debilitating Holiness. That this chaos
curse would outstrip him in title would sting the arrogant
cleric, and Aballister would enjoy that spectacle. Barjin and
his band had been at the castle for only a year. The priest had
traveled all the way from Damara, homeless and broken and
with no god to call his own since a new order of paladin kings
had banished his vile deity back to the lower planes. Like
Aballister, Barjin claimed to have encountered the avatar of
Talona and that it was she who had shown him the way to
Castle Trinity.

Barjin's dynamism and powers were considerable, and his
followers had carried uncounted treasures along with them
on their journey. When they first had arrived, the ruling triumvirate, particularly Aballister, had welcomed them with
open arms, thinking it grand that Talona had brought together so powerful a union, a marriage that would strengthen
the castle and provide the resources to complete Druzil's
recipe. Now, months later, Aballister had begun to foster
reservations about the union, particularly about the priest.
Barjin was a charismatic man, something frowned upon in an
order dedicated to disease and poison. Many of Talona's
priests scarred themselves or covered their skin with grotesque
tattoos. Barjin had done none of that, had sacrificed nothing to
his new goddess, but, because of his wealth and his uncanny
persuasive powers, he quickly had risen to the leadership of
the castle's clerics.

Aballister had allowed the ascent, thinking it Talona's will,
and had gone out of his way to appease Barjin—in retrospect,

he was not so certain of his choice. Now, however, he needed
Barjin's support to hold Castle Trinity together, and Barjin's
riches to fund the continuing creation of the chaos curse.

"I must see about the brewing of our ingredients for the
god-stuff," the wizard said with that thought in mind. "When
we find a quiet time, though, Druzil, I would like to learn a bit
of that full-flavored language you so often toss about."

"As you please, my master," replied the imp, bowing as
Aballister left the small room and closed the door behind him.

Druzil spoke his next words in his private tongue, the language of the lower planes, fearing that Aballister might be listening at the door, "*Quiesta bene tellemara, Aballister!*" The
mischievous imp couldn't help himself as he whispered, "But
you are too stupid," aloud, for no better reason than to hear
the words spoken in both tongues.

For all of the insults he so casually threw his master's way,
though, Druzil appreciated the wizard. Aballister was mar-
velously intelligent for a human, and the most powerful of his
order of three, and by Druzil's estimation those three wizards
were the strongest leg of the triumvirate. Aballister would
complete the cursing potion and supply the device to deliver
it, and for that, Druzil, who had craved this day for decades,
would be undyingly grateful. Druzil was smarter than most
imps, smarter than most people, and when he had come upon
the ancient recipe in an obscure manuscript a century before,
he wisely had kept it hidden from his former master, another
human. That wizard hadn't the resources or the wisdom to
carry through the plan and properly spread the cause of
chaos, but Aballister did.

* * * * *

Aballister felt a mixture of hope and trepidation as he
stared hard at the reddish glow emanating from within the
clear bottle. This was the first test of the chaos curse, and all
of the wizard's expectations were tempered by the huge

expense of putting this small amount together.

"One more ingredient," whispered the anxious imp, sharing none of his master's doubts. "Add the *yote*, then we may release the smoke."

"It is not to be imbibed?" Aballister asked.

Druzil paled noticeably. "No, master, not that," he rasped. "The consequences are too grave. Too grave!"

Aballister spent a long moment studying the imp. In the two years Druzil had been beside him, he could not recall ever seeing the imp so badly shaken. The wizard walked across the room to a cabinet and produced a second bottle, smaller than the plain one holding the potion, but intricately decorated with countless magical runes. When Aballister pulled off the stopper, a steady stream of smoke issued forth.

"It is ever-smoking," the wizard explained. "A minor item of magical . . ."

"I know," Druzil interrupted. "And I have already come to know that the flask will mate correctly with our potion."

Aballister started to ask how Druzil could possibly know that, how Druzil could even know about his ever-smoking bottle, but he held his questions, remembering that the mischievous imp had contacts on other planes that could answer many things.

"Could you create more of those?" Druzil asked, indicating the wondrous bottle.

Aballister gritted his teeth at yet another added expense, and his expression alone answered the question.

"The chaos curse is best served in mist, and with its magical properties, the bottle will continue to spew it forth for many years, though its range will be limited," Druzil explained. "Another container will be necessary if we mean to spread the intoxicant properly."

"Intoxicant?" Aballister balked, on the verge of rage. Druzil gave a quick flap of his leathery wings, putting him farther across the room from Aballister—not that distance mattered much where the powerful wizard was concerned.

"Intoxicant?" Aballister said again. "My dear, dear Druzil, do you mean to tell me that we have spent a fortune in gold, that I have groveled before Barjin and those utterly wretched priests, just to mix a batch of elvish wine?"

"*Bene tellemara,*" came the imp's exasperated reply. "You still do not understand what we have created? Elvish wine?"

"Dwarvish mead, then?" Aballister snarled sarcastically. He took up his staff and advanced a threatening step.

"You do not understand what will happen when it is loosed," Druzil barked derisively.

"Do tell me."

Druzil snapped his wings over his face, then back behind him again, a movement that plainly revealed his frustration. "It will invade the hearts of our targets," the imp explained, "and exaggerate their desires. Simple impulses will become god-given commands. None will be affected in quite the same way, nor will the effects remain consistent to any one victim. Purely chaotic! Those affected will . . ."

Aballister raised a hand to stop him, needing no further explanation.

"I have given you power beyond your greatest hopes!" the imp growled forcefully. "Have you forgotten Talona's promise?"

"The avatar only suggested that I summon you," Aballister countered, "and only hinted that you might possess something of value."

"You cannot begin to understand the potency of the chaos curse," Druzil replied smugly. "All the races of the region will be yours to control when their own inner controls have been destroyed. Chaos is a beautiful thing, mortal master, a force of destruction and conquest, the ultimate disease, the Most Fatal Horror. Orchestrating chaos brings power to he who remains beyond its crippling grip!"

Aballister leaned on his staff and looked away. He had to believe Druzil, and yet he feared to believe. He had given so much to this unknown recipe.

"You must learn," the imp said, seeing that Aballister

was not impressed. "If we are to succeed, then you must believe."

He folded his leathery wings over his head for a moment, burying himself in thought. "That young fighter, the arrogant one?" he asked suddenly.

"Haverly," Aballister answered.

"He thinks himself Ragnor's better," Druzil said, a wicked, toothy smile spreading over his face. "He desires Ragnor's death so that he might assume captainship of the fighters."

Aballister did not argue. On several occasions, young Haverly, drunken with ale, had indicated those very desires, though he had never gone so far as to threaten the ogrillon.

Even arrogant Haverly was not that stupid.

"Call him to us," Druzil begged. "Let him complete our test. Tell him that this potion could strengthen his position in the triumvirate. Tell him that it could make him even stronger than Ragnor."

Aballister stood quietly for a few moments to consider his options. Barjin had expressed grave doubts about the whole project, despite Aballister's claims that it would serve Talona beyond anything else in all the world. The priest had only funded Aballister's treasure hunt on the wizard's promise, made before a dozen witnesses, that every copper piece would be repaid if the priest was not overjoyed with the results. Barjin had lost much in his flight from the northern kingdom of Damara: his prestige, his army, and many valuable and powerful items, some enchanted. His retained wealth alone had played the major role in preserving a measure of his former power.

Now, as the weeks dragged on with rising expenses and no measurable results, Barjin grew increasingly impatient.

"I will get Haverly at once," Aballister replied, suddenly intrigued. Neither the wizard nor Barjin held any love for either Ragnor, whom they considered too dangerous to be trusted, or Haverly, whom they considered too foolish, and any havoc that the test wreaked on that pair could help to diminish Barjin's doubts.

Besides, Aballister thought, it might be fun to watch.

*   *   *   *   *

Druzil sat motionless on Aballister's great desk, watching the events across the room with great interest. The imp wished he could play a larger role in this part of the test, but only the other wizards knew of his position as Aballister's familiar, or that he was alive at all. The fighters of the triumvirate, even the clerics, thought the imp merely a garish statue, for on the few occasions that any of them had entered Aballister's private quarters, Druzil had sat perfectly motionless on the desk.

"Bend low over the beaker as you add the final drop," Aballister bade Haverly, looking back to Druzil for confirmation.

The imp nodded imperceptibly and flared his nostrils in anticipation.

"That is correct!" Aballister said to Haverly. "Breathe deeply as you pour."

Haverly stood straight and cast a suspicious gaze at the wizard. He obviously didn't trust Aballister—certainly the wizard had shown him no friendship before now. "I have great plans," he said threateningly, "and being turned into a newt or some other strange creature is not part of them."

"You doubt?" Aballister roared suddenly, knowing that he must scare off the young fighter's doubts without hesitation. "Then go away! Anyone can complete the brewing. I thought that one as ambitious as you . . ."

"Enough," Haverly interrupted, and Aballister knew his words had hit home. Haverly's suspicion was no match for his hunger for power. "I will trust you, wizard, though you have never given me cause to trust you," Haverly finished.

"Nor have I ever given you cause not to trust me," Aballister reminded him.

Haverly stared a moment longer at Aballister, his grimace not softening, then bent low over the beaker and poured the final drops. As soon as the liquids touched, the red-glowing elixir belched a puff of red smoke right in Haverly's face. The fighter jumped back, his hand going straight to his sword.

"What have you done to me?" he demanded.

"Done?" Aballister echoed innocently. "Nothing. The smoke was harmless enough, if a bit startling."

Haverly took a moment to inspect himself to be sure that he had suffered no ill effects, then he relaxed and nodded at the wizard. "What will happen next?" he asked sharply. "Where is the power you promised me?"

"In time, dear Haverly, in time," replied Aballister. "The brewing of the elixir is only the first process!"

"How long?" demanded the eager fighter.

"I could have invited Ragnor instead of you," Aballister pointedly reminded him.

Haverly's transformation at the mention of Ragnor forced the wizard back several steps: The young fighter's eyes widened grotesquely; he bit his lip so hard that blood dripped down his chin. "Ragnor!" he growled through gritted teeth. "Ragnor the imposter! Ragnor the pretender! You would not invite him, for I am his better!"

"Of course you are, dear Haverly," the wizard cooed, trying to soothe the wild-eyed man, recognizing that Haverly was on the verge of explosion. "That is why . . ." Aballister never finished, for Haverly, muttering under his breath, drew his sword and charged out of the room, nearly destroying the door as he passed. Aballister stared into the hallway, blinking in disbelief.

"Intoxicant?" came a sarcastic query from across the room.

Drawn away by the screams of "Ragnor!" Aballister didn't bother to answer the imp. The wizard rushed out, not wanting to miss the coming spectacle, and soon found his two colleagues as they made their way through the halls.

"It is Haverly, the young fighter," said Dorigen, the only female wizard in the castle. Aballister's evil smile stopped her and her companion in their tracks.

"The potion is completed?" Dorigen asked hopefully, her amber eyes sparkling as she tossed her long black hair back over her shoulder.

"Chaos curse," Aballister confirmed as he led them on.

When they arrived at the complex's large dining hall, they found that the fighting had already begun. Several tables had been flung about and a hundred startled men and orcs, and even a few giants, lined the room's perimeter, watching in amazement. Ragnor and Haverly stood facing each other in the center of the room, swords drawn.

"The fighters will need a new third in their ruling council," Dorigen remarked. "Surely either Ragnor or Haverly will fall this day, leaving only two."

"Ragnor!" Haverly proclaimed loudly. "Today I take my place as leader of the fighters!"

The other warrior, a powerfully built ogrillon, having ancestors both ogre and orc, and carrying the scars of a thousand battles, hardly seemed impressed. "Today you take your place among your ancestors," he chided.

Haverly charged, his foolishly straightforward attack costing him so deep a gash on one shoulder that his arm was nearly severed. The crazed fighter didn't even grimace, didn't even notice the wound or the pain.

Though plainly amazed that the vicious wound had not slowed his opponent, Ragnor still managed to deflect Haverly's sword and get in close to the man. He caught Haverly's sword arm with his free hand and tried to position his own weapon for a strike.

Gasps of astonishment arose throughout the gathering as Haverly somehow managed to lift his brutally torn arm and similarly block Ragnor's strike.

Haverly was almost as tall as Ragnor, but many pounds lighter and not nearly as strong. Still, and despite the wicked wound, he held Ragnor at bay for many moments.

"You are stronger than you seem," Ragnor admitted, somewhat impressed, but showing no concern; on the few occasions that his incredible strength had failed him, the ogrillon had always found a way to improvise. He pressed a disguised button on his sword hilt, and a second blade, a long, slender dirk, appeared, protruding straight down from the sword hilt, right in line with Haverly's unhelmeted head.

Haverly was too engrossed to even notice. "Ragnor!" he screamed again, hysterically, his face contorted. He slammed his forehead into Ragnor's face, squashing the ogrillon's nose.

Haverly's head came crashing in again, but Ragnor managed to ignore the pain and keep his concentration on the more lethal attack. Haverly's head came back in line a third time. Ragnor, tasting his own blood, savagely twisted his sword arm free and plunged straight down, impaling the dirk deeply into Haverly's skull.

* * * * *

The three priests of the ruling triumvirate entered the room then, led by Barjin, who was obviously not pleased by the combat.

"What is the meaning of this?" he demanded of Aballister, understanding that the wizard had played a role here.

"A matter for the fighters to explain, it would seem," Aballister replied with a shrug. Seeing that the priest was about to intervene in the continuing battle, Aballister bent over and whispered, "The chaos curse," in Barjin's ear.

Barjin's face brightened immediately and he watched the bloody battle with sudden enthusiasm.

* * * * *

Ragnor could hardly believe that Haverly still struggled. His foot-long dirk was bloodied right to the pommel, but his opponent stubbornly backed away, thrashing to free himself of the blade.

Ragnor let him go, thinking Haverly in his death throes. But, to the continuing gasps of the onlookers—Barjin's heard most loudly—Haverly did not topple.

"Ragnor!" he growled, slurring badly and spitting thick blood with every syllable. Blood filled one of his eyes and poured from his head wound, matting his brown hair, but he raised his sword and stumbled in.

Ragnor, terrified, struck first, taking advantage of Haverly's partial blindness and hacking at his already wounded arm. The force of the blow severed the arm completely, just below the shoulder, and knocked Haverly several feet to the side.

"Ragnor!" Haverly sputtered again, barely keeping his balance. Again he came in, and again Ragnor beat him back, this time slicing through Haverly's exposed ribs, digging at his heart and lungs.

Haverly's cries became unintelligible wheezes as he continued his advance. Ragnor frantically rushed out to meet him, locking him in a tight embrace that rendered both long swords useless. Haverly had no defenses against Ragnor's free hand, now holding a dirk, and the weapon dug repeatedly, viciously, at his back. Still, many minutes passed before Haverly finally tumbled dead to the floor.

"A worthy adversary," one bold orc remarked, coming over to inspect the body.

Covered in Haverly's blood, and with his own nose broken, Ragnor was in no mood to hear any praises for Haverly. "A stubborn fool!" he corrected, and he lopped off the orc's head with a single strike.

Barjin nodded at Aballister. "Talona watches with pleasure. Perhaps your chaos curse will prove worth the expense."

"Chaos curse?" Aballister replied as though a notion had struck him. "That is not a fitting title for such a powerful agent of Talona. *Tuanta Miancay*, perhaps . . . no, *Tuanta Quiro Miancay*."

One of Barjin's associates, understanding the language and the implications of the title, gasped aloud. His companions stared at him, and he translated, "The Most Fatal Horror!"

Barjin snapped his gaze back on Aballister, realizing the wizard's ploy. Aballister had played the most important role in the brewing and, with a few simple words, had ranked the potion above Barjin. Already the other two clerics, fanatic followers of Talona, were nodding eagerly and whispering their praises for Aballister's creation.

"*Tuanta Quiro Miancay*," the cornered priest echoed, forcing a smile. "Yes, that will do properly."

Three

Danica

The obese wrestler rubbed a pudgy hand over his newest bruise, trying to ignore the growing taunts of his colleagues. "I have been too relaxed against you," he said to the young woman, "my being thrice your weight and you being a girl."

Danica brushed her hair out of her almond-shaped brown eyes and tried to hide her smile. She didn't want to humiliate the proud cleric, a disciple of Oghma. She knew his boasts were ridiculous. He had fought with all his fury, but it hadn't done him any good.

Danica looked like a wisp of a thing, barely five feet tall, with a floppy mop of curly strawberry-blond hair hanging just below her shoulders and a smile to steal a paladin's heart. Those who looked more closely found much more than "girl-ish" dressing, though. Years of meditation and training had honed Danica's reflexes and muscles to a fine fighting edge, as the clerics of Oghma, fancying themselves great wrestlers in the image of their god figure, were painfully discovering one after another.

Every time Danica needed information in the great Edificant Library, she found it offered only in exchange for a wrestling match. For the gain of a single scroll penned by a long-dead monk, Danica now found herself faced off against this latest adversary, a sweaty and smelly behemoth. She didn't really mind the play; she knew she could defeat this one as easily as she had dispatched all the others.

The fat man straightened his black-and-gold vest, lowered his round head, and charged.

Danica waited until he was right in front of her, and to the onlookers it looked as if the woman would be buried beneath mounds of flesh. At the last moment, she dipped her head under the fat man's lunging arm, caught his hand, and casually stepped behind him as he lumbered past. A subtle twist of her wrist stopped him dead in his tracks and, before he even realized what was happening, Danica kicked the back of both his knees, dropping him to a kneel.

While the big man went down, his arm, bent backward and held firmly in Danica's amazingly strong grasp, did not. Sympathetic groans and derisive laughter erupted from those gathered to watch.

"Eastern corner!" the big man cried. "Third row, third shelf from the top in a silver tube!"

"My thanks," Danica said, releasing her hold. She looked around, flashing that innocent smile. "Perhaps the next time I require information, you can fight me two against one."

The clerics of Oghma, fearing that their god was not pleased, grumbled and turned away.

Danica offered her hand to the downed priest, but he proudly refused. He struggled to his feet, nearly falling again for lack of breath, and rushed to catch up with the others.

Danica shook her head helplessly and retrieved her two daggers from a nearby bench. She took a moment to examine them, as she always did before putting them back into their respective boot sheaths. One had a hilt of gold, twisted into a tiger's head, while the other had one of silver, bearing an image of a dragon. Both sported transparent crystal blades and were enhanced by a wizard's spell to give them the strength of steel and perfect balance. They had been a very valuable and treasured gift from Danica's master, a man whom Danica dearly missed. She had been with Master Turkel since her parents had died, and the wizened old man had become all the family she had. Danica thought of him as she resheathed the weapons, vowing for the millionth time to visit him when she had completed her studies.

Danica Maupoissant had been raised amid the bustle of the Westgate marketplace, five hundred miles to the northeast of the Edificant Library, on the neck between the Lake of Dragons and the Sea of Fallen Stars. Her father, Pavel, was a craftsman, reputably the finest wagonmaker in the region, who, like many people of Westgate, possessed a stubborn and fierce independence and no small amount of pride. Theirs was a life of simple pleasures and unconditional love.

Danica was twelve when she left her parents to serve as an apprentice to the aged, white-bearded potter named Turkel Bastan. Only months later did Danica come to understand her parents' reasoning in sending her to him: they had foreseen what was to come.

She spent a year shuffling back and forth across the city, splitting her time between her extensive duties with Master Turkel and those rare opportunities she found to go home.

Then, suddenly, there was nowhere to go. The raid had come in the dark of night, and when the assassins had gone, so, too, were Danica's parents, the house she had grown up in, and the wagon shop that had been her father's lifelong toil.

Master Turkel showed little emotion when he told Danica the terrible news, but the young girl heard him crying later, in the solitude of his small room. Only then did Danica come to realize that Turkel and her parents had orchestrated her apprenticeship. She had assumed it an accidental thing, and had feared that perhaps her parents had simply shuffled her away for their own convenience. She knew that Turkel was from the far-off eastern land of Tabot, the mountainous region of some of her mother's ancestors, and she wondered if Turkel might be a distant relative. Whatever their relationship, Danica's apprenticeship with the master soon had taken on a different light. He had helped her through her grieving, then had begun her true instruction, lessons that had little to do with making pottery. Turkel was a Tabotan monk, a disciple of Grandmaster Penpahg D'Ahn, whose religion combined mental discipline with physical training to achieve harmony of the soul. Danica guessed Turkel to be no less than eighty years old, but he could move with the grace of a hunting cat and strike with his bare hands with the force of iron weapons. His displays more than amazed Danica; they consumed her. Quiet and unassuming, Turkel was as peaceful and contented a man as Danica had ever known, yet underneath that outward guise was a fighting tiger that could be brought roaring forth in times of need.

So, too, grew the tiger in Danica. She learned and practiced; nothing else mattered to her. She used her constant work as a litany against her memories, a barricade against the pain with which she could not yet come to terms. Turkel understood, Danica later realized, and he chose carefully when he would tell her more of her parents' demise.

The craftsmen and merchants of Westgate, along with, or perhaps because of, their fierce independence, were often bitter rivals, and Pavel had not escaped this fact of Westgate life.

There were several other wagonmakers—Turkel would not tell Danica their names—who were jealous of Pavel's continuing prosperity. They went to Pavel on a few occasions, threatening him with severe consequences if he would not share with them his long backlog of orders.

"If they had come as friends and fellow craftsmen, Pavel would have shared the wealth," Turkel had said, as though he and Danica's father had been much more than the slight acquaintances they pretended to be in public. "But your father was a proud man. He would not give in to threats, no matter how real the danger behind them."

Danica had never pressed Turkel for the identity of the men who had killed her parents—or, rather, had hired the dreaded Night Masks, the usual means of assassination in Westgate, and to this day, she did not know who they were. She trusted that the master would tell her when he felt she was prepared to know, prepared to take revenge, if that was her choice, or when he believed she was willing to let go of the past and build on the future. Turkel had always indicated that to be his preference.

The image of the aged master came clearly to Danica's mind as she stood there, holding the magnificent daggers. "You have outgrown me," he had said to her, and there was no remorse, only pride, in his tone. "Your skills surpass my own in so many areas."

Danica remembered vividly that she had thought the time of revelation at hand, that Turkel would tell her the names of the conspirators who had killed her parents and tell her to go out and seek revenge.

Turkel had other ideas.

"There remains only one master who can continue to instruct you," Turkel had said, and as soon as he mentioned the Edificant Library, Danica knew what was to come. The library was home to many of Grandmaster Penpahg D'Ahn's rare and priceless scrolls; Turkel wanted her to learn directly from the records of the long-dead grandmaster. It was then that Turkel had given her the two magnificent daggers.

So she had left Westgate, barely more than a child, to build on her future, to attain new heights of self-discipline. Once again, Master Turkel had shown his love and respect for her, placing her needs above his own obvious despair at her departure.

Danica believed that she had accomplished much in her first year at the library, both in her studies and in her understanding of other people, of the world that suddenly seemed so very large. She thought it ironic that her education of the wide world would come in a place of almost monastic seclusion, but she couldn't deny that her views had matured considerably in the year she had spent at the library. Before she had lived in the private desire for revenge; now Westgate and the hired assassins seemed so very far away, and so many other, more positive, opportunities were opened to her.

She dismissed those dark memories now, left them with a final image of her father's calm smile, her mother's almond eyes, and the many wrinkles of Master Turkel's wizened old face. Then even those pleasing images dissipated, buried beneath Danica's many responsibilities to her craft.

The library was a massive room supported by dozens and dozens of arched pillars, which were even more confusing because of the thousands of distracting bas-reliefs carved into each one. It took Danica many minutes to determine which was the eastern corner. When she finally got there, moving down a narrow isle of tightly packed books, she found someone waiting for her.

Cadderly couldn't hide his smile; he never could when he looked upon Danica, since the very first time he had seen her.

He knew she had come from Westgate, several hundred miles to the northeast. That alone made her worldly by his standards, and there were so many other things about her that piqued his imagination. Although Danica's features and mannerisms were mostly Western and not so different from the norm in the central realms, the shape of her eyes revealed some ancestry in the far and exotic East.

Cadderly often wondered if that was what had initially attracted him to Danica. Those almond eyes had promised adventure to him, and he was a man sorely in need of adventure.

He had passed his twenty-first birthday and had been off the grounds of the Edificant Library only a few dozen times— and on those occasions, he had always been accompanied by at least one of the headmasters, usually Avery, and several other priests. Sometimes Cadderly thought himself pitifully bereft of any real experiences. To him, adventures and battles were events to be read about. He had never even seen a living orc, or monster of any kind.

Enter mysterious Danica and those alluring promises.

"It took you long enough," Cadderly remarked slyly.

"I have been at the library just a year," Danica retorted, "but you have lived here since before your fifth birthday."

"I had the library figured out in a week, even at that age," Cadderly assured her with a snap of his fingers. He fell into step beside her as she walked briskly toward the corner.

Danica glanced up at him, then bit back her sarcastic reply, not certain if the amazing Cadderly was teasing her or not.

"So you are fighting the big ones now?" Cadderly asked. "Should I be concerned?"

Danica stopped suddenly, pulled Cadderly's face down to her own, and kissed him eagerly. She moved back from him just a few inches, her almond eyes, striking and exotic, boring into him.

Cadderly silently thanked Deneir that neither he nor Danica were of a celibate order, but, as always when they kissed, the contact made both of them nervous. "Fighting excites you," Cadderly remarked coyly, stealing the romance and relieving the tension. "Now I am concerned."

Danica pushed him back but did not let go of his tunic.

"You should be careful, you know," Cadderly went on, suddenly serious. "If any of the headmasters caught you wrestling . . ."

"The proud young loremasters do not leave me much choice," Danica replied, casually tossing her hair and pulling it back from her face. She hadn't really worked up much of a sweat against her latest opponent. "In this maze you call a library, I could not find half of what I need in a hundred years!" She rolled her eyes about to emphasize the vastness of the pillared room.

"Not a problem," Cadderly assured her. "I had the library figured out . . ."

"When you were five!" Danica finished for him and she pulled him close again. This time Cadderly decided that her attention might bring some added benefits. He prudently moved around to Danica's right side—he scribed left-handed, and the last time he had attempted this with his left hand, he had not been able to work for several days. Cadderly had been thrilled by what Danica called her "Withering Touch" for many months, considering it the most effective nonlethal attack form he had ever witnessed. He had begged Danica to teach it to him, but the skilled monk carefully guarded her fighting secrets, explaining to Cadderly that her fighting methods were but a small part of her religion, as much a discipline of the mind as of the body. She would not allow others to copy simple techniques without first achieving the mental preparation and philosophical attitudes that accompanied them.

In the middle of the kiss, Cadderly rubbed his hand across Danica's belly, under the bottom of her short vest. As always, the young priest was amazed by the hard, rolling muscles of her stomach. A moment later, Cadderly started moving his hand slowly upward.

Danica's reaction came in the blink of an eye. Her hand, one finger extended, snapped out across Cadderly's chest and drove into his shoulder.

Under the vest, Cadderly's hand stopped immediately, then fell lifeless to hang by his side. He grimaced for a moment as the burning pain became a general numbness the length of his arm.

"You are such a . . ." Danica stammered, "a . . . a boy!"

At first, Cadderly thought her anger just the expected reaction to his bold advance, then Danica stunned him completely.

"Can you never forget your studies?"

"She knows!" a horrified Cadderly muttered to himself as Danica stormed away. Expecting the attack, he had carefully watched out of the corner of his eye and believed he knew precisely where Danica's finger had struck. Until that moment, he had considered this attempt a success, despite the continuing pain. But now Danica knew!

The young scholar paused a moment to consider the implications, then was relieved when he heard Danica's soft laughter from just beyond the next bookshelf. He took a step toward her, meaning to amend things, but Danica spun as soon as he rounded the corner, her finger poised to strike.

"The touch will work on your head as well," the young woman promised, her light brown eyes sparkling eagerly.

Cadderly didn't doubt that for a moment, and he surely didn't want Danica to prove her words. It always amazed him that Danica, barely half his weight, could so easily take him down. He looked upon her with sincere admiration, even envy, for Cadderly dearly wished that he possessed Danica's direction and dedication, her passion for her studies. While Cadderly went through his life busy but distracted, Danica's vision of the world remained narrowly focused, based in a rigid and philosophical religion little-known in the western realms. That passion, too, enhanced the enchantment Danica had cast over Cadderly. He wanted to open her mind and her heart and look into both, knowing that only there would he find answers to fill the missing elements of his own life.

Danica embodied his dreams and his hopes; he didn't even try to remember how sorely empty his life had been before he had met her. He backed away slowly, lifting his palms and holding them open and out wide to show that he wanted no part of any further displays.

"Stand!" Danica commanded as sharply as her melodious voice allowed. "Have you nothing to say to me?"

Cadderly thought for a moment, wondering what she wanted to hear. "I love you?" he asked as much as declared.

Danica nodded and smiled disarmingly, then dropped her hand. Cadderly's gray eyes returned the smile tenfold and he took a step toward her.

The dangerous finger shot up and waved about, resembling some hellish viper.

Cadderly shook his head and ran from the room, pausing only to grab a scrap of parchment and dip the quill he kept stuck under his hat band into an open inkwell. He had witnessed the Withering Touch perfectly, and he wanted to sketch the image while it was fresh in his mind.

This time, Danica's laughter was not so soft.

Four

Canticle

"They are singing to it!" Druzil cried in amazement, not certain of whether that was a good thing or not.

The religious fanatics of Castle Trinity had taken the potion to heart; even the not-so-faithful, such as Ragnor and, by Aballister's estimation, Barjin, had been swept up in the zealous flow. "Though not very well, I fear." The imp put his wings over his ears to lessen the sound.

Aballister, too, did not enjoy the discordant wails that resounded throughout the castle complex with a zeal that walls and doors could not diminish, but he tolerated the clerics better than his worrisome imp. The wizard, too, was not without his reservations, though. Ever since the battle in the dining hall four weeks before, Barjin had forcefully taken the project as his own and had led the chorus of chants to the Most Fatal Horror.

"Barjin has the wealth," Druzil reminded the wizard, as though the imp had sensed Aballister's thoughts.

Aballister replied with a grim nod. "I fear that my insult has been turned back on me," he explained, moving slowly to the window and looking out over the Shining Plains. "By naming the chaos curse the Most Fatal Horror, I sought to demean Barjin, to weaken his position, but he has weathered the torment and resisted his prideful urging better than I had expected. All the followers believe his sincerity, to Talona and to the chaos curse." Aballister sighed. On the one hand, he was disappointed that his ploy had not stung Barjin, at least not outwardly, but on the other hand, the priest leader, sincere or not, was surely preparing Castle Trinity for the coming trials and thus was furthering Talona's will.

"If the followers believe our mixture is a simple magical concoction, no matter how potent, they will not so readily give their lives to the cause," Aballister reasoned, turning back on Druzil. "There is nothing like religion to rouse the rabble."

"You do not believe the elixir is an agent of Talona?" Druzil asked, though he already knew the answer.

"I know the difference between a magical concoction and a sentient shield man," Aballister replied dryly. "The elixir will indeed serve the Lady of Poison's cause, and so its title is a fitting one."

"Barjin has put all the forces of Castle Trinity behind him," Druzil quickly responded, his tone ominous. "Even Ragnor does not dare go against him."

"Why would he, or anyone else, want to?" Aballister replied. "The chaos curse soon will be put to proper use, and Barjin has played a major role in that."

"At what price?" the imp demanded. "I gave the recipe for the chaos curse to you, my master, not the priest. Yet it is the priest who controls its fate and uses you and the other wizards to serve his own designs."

"We are a brotherhood, sworn to loyalty."

"You are a gathering of thieves," Druzil retorted. "Be not so swift in presuming the existence of honor. If Ragnor did not fear you, and did not see profit in keeping you, he would cut you down. Barjin—" Druzil rolled his bulbous eyes "—Barjin cares for nothing except Barjin. Where are his scars? His tattoos? He does not deserve his title, nor the leadership of the priests. He falls to his knees for the goddess only because doing so makes those around him praise him for his holiness. There is nothing religious—"

"Enough, dear Druzil," soothed the wizard, waving one hand calmly.

"Do you deny that Barjin controls the chaos curse?" Druzil retorted. "Do you believe that Barjin would show any loyalty to Aballister if he did not need Aballister?"

The wizard walked away from the small window and fell back into his wooden chair, unable to argue those points. But even if he admitted that he had miscalculated, he could do little now to stop events from following their course. Barjin had the elixir and the money, and if Aballister meant to recapture control of the potion for himself, he might have to fight a war within the triumvirate. Aballister and his wizard comrades were powerful, but they were only three. With Barjin whipping the hundreds of Castle Trinity soldiers into religious fervor, the wizards had become somewhat secluded within the complex.

"They have added rituals and conditions," the imp went on, spitting every word with distaste. "Did you know that Barjin has placed warding glyphs on the flask, so that it might be opened only by an innocent?"

"That is a typical priestly ploy," Aballister replied casually, trying to alleviate Druzil's worries.

"He does not understand the power under his control," Druzil retorted. "The chaos curse needs no 'priestly ploys.' "

Aballister gave an unconcerned shrug, but he, too, had not agreed with Barjin's decision concerning those glyphs. Barjin thought that allowing an innocent to serve as an unintentional catalyst was fitting for the agent of the chaotic goddess, but Aballister feared that the cleric was simply adding conditions to an already complicated process.

"*Barjin quiesta pas tellemara*," Druzil muttered.

Aballister narrowed his eyes. He had heard that obviously

unflattering phrase in many different contexts these last few weeks, most often aimed at him. He kept his suspicions to himself, though, realizing that many of Druzil's complaints were valid.

"Perhaps it is time for the Most Fatal Horror to go out and perform Talona's will beyond this pile of rocks," Aballister said. "Perhaps we have spent too long in preparation."

"Barjin's power is too consolidated," Druzil said. "Do not underestimate him."

Aballister nodded, then rose and walked across the room.

"You should not underestimate," he pointed out to the imp, "the advantages in convincing people that there is a higher purpose to their actions, a higher authority guiding their leaders' decisions." The wizard opened the heavy door, and the unholy canticle drowned out his next words. More than Barjin's handful of clerics were singing; the canticle was a hundred screaming voices strong, echoing off the stone walls with frantic urgency. Aballister shook his head in disbelief as he exited.

Druzil could not deny Barjin's effectiveness in preparing the force for the tasks ahead, but the imp still held reservations about the Most Fatal Horror and all the complications that title implied. The imp knew, if the wizard did not, that Aballister would not have an easy time of walking away with the elixir bottle.

* * * * *

"More like this one," Cadderly said to Ivan Bouldershoulder, a square-shouldered dwarf with a yellow beard hanging low enough to trip him if he didn't watch his step. The two were beside Cadderly's bed—Cadderly kneeling and Ivan standing— examining a tapestry depicting the legendary war wherein the elvish race had been split into surface and drow. Only half unrolled, the huge woven cloth still covered the bed. "The design is right, but its shaft might be a little tight for my darts."

Ivan pulled out a small-stick, notched at regular intervals, and took some measurements of the hand-held crossbow Cadderly had indicated, then of the arm of the drow elf holding it.

"They'll fit," the dwarf replied, confident of his work. He looked across the room to his brother, Pikel, who busied himself with several models Cadderly had constructed. "You got the bow?"

Engrossed in his play, Pikel didn't even hear him. He was older than Ivan by several years, but he was by far the less serious of the two. They were about the same size, though Pikel was a bit more round-shouldered, an attribute exaggerated by his loose-fitting, drooping robes. His beard was green this week, for he had dyed it in honor of the visiting druids.

Pikel liked druids, a fact that made his brother roll his eyes and blush. It wasn't usual that a dwarf would get on well with woodland folk, but Pikel was far from usual. Rather than let his beard hang loose to his toes, as did Ivan, he parted it in the middle and pulled it back over his huge ears, braiding it together with his hair to hang halfway down his back. It looked rather silly to Ivan, but Pikel, the library's cook, thought it practical for keeping his beard out of the soup. Besides, Pikel didn't wear the boots common to his race; he wore sandals—a gift from the druids—and his long beard tickled his free-wiggling, gnarly toes.

"Oo oi," Pikel chuckled, rearranging the models. One was remarkably similar to the Edificant Library, a squat, square, four-storied structure with rows of tiny windows. Another model was a displaced wall like those in the library, supported by huge, heavily blocked arches. It was the third and tallest model that intrigued Pikel. It, too, was of a wall, but unlike anything the dwarf, no novice to masonry, had ever seen. The model stood straight to half the dwarf's four-foot height but was not nearly as wide or bulky as the other, shorter, wall.

Slender and graceful, it was really two structures: the wall and a supporting pillar, connected by two bridges, one halfway up and the other at the very top.

Pikel pushed down hard on the model, but, fragile though it appeared, it did not bend under his considerable strength.

"Oo oi!" the delighted dwarf squealed.

"The crossbow?" demanded Ivan, now standing behind Pikel. Pikel fumbled about the many pockets in his cook's apron, finally handing over a small wooden coffer.

Pikel squeaked at Cadderly, pointed to the strange wall, and gave an inquisitive look.

"Just something I investigated a few months ago," Cadderly explained. He tried to sound nonchalant, but a clear trace of excitement rang in his voice. With all that had been going on lately, he had almost forgotten the models, though the new design had shown remarkable promise. The Edificant Library was far from a mundane structure. Elaborate sculptures, enhanced by the ivy, covered its walls, and some of the most wondrous gargoyles in all the Realms completed its intricate and effective gutter system. Many of the finest minds in the region had designed and constructed the place, but whenever Cadderly looked upon it, all that he could see were its limitations. For all its detail, the library was square and squat, and its windows were small and unremarkable.

"An idea for expanding the library," he explained to Pikel.

He gathered up a nearby blanket and slipped it under the model of the library, folding its sides to resemble the rough surrounding mountain terrain.

Ivan shook his head and walked back to the bed, knowing that Cadderly and Pikel could continue their outlandish conversations for hours on end.

"Centuries ago, when the library was built," Cadderly began, "no one had any idea it would grow so large. The founders wanted a secluded spot where they could study in private, so they chose the high passes of the Snowflake Mountains.

"Most of the northern and eastern wings, as well as the third and fourth stories were added much later, but we have run out of room. To the front and both sides, the ground

slopes too steeply to allow further expansion without sup-
ports, and to the west, behind us, the mountain stone is too
tough to be properly cleared away."

"Oh?" muttered Pikel, not so sure of that. The Bouldershoulder brothers had come from the forbidding Galena
Mountains, far to the north beyond Vaasa, where the ground
was ever frozen and the stones were as tough as any in the
Realms. But not too tough for a determined dwarf! Pikel kept
his thoughts private, though, not wanting to halt Cadderly's
mounting momentum.

"I think we should go up," Cadderly said casually. "Add a
fifth, and possibly sixth level."

"It'd never hold," grumbled Ivan from the bed, not so intrigued and wanting to get back to the business of the crossbow.

"Aha!" said Cadderly, pointing a finger straight up in the air.

Ivan knew by the look on Cadderly's face that he had
played right into the young man's hopes. Cadderly did so love
doubters where his inventions were concerned.

"The aerial buttress!" the young priest proclaimed, holding his hands out to the strange, two-structured wall.

"Oo oi!" agreed Pikel, who had already tested the wall's
strength.

"There's one for the faeries," grumbled a doubting Ivan.

"Look at it, Ivan," Cadderly said reverently. "One for the
faeries, indeed, if that phrase implies grace. The strength of
the design cannot be underestimated. The bridges displace
stress so that the walls, with minimal stonework, can hold
much more than you might believe, leaving incredible possibilities for window designs."

"Sure, from the top," the dwarf replied gruffly, "but how
might it take a giant's ram on the side? And what about the
wind? There are mighty cross-breezes up here, and mightier
still if you go building higher!"

Cadderly spent a long moment considering the aerial buttress. Every time he looked upon the model, he was filled with

hope. He thought that a library should be an enlightening place, physically and mentally, and while the Edificant Library was surrounded by impressive grounds and mountain views, it remained a dark and thick-stoned place. The popular architecture of the time required massive stone foundations and did not allow for large windows. In the world of the Edificant Library, sunlight was something to be enjoyed outside.

"Scholars should not sit squinting by candlelight, even at midday, to read their tomes," Cadderly argued.

"The greatest weapons in all the world were forged in deep holes by my ancestors," Ivan countered.

"It was just the beginnings of an idea," mumbled Cadderly defensively, suddenly agreeing with Ivan that they should get back to the crossbow. Cadderly did not doubt his design's potential, but he realized that he would have a hard time convincing a dwarf, who had lived a century in tight tunnels, of the value of sunlight.

Ever sympathetic, Pikel put a hand on Cadderly's shoulder.

"Now for the bow," Ivan said, opening the wooden coffer. The dwarf gently lifted a small, nearly completed crossbow, beautifully constructed and resembling the bow depicted on the tapestry. "The work's making me thirsty!"

"The scroll is nearly translated," Cadderly assured him, not missing the reference to the ancient dwarven mead recipe he had promised in return for the crossbow. Cadderly had actually translated the recipe many weeks before but had held it back, knowing that Ivan would complete the bow more quickly with such a prize dangling just out of his reach.

"That's good, boy," Ivan replied, smacking his lips. "You get your bow in a week, but I'll need the picture to finish it. You got something smaller showing it?"

Cadderly shook his head. "All I have is the tapestry," he admitted.

"You want me to walk through the halls with a stolen tapestry under me arm?" Ivan roared.

"Borrowed," Cadderly corrected.

"With Headmistress Pertelope's blessings?" Ivan asked sarcastically.

"Uh oh," added Pikel.

"She will never miss it," Cadderly replied, unconvincingly. "If she does, I will tell her that I needed it to confirm some passages in the drow tome I am translating."

"Pertelope knows more of drow than does yerself," Ivan reminded him. "She's the one who gave you the book!"

"Uh oh," Pikel said again.

"The mead is blacker than midnight," Cadderly said offhandedly, "so the recipe says. It would kill a fair-sized tree if you poured only a pint of it along the roots."

"Get the other end," Ivan said to Pikel. Pikel pulled his mushroom-shaped cook's cap over the tangle of green hair, which made his ears stick out even farther, then helped Ivan roll the tapestry up tight. They hoisted it together while Cadderly cracked open the door and made sure that the hall was empty. Cadderly glanced over his shoulder at the diminishing angle of the shining sun through his window. His floor was marked in measured intervals to serve as a morning clock. "A few minutes to noon," he said to the dwarves. "Brother Chaunticleer will begin the midday canticle soon. All the host priests are required to attend and most of the others usually go. The way should be clear."

Ivan gave Cadderly a sour look.

"Tut-tut," muttered Pikel, shaking his furry face and wagging a finger at Cadderly.

"I will get there!" Cadderly growled at them. "No one notices if I am just a few moments late."

The melody began then, Brother Chaunticleer's perfect soprano wafting gently through the corridors of the ancient library. Every noon, Chaunticleer ascended to his place at the podium of the library's great hall to sing two songs, the respective legends of Deneir and Oghma. Many scholars came to the library to study, it was true, but many others came to hear the renowned Chaunticleer. He sang a cappella but could fill the great hall and the rooms beyond with his amazing four-octave voice so fully that listeners had to look at him often just to make sure that no choir stood behind him.

Oghma's song was first this day, and under the cover of that energetic and rousing tune, the brothers Bouldershoulder bounced and stumbled their way down two curving stairways and through a dozen too-tight doorways to their quarters beside the library's kitchen.

Cadderly entered the great hall at about the same time, slipping quietly through the high oaken double doors and moving to the side, behind a large arch support.

"Aerial buttress," he couldn't help but mutter, shaking his head in dismay at the bulky pillar. He realized then that he had not entered unnoticed. Kierkan Rufo smiled at him from the shadows of the next nearest arch.

Cadderly knew that the conniving Rufo had waited for him, seeking new fuel for Headmaster Avery's ire, and he knew that Avery would not excuse his tardiness. Cadderly pretended not to care, not wanting to give Rufo the satisfaction. He pointedly looked away and pulled out his spindle-disks, an archaic weapon used by ancient halfling tribesmen of southern Luiren. The device consisted of two circular rock crystal disks, each a finger's breadth wide and a finger's length in diameter, joined in their centers by a small bar on which was wrapped a string. Cadderly had discovered the weapon in an obscure tome and had actually improved on the design, using a metal connecting bar with a small hole through which the string could be threaded and knotted rather than tied.

Cadderly slipped his finger through the loop on the string's loose end. With a flick of his wrist, he sent the spindle-disks rolling down the length of the string, then brought them spinning back to his hand with a slight jerk of his finger.

Cadderly sneaked a look out of the corner of his eye. Knowing that he had Rufo's attention, he sent the disks down again, quickly looped the string over the fingers of his free hand to form a triangle, and held the still-spinning disks in the middle, rocking them back and forth like a baby's cradle. Rufo was leaning forward now, mesmerized by the game, and Cadderly didn't miss the opportunity.

He released the string from his cradling hand, gathering the spindle-disks too suddenly for the eye to follow, then flicked them out straight at his rival. The string brought the flying device back to Cadderly's hand before it got halfway to Rufo, but the startled man stumbled backward and toppled. Cadderly congratulated himself for his timing, for Rufo's noisy descent coincided with the most dramatic pause in Brother Chaunticleer's song.

"Ssshhh!" came the angry hisses from every direction, and Cadderly's was not the least among them. It seemed that Headmaster Avery would have two students to discipline that night.

Five

To Know Your Allies

The meeting chamber at Castle Trinity was quite different from the great and ornate hall of the Edificant Library. Its ceiling was low and its door squat and barred and heavily guarded. A single triangular table dominated the room, with three chairs on each side, one group for the wizards, one for the fighters, and one for the clerics.

Scan the room, Druzil suggested telepathically to Aballister, who was in the room. The imp surveyed through the wizard's eyes, using their telepathic link to view whatever Aballister was looking at. Aballister did as he was bidden, moving his gaze around the triangular table, first to Ragnor and the other two fighters, then to Barjin and his two cleric companions.

Druzil broke the mental connection suddenly and hissed a wicked laugh, knowing that he had left Aballister in complete confusion. He could feel the wizard trying to reestablish the mental link, could hear Aballister's thoughts calling to him.

But Aballister was not in command of their telepathy; the imp had used this mental form of communication for more decades than Aballister had been alive and it was he who decided when and where he and the wizard would link. For now, Druzil had no reason to continue contact; he had seen all that he needed to see. Barjin was in the meeting hall and would be busy there for some time. Druzil found his center of magic, his otherworldly essence, which allowed him to transcend the physical rules governing creatures of this host plane. A few seconds later, the imp faded from sight, becoming transparent, then he was off, flapping down the hallways to a wing of Castle Trinity to which he rarely traveled.

It was risky business, Druzil knew, but if the chaos curse was to be in the priest's hands, then Druzil needed to know more about him.

Druzil knew that Barjin's door would be locked and heavily warded against intrusion, but he considered that a minor problem with one of Barjin's bodyguards standing rigid in the hall just outside it. Druzil entered the man's thoughts just long enough to plant a suggestion, a magical request.

"*There is an intruder in Barjin's room,*" came Druzil's silent beckon.

The guard glanced about nervously for a moment, as if seeking the source of the call. He stared long at Barjin's door looking right through the invisible imp—then hastily fumbled with some keys, spoke a command word to prevent the warding glyphs from exploding, and entered.

Druzil quietly mouthed the same command word and walked in behind.

After a few minutes of inspecting the apparently empty room, the guard shook his head and left, locking the door behind him.

Druzil snickered at how easily some humans could be controlled. The imp didn't have the time or inclination to gloat, though, not with all of the mysterious Barjin's secrets open for his inspection.

The room was ordinary enough for one of Barjin's stature. A large canopy bed dominated the wall opposite the door, with a night table beside it. Druzil rubbed his hands together eagerly as he headed for the table. Atop it, next to the lamp, was a black-bound book and, next to that, several quills and an inkwell.

"How thoughtful of you to keep a journal," Druzil rasped, carefully opening the work. He read through the first entries, dated two years earlier. They were mostly lamentations by Barjin, accounts of his exploits in the northern kingdoms of Vaasa, Damara, and Narfell, to the north. Druzil's already considerable respect for the priest grew as he devoured the words. Barjin once had commanded an army and had served a powerful master—he gave no direct references to the man, if it was a man—not as a cleric, but as a wizard!

Druzil paused to consider this revelation, then hissed and read on. Although formidable, Barjin admitted that he had not been the most powerful of the wizards in his master's service—again a vague reference to the mysterious master, giving Druzil the impression that perhaps Barjin, even years later, feared to speak the creature's name aloud or write it down. Barjin's rise to power had come later, when the army had taken on a religious zeal and his master apparently had assumed godlike proportions.

Druzil couldn't contain a snicker at the striking parallels between the priest's ascent and the chaos curse's transformation into a goddess's direct agent.

Barjin had become a priest and headed an army to fulfill his evil master's desire to conquer the whole of the northland. The plans had fallen through, though, when an order of paladins—Druzil hissed aloud when he read that cursed word—arose in Damara and organized an army of its own. Barjin's master and most of his cohorts had been thrown down, but Barjin had barely escaped with his life and a portion of the evil army's accumulated wealth.

Barjin had fled south, alone but for a few lackeys. Since his proclaimed "god" had been dispatched, his clerical powers had greatly diminished. Druzil spent a while musing over this revelation; nowhere did Barjin mention his claimed meeting with Talona's avatar. The journal went on to tell of Barjin's joining the triumvirate at Castle Trinity—again with no mention of the avatar. Druzil snickered aloud at Barjin's opportunism. Even a year ago, coming in as a pitiful refugee, Barjin had duped Castle Trinity's leaders, had used their fanaticism against them.

After only a month in the castle, Barjin had ascended to the third rank in the priestly hierarchy, and after only a few more weeks, Barjin had taken over undisputed command as Talona's chief representative. And yet, Druzil realized as he flipped quickly through the pages, Barjin thought not enough about his goddess to give her more than a few passing references in his journal.

Aballister was correct: Barjin was a hypocrite, a fact that hardly seemed to matter. Again Druzil snickered aloud at the irony, at the pure chaos.

Druzil knew the rest of Barjin's story well enough; he had been present long before Barjin ever arrived. The journal, sadly, did not offer any further revelations, but the imp was not disappointed when he closed the book; there were too many other items to be investigated.

Barjin's new vestments, a conical cap and expensive purple robes embroidered in red with the new insignia of the triumvirate, hung beside the bed. An offspring of Talona's symbol, the three teardrops inside a triangle's points, this one sported a trident, its three prongs tipped by teardrop-shaped bottles, much like the one carrying the chaos curse. Barjin had designed it personally, and only Ragnor had offered any resistance.

"So you do plan to spread the word of your god," Druzil muttered a few moments later when he discovered Barjin's bedroll, folded tent, and stuffed backpack under the bed. He reached for the items, then jumped back suddenly, sensing a presence in that pile. He felt the beginnings of a telepathic communication, but not from Aballister. Eagerly, the imp reached under the bed and pulled the items out, recognizing the telepathic source immediately as Barjin's magical mace.

"Screaming Maiden," Druzil said, echoing the item's telepathic declaration and examining the crafted item. Its obsidian head was that of a pretty young girl, strangely innocuous and appealing. Druzil saw through the grotesque facade. He knew this was not a weapon of the material plane, but one that had been forged in the Abyss, or in the Nine Hells, or in Tarterus, or in one of the other lower planes. It was sentient, obviously, and hungry. More than anything else, Druzil could feel its hunger, its blood-lust. He watched in joyful amazement as the mace enhanced that point, its obsidian head twisting into a leering visage, a fanged maw opening wide.

Druzil clapped his padded hands together and smiled wickedly. His respect for Barjin continued to mount, for any mortal capable of wielding such a weapon must be powerful indeed.

Rumors around the fortress expressed disdain that Barjin did not favor the poisoned dagger, the usual weapon of Talona's clerics, but, seeing this mace up close and sensing its terrible power, Druzil agreed with the priest's choice.

Inside the rolled tent Druzil found a brazier and tripod nearly as intricate and rune-covered as Aballister's. "You are a sorcerer, too, Barjin," the imp whispered, wondering what future events that might imply. Already Druzil imagined what his life might be like if he had stepped through the brazier to Barjin's call instead of Aballister's.

The thick backpack held other wondrous items. Druzil found a deep, gem-encrusted bowl of beaten platinum, no doubt worth a king's fortune. Druzil placed it carefully on the floor and reached back into the pack, as exuberant as a hungry orc shoving its arm down a rat hole.

He pulled out a solid and heavy object, fist-sized and wrapped in black cloth. Whatever was inside clearly emanated magical energies, and Druzil took care to lift only one corner of the cloth to peek in. He beheld a huge black sapphire, recognized it as a necromancer's stone, and quickly rewrapped it in the shielding cloth. If exposed, such a stone could send out a call to the dead, summoning ghosts or ghouls, or any other netherworld monsters in the area.

Of similar magical properties was the small ceramic flask that Druzil inspected next. He unstoppered it and sniffed, sneezing as some ashes came into his ample nose.

"Ashes?" the imp whispered curiously, peering in. Under the black cloth, the necromancer's stone pulsed, and Druzil understood. "Long dead spirit," he muttered, quickly closing the flask.

Nothing else showed to be of any particular interest, so Druzil carefully rewrapped and replaced everything as he had found it. He hopped up on the comfortable bed, secure with his invisibility, and relaxed, pondering all that he had learned. This Barjin was a diversified human-priest, wizard, general, dabbling in sorcery, necromancy, and who could guess what else.

"Yes, a very resourceful human," Druzil decided. He felt better about Barjin's involvement in the chaos curse. He checked in telepathically with Aballister for just a moment, to make certain that the meeting was in full swing, then congratulated himself on his cunning and folded his plump hands behind his head.

Soon he was fast asleep.

* * * * *

"We have only the one suitable bottle," said Aballister, representing the wizards. "The ever-smoking devices are difficult to create, requiring rare gems and metals, and we all know how costly it was to brew even a small amount of the

elixir." He felt Barjin's stare boring into him at the reference
to the cost.

"Do not speak of the Most Fatal Horror as an elixir," the
clerical leader commanded. "Once it may have been just a
magical potion, but now it is much more."

"*Tuanta Quiro Miancay*," chanted the other two priests,
scarred and ugly men with blotchy tattoos covering nearly
every inch of their exposed skin.

Aballister returned Barjin's glare. He wanted to scream
at Barjin's hypocrisy, to shake the other clerics into action
against him, but Aballister wisely checked his outburst. He
knew that any accusations against Barjin would produce the
opposite results and that he would become the target of the
faithful. Druzil's estimation of Barjin had been correct, Aballister had to admit. The priest had indeed consolidated his
power.

"Brewing the Most Fatal Horror," conceded Aballister,
"has depleted our resources. To begin again and create more,
and also acquire another bottle, could well prove beyond our
limits."

"Why do we need these stupid bottles?" interrupted
Ragnor. "If the stuff's a god as you say, then . . ."

Barjin was quick to answer. "The Most Fatal Horror is
merely an agent of Talona," the priest explained calmly. "In
itself, it is not a god, but it will aid us to comply with Talona's
edicts."

Ragnor's eyes narrowed dangerously. It was obvious that
the volatile ogrillon's patience had just about expired.

"All of your followers embrace *Tuanta Quiro Miancay*,"
Barjin reminded Ragnor, "embrace it with all their hearts."
Ragnor eased back in his seat, flinching at the threatening im-
plications.

Aballister studied Barjin curiously for a long while, awed
by how easily the priest had calmed the ogrillon. Barjin was
tall, vigorous, and imposing, but he was no match physically
for Ragnor. Usually, physical strength was all that mattered to

the powerful fighter; Ragnor normally showed the clerics and wizards less respect than he gave to even his lowliest soldiers.

Barjin seemed to be the exception, though; especially of late, Ragnor had not openly opposed him on any issue.

Aballister, while concerned, was not surprised. He knew that Barjin's powers went far beyond the priest's physical abilities. Barjin was a charmer and a hypnotist, a careful strategist who weighed his opponent's mind-set above all else and used spells as often for simple enhancement of a favorable situation as to affect those he meant to destroy. Just a few weeks earlier, a conspiracy had been discovered within the evil triumvirate. The single prisoner had resisted Ragnor's interrogations, at the price of incredible pain and several toes, but Barjin had the wretch talking within an hour, willingly divulging all that he knew about his fellow conspirators. Whispers said that the tortured man actually believed Barjin was an ally, right up until the priest casually bashed in his skull.

Aballister did not doubt those whispers and was not surprised. That was how Barjin worked; few could resist the priest's hypnotic charisma. Aballister did not know much of Barjin's former deity, lost in the wastelands of Vaasa, but what he had seen of the refugee priest's spell repertoire was beyond the norm that he would expect of clerics. Again Aballister referred to the whispers for his answers, rumors that indicated Barjin dabbled in wizardry as well as clerical magic.

Barjin was still speaking reverently of the elixir when Aballister turned his attention back to the meeting. The priest's preaching held the other clerics, and Ragnor's two fighter companions, awestruck. Aballister shook his head and dared not interrupt. He considered again the course that his life had taken, how the avatar had led him to Druzil, and Druzil had delivered the recipe. Then the avatar had led Barjin to Castle Trinity. That was the part of the puzzle that did not fit in Aballister's reasoning. After a year of watching the priest, Aballister remained convinced that Barjin was no true disciple of Talona, but again he reminded himself that

Barjin, sincere or not, was furthering the cause, and that because of Barjin's purse and influence, all the region might soon be claimed in the goddess's name.

Aballister let out a profound sigh; such were the paradoxes of chaos.

"Aballister?" Barjin asked. The wizard cleared his throat nervously and glanced around, realizing he had missed much of the conversation.

"Ragnor was inquiring about the necessity of the bottles," Barjin politely explained.

"The bottles, yes," Aballister stuttered. "The elix— . . . the Most Fatal Horror is potent with or without them. Minute amounts are all that are required for the chaos curse to take effect, but it will last only a short while. With the ever-smoking bottles, the god-stuff is released continually. We have created just a few drops, but I believe there is enough liquid to fuel the ever-smoking bottle for months, perhaps years, if the mixture within the bottle is correct."

Barjin looked around and exchanged nods with his clerical companions. "We have decided that Talona's agent is ready," he declared.

"You have . . ." the wizard Dorigen stammered in disbelief.

Aballister stared long and hard at Barjin. He had meant to take command of the meeting and suggest just what the priest was getting at; again Barjin had thought one step ahead of him, had stolen his thunder.

"We are the representatives of Talona," Barjin coolly replied to Dorigen's outrage. His companions bobbed their heads stupidly.

Aballister's clenched fingers nearly tore a chunk out of his oaken chair.

"The goddess has spoken to us, has revealed her wishes," Barjin continued smugly. "Our conquests will soon begin!"

Ragnor beat a fist on the table in excited agreement; now the priest was speaking in terms the ogrillon warrior could understand. "Who are you planning for carrying the bottle?" Ragnor asked bluntly.

"I will carry it," Aballister quickly put in. He knew as soon as he heard his own words that his claim sounded desperate, a last attempt to salvage his own position of power.

Barjin shot him an incredulous look.

"It was I who met Talona's avatar," Aballister insisted, "and I who discovered the recipe for the Most Fatal Horror."

"For that, we thank you," remarked the priest in a condescending tone. Aballister started to protest, but sank back in his chair as a magical message was whispered into his ear. *Do not fight with me over this, wizard*, Barjin quietly warned.

Aballister knew that the critical moment was upon him. If he gave in now, he felt he might never recover his standing in Castle Trinity, but if he argued against Barjin, against the religious fury that the priest had inspired, he would surely split the order and might find himself badly outnumbered.

"The priests of Talona will carry the bottle, of course," Barjin answered Ragnor. "We are the true disciples."

"You are one leg of a ruling triumvirate," Aballister dared to remind him. "Do not claim the Most Fatal Horror solely as your own."

Ragnor did not see things quite the same way. "Leave it to the priests," the ogrillon demanded.

Aballister's surprise disappeared as soon as he realized that the brutish fighter, suspicious of magic, was simply relieved that he would not have to carry the bottle.

"Agreed," Barjin quickly put in. Aballister started to speak out, but Dorigen put a hand over his arm and gave him a look that begged him to let it go.

"You have something to say, good wizard?" Barjin asked.

Aballister shook his head and sank even deeper into his chair—and even deeper into despair.

"Then it is settled," said Barjin. "The Most Fatal Horror will descend upon our enemies, carried by my second—" he nodded to the priests on his right and on his left "—and my third."

"No!" Aballister blurted, seeing a way to salvage something of this disaster. All gazes descended upon him; he saw Ragnor put a hand to his sword hilt. "Your second?" the wizard asked, and now it was he who feigned an incredulous tone. "Your third?" Aballister rose from his chair and held his arms outstretched.

"Is this not the direct agent of our goddess?" he preached. "Is this not the beginning of our greatest ambitions? No, only Barjin is fit to carry such a precious artifact. Only Barjin can properly begin the reign of chaos." The gathering turned as one to Barjin, and Aballister returned to his seat, thinking that he had at last outmaneuvered the clever priest. If he could get Barjin out of Castle Trinity for a time, he could reestablish his claim as the chief speaker for the brotherhood.

Unexpectedly, the priest didn't argue. "I will carry it," he said. He looked to the other, startled clerics and added, "and I will go alone."

"All the fun for you?" Ragnor complained.

"Merely the first battle of the war," Barjin responded.

"My warriors desire battle," Ragnor pressed. "They hunger for blood!"

"They will have all that they can drink and more!" Barjin snapped. "But I will go first and cripple our enemies. When I return, Ragnor can lead the second assault."

This seemed to satisfy the ogrillon, and now Aballister understood Barjin's salvaging ploy. By going alone, the priest would not only leave his clerical cohorts to keep an eye on things, but he would leave Ragnor and his soldiers. Always vying for power, the ogrillon, with the prodding of the remaining clerics, would not allow Aballister and the wizards to regain a firm foothold.

"Where will you loose it?" Aballister asked. "And when?"

"There are preparations to be made before I leave," Barjin answered, "things that only a priest, a true disciple, would understand. As to where, let it be of no concern to you."

"But—" Aballister started, only to be interrupted sharply.

"Talona alone will tell me," Barjin growled with finality.

Aballister glared in outrage but did not respond. Barjin was a slippery opponent; every time Aballister had him cornered, he merely invoked the name of the goddess, as if that answered everything.

"It is decided," Barjin continued, seeing no response forthcoming. "This meeting is at an end."

* * * * *

"Oh, go away," Druzil slurred, both audibly and telepathically. Aballister was looking for him, trying to get into his thoughts. Druzil smiled at his superiority in keeping the wizard out and lazily rolled over.

Then the imp realized what Aballister's call might signify. He sat up with a start and looked into Aballister's mind just long enough to see that the wizard had returned to his own room.

Druzil hadn't meant to sleep this long, had wanted to be far from this place before the meeting adjourned.

Druzil held very still when the door opened and Barjin entered the room.

If he had been more attentive, the priest might have sensed the invisible presence. Barjin had other things on his mind, though. He rushed for the bed and Druzil recoiled, thinking Barjin meant to attack him. But Barjin dropped to his knees and reached eagerly for his pack and his enchanted mace.

"You and I," Barjin said to the weapon, holding it out before him, "will spread the word of their goddess and reap the rewards of chaos. It has been too long since you feasted on the blood of humans, my pet, far too long." The mace couldn't audibly reply, of course, but Druzil thought he saw a smile widen on the pretty girl's sculpted face.

"And you," Barjin said into the backpack, to the ceramic, ash-filled flask as far as Druzil could tell. "Prince Khalif. Could it be the time for you to walk the earth again?" Barjin snapped the backpack shut and roared with such sincere and exuberant laughter that Druzil almost joined in.

The imp promptly reminded himself that he and Barjin were not, as yet, formally allied, and that Barjin would most definitely prove a dangerous enemy. Fortunately for the imp, Barjin, in his haste, had not closed the door behind him. Druzil crawled off the bed, using Barjin's laughter as cover, and slipped out the door, wisely uttering the password for the warding glyph as he crossed the threshold.

* * * * *

Barjin left Castle Trinity five days later, bearing the ever-smoking bottle. He traveled with a small entourage of Ragnor's fighters, but they would only serve as escorts as far as the human settlement of Carradoon, near Impresk Lake on the southeastern edge of the Snowflake Mountains. Barjin would go alone from there to his final destination, which he and his clerical conspirators would still not reveal to the other leaders of Castle Trinity.

Back at the fortress, Aballister and the wizards waited as patiently as possible, confident that their turn would come.

Ragnor's force was not so patient, though. The ogrillon wanted battle, wanted to begin the offensive right away. Ragnor was not a stupid creature, though. He knew that his small force, only a few hundred strong unless he managed to entice the neighboring goblinoid tribes to join in, would not have an easy time of conquering the lake, the mountains, and the forest.

Still, and despite all his reasoning, Ragnor was hungry.

Since his very first day at Castle Trinity, nearly five years before, the ogrillon had vowed revenge on Shilmista Forest, on the elves who had defeated his tribe and driven him and the other refugees far from the wood.

Every member of Castle Trinity, from lowly soldier to wizard to priest, had spoken often of the day they would rise from their disguised holes and blacken the region. All now held their breath, awaiting Barjin's return, awaiting confirmation that the conquest had begun.

Six

Water and Dust

The cloaked figure moved slowly toward Danica.

Thinking it a monk of some obscure and eccentric scct—and such monks were usually hostile and dangerous, determined to prove their fighting prowess against any other monks they encountered—the woman gathered up the pile of parchments she had been studying and quickly moved to another table.

The tall figure, cowl pulled low to hide its face, turned to pursue, its feet making unrecognizable scuffling noises on the stone floor.

Danica looked around. It was late; this study hall, on the second floor above the library, was nearly empty and Danica decided that it might be time for her to retire, too. She realized that she was exhausted, and she wondered if she might be imagining things.

The figure came on, slowly, menacingly, and Danica thought that perhaps it was not some other monk. What horrors might that low cowl be hiding? she wondered. She gathered the parchments again and started boldly for the main aisle, though that course meant passing right by the figure.

A hand shot out and caught her shoulder. Danica stifled a startled cry and spun about—to face the shadowy cowl, losing many of her scrolls in the action. As she collected her wits, though, Danica realized that it was no skeletal apparition holding her in an icy, undead grip. It was a human hand, warm and gentle, and showing signs of ink near the fingernails.

The hand of a scribe.

"Fear not!" the specter rasped.

Danica knew that voice too well to be deceived by the breathless mask. She scowled and crossed her arms over her chest.

Understanding that the joke was ended, Cadderly removed his hand from Danica's shoulder and quickly pulled back the cowl. "Greetings!" he said, smiling widely into Danica's frown as though he hoped his mirth to be a contagious thing. "I thought I might find you here."

Danica's silence did not promise reciprocal warmth.

"Do you like my disguise?" Cadderly went on. "It had to be convincing for me to get past Avery's spies. They are everywhere, and Rufo watches my every move even more closely now, though he shared equal punishment."

"You both deserved it!" Danica snapped back. "After your behavior in the great hall."

"So now we clean," Cadderly agreed with a resigned shrug. "Everywhere, every day. It has been a long two weeks, with a longer two still to come."

"More than that if Headmaster Avery catches you here," Danica warned.

Cadderly shook his head and threw up his hands. "I was cleaning the kitchen," he explained. "Ivan and Pikel threw me out. 'It's me kitchen, boy!' Cadderly said in his best dwarven voice, slamming his fists on his hips and puffing out his chest. " 'If there's any cleanin' to be done, it'll be done by meself! I'm not needing a . . .' "

Danica reminded him where he was to quiet him and pulled him to the side, behind the cover of some book racks.

"That was Ivan," Cadderly said. "Pikel did not say much. So the kitchen will be cleaned by the dwarves if it is to be cleaned at all, and a good thing, I say. An hour in there could put an end to my appetite for some time to come!"

"That does not excuse you from your work," Danica protested.

"I am working," Cadderly retorted. He pulled aside the front of his heavy woolen cloak and lifted a foot, revealing a sandal that was half shoe and half scrubbing brush. "Every step I take cleans the library a little bit more."

Danica couldn't argue with Cadderly's unending stream of personalized logic. In truth, she was glad that Cadderly had come to visit her. She hadn't seen much of him in the last two weeks and found that she missed him dearly. Also, on a more practical level, Danica was having trouble deciphering some important parchments and Cadderly was just the person to help her.

"Could you look at these?" she asked, retrieving the fallen scrolls.

"Master Penpahg D'Ahn?" Cadderly replied, hardly surprised. He knew that Danica had come to the Edificant Library more than a year before to study the collected notes of Penpahg D'Ahn of Ashanath, the grandmaster monk who had died five hundred years before. Danica's order was small and secretive, and few in this part of the Realms had ever heard of Penpahg D'Ahn, but those who studied the grandmaster's fighting and concentration techniques gave their lives over to his philosophies wholeheartedly. Cadderly had only seen a fraction of Danica's notes, but those had intrigued him, and he certainly could not dispute Danica's fighting prowess. More than half of the proud Oghman clerics had been walking around rubbing numerous bruises since the fiery young woman had come to the library.

"I am not quite certain of this interpretation," Danica

explained, spreading a parchment over a table.

Cadderly moved to her side and examined the scroll. It began with a picture of crossed fists, which indicated that it was a battle technique, but then showed the single open eye indicating a concentration technique. Cadderly read on. "Gigel Nugel," he said aloud, then he thought that over for a moment.

"Iron Skull. The maneuver is called Iron Skull."

Danica banged a fist onto the table. "As I believed!" she said.

Cadderly was almost afraid to ask. "What is it?"

Danica held the parchment up over the table's lamp, emphasizing a small, nearly lost sketch in the lower corner. Cadderly eyed it closely. It appeared to be a large rock sitting atop a man's head. "Is that supposed to be a representation of Penpahg D'Ahn?" he asked.

Danica nodded.

"So now we know how he died," Cadderly snickered.

Danica snapped the parchment away, not appreciating the humor. Sometimes Cadderly's irreverence crossed the boundaries of her considerable tolerance.

"I am sorry," Cadderly apologized with a low bow. "Truly Penpahg D'Ahn was an amazing person, but are you saying he could break stone with his head?"

"It is a test of discipline," Danica replied, her voice edged with mounting excitement. "As are all of Grandmaster Penpahg D'Ahn's teachings. The grandmaster was in control of his body, of his very being."

"I am quite certain that you would forget my very name if Master Penpahg D'Ahn returned from the grave," Cadderly said mournfully.

"Forget who's name?" Danica replied calmly, not playing into his game.

Cadderly cast a hard glare at her but smiled as she smiled, unable to resist her charms. The young scholar grew suddenly serious, though, and looked back to the parchment. "Promise me that you are not intending to smash your face into a stone," he said.

Danica crossed her arms over her chest and tilted her head in an obstinate way, silently telling Cadderly to mind his own business.

"Danica," Cadderly said firmly.

In reply, Danica extended one finger and placed it down on the table. Her thoughts turned inward; her concentration had to be complete. She lifted herself by that single extended digit, bending at the waist and bringing her legs up even with the table top. She held the pose for some time, glad for Cadderly's amazed gape.

"The powers of the body are beyond our comprehension and expectations," Danica remarked, shifting to a sitting position on the table and wiggling her finger to show Cadderly that it had suffered no damage. "Grandmaster Penpahg D'Ahn understood them and learned to channel them to fit his needs. I will not go out this night, nor any night soon, and attempt the Iron Skull, that much I can promise you. You must understand that Iron Skull is but a minor test compared to what I came here to achieve."

"Physical suspension," Cadderly muttered with obvious distaste.

Danica's face brightened. "Think of it!" she said. "The grandmaster was able to stop his heart, to suspend his very breathing."

"There are priests who can do the very same thing," Cadderly reminded her, "and wizards, too. I saw the spell in the book I inscribed . . ."

"This is not a spell," Danica retorted. "Wizards and priests call upon powers beyond their own minds and bodies. Think, though, of the control necessary to do as Grandmaster Penpahg D'Ahn did. He could stop his heart from beating at any time, using only his own understanding of his physical being. You above all should appreciate that."

"I do," Cadderly replied sincerely. His visage softened and

he ran the back of his hand gently across Danica's soft cheek. "But you scare me, Danica. You are relying on tomes a half millennium old for techniques that could be tragic. I do not remember with fondness how my life was before I met you, and I do not want to think of what it would be without you."

"I cannot change who I am," Danica replied quietly, but without compromise, "nor will I surrender the goals I have chosen for my life."

Cadderly considered her words for a few moments, weighing them against his own feelings. He respected everything about Danica, and above all else it was her fire, her willingness to accept and defeat all challenges, that he most loved. To tame her, to put out that fire, Cadderly knew, would be to kill this Danica, his Danica, more surely than any of Penpahg D'Ahn's seemingly impossible tests ever could.

"I cannot change," Danica said again.

Cadderly's reply came straight from his heart. "I would not want you to."

* * * * *

Barjin knew that he could not enter the ivy-streaked building through any of its windows or doors. While the Edificant Library was always open to scholars of all nonevil sects, warding glyphs had been placed over every known entrance to protect against those not invited—persons, such as Barjin, dedicated to the spread of chaos and misery.

The Edificant Library was an ancient building, and Barjin knew that ancient buildings usually held secrets, even from their present inhabitants.

The priest held the red-glowing bottle aloft before his eyes.

"We have come to our destination," he said, speaking as if the bottle could hear him, "to where I will secure my position of rulership over Castle Trinity, and over all the region once our conquest is completed." Barjin wanted to rush in, find his catalyst, and set the events in motion. He really didn't believe the elixir was an agent of Talona, but then, Barjin didn't consider himself an agent of Talona, though he had joined her clerical order. He had adopted the goddess for convenience, for mutual benefit, and knew that as long as his actions furthered the Lady of Poison's evil designs, she would be content.

Barjin spent the rest of the day, which was drizzly and dreary for late spring, in the shadows behind the trees lining the wide road. He heard the midday canticle, then watched many priests and other scholars exit alone or in groups for an early afternoon stroll.

The evil priest took a few precautionary measures, casting simple spells that would help him blend into his background and remain undetected. He listened to the casual banter of the passing groups, wondering with amusement how their words might change when he loosed the Most Fatal Horror in their midst.

The figure that soon caught Barjin's attention, though, was neither priest nor scholar. Disheveled and gray haired, with a dirty and stubbly face and skin wrinkled and browned from many years in the sun, Mullivy, the groundskeeper, went about his routines as he had for four decades, sweeping the road and the stairs to the front doors, heedless of the drizzle.

Barjin's wicked grin spread wide. If there was a secret way into the Edificant Library, this old man would know of it.

* * * * *

The clouds had broken by sunset, and a beautiful crimson patina lined the mountains west of the library. Mullivy hardly noticed it, though, having seen too many sunsets to be impressed anymore. He stretched the aches out of his old bones and strolled to his small workshed off to the side of the library's huge main building.

"You're getting old, too," the groundskeeper said to the

shack as the door opened with a loud creak. He reached inside, meaning to replace his broom, then stopped abruptly, frozen in place by some power he did not understand.

A hand reached around him, prying the broom from his stubborn grasp. Mullivy's mind shouted warnings, but he could not bring his body to react, could not shout or spin to face the person guiding that unexpected hand. He then was pushed into the shed—fell face down, not able to lift an arm to break the fall—and the door closed behind him. He knew he was not alone.

* * * * *

"You will tell me," the sinister voice promised from the darkness.

Mullivy hung by his wrists, as he had for several hours. The room was totally black, but the groundskeeper sensed the awful presence all too near.

"I could kill you and ask your corpse," Barjin said with a chuckle. "Dead men talk, I assure you, and they do not lie."

"There's no other way in," Mullivy said for perhaps the hundredth time.

Barjin knew the old man was lying. At the beginning of the interrogation, the priest had cast spells to distinguish truth from falsehood and Mullivy had failed that test completely.

Barjin reached out and gently grabbed the groundskeeper's stomach in one hand.

"No! No!" he begged, thrashing and trying to wiggle out of that grip. Barjin held tight and began a soft chant, and soon Mullivy's insides felt as if they were on fire, his stomach ripped by agony that no man could endure. His screams, primal, hopeless, and helpless, emanated from that pained area.

"Do cry out," Barjin chided him. "All about the shed is a spell of silence, old fool. You will not disturb the slumber of those within the library. But then, why would you care for their sleep?" Barjin asked quietly, his voice filled with feigned sympathy. He released his grip and softly stroked Mullivy's wounded belly.

Mullivy stopped thrashing and screaming, though the pain of the sinister spell lingered.

"To them you are insignificant," Barjin purred, and his suggestion carried the weight of magical influences. "The priests think themselves your betters. They allow you to sweep for them and keep the rain gutters clean, but do they care for your pain? You are out here suffering terribly, but do any of them rush to your aid?"

Mullivy's heaving breaths settled into a calmer rhythm.

"Still you defend them so stubbornly," Barjin purred, knowing that his torture was beginning to wear the groundskeeper down. "They would not defend you, and still you will not show me your secret, at the cost of your life."

Even in his most lucid state, Mullivy was not a powerful thinker. His best friend most often was a bottle of stolen wine, and now, in his agony-racked jumble of thoughts, this unseen assailant's words rang loudly of truth. Why shouldn't he show this man his secret, the damp, moss-and-spider-filled dirt tunnel that led to the lowest level of the library complex, the ancient and unused catacombs below the wine cellar and the upper dungeon level? Suddenly, as Barjin had planned, Mullivy's imagined appearance of the unseen assailant softened. In his desperation, the groundskeeper needed to believe that his tormentor could actually be his ally.

"You won't tell them?" Mullivy asked.

"They will be the last to know," Barjin promised hopefully.

"You won't stop me from getting at the wine?"

Barjin backed off a step, surprised. He understood the old man's initial hesitance. The groundskeeper's secret way into the library led to the wine cellar, a stash that the wretch would not easily part with. "Dear man," Barjin purred, "you may have all the wine you desire—and much more, so much more."

* * * * *

They had barely entered the tunnel when Mullivy, carrying the torch, turned and waved it threateningly at Barjin.

Barjin's laughter mocked him, but Mullivy's voice remained firm. "I showed you the way," the groundskeeper declared. "Now I'm leaving."

"No," Barjin replied evenly. A shrug sent the priest's traveling cloak to the floor, revealing him in all his splendor. He wore his new vestments, the purple silken robes depicting a trident capped by three red flasks. On his belt was his peculiar mace, its head a sculpture of a young girl. "You have joined me now," Barjin explained. "You will never be leaving."

Terror drove Mullivy's movements. He slapped the burning torch against Barjin's shoulder and tried to push by, but the priest had prepared himself well before handing the torch to the groundskeeper. The flames did not touch Barjin, did not even singe his magnificent vestments, for they were defeated by a protection spell.

Mullivy tried a different tactic, slamming the torch like a club, but the vestments carried a magical armor as solid as metal plate mail and the wooden torch bounced off Barjin's shoulder without so much as causing the priest to flinch.

"Come now, dear Mullivy," Barjin cajoled, taking no offense. "You do not want me as an enemy."

Mullivy fell back and nearly dropped the torch. It took him a long moment to get past his terror, to even find his breath.

"Lead on," Barjin bade him. "You know this tunnel and the passages beyond. Show them to me."

Barjin liked the catacombs—dusty and private and filled with the remains of long-dead priests, some embalmed and others only cobweb-covered skeletons. He would have use for them.

Mullivy led him through a tour of the level, including the rickety stairwell that led up to the library's wine cellar and a medium-sized chamber that once had been used as a study for the original library. Barjin thought this room an excellent place to set up his unholy altar, but first he had to see exactly how useful the groundskeeper might prove.

They lit several torches and set them in wall sconces, then Barjin led Mullivy to an ancient table, one of many furnishings in the room, and produced his precious baggage. The bottle had been heavily warded back at Castle Trinity; only disciples of Talona or someone of pure heart could even touch it, and only the latter could open it. Like Aballister, Barjin knew this to be an obstacle, but unlike the wizard, the priest believed it a fitting one. What better irony than to have one of pure heart loose the chaos curse?

"Open it, I pray you," Barjin said.

The groundskeeper studied the flask for a moment, then looked curiously at the priest.

Barjin knew Mullivy's weak spot. "It is ambrosia," the priest lied. "The drink of the gods. One taste of it and forever after wines will taste to you ten times as sweet, for the lingering effects of ambrosia will never diminish. Drink, I pray you. You have certainly earned your reward."

Mullivy licked his lips eagerly, took one final look at Barjin, then reached for the glowing bottle. A jolt of electricity shot into him as he touched it, blackening his fingers and throwing him across the room to where he slammed into a wall. Barjin went over and dropped one arm under Mullivy's shoulder to help him stand.

"I thought not," the priest muttered to himself.

Still twitching from the blast, his hair dancing wildly with lingering static, Mullivy could not find his voice to reply.

"Fear not," Barjin assured him. "You will serve me in other ways." Mullivy noticed then that the priest held his girl's-head mace in his other hand.

Mullivy fell back against the wall and put his arms up defensively, but they were hardly protection from Barjin's foul weapon. The innocent looking head swung in at the doomed groundskeeper, transforming as it went. The weapon's image became angular, evil, the Screaming Maiden, her mouth opening impossibly wide, to reveal long, venom-tipped fangs.

She bit hungrily through the bone in Mullivy's forearm and plowed on, crushing and tearing into the man's chest. He twitched wildly for several agonizing moments, then he slid down the wall and died.

Barjin, with many preparations still to make, paid him no heed.

* * * * *

Aballister leaned back in his chair, breaking his concentration from his magical mirror but not breaking the connection he had made. He had located Barjin and had recognized the priest's surroundings: the Edificant Library. Aballister rubbed his hands through his thinning hair and considered the revelation, news that he found more than a little disturbing.

The wizard had mixed emotions concerning the library, unresolved feelings that he did not care to examine at this important time. Aballister had actually studied there once, many years before, but his curiosity with denizens of the lower planes had ended that relationship. The host priests thought it a pity that one of Aballister's potential had to be asked to leave, but they expressed their concerns that Aballister had some trouble distinguishing between good and evil, between proper studies and dangerous practices.

The expulsion did not end Aballister's relationship with the Edificant Library, though. Other events over the ensuing years had served to increase the wizard's ambiguous feelings toward the place. Now, in the overall plan of regional conquest, Aballister would have greatly preferred to leave the library for last, with him personally directing the attack. He never would have guessed that Barjin would be so daring as to go after the place in the initial assault, believing that the priest would venture to Shilmista, or to some vital spot in Carradoon.

"Well?" came a question from across the room.

"He is in the Edificant Library," Aballister answered grimly. "The priest has chosen to begin our campaign against our most powerful enemies."

Aballister anticipated Druzil's reply well enough to mouth "*bene tellemara*" along with the imp.

"Find him," Druzil demanded. "What is he thinking?"

Aballister put a curious gaze the imp's way, but if he had any notion to reprimand Druzil, it was lost in his agreement with the demand. He leaned forward again toward the large mirror and scried deeper, into the library's lower levels, through the cobweb-covered tunnels to the room where Barjin had built his altar.

Barjin glanced around nervously for a moment, then apparently recognized the source of the mental connection. "Well met, Aballister," the priest said smugly.

"You take great chances," the wizard remarked.

"Do you doubt the power of *Tuanta Quiro Miancay*?" Barjin asked. "The agent of Talona?"

Aballister had no intentions of reopening that unresolvable debate. Before he could respond, another figure moved into the picture, pallid and unblinking, with one broken arm hanging grotesquely and blood covering the left side of its chest.

"My first soldier," Barjin explained, pulling Mullivy's body close to his side. "I have a hundred more awaiting my call."

Aballister recognized the "soldier" as an animated corpse, a zombie, and, knowing that Barjin was in catacombs no doubt laced with burial vaults, the wizard did not have to ask where he intended to find his army. Suddenly Barjin's choice to assault the library did not seem so foolhardy; Aballister had to wonder just how powerful his conniving rival might be, or might become. Again the wizard's mixed feelings about the Edificant Library flooded over him. Aballister wanted to order Barjin out of the place at once, but of course, he had not the power to enforce the demand.

"Do not underestimate me," Barjin said, as though he had read the wizard's mind. "Once the library is defeated, all the region will be opened to us. Now be gone from here; I have duties to attend that a simple wizard cannot understand."

Aballister wanted to voice his protest at Barjin's demeaning tone, but again, he knew that words would carry no real weight. He broke the connection immediately and fell back in his chair, memories welling inside him.

"Bene tellemara," Druzil said again.

Aballister looked over to the imp. "Barjin may bring us a great victory much earlier than we expected," the wizard said, but there was little excitement in his voice.

"It is an unnecessary risk," Druzil spat back. "With Ragnor's forces ready to march, Barjin could have found a better target. He could have gone to the elves and loosed the curse there—Ragnor certainly hates them and intends to make them his first target. If we took Shilmista Forest, we could march south around the mountains to isolate the priests, surround the powerful library before they ever even realized that trouble had come to their land."

Aballister did not argue and wondered again if he had been wise in so easily relinquishing control of the elixir to Barjin. He had justified each action, each failing, but he knew in his heart that his cowardice had betrayed him.

"I must go to him," Druzil remarked unexpectedly.

After taking a moment to consider the request, Aballister decided not to contest it. Sending Druzil would be a risk, the wizard knew, but he realized, too, that if he had found the strength to take more risks in his earlier meetings with Barjin, he might not now be in so awkward a position.

"Dorigen informed me that Barjin carried an enchanted brazier with him," the wizard said, rising and taking up his staff. "She is the best with sorcery. She will know if Barjin opens a gate to the lower planes in search of allies. When Dorigen confirms the opening, I will open a gate here. Your journey will be a short one. Barjin will not know you as my emissary and will think that he freely summoned you and that it is he who controls you."

Druzil snapped his batlike wings around him and wisely held his tongue until Aballister had exited the room.

"Your emissary?" the imp snarled at the closed door.

Aballister had a lot to learn.

Seven

Sunlight and Darkness

Newander felt invigorated as soon as he walked out the building's front doors, into the morning sunshine. He had just completed his turn at translating the ancient moss tome, hours huddled over the book with walls closing in all about him. For all his doubts concerning his own views about civilization, Newander knew with certainty that he preferred the open sky to any ceiling.

He was supposed to be in the small chamber, resting now, while Cleo worked at the book and Arcite performed the daily druidic rituals. Newander didn't often go against Arcite's orders, but he could justify this transgression; he was much more at rest walking along the mountain trails than in any room, no matter how comfortable its bed.

The druid found Percival skipping through the branches along the tree-lined lane. "Will you come and talk with me, white one?" he called.

The squirrel looked Newander's way, then glanced back to a different tree. Following the gaze, Newander saw another squirrel, this one a normal gray female, sitting very still and watching him.

"A thousand pardons," Newander piped to Percival. "I did not know that you were engaged, so to speak." He gave a low bow and went on his merry way down the mountain road.

Percival chattered at the departing druid for a few moments, then hopped back toward his mate.

The morning turned into afternoon and still the druid walked, away from the Edificant Library. He had broken off the main road some time ago, following a deer trail deep into the wilderness. Here he was at home and at peace, and he was confident that no animal would rise against him.

Clouds gathered over distant ridges, promising another of the common spring thunderstorms. As with the animals, the druid did not fear the weather. He would walk in a downpour and call it a bath, skip and slide along snow-covered trails and call it play. While the gathering storm clouds did not deter the druid, they did remind him that he still had duties back at the library and that Arcite and Cleo soon would realize that he was gone. "Just a little bit farther," he promised himself.

He meant to turn back a short while later but caught sight of an eagle, soaring high on the warm updrafts. The eagle spotted him, too, and swooped down low at him, cawing angrily. At first, Newander thought the bird meant to attack, but then he sorted through enough of its excited chatter to realize that it had recognized him as a friend.

"What is your trouble?" Newander asked the bird. He was fairly adept at understanding bird calls, but the eagle was too agitated and spoke too rapidly for Newander to hear anything but a clear warning of danger.

"Show me," the druid replied, and he whistled and cawed to ensure that the eagle understood. The great bird rushed off, climbing high into the sky so that Newander would not lose sight of it as it soared ever deeper, and ever higher, into the mountains.

When he came out on a high and treeless ridge, the wind buffeted his green cloak fiercely and the druid realized the cause of the eagle's distress. Across a deep ravine, three filthy gray, monkeylike creatures scrambled up the side of a tall, sheer cliff, using their prehensile tails and four clawed paws to gain a secure hold on even the tiniest juts and cracks.

On a shallow ledge near the top of the cliff sat a great pile of twigs and sticks, an eagle aerie. Newander could guess what was inside that nest.

The infuriated eagle dove at the intruders repeatedly, but the monsters only spat at it as it helplessly passed, or swiped at it with their formidable claws.

Newander recognized these creatures as su-monsters, but he had no direct knowledge of them and had never encountered them before. It was widely agreed that they were vicious and bloodthirsty, but the druids had taken no formal stance concerning them. Were they an intelligent, evil group, or just a superbly adapted predator, feared because of their prowess? Animal or monster?

To many, the distinction would mean nothing, but to a druid, that question concerned the very tenets of his or her religion.

If the su-monsters were animal, then terms such as "evil" did not apply to them and Newander could play no role in aiding the pitiful eagle. Watching their eager climb, saliva dripping from their toothy maws, Newander knew that he must do something. He called out a few of the more common natural warning cries, and the su-monsters stopped suddenly and looked at him, apparently noticing him for the first time. They hooted and spat and waved their claws threateningly, then resumed their climb.

Newander called out again. The su-monsters ignored him.

"Guide me, Silvanus," Newander begged, closing his eyes.

He knew that the greatest druids of his order had held council about these rare but nightmarish creatures, and that they had come to no definite conclusions. Thus, the common practice among the order, though no edict had been issued, was to interfere with su-monsters only if threatened directly.

In his heart, though, Newander knew that the scene before him was unnatural.

He called again to Silvanus, the Oak Father, and, to his utter amazement, he believed that he was answered. He looked to the nearest thunderhead, gauging the distance, then back to the su-monsters.

"Halt!" Newander cried out. "Go no farther!"

The su-monsters turned at once, startled perhaps by the urgency, the power, in the druid's voice. One found a loose stone and heaved it Newander's way, but the ravine was wide as well as deep and the missile fell harmlessly.

"I warn you again," the druid cried, sincerely desiring no battle. "I have no fight with you, but you'll not get to the aerie."

The monsters spat again and clawed ferociously at the empty air.

"Be gone from here!" Newander cried. Their reply came in the form of spittle and they turned and started up again.

Newander had seen enough; the su-monsters were too close to the aerie for him to waste any more time screaming warnings. He closed his eyes, clutched the oak leaf holy symbol hanging on a leather cord about his neck, and called out to the thunderstorm.

The su-monsters paid him no heed, intent on the egg-filled nest just a few dozen yards above them.

Druids considered themselves the guardians of nature and the natural order. Unlike wizards and priests of many other sects, druids accepted that they were the watchdogs of the world and that the powers they brought were more a call for help to nature than any manifestation of their own internal power. So it was as Newander called again to the heavy black cloud, directing its fury.

The thunderstroke shook the mountains for many miles around, sent the surprised eagle spinning away blindly, and nearly knocked Newander from his feet. When his sight returned, the druid saw that the cliff face was clear, the aerie was safe. The su-monsters were nowhere to be seen, and the only evidence that they had ever been there was a long scorch mark, a dripping crimson stain along the mountain wall, and a small tuft of fur, a severed tail perhaps, burning on a shallow ledge.

The eagle flew to its nest, squawked happily, and soared down to thank the druid.

"You are very welcome," the druid assured the bird. In conversing with the eagle, he felt much better about his own destructive actions. Like most druids, Newander was a gentle sort, and he was always uncomfortable when called to battle.

The fact that the cloud had answered his summons, a calling power that he believed came from Silvanus, also gave him confidence that he had acted correctly, that the su-monsters were indeed monsters and no natural predators.

Newander interpreted the next series of the eagle's caws as an invitation to join the bird at its aerie. The druid would have loved that, but the cliff across the way was too formidable a barrier with night fast approaching.

"Another day," he replied.

The eagle cackled a few more thanks, then, explaining that many preparations were still needed for the coming brood, bade the druid farewell and soared off. Newander watched the bird fly away with sincere lament. He wished that he was more skilled at his religion; druids of higher rank, including both Arcite and Cleo, could actually assume the form of animals. If Newander were as skilled as either of them, he could simply shed his light robes and transform himself into an eagle, joining his new friend on the high, shallow ledge. Even more enticing, as an eagle Newander could explore these majestic mountains from a much improved viewpoint, with the wind breaking over his wings and eyes sharp enough to sort out the movements of a field mouse from a mile up.

He shook his head and shook away, too, his laments for what could not be. It was a beautiful day, with a cleansing shower close at hand, full of new-blossoming flowers, chattering birds, fresh air on a chill breeze, and clear and cold mountain spring water around every bend—all the things that the druid loved best.

He stripped off his robes and put them under a thick bush, then sat cross-legged out on a high and open perch, awaiting the rain. It came in a torrential downpour, and Newander considered its patter on the stones the sweetest of nature's many songs.

The storm broke in time for a wondrous sunset, scarlet fading to pink, and filling every break in the towering mountain peaks to the west.

"I fear that I am late in returning," Newander said to himself. He gave a resigned shrug and could not prevent a boyish grin from spreading over his face. "The library will still be there on the morrow," he rationalized as he retrieved his robes, found a comfortable spot, and settled in for the night.

* * * * *

Barjin hung the brazier pot in place on the tripod and put in the special mixture of wood chips and incense blocks. He did not light the brazier at this time, though, uncertain of how long it would take him to find a proper catalyst for the chaos curse.

Denizens of lower planes could be powerful allies, but they were usually a wearisome lot, demanding more of their summoner's time and energy than Barjin now had to give.

Similarly, Barjin kept his necromancer's stone tightly wrapped in the shielding cloth. As with lower-plane creatures, some types of undead could prove difficult to control, and, like the gate created by the enchanted brazier, the necromancer's stone could summon an assortment of monsters, anything from the lowliest, unthinking skeletons and zombies to cunning ghosts.

Still, for all his glyphs and wards, Barjin felt insecure about leaving the altar room, and the precious bottle, with nothing more intelligent and powerful than Mullivy to stand guard. He needed an ally, and he knew where to find it.

"Khalif," the evil priest muttered, retrieving the ceramic flask. He had carried it for years, even before his days in Vaasa and before he had turned to Talona. He had found the ash urn among some ancient ruins while working as an apprentice to a now dead wizard. Barjin, by the terms of his apprenticeship, was not supposed to claim any discoveries as his own, but then, Barjin had never played by any rules but his own. He had kept the ceramic urn, filled with the ashes of Prince Khalif, a noble of some ancient civilization according to the accompanying parchment, private and safe through many years.

Barjin hadn't fully come to appreciate the potential value of such a find until after he began his training in clerical magic. Now he understood what he could do with the ashes; all he needed was a proper receptacle.

He led Mullivy out into the passageway beyond the altar room's door, a wide corridor lined with alcoves, burial vaults of the highest-ranking founders of the Edificant Library. Unlike the other vaults Barjin had seen down here, these were not open chairs, but elaborately designed caskets, sarcophagi, gem-studded and extravagant. Barjin could only hope, as he instructed Mullivy to open the closest sarcophagus, that the early scholars had spared no expenses on the contents within the casket as well, that they had used some embalming techniques.

Mullivy, for all his strength, could not begin to open the first sarcophagus, its lock and hinges rusted fast. The zombie had better luck with the second, for its cover simply fell away under Mullivy's heavy tug. As soon as the door opened, a long tentacle shot out at Mullivy, followed by a second and a third. They did no real damage, but Barjin was glad that the zombie, and not he, had opened the lid.

Inside was a carrion crawler, a monstrous wormlike beast with eight tentacles tipped with paralyzing poison. Undead Mullivy could not be affected by such an attack and, beyond the tentacles, the carrion crawler was virtually defenseless.

"Kill it!" Barjin instructed. Mullivy pounded away with his one good arm. The carrion crawler was no more than a lifeless lump at the bottom of the casket when Mullivy at last backed away.

"This one will not do," Barjin mumbled, inspecting the empty husk inside the sarcophagus. There was no dismay in his voice, though, for the body, ruined by the carrion crawler, had been carefully wrapped in thick linen, a sure sign that the ancient scholars had used some embalming techniques. Barjin also found a small hole at the back of the sarcophagus, and he correctly assumed that the carrion crawler had come in there, gorged itself for months, perhaps even years, on the full corpse, then had grown too large to crawl back out.

Barjin pulled Mullivy along eagerly, seeking another sarcophagus, one with no obvious external holes. The third time paid for all, as the saying goes, for, with help from the Screaming Maiden, Barjin and Mullivy were able to break through the locks of the next casket. Inside, wrapped in linen, lay a well-preserved corpse, the receptacle that Barjin needed.

Barjin instructed Mullivy to carry the corpse gently into the altar room—he did not want to touch the scabrous thing himself—then to rearrange the sarcophagi so that this one's would be closest to the altar room door.

Barjin shut the door behind his zombie, not wanting to be distracted by the noises outside. He took out his clerical spellbook, turned to the section on necromantic practices, and took out his necromancer's stone, thinking its summoning powers to be helpful in calling back the spirit of Prince Khalif.

The priest's chanting went on for more than an hour, and all the while he dropped pinches of the ash onto the wrapped corpse. When the ceramic urn was emptied, the priest broke it apart, rubbing it clean on the receptacle body's linen. Khalif's spirit had been contained in the whole of the ash; the absence of the slightest motes could prove disastrous.

Barjin became distracted by the necromancer's stone, for

it began to glow with an eerie, purple-black light. The priest snapped his gaze back to the mummy, his attention caught by the sudden red glow as two dots of light appeared behind the linen wrappings that covered the corpse's eyes. Barjin covered his hand in clean cloth and carefully pulled away the linen.

He fell back with a start. The mummy rose before him.

It looked upon the priest with utter hatred, its eyes burning as bright red dots. Barjin knew that mummies, like most monsters of the netherworld, hated all living things, and Barjin, for the moment anyway, was a living thing.

"Back, Khalif!" Barjin commanded as forcefully as he could manage. The mummy took another stiff-legged step forward.

"Back, I say!" Barjin snarled, replacing his fear with determined anger. "It was I who retrieved your spirit, and here in my service you shall stay until I, Barjin, release you to your eternal rest!"

He thought his words pitifully inept, but the mummy responded, sliding back to its original position.

"Turn away!" Barjin cried, and the mummy did.

A smile spread wide over the evil priest's face. He had dealt with denizens of the lower planes many times before and had animated simple undead monsters, like Mullivy, but this was a new and higher step for him. He had called to a powerful spirit, torn it from the grave and forced it under his control.

Barjin moved back to the door. "Come in, Mullivy," he ordered in a mirthful tone. "Come and meet your new brother."

Eight

Catalyst

P ikel just shook his hairy head and continued stirring the cauldron's contents with his huge wooden spoon as Cadderly considered Ivan's grim news.

"Can you finish the crossbow?" Cadderly asked.

"I can," Ivan replied, "but me thinkin's that you should be more worried about yer own fate, boy. The headmistress was not smiling much when she found her tapestry in my kitchen—not smiling a bit when she saw that Pikel had spilled gravy on one corner."

Cadderly flinched at that remark. Headmistress Pertelope was a tolerant woman, especially of Cadderly and his inventions, but she prized her art collection above all else. The tapestry depicting the elven war was one of her favorites.

"I am sorry if I have caused you two any problems," Cadderly said sincerely, though the honest lament did not stop him from dipping his fingers into a bowl that Ivan had recently used for cake baking. "I did not believe . . ."

Ivan waved his concerns away. "Not a problem," the dwarf grunted. "We just blamed everything on yerself."

"Just finish the crossbow," Cadderly instructed with a half-hearted chuckle. "I will go to Headmistress Pertelope and set things right."

"Perhaps Headmistress Pertelope will come to you," came a woman's voice from the kitchen's doorway, behind Cadderly.

The young scholar turned slowly and winced even more when he saw that Headmaster Avery stood beside Pertelope.

"So you have elevated your mischief to theft," Avery remarked. "I fear that your time in the library may be drawing to an end, Brother Cadderly, though that unfortunate conclusion was not altogether unexpected, given your heri—"

"You must be given the opportunity to explain," Pertelope interrupted, flashing a sudden dark glare Avery's way. "I am not pleased, whatever excuse you might offer."

"I had . . ." Cadderly stuttered. "I meant to . . ."

"Enough!" Avery commanded, glowering at both Cadderly and the headmistress. "You may explain about Headmistress Pertelope's tapestry later," he said to Cadderly. "First, do tell me why are you here. Have you no work to do? I thought that I had given you enough to keep you busy, but if I thought wrong, I can surely correct the situation!"

"I am busy," Cadderly insisted. "I only wanted to check on the kitchen, to make certain that I had not missed anything in my cleaning." As soon as Cadderly glanced around, he realized how ludicrous his claim sounded. Ivan and Pikel never kept an overly neat shop. Half the floor was covered with spilled flour, the other half with assorted herbs and sauces. Fungus-lined bowls, some empty and some half full of last week's meals some from meals even older than that—sat on every available space, counter, or table.

Avery's brow crinkled as he recognized the lie for what it was. "Do make certain that the task was done correctly, Brother Cadderly," the headmaster crooned with dripping sarcasm. "Then you may join Brother Rufo in his inventory of the wine cellar. You will be informed of how Dean Thobicus will proceed concerning your greater transgression." Avery turned and stalked away, but Pertelope did not immediately follow.

"I know that you meant to return the tapestry," the stately older woman said. "Might I know why you saw the need to appropriate it at all? You might have asked."

"We only needed it for a few days," Cadderly replied. He looked to Ivan and indicated the drawer, and the dwarf reached into it and produced the nearly completed crossbow. "For this."

Pertelope's hazel eyes sparkled at the sight. She moved across the room and tentatively took the small weapon from the dwarf. "Exquisite," she muttered, truly awed by the reproduction.

"My thanks," Ivan replied proudly.

"Oo oi!" Pikel added in a triumphant tone.

"I would have shown it to you," Cadderly explained, "but I thought the surprise would prove more pleasurable when it was completed."

Pertelope smiled warmly at Cadderly. "Can you complete it without the tapestry?"

Cadderly nodded.

"I will want to see it then, when it is done," said the headmistress, suddenly businesslike. "You should have asked for the tapestry," she scolded, then she glanced around and added under her breath, "Do not fear too much for Headmaster Avery. He is excitable, but he forgets quickly. He likes you, whatever his bluster. Go, now, to your duties."

*   *   *   *   *

Barjin crept from cask to cask, studying the angular man at work sorting wine bottles. The evil priest had suspected that his victim, the catalyst for the chaos curse, would come from the cellar, but he was no less delighted when he found this man unexpectedly at work here on his very first trip up the rickety stairway. The door to the lower dungeons was cleverly concealed—no doubt by the thirsty groundskeeper—in a thickly packed and remote corner of the huge chamber. The portal probably had been long forgotten by the priests of the library, allowing Barjin easy and secret access.

Barjin's delight diminished considerably when he worked his way far enough around the room to cast some detection spells on the man. The same spells had been ambiguous on the groundskeeper—Barjin had not known for certain whether the old wretch would suffice until the warding glyphs had blown him back from the bottle, but the spells were not so ambiguous concerning Kierkan Rufo. This man was not possessed of innocence and would have no more luck with the magic bottle than did the groundskeeper.

"Hypocrite," Barjin grumbled silently. He rested back in the shadows and wondered how he might still find some use for the angular man. Certainly visitors to the wine cellar were not commonplace and Barjin could not allow anyone to pass through without extracting some benefit.

He was still contemplating things when a second priest unexpectedly came skipping down the stairwell. Barjin watched curiously as this smiling young man, hair bouncing about his shoulders under a wide-brimmed hat, moved to confer with the angular worker. Barjin's detection spells had not yet expired and when he focused on this newest arrival, his curiosity turned to delight.

Here was his catalyst.

He watched a bit longer—long enough to discern that there was some tension between the two—then sneaked back to the concealed door. He knew that his next critical moves must be planned carefully.

* * * * *

"Should we work together?" Cadderly offered in an exaggerated, bubbly voice.

Kierkan Rufo glared at him. "Have you any tricks planned for me now?" he asked. "Any new baubles to show off at my expense?"

"Are you saying that you did not deserve it?" Cadderly asked. "You started the battle when you brought Avery to my room."

"Pity the mighty scribe," came the sarcastic reply.

Cadderly started to respond, but held his tongue. He sympathized with Rufo, truly an attentive priest. Cadderly knew that the headmasters had pushed Rufo aside after Cadderly's success with the wizard's spellbook. The wound was too fresh to mend it here, Cadderly knew, and neither he nor Rufo had any desire to work together.

Rufo explained his logging system for the inventory so that their lists might be compatible. Cadderly saw several possibilities for improvement but again said nothing. "Do you understand?" Rufo asked, handing Cadderly a counting chart.

Cadderly nodded. "A good system," he offered.

Rufo bruskly waved him away, then continued his inventory, working his way slowly around the long and shadowy racks.

A flash of light in a distant corner caught the angular man's attention, but it was gone as fast as it had appeared. Rufo cocked his head, took up his torch, and inched his way over. A wall of casks confronted him, but he noticed an opening around to the side.

"Is anyone there?" Rufo asked, a bit nervously. Torch leading the way, he peeked into the opening and saw the ancient portal. "What is it?" came a voice behind him. Rufo jumped in surprise, dropped his torch at his feet, and upset a cask as he danced away from the flames. He was not comforted when the crashing had ended and he looked back into Cadderly's grinning face.

"It is a door," Rufo replied through gritted teeth.

Cadderly picked up the torch and peered in. "Now where might that lead?" he asked rhetorically.

"It is none of our concern," Rufo said firmly.

"Of course it is," Cadderly retorted. "It is part of the library and the library is our concern."

"We must tell a headmaster and let him decide the proper way to investigate it," Rufo offered. "Now give me the torch."

Cadderly ignored him and advanced to the small wooden portal. It opened easily, revealing a descending stairway, and Cadderly was surprised and delighted once more.

"You surely will get us into even more trouble!" Rufo complained at his back. "Do you wish to count and clean until your hundredth birthday?"

"To the lowest levels?" Cadderly said excitedly, ignoring the warning. He looked back at Rufo, his face glowing brightly in the near torchlight.

The nervous Rufo backed away from the weirdly shadowed specter. He seemed not to understand his companion's excitement.

"The lowest levels," Cadderly repeated as though those words should hold some significance. "When the library was originally built, most of it was below ground. The Snowflakes were wilder back then, and the founders thought an underground complex more easily defended. The lowest catacombs were abandoned as the mountains were tamed and the building expanded, and eventually it was believed that all the exits had been sealed." He looked back to the enticing stair. "Apparently that was not the case."

"Then we must tell a headmaster," Rufo declared nervously. "It is not our place to investigate hidden doorways."

Cadderly shot him an incredulous stare, hardly believing the man to be so childish. "We will tell them," the young scholar agreed, poking his head through the dusty opening. "In time."

* * * * *

A short distance away, Barjin watched the two men with nervous anticipation, one hand holding tight to the security of his cruel mace. The evil priest knew that he had taken quite a chance in calling up the magical light signaling the portal's location. If the two men decided to go and tell their masters, Barjin would have to intercept them—forcefully. But Barjin had never been patient, which was why he had come directly to the Edificant Library in the first place. There was a degree of danger in his gamble, both in coming here and in revealing the door, but the potential gains of both actions could not be ignored. If these two decided to explore, then Barjin would be one giant step closer to realizing his desires.

They disappeared from sight around the barricading casks, so Barjin crept closer. "The stairs are fairly solid, though they are ancient," he heard Cadderly call back, "and they go down a long, long way."

Appearing skeptical, even afraid, the angular priest slowly backed out of the concealed area. "The headmaster," he muttered softly and turned abruptly for the stairs.

Barjin stepped out before him.

Before Rufo could even cry out, the evil priest's spell fell over him. Rufo's gaze locked fast to the evil priest's dark eyes, held in place by Barjin's hypnotic stare. In his studies of wizardry, charms had always been the charismatic Barjin's strength. His adoption of Talona had not diminished that touch, though the Lady of Poison's clerics were not normally adept at such magic, and Kierkan Rufo was not a difficult opponent.

Nor were Barjin's magically enhanced suggestions to the enthralled Rufo contrary to the angular man's deepest desires.

* * * * *

Cadderly creeped slowly toward the open door, never taking his gaze from the enticing blackness beyond the meager limits of his torchlight. What wonders remained down there in the oldest rooms of the Edificant Library? he wondered. What secrets long forgotten about the founders and initial scholars?

"We should investigate—we'll be working down here for many days," Cadderly said, leaning forward and peering over the stairs. "No one would have to know until we decided to tell them."

Despite his consuming curiosity for the mysteries before him, Cadderly kept enough wits about him to realize that he had been betrayed as soon as he felt a boot against his lower back. He grabbed the flimsy railing, but the wood broke away in his hand. He managed to look back for just an instant and saw Rufo crouched in the low doorway, a weird, emotionless expression on his dark and hollowed face.

Cadderly's torch flew away, and he tumbled into the blackness, bouncing down the stairs and coming to rest heavily on the stone floor below. All the world fell into blackness; he did not hear the door close above him.

* * * * *

Kierkan Rufo went right from the wine cellar to his room that night, wanting to confront no one and respond to no questions. The recent events were but a blur to the charmed man.

He vaguely remembered what he had done to Cadderly, though he couldn't be certain if it had been real or a dream. He remembered, too, closing and blocking off the hidden door.

There was something else, or someone else, though, in the picture, hovering off to the side in the shadows just out of reach of Rufo's consciousness.

Try as he may, poor Rufo could not remember anything about Barjin, as a result of the enchanting priest's devious instructions. In the back of his mind, Rufo retained the strange sensation that he had made a friend this night, one who understood his frustrations and who agreed that Cadderly was an unworthy man.

Nine

Barjin's World

C adderly awoke in utter darkness; he could not see his hand if he waved his fingers just an inch in front of his face. His other senses told him much, though. He could smell the thick dust and feel the sticky lines of cobwebs hanging all about.

"Rufo!" he called, but his voice carried nowhere in the dead air, just reminded him that he was alone in the dark. He crawled to his knees and found that he was sore in a dozen places, particularly on the side of his head, and that his tunic was crusted as if with dried blood. His torch lay beside him, but in pawing about it, Cadderly realized that it had expired many hours before.

Cadderly snapped his fingers, then reached down to his belt.

A moment later, he popped the cap from a cylindrical tube and a ray of light cut through the darkness. Even to Cadderly, the light seemed an intruder in these corridors, which had known only darkness for centuries uncounted. A dozen small creatures scuttled away on the edges of Cadderly's vision, just out of the light. Better to have them scurry away, Cadderly thought, than to have them lay in wait in the darkness for him to pass.

Cadderly examined his immediate surroundings with the light tube's aperture wide open, mostly focusing on the shattered stairway beside him. Several stairs remained attached at the top, near the closed door, but most of the boards lay scattered about, apparently shattered by Cadderly's heavy descent. No easy path back that way, he told himself, and he narrowed the beam to see down the greater distances. He was in a corridor, one of many crisscrossing and weaving together to form a honeycomb-type maze, judging from the many passages lining both walls. The supporting arches were similar to those of the library above, but, being an earlier architectural design, they were even thicker and lower, and seemed lower still covered with layers of dust, hanging webs, and promises of crawly things.

When Cadderly took the time to examine himself, he saw that his tunic was, as he expected, crusted with his own blood.

He noticed a broken board lying next to him, sharply splintered and darkly stained. Tentatively, the young priest unbuttoned his tunic and pulled it aside, expecting a garish wound.

What he found instead was a scab and a bruise. Although the more dutiful priests of Deneir, even those Cadderly's age, were accomplished healers, Cadderly was hardly practiced in the medicinal arts. He could tell, though, by the stains on the splintered board that his wound had been deep and it was obvious from his soaked shirt alone that he had lost quite a bit of blood. The wound was undeniably on the mend, though, and if it once had been serious, it was not now.

"Rufo?" Cadderly called again, wondering if his companion had come down behind him and healed him. There was no answer, not a sound in the dusty corridor. "If not Rufo, then who?" Cadderly asked himself softly. He shrugged his shoulders a moment later; the riddle was quite beyond him.

"Young and strong," Cadderly congratulated himself,

having no other answer. He stretched the rest of his aches out and finished his survey of the area, wondering if there might be some way to reconstruct enough of the stairway to get back near the door. He set his light tube on the floor and pieced together some boards. The wood was terribly deteriorated and smashed beyond repair—too much so, Cadderly thought, to have been caused just by his fall. Several pieces were no more than splinters, as though they had been battered repeatedly.

After a short while, Cadderly gave up the idea of going back through the wine cellar. The old, rotted wood would never support his weight even if he could find some way to piece it back together. "It could be worse," he whispered aloud, picking up his light tube and taking his spindle-disks from a pouch.

He took a deep breath to steady himself and started off—any way seemed as good as another.

Crawling things darted to dark holes on the perimeter of the light beam, and a shudder coursed along Cadderly's spine as he imagined again what this journey might be like in darkness.

The walls were of brickwork in most of the passages, crushed under uncountable tonnage and cracked in many places. Bas-reliefs had worn away, the lines of an artist's chisel filled in by the dust of centuries, the fine detail of sculptures replaced by the artwork of spiderwebs. Somewhere in the dark distance, Cadderly heard the drip of water, a dull and dead *thump-thump*. "The heartbeat of the catacombs," Cadderly muttered grimly, and the thought did not comfort him.

He wandered for many minutes, trying to formulate some logical scheme for conquering the tunnel layout. While the builders of the original library had been an orderly group and had carefully thought out the catacomb design, the initial purposes, and courses, of the various tunnels had been adapted over the decades to fit the changing needs of the structure above.

Every time Cadderly thought he had some sense of where he might be, the next corner showed him differently. He moved along one low and wide corridor, taking care to keep away from the rotting crates lining the walls. If this was the storage area, he reasoned, there might be an outside exit nearby, a tunnel large enough for wagons, perhaps.

The corridor ended at a wide arch that fanned out diagonally under two smaller arches to the left and the right. These were congested by webs so thick that Cadderly had to retrieve a plank from the crates just to poke his way through.

The passages beyond the arched intersection were identical, layered stonework and only half as wide as the corridor he had just traveled. His instinct told him to go left, but it was just a guess, for in the winding ways Cadderly really had little idea of where he was in relation to the buildings above him.

He kept his pace swift, following the narrow beam faithfully and trying to ignore the rat squeaks and imagined perils to the sides and behind him. His fears were persistent, though, and each step came with more effort. He shifted the beam from side to side and saw that this passage's walls were lined with dark holes, alcoves. Hiding places, Cadderly imagined, for crouched monsters.

Cadderly turned slowly, bringing his light to bear, and realized that in his narrow focus on the path ahead, he had crossed the first few sets of these alcoves. A shudder ran through his spine, for he figured out the purpose of the alcoves before his light ever angled properly for him to see inside one.

Cadderly jumped back. The distant *thump-thump* of the catacomb heartbeat remained steady, but the young scholar's own heart missed a few beats, for the beam of light fell upon a seated skeleton just a few feet to Cadderly's side. If this passage had been intended for storage, its goods were macabre indeed! Where once may have been stored crates of food, now there was only food for the carrion eaters. Cadderly had entered the crypts, he knew, the burial vaults for the earliest scholars of the Edificant Library.

The skeleton sat impassive and oblivious in its tattered shroud, hand bones crossed over its lap. Webs extended from a dozen angles in the small alcove, seeming to support the skeleton in its upright posture.

Cadderly sublimated his mounting terror, reminded himself that these were simply natural remains, the remains of great men, good-hearted and thinking men, and that he, too, one day would resemble the skeleton seated before him. He looked back and counted four alcoves on either side of the corridor behind him and considered whether he should turn back.

Stubbornly, Cadderly dismissed all his fears as irrational and focused again on the path before him. He kept his light in the middle of the passage, not wanting to look into any more of the alcoves, not wanting to test his determination any further. But his eyes inevitably glanced to the side, to the hushed darkness. He imagined skeletal heads turning slowly to watch him pass.

Some fears were not so easily conquered.

A scuffle behind and to his left spun Cadderly about, his spindle-disks at the ready. His defensive reflexes launched the weapon before his mind could register the source of the noise: a small rat crawling across a wobbling skull.

The rodent flew away into webs and darkness when the disks struck full on the skull's forehead. The wobbly skull flew, too, rebounding off the alcove's back wall, rolling down the front of its former possessor, and coming to a rattling stop between the seated skeleton's legs.

A chuckle burst from Cadderly's mouth, relieved laughter at his own cowardice. The sound died away quickly as the dusty stillness reclaimed the ancient passage, and Cadderly relaxed . . . until the skeleton reached down between its legs and retrieved its fallen head.

Cadderly stumbled backward against the opposite wall—and promptly felt a bony grip on his elbow. He tore away, snapped his spindle-disks at this newest foe, and turned to flee, not pausing to note the damage his weapon had exacted. As his light swung about, though, Cadderly saw that the skeletons he had passed had risen and congregated in the corridor, and were now advancing, their faces locked in lipless grins, their arms outstretched as though they desired to pull Cadderly fully into their dark realm.

He had only one path open and he went with all speed, trying to keep his eyes ahead, trying to ignore the rattling of still more skeletons rising from every alcove he passed. He could only hope that no monstrous spiders were nearby as he charged right through another heavily webbed archway, tasting webs and spitting them out in disgust. He stumbled and fell more than once but always scrambled back to his feet, running blindly, knowing not where he should run, only what he must keep behind him.

More passages. More crypts. The rattling mounted behind him and he heard again, startlingly clear, the *thump-thump* water-drop heartbeat of the catacombs. He burst through another webbed archway, and then another, then came to a three-way intersection. He turned to the left but saw that the skeletons down that passage had already risen to block his way.

To the right he ran, too afraid to sort out any patterns, too distracted to realize that he was being herded.

He came to another low archway, noted that this one had no webs, but hadn't the time to pause and consider the implications. He was in a wider, higher passage, a grander hall, and saw that the alcoves here were filled not by raggedly shrouded skeletons, but by standing sarcophagi, exquisitely detailed and gilded in precious metals and gemstones.

Cadderly only noticed them for a moment, for down at the end of the long hallway he saw light—not daylight, which he would have welcomed with open arms, but light nonetheless peeking out at him from the cracks and loosened seals of an ancient door.

The rattling intensified, booming all about him. An eerie red mist appeared at Cadderly's feet, following his progress, adding a surreal and dreamlike quality. Reality and nightmare battled in his rushing thoughts, reason fighting fear. The resolution to that battle lay in the light, Cadderly knew.

The young scholar staggered forward, his feet dragging as though the mist itself weighed heavily upon them. He lowered his shoulder, meaning to push right through the door, to charge right into the light.

The door squeaked open just before he collided, and he stumbled in, sinking down to his knees on the clean floor within. Then the door swung closed of its own accord, leaving the red mist and the macabre rattle out in the darkness. Cadderly remained very still for a long moment, confused and trying to slow his racing heart.

After a moment, Cadderly rose shakily to survey the room, hardly even registering that the door had closed behind him.

He was struck by the cleanliness of this room, so out of place in the rest of the dungeons. He recognized the place as a former study hall; it was similar in design and contained similar furniture to those studies still in use in the library proper. Several small cabinets, worktables, and free-standing two-sided bookcases sat at regular intervals about the room, and a brazier rested on a tripod along the right-hand wall. Torches burned in two sconces, and the walls were lined with bookshelves, empty except for a few scattered parchments, yellow with age, and an occasional small sculpture, once a book end, perhaps.

Cadderly's gaze went to the brazier first, thinking it oddly out of place, but it was the display in the center that ultimately commanded his attention.

A long and narrow table had been placed there, with a purple and crimson blanket spread over it and hanging down the front and sides. Atop the table was a podium, and on this sat a clear bottle sealed with a large cork and filled with some red glowing substance. In front of the bottle was a silvery bowl, platinum perhaps, intricately designed and covered with strange runes.

Cadderly was hardly surprised, or alarmed, at the blue mist he noted covering the floors and swirling about his legs. This entire adventure had taken on a blurry feeling of unreality to him. Rationally, he could tell himself that he was wide awake, but the dull ache on the side of his skull made him wonder just how badly he had banged his head. Whatever this was, though, Cadderly was now more intrigued than afraid, so, with great effort, he forced himself to his feet and took a cautious step toward the central table.

There were designs, tridents capped by three bottles, woven into the blanket. He noticed that the bottles of the designs were similar to the real one atop the table. Cadderly thought he knew most of the major holy symbols and alliance crests of the central Realms, but this was totally foreign. He wished he had prepared some spells that might reveal more of the strange altar, if it was an altar. Cadderly smiled at his own ineptitude. He rarely prepared any spells at all, and even when he took the time, his accomplishments with clerical magic were far from highly regarded. Cadderly was more scholar than priest, and he viewed his vows to Deneir more as an agreement of attitude and priorities than a pledge of devotion.

As he approached the table, he saw that the silvery bowl was filled with a clear liquid—probably water, though Cadderly did not dare dip his fingers into it. More intrigued by the glowing bottle behind it, Cadderly meant to pay it little heed at all, but the reflection of the flask in that strange rune-covered bowl captured his attention suddenly and for some reason would not let go.

Cadderly felt himself drawn toward that reflected image. He moved right up to the bowl and bent low, his face nearly touching the liquid. Then, as if a tiny pebble had fallen into the bowl, little circular ripples rolled out from the exact center.

Far from breaking Cadderly's concentration on the reflection, the watery dance only enhanced it. The light bounced and rolled around the tiny waves and the image of the bottle elongated and bent, side to side.

Cadderly knew somehow that the water was pleasantly warm. He wanted to immerse himself in the bowl, to silence all the noises of the world around him in watery stillness and feel nothing but the warmth.

Still there was the image, swaying enticingly, capturing Cadderly's thoughts.

Cadderly looked up from the bowl to the bottle. Somewhere deep inside him he knew that something was amiss and that he should resist the strangely comforting sensations. Inanimate objects were not supposed to offer suggestions.

Open the bottle, came a call within his head. He did not recognize the soothing voice, but it promised only pleasure. *Open the bottle*.

Before he realized what he was doing, Cadderly had the bottle in his hands. He had no idea what the bottle truly was, or how and why this unknown altar had been set up. There was a danger here—Cadderly sensed it—but he could not sort it out clearly; the ripples in the silvery bowl had been so enthralling.

Open the bottle, came the quiet suggestion a third time.

Cadderly simply could not determine whether or not he should resist and that indecision weakened his resolve. The cork stopper was stubborn, but not overly so, and it came out with a loud *foomp*!

That pop cut through the smoky confusion in the young scholar's brain, rang out like a clarion call of reality, warning him of the risk he had taken, but it was too late.

Red smoke poured out of the flask, engulfing Cadderly and spreading to fill the room. Cadderly realized his error at once and he moved to replace the cork, but watching from behind the cabinet, an unseen enemy was already at work.

"Hold!" came an undeniable command from the side of the room.

Cadderly had the cork almost back to the bottle when his hands stopped moving. Still the smoke poured out. Cadderly could not react, could not move at all, could not even make his eyes look away. His whole body grew weirdly numb, tingled in the grasp of a magical grip. A moment later, Cadderly saw a hand reach around him but did not even feel the bottle being pried from his grasp. He then was forcefully turned about to face a man he did not know.

The man was waving and chanting, though Cadderly could not hear the words. He recognized the movements as some sort of spellcasting and knew that he was in dire peril. His mind struggled against the paralysis that had overcome him.

It was a futile effort.

Cadderly felt his eyes drooping. The sensations suddenly came rushing back to his limbs, but all the world grew dark around him and he felt himself falling, forever falling.

*   *   *   *   *

"Come, groundskeeper," Barjin called. From out of the same cabinet in which Barjin had hidden came Mullivy's pallid corpse.

Barjin spent a moment inspecting his latest victim. Cadderly's light tube and spindle-disks, along with a dozen other curiosities, intrigued the priest, but Barjin quickly dismissed the idea of taking anything. He had used the same spell of forgetfulness on this man as he had on the tall, angular man back in the wine cellar. Barjin knew that this man, unlike the other, was strong of mind and will, and would unconsciously battle such a spell. Missing items might aid his fight to regain the blocked parts of his memory, and for the priest, alone and beneath a virtual army of enemies, that could prove disastrous.

Barjin dropped a hand to his hungry mace. Perhaps he

should kill this one now, add this young priest to his undead army so that he would bring Barjin no trouble in the future.

The evil priest dismissed the idea as quickly as it had come to him; his goddess, a deity of chaos, would not approve of eliminating the excruciating irony. This man had served as catalyst for the curse; let him see the destruction wrought of his own hands!

"Bring him," Barjin instructed, dropping Cadderly to his zombie. With one stiff arm and little effort, Mullivy lifted Cadderly from the floor.

"And bring the old ladder," Barjin added. "We must get back up to the wine cellar. We have much work to do before the dawn."

Barjin wrung his hands with mounting excitement. The primary component of the ritual had been executed easily; all that remained to complete the curse, to fully loose the Most Fatal Horror upon the Edificant Library, were a few minor ceremonies.

Ten

The Puzzle

Danica knew by the approaching headmaster's expression, and by the fact that Kierkan Rufo shuffled along at Avery's heels, that Cadderly had done something wrong again. She pushed away the book she was reading and folded her arms on the table in front of her.

Avery, normally polite to guests of the library, came quickly and bluntly to his point. "Where is he?" the headmaster demanded.

"He?" Danica replied. She knew perfectly well that Avery was referring to Cadderly, but she didn't appreciate the headmaster's tone.

"You know . . ." Avery began loudly, but then he realized Danica's objections and caught himself, looked around, and blushed with embarrassment.

"I am sorry, Lady Danica," he apologized sincerely. "I had only thought . . . I mean, you and . . ." He stomped hard with one foot to steady himself and proclaimed, "That Cadderly frustrates me so!"

Danica accepted the apology with a grin and a nod,

understanding, even sympathizing, with Avery's feelings. Cadderly was an easily distracted free spirit, and, like most formal religious organizations, the Order of Deneir was firmly based on discipline. It was not a difficult task for Danica to remember just a few of the many times she had waited for Cadderly at an appointed place and time, only to eventually give up and go back to her chambers alone, cursing the day she ever saw his boyish smile and inquisitive eyes.

For all her frustrations, though, the young woman could not deny the pangs in her heart whenever she looked upon Cadderly. Her smile only widened as she thought of him now, flying in the face of Avery's bubbling anger. As soon as Danica turned her attention back to the present and looked over Avery's shoulder, though, her grin disappeared. There stood Kierkan Rufo, leaning slightly to one side, as always, but wearing a mask of concern rather than the normally smug expression he displayed whenever he had one-upped his rival.

Danica locked stares with the man, her unconscious grimace revealing her true feelings toward him. She knew that he was Cadderly's friend—sort of—and she never spoke out against him to Cadderly, but in her heart she didn't trust the man, not at all.

Rufo had made many advances on Danica, beginning on her very first day at the Edificant Library, the first time the two had ever met. Danica was young and pretty and not unused to such advances, but Rufo had unnerved her on that occasion.

When she had politely turned Rufo down, he just stood towering over her, tilting his head and staring, for many minutes with that same frozen, unblinking stare on his face. Danica didn't know exactly what it was that had caused her to rebuff Rufo way back then, but she suspected it was his dark, deepset eyes. They showed the same inner light of intelligence as Cadderly's, but if Cadderly's were inquisitive, then

Rufo's were conniving. Cadderly's eyes sparkled joyfully as if in search of answers to the uncounted mysteries of the world; Rufo's, too, collected information, but his, Danica believed, searched for advantage.

Rufo had never given up on Danica, even after her budding relationship with Cadderly had become common talk in the library. Rufo still approached her often, and still she sent him away, but sometimes she saw him, out of the corner of her eye, sitting across the room and staring at her, studying her as though she were some amusing book.

"Do you know where he is?" Avery asked her, his tone more controlled.

"Who?" Danica answered, hardly hearing the question.

"Cadderly!" cried the flustered headmaster.

Danica looked at him, surprised by the sudden outburst.

"Cadderly," Avery said again, regaining his composure. "Do you know where Cadderly might be found?"

Danica paused and considered the question and the look on Rufo's face, wondering if she should be worried. As far as she knew, Avery was the one directing Cadderly's movements.

"I have not seen him this morning," she answered honestly. "I thought that you had put him to work—in the wine cellar, by the words of the dwarven brothers."

Avery nodded. "So, too, did I believe, but it seems as if our dear Cadderly has had enough of his labors. He did not report to me this morning, as he had been instructed, nor was he in his room when I went to find him."

"Had he been in his room at all this morning?" Danica asked. She found her gaze again drawn to Kierkan Rufo, fearing for Cadderly and somehow guessing that if trouble had befallen him, Rufo was involved.

Rufo's reaction did not diminish her suspicions. He blinked—one of the few times Danica had ever seen him blink—and tried hard to appear unconcerned as he looked away.

"I cannot say," Avery replied and he, too, turned to Rufo for some answers.

The angular man only shrugged. "I left him in the wine cellar," he said. "I was down there working long before he arrived. I thought it fitting that I retire earlier than he."

Before Avery could even suggest that they go search the wine cellar, Danica had pushed past him and started on her way.

* * * * *

The darkness and the weight. Those were the two facts of Cadderly's predicament: the darkness and the weight. And the pain. There was pain, too. He didn't know where he was or how he had gotten to this dark place or why he could not move. He was lying face down on the stone floor, buried by something. He tried calling out several times but found little breath.

Images of walking skeletons and thick spiderwebs flitted about his consciousness as he lay there, but they had no real definition, nor any solid place in his memory. Somewhere—in a dream?—he had seen them, but whether that place had anything to do with this place, he could not guess.

Then he saw the flicker of torchlight, far away but coming down toward him, and as the shadows revealed tall and open racks, he at last recognized his surroundings.

"The wine cellar," Cadderly grunted, though the effort sorely hurt. "Rufo?" It was all a blur. He remembered coming down from the kitchen to join Rufo in his inventory, and remembered beginning his work, away from the angular man, but that was all. Something obviously had happened subsequent to that, but Cadderly had no recollection of it, or of how he might possibly have gotten in his current predicament.

"Cadderly?" came a call, Danica's voice. Not one, but three torches had entered the large wine cellar.

"Here!" Cadderly gasped with all his breath, though the wheeze was not nearly loud enough to be heard. The torches fanned out in different directions, sometimes disappearing from Cadderly's sight, other times flickering at regular intervals as they moved behind the open, bottle-filled racks. All three bearers—Avery, Rufo, and Danica, Cadderly realized, called out now.

"Here!" he gasped as often as he could. Still, the cellar was wide and sectioned by dozens of tall wine racks, and it was many minutes before Cadderly's call was heard.

Kierkan Rufo found him. The tall man seemed more ghastly than ever to Cadderly as he looked up at the shadows splayed across Rufo's angular features. Rufo appeared surprised to find Cadderly, then he glanced all about, as if undecided as to how to react.

"Could you . . ." Cadderly began, and he paused to catch his breath. "Please get . . . me . . . get this off me."

Still Rufo hesitated, confusion and concern crossing his face.

"Over here," he called out finally. "I have found him."

Cadderly didn't note much relief in Rufo's tone.

Rufo laid his torch down and began removing the pile of casks that were pinning Cadderly. Over his shoulder, Cadderly noticed Rufo tipping one heavy cask over him, and the thought came to him for just an instant that the angular man had tilted it purposely and meant to drop it on his head. Then Danica came running up, and she helped Rufo push it away.

All the casks were cleared before Headmaster Avery ever got there, and Cadderly started to rise.

Danica held him down. "Do not move!" she instructed firmly. Her expression was grave, her brown almond eyes intense and uncompromising. "Not until I have inspected your wounds."

"I am all right," Cadderly tried to insist, but he knew his words fell on deaf ears. Danica had been scared, and the stubborn woman rarely bothered to argue when she was scared.

Cadderly tried halfheartedly to rise again, but this time Danica's strong hand stopped him, pressing on a particularly vulnerable area on the back of his neck.

"I have ways of stopping you from struggling," Danica promised, and Cadderly didn't doubt her. He put his cheek down on folded arms and let Danica have her way.

"How did this happen?" demanded the chubby, red-faced Avery, huffing up to join them.

"He was counting bottles when I left," Rufo offered nervously.

Cadderly's face crinkled in confusion as he tried again to sort through the blur of his memories. He got the uncomfortable feeling that Rufo expected his explanation to sound like an accusation, and Cadderly himself wondered what part Rufo might have had in his troubles. A feeling of something hard—a boot?—against his back slipped past him too quickly to make any sense.

"I know not," Cadderly answered honestly. "I just cannot remember. I was counting . . ." He stopped there and shook his head in frustration. Cadderly's existence depended on knowledge; he didn't like illogical puzzles.

"And you wandered away," Avery finished for him. "You went exploring when you should have been working."

"The wounds are not too severe," Danica cut in suddenly.

Cadderly knew that she had purposely deflected the headmaster's rising agitation, and he smiled his thanks as Danica helped him to his feet. It felt good to be standing again, though Cadderly had to lean on Danica for support for several minutes.

Somehow Avery's supposition didn't fit into Cadderly's memories—whatever they might be. He did not believe that he had just "wandered away" to fall into trouble. "No," he declared. "Not like that. There was something here." He looked at Danica, then to Rufo. "A light?"

Hearing the word triggered another memory for Cadderly.

"The door!" he cried suddenly.

If the torchlight had been stronger, they all would have noticed the blood drain from Kierkan Rufo's face.

"The door," Cadderly said again. "Behind the wall of casks."

"What door?" Avery demanded.

Cadderly paused and thought for a moment but had no answers. His considerable willpower subconsciously battled Barjin's memory blocking spell, but all he could remember was the door, some door, somewhere. And wherever that portal might have led, Cadderly could only guess. He resolved to find out again, as soon as he rounded the casks and opened it.

It was gone.

Cadderly stood for a long while, staring at the dusty bricks of the solid wall.

"What door?" the impatient headmaster asked again.

"It was here," Cadderly insisted with as much conviction as he could muster. He moved closer to the wall and felt it. That, too, proved futile. "I remember . . ." Cadderly started to protest. He felt an arm reach under his shoulder.

"You have been hurt in the head," Danica said quietly. "Confusion is not unexpected after such a blow, nor usually lasting," she added quickly to comfort him.

"No, no," Cadderly protested, but he let Danica lead him out.

"What door?" the flustered Avery asked a third time.

"He has hurt his head," Danica interjected.

"I thought . . ." Cadderly began. "It must have been a dream—" he looked at Avery directly "—but what a strange dream."

Rufo's sigh was audible. "He is not hurt too badly?" the tall man asked embarrassedly when curious expressions turned toward him.

"Not too badly," replied Danica, the tone of her voice indicating her suspicions.

Cadderly hardly noticed, too engrossed was he with trying to remember. "What would be below here?" he asked on impulse.

"Nothing to concern you," Avery replied sharply.

Skeletons walked intangibly through Cadderly's subconscious again. "Crypts?" he asked.

"Nothing to concern you!" Avery answered sternly. "I grow tired of your curiosity, brother."

Cadderly, too, was annoyed, not enjoying the puzzles within his own mind. Avery's glare was uncompromising, but Cadderly was too upset to be scared off. "Sssh!" he hissed sarcastically, putting a finger to his pursed lips. "You would not want Deneir, whose edict is the seeking of knowledge, to hear you say that."

Avery's face turned so red that Cadderly almost expected it to burst. "Go and see the healers," the headmaster growled at Cadderly, "then come back to see me. I have a thousand tasks prepared for you." He spun about and stormed away, Rufo close on his heels, though all the way to the stairs, Rufo kept glancing back over his shoulder.

Danica gave Cadderly a forceful nudge—and a painful one against his sorely bruised ribs. "You never know when to hold your tongue," she scolded. "If you keep talking so to Headmaster Avery, we will never find the opportunity to see each other!" With her torch in one hand and her other wrapped about Cadderly's back, she pulled him roughly toward the distant stairs.

Cadderly looked down at her, thinking that he owed her an apology, but he saw that Danica was biting back laughter and he realized that she hadn't truly disapproved of his sarcasm.

* * * * *

Barjin watched the steady stream of reddish smoke rise from the opened flask and slip into cracks in the ceiling, making its way up into the library above. The evil priest still had several ceremonies to perform to complete the formal ritual, as agreed upon back in Castle Trinity, but these were merely a formality. The Most Fatal Horror had been released, and the chaos curse was under way.

It would take longer to exact a toll here, Barjin knew, than it had with Haverly back at Castle Trinity. According to Aballister, Haverly had taken a concentrated dose right in the face. Producing the elixir was far too expensive to duplicate those effects on enemy after enemy, thus the mixture in the ever-smoking bottle had been greatly diluted. The priests here would absorb the elixir gradually, each hour bringing them closer to the edge of doom. Barjin held no reservations, though. He believed in the powers of the elixir, in the powers of his goddess—particularly with himself serving as her agent.

"Let us see how these pious fools behave when their truest emotions are revealed," he snickered to Mullivy. The zombie did not respond, of course. He just stood very still, unblinking and unmoving. Barjin gave him a sour look and turned his gaze back to the ever-smoking bottle.

"The next day will be the most dangerous," he whispered to himself. "Beyond that, the priests will have no power to stand against me." He looked back to Mullivy and grinned wickedly.

"We will be ready," Barjin promised. He already had animated dozens of skeletons and had enacted further spells upon Mullivy's corpse to strengthen it. And, of course, there was Khalif, Barjin's prized soldier, awaiting the priest's command from the sarcophagus just outside the altar room door.

Barjin meant to add new and more horrible monsters to his growing army. First, he would uncover the necromancer's stone and see what undead allies it might bring in. Then, taking Aballister's advice, he would open a gate to the least of the lower planes, summoning minor monsters to serve as advisers and scouts for his expanding evil network.

"Let the foolish priests come after us," Barjin said, taking an ancient and evil tome, a book of sorcery and necromancy, out of the folds of his robes. "Let them see the horror that has befallen them!"

Eleven

Oddities

Cadderly sat before his open window, watching the dawn and feeding Percival cacasa-nut-and-butter biscuits. The Shining Plains lived up to their name this morning, with dew-speckled grass catching the morning sunlight and throwing it back to the sky in a dazzling dance. The sun climbed higher and the line of brightness moved up into the foothills of the Snowflake Mountains. Pockets of darkness, valleys, dotted the region and a wispy mist rose to the south, from the valley of the Impresk River, feeding the wide lake to the east.

"Ow!" Cadderly cried, pulling his hand away from the hungry squirrel. Percival had gotten a bit too eager, nipping through the biscuit and into Cadderly's palm. Cadderly pinched the wound between his thumb and forefinger to stem the blood flow.

Busily licking the last of the cacasa-nut from his paws, Percival hardly seemed to notice Cadderly's discomfort.

"It is my own fault, I suppose," Cadderly admitted. "I cannot expect you to behave rationally when there is cacasa-nut and butter to be won!"

Percival's tail twitched excitedly, but that was the only indication Cadderly had that the squirrel was even listening. The young man turned his attention again to the world outside.

The daylight had reached the library, and though Cadderly had to squint against its fresh brightness, it felt warm and wonderful upon his face.

"It will be another beautiful day," he remarked, and even as he spoke the words, he realized that he probably would spend the whole of it in the dark and dreary wine cellar, or in some other hole that Headmaster Avery found for him.

"Perhaps I can trick him into letting me tend the grounds this morning," Cadderly said to the squirrel. "I could help old Mullivy."

Percival chittered excitedly at the mention of the groundskeeper.

"I know," Cadderly offered comfortingly. "You do not like Mullivy." Cadderly shrugged and smiled, remembering the time he had seen the crooked old groundskeeper waving a rake and spitting threats at the tree that Percival and other squirrels were sitting in, complaining about the mess of acorn husks all over his freshly raked ground.

"Here you go, Percival," Cadderly said, pushing the rest of the biscuit to the windowsill. "I have many things to attend to before Avery catches up with me." He left Percival sitting on the sill, and the squirrel went on munching and crunching and licking his paws, and basking in the warm daylight, apparently having already dismissed any uneasiness at the mention of Mullivy.

* * * * *

"Ye're bats!" Ivan yelled. "Ye can't be one of them!"

"Doo-dad!" Pikel replied indignantly.

"Ye think they'd have ye?" Ivan roared. "Tell him, boy!" he cried at Cadderly, who had just entered the kitchen. "Tell the fool that dwarves can't be druids!"

"You want to be a druid?" Cadderly asked with interest.

"Oo oi!" piped a happy Pikel. "Doo-dad!"

Ivan had heard enough. He hoisted a frying pan—dumping its half-cooked eggs on the floor—and heaved it at his brother.

Pikel wasn't quick enough to get out of the way of the missile, but he managed to bow into it, taking the blow on the top of his head and suffering no serious damage.

Still fuming, Ivan reached for another pan, but Cadderly grabbed his arm to stop him. "Wait!" Cadderly pleaded.

Ivan paused for just a moment, even whistled to show his patience, then cried, "Long enough!" and pushed Cadderly to the floor. The dwarf hoisted the pan and charged, but Pikel, now similarly armed, was ready for him.

Cadderly had read many tales of valor describing the ring of iron on iron, but he had never imagined the sound attributed to two dwarves sparring with frying pans.

Ivan got the first strike in, a wicked smash to Pikel's forearm. Pikel grunted and retaliated, slamming his pan straight down on top of Ivan's head.

Ivan backed up a step, trying to stop his eyes from spinning. He looked to the side, to a littered table, and was struck with a sudden inspiration, no doubt from the head blow. Pikel returned his smile. "Pots?" Ivan asked.

Pikel nodded eagerly and the two rushed to the table to find one that fit properly. Food went flying everywhere, followed by pots that had proven too small or too big. Then Ivan and Pikel faced off again, wielding their trusty pans and helmeted in the cookware of last night's stew.

Cadderly watched it all in blank amazement, not quite certain of how to take the actions. It seemed a comedy at times, but the growing welts and bruises on Ivan and Pikel's arms and faces told a different tale. Cadderly had seen the brothers argue before, and certainly he had come to expect all sorts of strange things from dwarves, but this was too wild, even for

Ivan and Pikel.

"Stop it!" Cadderly yelled at them. Pikel's answer came in the form of a hurled cleaver that narrowly missed Cadderly's head and buried itself an inch deep in the oaken door beside him. Cadderly stared in disbelief at the deadly instrument, still shuddering from the force of Pikel's throw, and knew that something was terribly wrong here, and terribly dangerous.

The young priest didn't give up, though. He just redirected his efforts. "I know a better way to fight!" he cried, moving cautiously toward the dwarves.

"Eh?" asked Pikel.

"Better way?" Ivan added. "For fighting?"

Ivan seemed already convinced—Pikel was winning the cookware battle—but Pikel only used Ivan's ensuing hesitation to press him even harder. Pikel's pan hummed as it dove in at a wide arc, smashing Ivan's elbow and knocking the yellow bearded dwarf off balance. Pikel recognized his clear advantage. His wicked pan went up high again for a follow-up strike.

"Druids do not fight with metal weapons!" Cadderly yelled.

"Oo," Pikel said, halting in midswing. The brothers looked at each other, shrugged once, and tossed their pots and pans to the ground.

Cadderly had to think quickly. He brushed off a section of the long table. "Sit here," he instructed Ivan, pulling up a stool.

"And you over here," he said to Pikel, indicating a second seat across from Ivan.

"Put the elbows of your right arms on the table," Cadderly explained.

"Arm-pulling?" Ivan scoffed incredulously. "Get me back me pan!"

"No!" Cadderly shouted. "No. This is a better way, a true test of strength."

"Bah!" snorted Ivan. "I'll clobber him!"

"Oh?" said Pikel.

They clasped hands roughly and started pulling before Cadderly could give any signal, or even line them up. He considered them for a moment, wanting to stay and see things through to conclusion, but the brothers were evenly matched, Cadderly realized, and their contest might last a while. Cadderly heard other priests shuffling by outside the open kitchen door; it was time for the midday canticle. Whatever the emergency, Cadderly simply could not be late for the required ceremony again. He watched the struggle a moment longer, to ensure that the dwarves were fully engaged, then shook his head in confusion and walked away. He had known Ivan and Pikel for more than a decade, since his childhood days, and had never seen either one of them lift a fist at the other. If that had not been bad enough, the cleaver, still wobbling in the door, vividly proved that something was terribly out of sorts.

*   *   *   *   *

Brother Chaunticleer's voice rang out with its usual quality, filling the great hall with perfect notes and filling the gathering of priests and scholars with sincere pleasure, but those most observant among the group, Cadderly included, glanced around at the crowd's reaction, as if they noticed something missing in Chaunticleer's delivery. The key was perfect and the words correct, but there seemed to be a lacking in the strength of the song.

Chaunticleer didn't notice them. He performed as always, the same songs he had sung at midday for several years. This time, though, unlike any of the others, Chaunticleer was indeed distracted. His thoughts drifted down to the rivers in the mountain foothills, still swollen from the winter melt and teeming with trout and silver perch. It had always been said that fishing was second only to singing in Brother Chaunticleer's heart. The priest was learning now that the perceived order of his desires might not be so correct.

Then it happened.

Brother Chaunticleer forgot the words.

He stood at the podium of the great hall, perplexed, as undeniable images of rushing water and leaping fish added to his confusion and put the song farther from his thoughts.

Whispers sprang up throughout the hall; mouths dropped open in disbelief. Dean Thobicus, never an excitable man, calmly moved up toward the podium. "Do go on, Brother Chaunticleer," he said softly, soothingly.

Chaunticleer could not continue. The song of Deneir was no match for the joyful sound of leaping trout.

The whispers turned to quiet giggles. Dean Thobicus waited a few moments, then whispered into Headmaster Avery's ear, and Avery, obviously more shaken than his superior, dismissed the gathering. He turned back to question Chaunticleer, but the singing priest was already gone, running for his hook and line.

*　*　*　*　*

Cadderly used the confusion in the great hall to get out from under Avery's watchful eye. He had spent a dreary morning scrubbing floors, but had completed the tasks and was free, at least until Avery found him idle and issued new orders. Avery was busy now, trying to figure out what had happened to Brother Chaunticleer. If Cadderly correctly understood the gravity of Chaunticleer's misfortunes, the headmaster would be busy with him for some time. Chaunticleer was considered among the most devout priests in the order of Deneir, and his highest duty, his only real priority, was the midday canticle.

Cadderly, too, was concerned by the events at the ceremony, especially after his visit with the dwarves that morning.

More disturbing than Chaunticleer's problems with the

songs, Danica had not been at the canticle. She was not associated with either the Oghman or Deneir sects and therefore not required to attend, but she rarely missed the event, and never before without telling Cadderly that she would not attend.

Even more disquieting, Kierkan Rufo had not been in attendance.

Since the main library was on the first floor and not far from the great hall, Cadderly decided to begin his search there. He skipped along briskly, his pace quickening as his suspicions continued to gnaw at him. A moaning sound from a side corridor stopped him abruptly.

Cadderly peeked around the corner to see Kierkan Rufo coming down the stairs, leaning heavily on the wall. Rufo seemed barely coherent; his face was covered in blood and he nearly toppled with each step.

"What happened?" Cadderly asked, rushing to help the man.

A wild light came into Rufo's eyes and he slapped Cadderly's reaching hands away. The action cost the disoriented man his balance and he tumbled down the last few steps to the floor.

The manner in which Rufo fell revealed much to Cadderly. Rufo had reached out to catch himself with one arm, the same arm he had used to slap at Cadderly, but his other arm remained limp at his side, useless.

"Where is she?" Cadderly demanded, suddenly very afraid.

He grabbed Rufo by the collar, despite the man's protests, and pulled him to his feet, viewing up close the damage to his face. Blood continued to flow from Rufo's obviously broken nose, and one of his eyes was swollen and purple and nearly closed. The man had numerous other bruises, and the way he flinched when Cadderly straightened him indicated other wounds in his abdomen or just a little bit lower.

"Where is she?" Cadderly said again.

Rufo gritted his teeth and turned away.

Cadderly forcibly turned him back. "What is wrong with you?" he demanded.

Rufo spat in his face.

Cadderly resisted the urge to strike out. There had always been tension in his friendship with Rufo, an element of rivalry that had only heightened when Danica came to the library.

Cadderly, usually getting the upper hand with Danica and the headmasters, realized that he often upset Rufo, but never before had the tall man shown him any open hostility.

"If you hurt Danica, I will come back to find you," Cadderly warned, though he thought that highly improbable. He let go of Rufo's wet tunic and ran up the stairs.

Rufo's blood trail led him to the south wing of the third floor, the library's guest quarters. Despite his urgency, Cadderly stopped his tracking as he neared Histra's room, for he heard cries emanating from within. At first Cadderly thought the priestess of Sune to be in peril, but as he reached for the door handle, he recognized the sounds as something other than pain.

Down the hall he rushed, too worried to be embarrassed.

The blood trail led to Danica's door, as he had feared it would.

He knocked loudly on the door and called out, "Danica?"

No answer.

Cadderly banged more urgently. "Danica?" he yelled. "Are you in there?"

Still no answer.

Cadderly lowered his shoulder and easily plowed through the unlocked door.

Danica stood perfectly still in the middle of the small room on the thick carpet she used for exercising. She held her open hands out in front of her, a meditative pose, and she did not even acknowledge that someone had entered the room. Her concentration was straight ahead, on a solid block of stone supported between two sawhorses.

"Danica?" Cadderly asked again. "Are you all right?" He moved over to her tentatively.

Danica turned her head, and her blank stare fell over him.

"Of course," she said. "Why would I not be?"

Her blond locks were matted with sweat and her hands were caked in drying blood.

"I just saw Kierkan Rufo," Cadderly remarked.

"As did I," Danica said calmly.

"What happened to him?"

"He tried to put his hands where they did not belong," Danica said casually, turning to stare back at the stone block. "I stopped him."

None of it made any sense to Cadderly; Rufo had leered and stared, but had never been foolish enough to make a move toward Danica. "Rufo attacked you?" he asked.

Danica laughed hysterically, and that, too, unnerved the young priest. "He tried to touch me, I said."

Cadderly scratched his head and looked around the room for some further clues as to what had transpired. He still couldn't believe that Rufo would make an open advance toward Danica, but even more remarkable had been Danica's response. She was a controlled and disciplined warrior. Cadderly would never expect such overkill as the beating she had apparently given Rufo.

"You hurt him badly," Cadderly said, needing to hear Danica's explanation.

"He will recover," was all that the woman replied.

Cadderly grabbed her arm, meaning to turn her about to face him. Danica was too quick. Her arm flicked back and forth, breaking the hold, then she snapped her hand onto Cadderly's thumb and bent it backward, nearly driving him to his knees. Her ensuing glare alone would have backed Cadderly away, and he honestly believed that she would break his finger.

Then Danica's look softened, as if she suddenly recognized the man at her side. She released her grip on his thumb and grabbed around his head instead, pulling him close. "Oh Cadderly!" she cried between kisses. "Did I hurt you?"

Cadderly pushed her back to arm's length and stared at her for a long while. She appeared fine, except for Rufo's blood on her hands and a curious, urgent look in her eyes.

"Have you been drinking any wine?" Cadderly asked.

"Of course not," Danica replied, surprised by the question. "You know that I am allowed only one glass . . ." Her voice trailed off as the hard glare returned. "Are you doubting my loyalty to oath?" she asked sharply.

Cadderly's face crinkled in confusion.

"Let go of me."

Her tone was serious, and when the stunned Cadderly did not immediately respond, she accentuated her point. She and Cadderly were only standing about two feet apart, but the limber monk kicked with her foot, up between them, and waved it threateningly in Cadderly's face.

Cadderly released her and fell back. "What is wrong with you?" he demanded.

Danica's visage softened again.

"You beat Rufo badly," Cadderly said. "If he made inappropriate advances—"

"He interrupted me!" Danica cut him off. "He . . ." she looked to the block of stone, then back to Cadderly, again glowering. "And now you are interrupting me."

Cadderly wisely backed away. "I will go," he promised, studying the block, "if you tell me what I am interrupting."

"I am a true disciple of Grandmaster Penpahg D'Ahn!" Danica cried as though that answered everything.

"Of course you are," said Cadderly.

His agreement calmed Danica. "The time has come for Gigel Nugel," she said, "Iron Skull, but I must not be interrupted in my concentration!"

Cadderly regarded the solid block for a moment—a block far larger than the one in the sketch of Penpahg D'Ahn—then eyed Danica's delicate face, trying unsuccessfully to digest the news. "You plan to smash that block with your head?"

"I am a true disciple," Danica reiterated.

Cadderly nearly swooned. "Do not," he begged, reaching for Danica.

Seeing her impending reaction, Cadderly pulled his arms back and qualified his statement. "Not yet," he pleaded. "This is a great event in the history of the library. Dean Thobicus should be informed. We could make it a public showing."

"This is a private matter," Danica replied. "It is not a curiosity show for the pleasures of unbelievers!"

"Unbelievers?" Cadderly whispered, and at this strange moment he knew that the label fit him, but for more reasons than his and Danica's differing faiths. He had to think quickly.

"But," he improvised, "surely the event must be properly witnessed and recorded."

Danica looked at him curiously.

"For future disciples," Cadderly explained. "Who will come to study Grandmaster Penpahg D'Ahn in a hundred years? Would that disciple not also benefit from the practices and successes of Grandmistress Danica? You cannot be selfish with this achievement. Surely that would not be in accord with Penpahg D'Ahn's teachings."

Danica mulled over his words. "It would be selfish," she admitted.

Even her acquiescence reinforced Cadderly's fears that something was terribly wrong. Danica was sharp thinking and never before so easily manipulated.

"I will wait for you to make the arrangements," she agreed, "but not for long! The time has come for Iron Skull. This I know is true. I am a true disciple of Grandmaster Penpahg D'Ahn."

Cadderly did not know how to proceed. He sensed that if he left Danica, she would go right back to her attempt. He looked all around, his gaze finally settling on Danica's bed. "It would be well for you to rest," he offered.

Danica looked to the bed, then back to Cadderly, a sly look

on her face. "I know something better than rest," she purred, moving much closer. The urgency of her unexpected kiss weakened Cadderly in the knees and promised him many wonderful things.

But not like this. He reminded himself that something was wrong with Danica, that something was apparently wrong with almost everything around him.

"I have to go," he said, pulling away. "To Dean Thobicus, to make the arrangements. You rest now. Surely you will need your strength."

Danica reluctantly let him go, honestly torn between her perception of duty and the needs of love.

*   *   *   *   *

Cadderly stumbled back down to the first level. The hallways were unnervingly empty and quiet, and Cadderly wasn't certain of where he should turn. He had few close friends in the library—he wasn't about to go to Kierkan Rufo with this problem, and he wanted to keep far away from the living and working quarters of Dean Thobicus and the headmasters, fearing an encounter with Avery.

In the end, he went back to the kitchen and found Pikel and Ivan, nearly collapsed with exhaustion, still stubbornly arm wrestling at the table. Cadderly knew that the dwarves were headstrong, but more than an hour had passed since they had begun their match.

When Cadderly approached, shaking his head in disbelief, he saw just how headstrong the Bouldershoulder brothers could be. Purplish bruises from popped veins lined their arms and their entire bodies trembled violently under the continuing strain, but their visages were unyieldingly locked.

"I'll put ye down!" Ivan snarled.

Pikel growled back and strained harder at the pull.

"Stop it!" Cadderly demanded. Both dwarves looked up from the match, realizing only then that someone had entered the kitchen.

"I can take him," Ivan assured Cadderly.

"Why are you fighting?" Cadderly asked, guessing that the dwarves would not remember.

"Yerself was here," Ivan replied. "Ye saw he was the one what started it."

"Oh?" Pikel piped in sarcastically.

"What did he start?" Cadderly asked.

"The fight!" growled an exasperated Ivan.

"How?"

Ivan had run out of answers. He looked at Pikel, who only shrugged in reply.

"Then why are you fighting?" Cadderly asked again with no answer forthcoming.

Both dwarves stopped at the same time and sat looking across the table at each other.

"Me brother!" Ivan cried suddenly, springing over the table. Pikel caught him in midflight and their hugs and pats on the back were nearly as vicious as the arm wrestling had been.

Ivan turned happily on Cadderly. "He's me brother!" the dwarf announced.

Cadderly strained a smile and figured that it might be best to divert the dwarves as he had diverted Danica. "It is not so far from suppertime," was all he had to say.

"Supper?" Ivan bellowed.

"Oo oi!" added Pikel, and they were off, whirling like little bearded tornados, sweeping the kitchen into order in preparation of the evening meal. Cadderly waited just a few minutes, to make sure that the dwarves wouldn't get back to their fighting, then he slipped out and headed back to check on Danica.

He found her in her room, sleeping contentedly. He pulled her blankets up over her, then went to the stone to see if he could find some way to remove it.

"How did you ever get this up here?" he asked, staring at

the heavy block. It would take at least two strong men to move it, and even then, or even with three men, the stairs would not be easily negotiated. For now, Cadderly figured that he could just drop the block down from the sawhorses, put it on the floor to stop Danica from making her Iron Skull attempt. He went back to the bed and took the heaviest blankets. He tied them together and wrapped them about the block, then threw both ends over a rafter in the low room.

Cadderly grabbed the dangling ends and hoisted himself right off the floor to kick at the block. The sawhorses leaned, then toppled and the rafter creaked in protest, but Cadderly's counterbalancing weight brought the blanketed block down slowly and quietly.

Using the sawhorse legs as levers, he managed to wiggle the blankets out from under the stone. Then he tucked Danica back in and headed away, his mind racing to find some logical reason for all the illogical events of the day.

* * * * *

It was a wondrous oak, a most excellent tree indeed, and Newander gently stroked each of its spreading branches as he made his way higher. The view from the uppermost branches was splendid, a scene that sent shivers of delight along the druid's spine.

When he turned about to regard the mountains to the southwest, though, Newander's smile disappeared.

There sat the Edificant Library, a barely seen square block far in the distance. Newander hadn't meant to be gone this long; for all the freedom and individuality their order offered, he knew that Arcite would not be pleased.

A bird flitted down and landed not far from the druid's head.

"I should be getting back," the druid said to it, though he wanted to remain out here in the wilderness, away from the temptations of civilization.

Newander started reluctantly down the tree. With the distant library removed from sight, he nearly headed off again in the opposite direction. He didn't, though. Chastising himself for his fears and weaknesses, he grudgingly started back toward the library, back to his duties.

* * * * *

Cadderly meant to lie down and rest for only a short while when he returned to his room. The afternoon was barely half over, but it already had been an exhausting day. Soon the young priest was snoring loudly.

But not contentedly. From the depths of his mist-filled dreams came the walking dead, skeletons and gruesome ghouls, reaching for him with sharp, bony hands and rotting fingers.

He sat up in pitch blackness. Cold trails of sweat lined his face, and his blankets were moist and clammy. He heard a noise to the side of the bed. He hadn't undressed when he lay down, and he fumbled about, finding his spindle-disks and then his light tube.

Something was close.

The end cap popped off and the light streamed out. Cadderly nearly flicked his spindle-disks out of sheer terror, but he managed to forego his attack when he recognized the white fur of a friend.

As startled as Cadderly, Percival rushed across the room, upsetting all sorts of things, and darted under the bed. The squirrel came up tentatively a moment later at Cadderly's feet and slowly moved up to nestle in the pit of the man's arm.

Cadderly was glad for the company. He recapped his light, but kept it in his hand, and soon was fast asleep.

The walking dead were waiting for him.

Twelve

The Time to Act

Barjin is preparing to open the gate," Dorigen told Aballister. "My contacts on the lower planes sense the beginnings of the portal."

"How long?" the wizard asked grimly. Aballister was glad that Druzil soon would be close to Barjin, keeping an eye on the dangerous man, but he was not pleased that Barjin had so quickly advanced to this level of preparedness. If Barjin meant to open a gate, then his plans were probably in full swing.

Dorigen shrugged. "An hour or two," she replied. "I cannot know which methods of sorcery the priest will employ." She looked over to Druzil, sitting comfortably atop Aballister's desk, appearing impassive, though both wizards knew better than to think that. "Do you really believe it's necessary to send the imp?"

"Do you trust Barjin" Aballister answered.

"Talona would not have allowed him to take the elixir if he was not loyal to our cause," Dorigen replied.

"Do not presume that the goddess is so directly interested in our cause," warned Aballister, rising from and walking nervously about his oaken chair. "The Time of Troubles has passed and much has changed. Talona's avatar was pleased to bring me into her dark fold, but I am not her only concern, and I do not presume to be her chief concern. She directed me to Druzil, and he provided the chaos curse. Its fate is in my . . . in our hands now."

"But if Barjin was not of Talona's clergy . . ." Dorigen argued, shifting tentatively from foot to foot and letting her companion complete the warning for himself.

Aballister considered Dorigen for a long moment, surprised that she was as fearful as he about Barjin. She was a middle-aged wizard, thin and drawn, with darting eyes and a tangle of graying black hair that she never bothered to brush.

"Perhaps he is of Talona's clergy," Aballister replied. "I believe that he is." Aballister had played these possible scenarios through his thoughts a hundred times over the last few days. "Do not let that fact comfort you. If Barjin stuck a poisoned dagger into my heart, Talona would not be pleased, but neither would she seek vengeance on the priest. That is the price of serving a goddess such as ours."

Dorigen considered those words for a few moments, then nodded her agreement.

"We vie for power with the priests," Aballister went on. "It has been that way since the beginning of Castle Trinity, and that contest intensified with Barjin's arrival. He gained control of the elixir from me. I admit my own failure in not anticipating his cunning, but I have not conceded defeat, I promise you. Now, go back to your chambers and converse with your contacts. Inform me at once if there is any change in Barjin's gate."

Aballister looked over to his magical mirror and considered whether he should scry into Barjin's altar room to confirm what Dorigen had told him. He decided against it, though, knowing that Barjin would easily sense the scrying and recognize its source. Aballister did not want Barjin to know how concerned he was, did not want the priest to understand how great an advantage he was gaining in their competition.

The wizard looked over his shoulder and nodded to Druzil.

"The priest is a daring one," Druzil remarked, "to open a gate right below so many enemies of magical power. *Bene tellemara*. If the priests of the library discover the gate . . ."

"It was not unexpected," Aballister retorted defensively. "We knew that Barjin was taking materials for sorcery."

"If he is opening the gate already," Druzil put in, "then perhaps the curse has begun!" The imp rubbed his pudgy, leathery hands eagerly at that prospect.

"Or perhaps Barjin's situation has become desperate," Aballister quickly replied.

Druzil wisely disguised his excitement.

"We must get the brazier prepared," Aballister said, "and quickly. We must be ready before Barjin begins his summoning." He moved over to his own burning brazier and picked up the closest bag, checking to ensure that the powder inside was blue.

"I will provide you with two powders," the wizard explained. "One to close Barjin's gate behind you as you pass through to join him, another to reopen it so that you may return to me."

"To ensure that I am his only catch?" Druzil asked, cocking his dog-faced head curiously.

"I am not as confident of Barjin's powers as he appears to be," Aballister replied. "If he summons too many denizens, even minor creatures, of the lower planes through to serve him, his control will be sorely taxed. No doubt he is bringing in undead to serve him as well. That type of an army could be beyond him when the priests of the Edificant Library strike back. I fear Barjin may be reaching too far. It all could crumble around him."

"Fear?" Druzil asked slyly. "Or hope?"

Aballister's hollowed eyes narrowed dangerously.

"Examine the situation from another point of view, my dear Druzil," he purred. "From your own. Do you wish to find competitors from your filthy home at Barjin's side? Might not another imp, or a midge perhaps, know you and know that you have been in service to me?"

The wizard enjoyed the way the imp's features suddenly seemed to droop.

"Barjin would know you as my agent then," Aballister went on. "If you were fortunate, he would only banish you."

Druzil looked over to Aballister's brazier and nodded his agreement.

"Get through as soon as Barjin opens his gate," Aballister instructed, dumping the blue powder into the burning brazier.

The flames roared and shifted through the colors of the spectrum. Druzil walked by the wizard, taking the two tiny bags and looping them over the foreclaws on his wing.

"Close Barjin's gate as you step out of the flames," Aballister continued. "He will not understand the sudden shift in his fire's hue. He will think it is the result of your passing."

Again Druzil nodded and then, eager to be away from Aballister, and even more eager to see exactly what was going on at the library, he jumped into the brazier and was gone.

"Aballister's plans serve everyone," Druzil muttered to himself a few minutes later, as he floated in the black void at the edge of the material plane, just waiting for Barjin's gate to open. The imp realized, too, that other things—jealousy and fear—guided the wizard's actions. Barjin had shown no signs of weakness throughout and Aballister knew as well as Druzil did that a gate to the lower planes would not seriously threaten the priest's successes. Still, Druzil was more than happy when he looked down at the magical powders Aballister had provided. The imp remained intrigued by Barjin's brashness and confidence. The priest's preliminary victories, both at Castle Trinity, against Aballister, and possibly in the dungeons of the library, could not easily be dismissed. While Aballister might fear for his own position, Druzil's only concern was the chaos curse, the recipe he had waited so very long to exploit.

Where the chaos curse was concerned, Barjin deserved some serious attention.

* * * * *

The terrible, clawed hand grabbed at Cadderly's heart. He dove to the side wildly, his arms flailing in futile defense.

He woke up when he hit the floor and spent several long moments trying to orient himself. It was morning, and Cadderly's nightmares faded fast under the sun's enlightening rays. Cadderly tried to hold on to them so that he might better decipher any hidden meaning, but they could not withstand the light of day.

With a resigned shrug, Cadderly focused his thoughts back to the previous afternoon, remembering the events before he had come for some rest.

Some rest! How much time had passed? he wondered frantically, looking at his clocking measurements on the floor. Fifteen hours?

Percival was still in the room but apparently had been up and about for some time. The squirrel sat on Cadderly's desk just inside the window, contentedly munching on an acorn. Below him lay the discarded husks of a dozen appetizers.

Cadderly sat up beside the bed and tried again to recover the fading blur of his dreams, seeking some clue to the confusion that had so suddenly come into his life. His light tube, opened and glowing faintly, lay under the thick jumble of bed covers.

"There is something here," Cadderly remarked to Percival, absently grabbing and recapping the tube. "Something I cannot yet understand." There was more confusion than determination in Cadderly's voice. Yesterday seemed a long time ago, and he seriously wondered where his memories ended and his dreams began. How unusual had yesterday's events really been? How much of the apparent strangeness was no more than Cadderly's own fear? Danica could be a stubborn one, after all, he reminded himself, and who could predict the actions of dwarves?

Unconsciously, Cadderly rubbed the deep bruise on the side of his head. The daylight streaming into his room made everything seem in order. They made all of his fears that something had gone awry in the secure library seem almost childish.

A moment later, he realized a new fear, one based surely in reality. There came a knock on his door and the call of a familiar voice. "Cadderly? Cadderly, boy, are you in there?"

Headmaster Avery.

Percival popped the acorn into a chubby cheek and skittered out the window. Cadderly hadn't gotten to his feet when the headmaster entered.

"Cadderly!" Avery cried, rushing to him. "Are you all right, my boy?"

"It is nothing," Cadderly replied tentatively, keeping out of Avery's reaching hands. "I just fell out of bed."

Avery's distress did not diminish. "That is terrible!" the headmaster cried. "We cannot have that, oh, no!" Avery's eyes darted about frantically, then he snapped his fingers and smiled widely. "We will get the dwarves to put up a railing. Yes, that is it! We cannot have you falling out of bed and injuring yourself. You are much too valuable an asset to the Order of Deneir for us to allow such potential tragedy!"

The young scholar looked at him blankly, uncertain whether this was sarcasm or strange reality.

"It is nothing," Cadderly replied timidly.

"Oh, yes," Avery spouted, "you would say that. Such a fine lad! Never concerned for your own safety!" Avery's exuberant pat on the back hurt Cadderly more than the fall.

"You have come to give me my list of duties," Cadderly reasoned, eager to change the subject. Somehow he liked Avery better when the headmaster was screaming at him. At least then he could be certain of Avery's intent.

"Duties?" Avery asked, seeming sincerely confused. "Why, I do not believe that you have any this day. Or, if you do, ignore them. We cannot have one of your potential busied by menial tasks. Make your own routines. Certainly you know better than any where you might be of greatest value."

Cadderly didn't believe a word of it. Or if he did allow himself to believe Avery's sincerity, he couldn't quite comprehend it anyway. "Then why are you here?" he asked.

"Do I need a reason to look in on my most-prized acolyte?" Avery answered, giving Cadderly a second rough pat. "No, no reason. I just came to say good morning, and I say it now. Good morning!" He started away, then stopped abruptly, spun about and wrapped a bear hug on Cadderly. "Good morning indeed!"

Avery, his eyes suddenly misted, put him out at arm's length. "I knew that you would grow to be a fine lad when first you came to us," he said.

Cadderly expected him to abruptly change the subject, as he always did when speaking of Cadderly's early days at the Edificant Library, but Avery rambled on.

"We feared that you would become just like your father— he was an intelligent one, just like you! But he had no guidance, you see." Avery's laughter erupted straight from his belly. "I called him a Gondsman!" the priest roared, slapping Cadderly's shoulder.

Cadderly failed to see the humor, but he was truly intrigued to hear about his father. That subject had always been avoided at the library, and Cadderly, with no recollections at all before his arrival, had never pressed it seriously.

"And indeed he was," Avery continued, becoming calm and grim. "Or worse, I fear. He could not remain here, you see. We could not allow him to take our knowledge and put it to destructive practice."

"Where did he go?" Cadderly asked.

"I know not. That was twenty years ago!" Avery replied. "We saw him only once after that, the day he presented Dean

Thobicus with his son. Do you understand, then, my boy, why I am always chasing after you, why I fear that your course might lead you astray?"

Cadderly didn't even try to find a voice to respond with, though he would have liked to learn more while he had the headmaster in so talkative a mood. He quickly reminded himself that these actions were out of sorts for Avery, and just further confirmation that something was going wrong.

"Well, then," the headmaster said. He slammed Cadderly with one more hug, then pushed the young man away, spinning briskly for the door. "Do not waste too much of this glorious day!" he roared as he entered the hall.

Percival came back to the window, working on a new acorn.

"Do not even ask," Cadderly warned him, but if the squirrel cared at all, he did not show it.

"So much for dreams," Cadderly remarked grimly. If ever he doubted his memories of the previous day, he did not now, not in light of Avery's outburst. Cadderly dressed quickly. He would have to check on Ivan and Pikel, to make sure they were not back at their fighting, and on Kierkan Rufo, to make sure the man had no designs against Danica.

The hallway was strangely quiet, though the morning was in full swing. Cadderly started for the kitchen but changed his direction suddenly when he got to the spiral stairway. The only change in the daily routines, the only unusual occurrence at the library before this inexplicable weirdness, had been the arrival of the druids.

They had been housed on the fourth floor. Normally that level was reserved for the novice priests of the host sects, the servants, and for storage, but the druids had expressed a desire to be away from the rest of the gathered scholars. Not without reservations, for he did not want to disturb the xenophobic group, Cadderly started up the stairs instead of down.

He didn't really believe that Arcite, Newander, and Cleo

were the source of the problems, but they were wise and experienced and might have some insight about what was going on.

The first sign Cadderly noticed that something up here, too, was amiss, was a growl and a scraping noise. He stood outside the door to the druids' quarters in a remote corner of the north wing, uncertain of whether to continue, wondering whether the woodland priests might be engaged in some private ritual.

Memories of Danica and Avery and Brother Chaunticleer spurred him on. He knocked lightly on the door.

No answer.

Cadderly turned the handle and opened the door a crack.

The room was a mess, the work of an obviously agitated brown bear. The creature squatted on the bed, which had broken under its great weight, and was now casually tearing apart a down-filled pillow. Shuffling slowly across the floor in front of it was a huge tortoise.

The bear seemed to pay little attention to him, so Cadderly boldly opened the door a bit wider. Newander sat on the windowsill, staring despairingly out at the wide mountains, his blond hair hanging limply about his shoulders.

"Arcite and Cleo," the druid remarked offhandedly. "Arcite is the bear."

"A ritual?" Cadderly asked. He remembered when the druid named Shannon had enacted such physical changes before his eyes years ago, and he knew that the shape-changing ability was common for the most powerful druids. Actually witnessing it again amazed him nonetheless.

Newander shrugged, not really knowing the answer. He looked at Cadderly, a saddened expression on his face.

Cadderly started to go to him, but Arcite, the bear, didn't seem to like that idea. He stood high and issued a growl that turned Cadderly right around.

"Keep yourself safely back from him," Newander explained. "I am not yet certain of his intentions."

"Have you asked?"

"He does not answer," Newander replied.

"Then can you be sure it is really Arcite?" Cadderly asked.

Shannon had explained that the druidic shape change was purely physical, with retention of the woodland priest's mental facilities. Shape-changed druids could even converse in the common tongue.

"It was," Newander replied, "and is. I recognize the animal. Perhaps it is Arcite now, more truly Arcite than Arcite ever was."

Cadderly could not exactly decipher those words, but he thought he understood the druid's basic meaning. "The turtle, then, is Cleo?" he asked. "Or is Cleo really the turtle?"

"Yes," Newander answered. "Both ways, as far as I can discern."

"Why is Newander still Newander?" Cadderly pressed, guessing the source of Newander's despair.

He saw that his question greatly wounded the still-human druid, and he figured that he had his answers. He bowed quickly, exited, and closed the door. He started to walk away, but changed his mind and ran instead.

Newander sat back against the windowsill and looked at his animal companions. Something had happened here, while he was gone, though he still wasn't certain whether it had been a good or a bad thing. Newander feared for his comrades, but he envied them, too. Had they found some secret while he was away, some measure by which they could slip fully into the natural order? He had seen Arcite in bear form before, and clearly recognized the druid, but never had it been like this.

This bear resisted Newander's every attempt to communicate; Arcite was fully a bear, in body and mind. The same held true of Cleo, the turtle.

Newander remained a human, alone now in a house of tempting civilization. He hoped that his friends would return soon; he feared he would lose his way without their guidance.

Newander looked back out the window, back to the mountains majestic and the world that he so loved. For all of that love, though, the druid still did not know where he fit in.

*   *   *   *   *

When he arrived at the kitchen, Cadderly found that the dwarves had resumed their fighting. Pots, pans, and kitchen knives hummed about the room, smashing ceramic items, clanging against iron ones, and knocking holes in the walls.

"Ivan!" Cadderly screamed, and the desperation in his voice actually stopped the barrage.

Ivan looked at Cadderly blankly and, from across the room, Pikel added, "Oo."

"What are you fighting about now?" Cadderly asked.

"That one's fault!" Ivan growled. "He spoiled me soup. Put in roots and leaves and grass and things. Says it's druidlike that way. Bah! A dwarven druid!"

"Put your desires on hold, Pikel," Cadderly advised solemnly. "Now is not the time to be thinking of joining a druidic order."

Pikel's big, round eyes narrowed dangerously.

"The druids are not in the mood for visitors," Cadderly explained, "even for aspiring druids. I just came from them." Cadderly shook his head. "Something very wrong is going on," he said to Ivan. "Look at you two, fighting. Never have you done that in all the years I have known you."

"Never before did me stupid brother claim that he's a druid!" Ivan replied.

"Doo-dad," Pikel pointedly added.

"Granted," said Cadderly, glancing curiously at Pikel, "but look around at the destruction in this kitchen. Do you not believe this is a bit out of hand?"

Tears flooded both Ivan and Pikel's eyes when they took a moment to survey their prized kitchen. Every pot had been upset; the spice rack was thoroughly smashed and all spices lost; their oven, Pikel's own design, was damaged so brutally that it could not possibly be repaired.

Cadderly was glad that his appeal had not gone unnoticed, but the dwarven tears made him shake his head in continued disbelief. "Everyone has gone mad," he said. "The druids are up in their room, pretending to be animals. Headmaster Avery acts as if I am his favorite protégé. Even Danica is out of sorts. She nearly crippled Rufo yesterday and has it in her mind to try this Iron Skull maneuver."

"That'd explain the block," remarked Ivan.

"You know about that?" Cadderly asked.

"Brought it up yesterday," Ivan explained. "Solid and heavy, that one! Yer lady was here this morning, needing to put the thing back up on the sawhorses."

"You didn't . . ."

"'Course we did," Ivan replied, puffing out his barrellike chest. "Who else'd be able to lift the thing . . .?" The dwarf stopped abruptly. Cadderly was already gone.

The renewed clamor from Histra's room haunted Cadderly when he got back to the third level. The priestess of Sune's cries had only intensified, taking on a primordial urgency that truly frightened Cadderly and made every running stride toward Danica's room seem a futile, dream-weighted step.

He burst through Danica's door, not even slowing to knock. He knew in his heart what he would find.

Danica lay on her back in the center of the floor, her forehead covered in blood. The stone block was not broken, but her pounding had moved the sawhorses back a few feet. Like Danica, the block was caked in blood in several places, indicating that the monk had slammed it repeatedly, even after splitting open her head.

"Danica," Cadderly breathed, moving to her. He tilted her head back and stroked her face, still delicate beneath her swollen and battered forehead.

Danica stirred just a bit, managing to drape one arm weakly over Cadderly's shoulder. One of her almond eyes cracked open, but Cadderly did not think she saw anything.

"What have you done to her?" came a cry from the doorway. Cadderly turned to see Newander glaring at him, quarterstaff leveled at the ready.

"I did nothing," Cadderly retorted. "Danica did it to herself. Against that block." He pointed to the bloodied stone, and the druid relaxed his grip on the staff. "What is happening?" Cadderly demanded. "With your friends, with Danica? With everyone, Newander? Something is wrong!"

Newander shook his head helplessly. "This is a cursed place," he agreed, dropping his gaze to the floor. "I have sensed it since my return."

"It?" Cadderly asked, wondering what Newander knew that he did not.

"A perversion," the druid tried to explain, though he stuttered over the words, as though he, himself, had not yet come to understand his fears. "Something out of the natural order, something . . ."

"Yes," Cadderly agreed. "Something not as it should be."

"A cursed place," Newander said again.

"We must figure out how it is cursed," reasoned Cadderly, "and why."

"Not we," Newander corrected. "I am a failure, good lad. You must find your own answers."

Cadderly wasn't even surprised anymore at the unexpected and uncharacteristic response, nor did he try to argue. He gently lifted Danica in his arms and carried her over to the bed, where Newander joined them.

"Her wounds are not too serious," the druid announced after a quick inspection. "I have some healing herbs." He reached into a belt pouch.

Cadderly grabbed his wrist. "What is happening?" he asked again, quietly. "Have all the priests gone mad?"

Newander pulled away and sniffled. "I care nothing for

your priests," he said. "It is for my own order that I fear, and for myself!"

"Arcite and Cleo," Cadderly remarked grimly. "Can you help them?"

"Help them?" Newander replied. "Surely it is not they who need help. It is me. They are of the order. Their hearts lie with the animals. Pity Newander, I say. He has found his voice and it is not the bay nor the growl, nor even the cackle of a bird!"

Cadderly's face crinkled at the absurd words. The druid considered himself a failure because he had not changed into some beast and crawled about on the floor!

"Newander, the druid," Newander went on, fully absorbed in self-pity. "Not so, I say. Not a druid by my own measure."

Cadderly had a definite feeling that time was running out for all of them. He had awakened that morning full of hope, but things certainly had not improved.

He looked closely at Newander. The druid considered himself a failure, but by Cadderly's observation, he remained the most rational person at the library. Cadderly needed some help now, desperately. "Then be Newander, the healer" he said. "Tend to Danica—on your word."

Newander nodded.

"Heal her, and do not let her back to that block!" As if in response to his own words, Cadderly rushed across the room and pushed the stone over, not even caring about the resounding crash or the damage to the floor.

"Do not let her do anything," Cadderly went on firmly.

"Would you put your trust in a failure?" the pitiful Newander asked.

Cadderly did not hesitate. "Self-pity does not become you," he scolded. He grabbed the druid roughly by the front of his green cloak. "Danica is the most important person in all the world to me," he said sincerely, "but I have some things I must do, though I fear I do not yet understand what they might be. Newander will care for Danica—there is no one else—on his word and with my trust."

Newander nodded gravely and put his hand back into his pouch.

Cadderly moved swiftly to the door, paused, and looked back at the druid. He didn't feel comfortable leaving Danica, even with Newander, whom he trusted despite the druid's self-doubts. Cadderly dismissed his protective urges. If he really wanted to help Danica, to help everyone in the library, he would have to find out what was going on, find the source of the infection that had apparently come over the place, and not merely bandage its symptoms. It was up to him, he decided.

He nodded to Newander and headed for his room.

Thirteen

Cryptic

The tunnel was fiery and swirling, but not so long for the imp. These were summoning flames and did not burn a creature of Druzil's otherworldly constitution. Barjin had opened his interplanar gate, exactly as Dorigen had predicted, and Druzil was quick to rush to the cleric's call.

A puff of red smoke—Druzil dropping the powder to effectively shut the gate behind him—signaled Barjin that his first summoned ally had arrived. He stared deeply into the brazier's orange flames at the grotesque face taking definite form.

A batlike wing extended from the side of the brazier, then another, and a moment later Druzil hopped through.

"Who has dared to call me?" the imp snorted, playing the part of an unwitting lower-planar creature caught by Barjin's magical call.

"An imp?" the priest retorted derisively. "I have extended all my efforts for the sake of summoning a mere imp?"

Druzil folded his wings around him and snarled, not appreciating Barjin's tone.

If Barjin exhibited sarcastic disdain, Druzil knew that that, too, was part of the summoning game. As with the summoned creature, if the summoner accepted the situation without grumbles, he would be giving a definite advantage to his counterpart. Sorcery, the magic of conjuring creatures from other planes, was a contest of wills, where perceived strength was often more important than actual strength.

Druzil knew that the priest was thrilled that his first call had been answered at all, and an imp, resourceful and clever, was no small catch. But Barjin had to seem disappointed, had to make Druzil believe he was capable of calling and controlling much larger and stronger denizens.

Druzil didn't appear impressed. "I may go?" he replied as he turned back to the brazier.

"Hold!" Barjin shouted at him. "Do not assume anything, I warn you. I have not dismissed you, nor shall I for many days to come. What is your name?"

"*Cueltar qui tellermar gwi*," Druzil replied.

"Lackey of the stupid one?" Barjin translated, laughing, though he did not fully understand the connotations of Druzil's words. "Surely you can concoct a better title than that for yourself!"

Druzil rocked back on his clawed feet, hardly believing that Barjin could understand the common language of the lower planes. This priest was full of surprises.

"Druzil," the imp replied suddenly, though he didn't quite understand why he had revealed his true name. Barjin's quiet chuckle told him that the priest might have mentally compelled such a truthful response.

Yes, Druzil thought again, this priest was full of surprises.

"Druzil," Barjin muttered, as though he had heard the name before, a fact that did not please the imp. "Welcome, Druzil," Barjin said sincerely, "and be glad that I have called you to my side. You are a creature of chaos, and you will not be disappointed by what you witness in your short stay here."

"I have seen the Abyss," Druzil reminded him. "You cannot imagine the wonders there."

Barjin conceded the point with a nod. No matter how completely the Most Fatal Horror engulfed the priests of the Edificant Library, it could not, of course, rival the unending hellish chaos of the Abyss.

"We are in the dungeons of a bastion dedicated to order and goodness," Barjin explained.

Druzil crinkled his bulbous nose sourly, acting as though Barjin had revealed something he did not already know.

"That is about to change," Barjin assured him. "A curse has befallen this place, one that will bring the goodly priests to their knees. Even an imp who has witnessed the Abyss should enjoy that spectacle."

The glimmer in Druzil's black eyes was genuine. This was the whole purpose in giving Aballister the recipe for the chaos curse. Aballister had expressed concerns, even distress over Barjin's choice of target and Barjin's apparent successes, but Druzil was not Aballister's stooge. If Barjin could indeed take down the Edificant Library, then Druzil would be much closer to realizing his hopes of throwing an entire region of the Realms into absolute disarray.

He looked around at the altar room, impressed by Barjin's work, particularly by the setup around the precious bottle. His gaze then went to the door, and he was truly amazed.

There stood Barjin's newest bodyguard, wrapped head to toe in graying linen. Some of the cloth had slipped, revealing part of the mummy's face, dried and hollowed skin on bone with several lesions where the skilled preservation techniques had not held up to the test of centuries.

"Do you like him?" Barjin asked.

Druzil did not know how to respond. A mummy! Mummies were among the most powerful of the undead, strong and disease ridden, hateful of all living things and nearly invulnerable to most attacks. Few could animate such a monster; fewer still would dare to, fearing that they could not begin to keep the monster under control.

"The priests and scholars above soon will be helpless, lost in their own confusion," Barjin explained, "then they will meet my army. Look at him, my new friend, Druzil," the priest said triumphantly, moving over to Khalif. He started to drape an arm over the scabrous thing, then apparently reconsidered the act and prudently pulled back. "Is he not beautiful? He does love me so." To illustrate his power, Barjin turned to the mummy and commanded, "Khalif, kneel!"

The monster stiffly dropped to its knees.

"There are other preserved corpses that offer similar promise," Barjin bluffed. He had no other ashes, and any attempts to animate a mummified corpse without such aid would prove futile or produce nothing more powerful than a simple zombie.

Druzil's growing admiration for Barjin did not diminish when the priest led him out on a tour of the catacombs. Cunning, explosive glyphs, both fiery and electrical, had been placed at strategic positions, and a virtual army of animated skeletons sat patiently in their open tombs, awaiting Barjin's commands or the predetermined conditions for action the priest had set upon them.

Druzil did not need to be reminded that all of these precautions could well be unnecessary. If the chaos curse continued to work effectively in the library above, no enemies would be likely to find their way down to bother Barjin.

"Caution," Barjin muttered as though he had read Druzil's thoughts when the two had returned to the altar room. "I always assume the worst, thus am I pleasantly surprised if anything better occurs."

Druzil could not hide his agreement or his excitement. Barjin's thinking had been complete; the priest had taken no chances.

"This library soon will be mine," Barjin assured the imp, and Druzil did not doubt his boasts. "With the Edificant

Library, the very cornerstone of the Impresk region, defeated, all the area from Shilmista Forest to Impresk Lake will fall before me."

Druzil liked what he heard, but Barjin's reference to "me" and not to the triumvirate was a bit unnerving. Druzil did not want any open warfare among the ruling factions of Castle Trinity, but if it did come, the imp had to make certain that he chose the winning side. He was even more glad now that Aballister had chosen to send him to Barjin, glad that he could view both sides of the coming storm.

"It is almost done," Barjin reiterated. "The curse grabs at the sensibilities of the priests above and the library soon will fall."

"How can you know what happens above?" Druzil asked him, for the tour had not included any windows or passages up into the library. The one stairway Barjin had shown him had been smashed into pieces, and the door it once had led to had been recently bricked off. The only apparent weakness in Barjin's setup was isolation, not knowing the exact sequence of events in the library above.

"I have only indications," Barjin admitted. "Behind the new wall I showed you lies the library's wine cellar. I have heard many priests passing through there for more than a day now, grabbing bottles at random—some of which are extraordinarily expensive—and apparently guzzling them down. Their talk and actions speak loudly of the growing chaos, for this certainly is not within the rules of behavior in the disciplined library. Yet you are correct in your observations, friend imp. I do indeed require more details to the events above."

"So you have summoned me," said Druzil.

"So I have opened the gate," Barjin corrected, flashing a sly look Druzil's way. "I had hoped for a more powerful ally."

More of the summoner's façade, Druzil thought, but he did not question Barjin's claims. Anxious to see for himself what effects the curse was having, Druzil was more than willing to serve Barjin in a scouting capacity. "Please, my master," the imp whined. "Let me go and see for you. Please, oh, please!"

"Yes, yes," Barjin chuckled condescendingly. "You may go above while I bring more allies through the gate."

"Does a path remain through the wine cellar?" the imp asked.

"No," Barjin explained, grabbing Mullivy by the arm. "My good groundskeeper has sealed that door well. Take my imp out the western tunnel," Barjin instructed the zombie. "Then return to me!" Mullivy's stinking, bloated corpse shuffled, stiff-legged, out of its guard position and through the altar room door. Not revolted in the least by the disgusting thing, Druzil flapped over and found a perch on Mullivy's shoulder.

"Take care, for it is daylight above," Barjin called after him.

In response, Druzil chuckled, whispered an arcane phrase, and became invisible.

Barjin moved excitedly back to the gate, hoping for continued good fortune in his summoning. An imp was a prized catch for so small a gate, though if Barjin had known the identity of this particular imp and his wizard master, or that Druzil had sealed the gate behind his entry, he would not have been so thrilled.

He tried for more than an hour, calling out general spells of summoning and the names of every minor denizen he knew.

Flames leaped and danced, but no forms appeared within their orange glow. Barjin wasn't too concerned. The brazier would burn for many days, and the necromancer's stone, though it had not yet produced results, continued to send out its call for undead. The priest would find many opportunities to add to his force.

* * * * *

Cadderly wandered the hallways of the building, stunned by the emptiness, the brooding quiet. Many priests, both

visitors and those of the host sects, such as Brother Chaunticleer, had left the library without explanation, and many of
those who had remained apparently preferred the solitude of
their rooms.

Cadderly did find Ivan and Pikel, in the kitchen, busily
cooking a variety of dishes.

"Your fights have ended?" Cadderly asked, grabbing a biscuit as he entered. He realized then that he hadn't eaten much
in nearly a day, and that Danica and Newander no doubt
would be hungry also.

"Fights?" Ivan balked. "No time for fighting, boy! Been
cooking since the eve. Not a many for supper, but them that's
there won't go away."

A terrible, sick feeling washed over Cadderly. He moved
through the kitchen to peek out the other door, which led to
the library's large dining hall. A score of people were in there,
Headmaster Avery among them, stuffing themselves hand
over hand. Several had fallen to the floor, so full that they
could hardly move, but still trying to shove more food into
their eager mouths.

"You are killing them, you know," Cadderly remarked to
the dwarves, his tone resigned. The young scholar was beginning to get an idea of what was going on. He thought of
Histra and her unending passion, of Danica's sudden obsession with lessons that were beyond her level of achievement,
and of the druids, Arcite and Cleo, so fanatic to their tenets
that they had lost their very identities.

"They will eat as long as you put food before them," Cadderly explained. "They will gorge themselves until they die."

Both Ivan and Pikel stopped their stirring and stared long
and hard at the young priest.

"Slow the meals down," Cadderly instructed them.

For the first time in a while, Cadderly noted some measure of comprehension. Both dwarves seemed almost repulsed
by their own participation in the food orgy. Together they
backed away from their respective pots.

"Slow the meals down," Cadderly asked again.

Ivan nodded gravely.

"Oo," added Pikel.

Cadderly studied the brothers for a long moment, sensing that they had regained their sanity, that he could trust them as he had trusted Newander.

"I will be back as soon as I can," he promised, then he took a couple of plates, packed a meal, and took his leave.

Anyone watching would have noticed a profound difference in the strides of the young scholar as he left the kitchen. Cadderly had come down tentatively, afraid of something he could not understand. He still had not figured out the curse or its cause, nor could he remember his trials in the lower catacombs, but, more and more, it was becoming evident to Cadderly that fate had placed a great burden upon him, and the price of his success or failure was terrifying indeed.

To his relief, Newander had the situation in Danica's room under control. Danica was still in her bed, conscious but unable to move, for the druid had compelled long vines of ivy to come in through the window and wrap the woman where she lay. Newander, too, seemed in better spirits, and his face brightened even more when Cadderly handed him the supper plate.

"You have done well," Cadderly remarked.

"Minor magic," the druid answered. "Her wounds were not so bad. What have you learned?"

Cadderly shrugged. "Little," he answered. "Whatever is wrong in this place grows worse by the moment. I have an idea, though, a way that I might learn what is happening."

Newander perked up, expecting some revelation.

"I am going to go to sleep."

The druid's fair face crinkled in confusion, but Cadderly's confident smile deflected any forthcoming questions. Newander took the plate and began eating, mumbling to himself with every bite.

Cadderly knelt beside Danica. She seemed barely coherent, but she managed to whisper, "Iron Skull."

"Forget Iron Skull," Cadderly replied quietly. "You must rest and heal. Something is wrong here, Danica, wrong with you and with all the library. I do not know why, but I seem to have not been affected." He paused, searching for the words.

"I think I did something," he said. Newander shuffled uneasily behind him. "I cannot explain. . . . I do not understand, but I have this feeling, this vagrant thought, that I somehow caused all of this."

"Surely you cannot blame yourself," Newander said.

Cadderly turned on him. "I am not looking to place any blame at all," he replied evenly, "but I believe I played a part in this growing catastrophe, whatever it might be. If I did, then I must accept that fact and search, not for blame, but for a solution."

"How do you mean to search?" the druid asked. His tone turned sarcastic. "By going to sleep?"

"It is hard to explain," Cadderly replied to the druid's stare. "I have been dreaming—vivid dreams. I feel there is a connection. I cannot explain."

Newander's visage softened. "You need not explain," he said, no longer doubting. "Dreams sometimes do have the power of prophecy, and we have no clearer trail to follow. Take your rest, then. I will watch over you."

Cadderly kissed Danica's pale cheek.

"Iron Skull," the woman whispered.

More determined than ever, Cadderly pulled a blanket to the corner of the room and lay down, placing an inkwell, quill, and parchments beside him. He threw an arm across his eyes and filled his thoughts with skeletons and ghouls, beckoning the nightmare.

* * * * *

The skeletons were waiting for him. Cadderly could smell the rot and the thick dust, and hear the scuffle of fleshless feet on the hard stone. He ran in a red fog, his legs heavy, too heavy. He saw a door down a long hallway, and there was light peeking through its cracks. His legs were too heavy; he could not get there.

Cold beads of sweat caked Cadderly's clothing and streaked his face. His eyes popped open and there, hovering over him, stood the druid.

"What have you seen, boy?" Newander asked. The druid quickly handed him the writing materials.

Cadderly tried to articulate the gruesome scene, but it was fast fading from his thoughts. He snatched up the quill and began writing and sketching, capturing as many of the images as he could, forcing his thoughts back into the dimming recesses of his nightmare.

Then it was daytime again, midafternoon, and the dream was no more. Cadderly remembered the skeletons and the smell of dust, but the details were foggy and indistinct. He looked down to the parchment and was surprised by what he saw, as if someone else had done the writing. At the top of the scroll were the words, "slow . . . red fog . . . reaching for me . . . too close!" and below these was a sketch of a long hallway, its sides lined by sarcophagi-filled alcoves and with a cracked door at its end.

"I know this place," Cadderly began tentatively, then he stopped abruptly, his elation and train of thought disrupted by Barjin's insidious and incessant memory-blocking spell.

Before Cadderly could fight back against the sudden lapse, a scream from the hallway froze him where he sat. He looked at Newander, who was equally disturbed.

"That was not the priestess of Sune," the druid remarked.

They rushed through the door and into the hallway.

There stood a gray-capped priest, holding his entrails in his hands, an eerie, almost ecstatic expression on his face. His tunic, too, was gray, though most of it now was blood-stained, and still more blood poured out of the man's opened belly with each passing second.

Cadderly and Newander could not immediately find the strength to go to him, knew the futility of it anyway. They watched in blank horror as the priest fell face down, a pool of blood widening around him.

Fourteen

Disturbing Answers

Mullivy was not a swift walker, and Druzil used this time away from Barjin to reestablish contact with his master. He sent his thoughts out across the miles to Castle Trinity and found an eager recipient awaiting them.

Greetings, my master, the imp communicated.

You have found Barjin?

In the catacombs, as you believed, Druzil replied.

The fool.

Druzil wasn't certain that he shared Aballister's appraisal, but the wizard didn't need to know that.

He has other allies, the imp imparted. *Undead allies, including a mummy.*

Druzil smiled widely as he sensed Aballister's reaction to that bit of news. The wizard didn't mean to communicate his next thoughts, but Druzil was deeply enough into his mind to hear them anyway.

I never would have believed that Barjin could achieve that.

Many emotions accompanied those words, Druzil knew, and fear was not the least among them.

The mighty Edificant Library is in peril, Druzil added, just to prod the wizard. *If Barjin succeeds, then the Most Fatal Horror will have put us on the path toward a great victory. All the region will fall without the guidance of the library's clerics.*

Aballister was wondering if the price was too high, Druzil realized, and the imp decided that he had told the wizard enough for this day. Besides, he could see the daylight up ahead as his zombie chauffeur neared the tunnel exit. He broke off direct communication, though he let the wizard remain in his mind and view through the imp's eyes. Druzil wanted Aballister to get a good look at the glory of the chaos curse.

* * * * *

The white squirrel kept high in the branches, unsure of what its keen senses were telling it. Mullivy came to the edge of the earthen tunnel, then immediately turned around and disappeared back into it. Another scent, an unfamiliar scent, lingered. Percival saw nothing, but like other foraging animals, low on the food chain, the squirrel had learned quickly to trust more than just its eyes.

Percival followed the scent—it was moving—to the tree-lined lane. The road was quiet, as it had been for the last two days, though the sun shone bright and warm in a clear blue sky. The squirrel's ears perked up and twitched nervously as the library's door opened, seemingly of its own accord, and the strange scent moved inside.

The unusualness of it all kept the squirrel sitting nervously still for many moments, but the sun was warm and the nuts and berries in the trees and shrubs were abundant, just waiting to be plucked. Percival rarely kept any thought for any length of time, and when he spotted a pile of acorns lying unattended on the ground, he was too relieved that the groundskeeper had stayed in the tunnel to worry about anything else.

*   *   *   *   *

Druzil's perceptions of the state of the Edificant Library were far different from Cadderly's. Unlike the young scholar, the imp thought the rising, paralyzing chaos a marvelous thing.

He found just a few priests in the study halls, sitting unmoving in front of open books, so riveted by their studies that they barely remembered to draw breath. Druzil understood the hold of the chaos curse better than any; if Barjin entered the hall with a host of skeletons at his back, these priests would offer no resistance, would probably not even notice.

Druzil enjoyed the spectacle in the dining hall most of all, where gluttonous priests sat on chairs set back from the table to accommodate their swelling bellies, and other priests lay semiconscious on the floor. At one end of the table, three priests were engaged in mortal combat over a single remaining turkey leg.

Arguments, particularly between priests of differing faiths, were general throughout the building, often becoming more serious encounters. The least faithful or studious simply wandered away from the library altogether, and few had a care to stop them. Those most faithful were so absorbed in their rituals that they seemed to notice nothing else. In another of the second-floor study chambers, Druzil found a pile of Oghman priests heaped together in a great ball, having wrestled until they were too exhausted even to move.

When Druzil left an hour later to report to Barjin, he was quite satisfied that the chaos curse had done its work to unpredictable perfection.

He felt the first insistent demands of his master when he rounded the northern side of the building, approaching the tunnel.

You have seen? his thoughts asked Aballister. He knew that if Aballister had been paying attention, the wizard would know the state of the library as well as Druzil did.

The Most Fatal Horror, Aballister remarked somewhat sourly.

Barjin has brought us a great victory, Druzil promptly reminded the ever-skeptical wizard.

Aballister was quick to reply. *The library is not yet won. Do not count our victory until Barjin is actually in control of the structure.*

Druzil replied by shutting the wizard completely out of his thoughts in midconversation. *"Tellemara,"* the imp muttered to himself. The curse was working. Already the few score priests remaining at the library probably would not be able to fend off Barjin's undead forces, and their potential for resistance lessened with each passing moment. Soon, many of them likely would kill each other and many others simply would wander away. How much more control did the wizard require before claiming victory?

Druzil paid no heed to Aballister's final warning. Barjin would win here, the imp decided, and he was thinking, too, that maybe he could find extra gains in his mission from Aballister, in spying on the powerful priest. Ever since the magical elixir had been dubbed an agent of Talona, the priests of Castle Trinity had enjoyed a more prominent role in the evil triumvirate. With the Edificant Library in Barjin's hands, and with Barjin controlling a strong undead army, that domination would only increase.

Aballister was an acceptable "master," as masters went, but Druzil was an imp from the domain of chaos, and imps owed no loyalty to anyone except themselves.

It was too early to make a definitive judgment, of course, but already Druzil was beginning to suspect that he would find more pleasure and more chaos at Barjin's side than at Aballister's.

* * * * *

"Do something for him!" Cadderly pleaded, but Newander only shook his head helplessly.

"Ilmater!" gasped the dying priest. "The . . . pain," he stammered. "It is so won—" He shuddered one final time and fell limp in Cadderly's arms.

"Who could have done this?" Cadderly asked, though he feared he knew the answer.

"Is not Ilmater the Crying God, a deity dedicated to suffering?" the druid asked, leading Cadderly to a clear conclusion.

Cadderly nodded gravely. "Priests of Ilmater often engage in self-flagellation, but it is usually a minor ritual of no serious consequence."

"Until now," Newander remarked dryly.

"Come on," Cadderly said, laying the dead priest onto the floor. The blood trail was easily followed, and both Cadderly and Newander could have guessed where it led anyway.

Cadderly didn't even bother knocking on the partly opened door. He pushed it in, then turned away, too horrified to enter.

In the middle of the floor lay the remaining five priests of the Ilmater delegation, torn and bloodied.

Newander rushed in to check on them but returned in only a few moments, shaking his head grimly.

"Priests of Ilmater never carry it this far," Cadderly said, as much to himself as to the druid, "and druids never go so far as to become, heart and body, their favored animals." He looked up at the druid, his gray eyes revealing that he thought his words important. "Danica was never so obsessed as to slam her face into a stone block repeatedly."

Newander was beginning to catch on.

"Why were we not affected?" Cadderly asked.

"I fear that I have been," replied the sullen druid.

When Cadderly looked more closely at Newander, he understood. The druid continued to fear not for his animal transformed friends, but for himself.

"I have not the true heart for my chosen calling," explained the druid.

"You make too many judgments," Cadderly scolded. "We know that something is wrong—" he waved toward the room of carnage "—terribly wrong. You have heard the priestess of Sune. You have seen these priests, and your own druid brothers. For some reason, we two have been spared—and perhaps I know of two others who have not been so badly affected— and that is not cause to lament. Whatever has happened threatens the whole library."

"You are wise for one so young," admitted Newander, "but what are we to do? Surely my druid brothers and the girl will be of no help."

"We will go to Dean Thobicus," Cadderly said hopefully. "He has overseen the library for many years. Perhaps he will know what to do." Cadderly didn't have to speak his hopes that Dean Thobicus, aged and wise, had not fallen under the curse also.

The journey down to the second floor only increased the companions' apprehension. The halls were quiet and empty, until a group of drunken rowdies appeared down at the other end of a long hallway. As soon as the mob spotted Cadderly and Newander, they set out after them. Cadderly and the druid did not know if the men meant to attack them or coerce them into joining the party, but neither of them had any intentions of finding out.

Newander turned back after rounding one corner and cast a simple spell. The group came in fast pursuit, but the druid had laid a magical trip-wire and the intoxicated mob had no defense against such a subtle attack. They tumbled in a twisting and squirming heap and came up too busily wrestling with each other to remember that they had been chasing somebody.

Cadderly considered the headmasters' area his best hope until he and Newander crossed through the large double doors at the southern end of the second level. The area was eerily quiet, with no one to be seen. Dean Thobicus's office door was among the few that were not open. Cadderly moved up slowly and knocked.

He knew in his heart that he would get no response.

Dean Thobicus was never an excitable man. His love was introspection, spending hours on end staring at the night sky, or at nothing at all. Thobicus's loves were in his own mind, and when Cadderly and Newander entered his office, that was exactly where they found him. He sat very still behind his large oaken desk and apparently hadn't moved for quite a while. He had soiled himself, and his lips were dry and parched, though a beaker full of water sat only inches away on his desk.

Cadderly called to him several times and shook him roughly, but the dean showed no sign of having heard him. Cadderly gave him one last shake, and Thobicus fell right over and remained where he dropped, as if he hadn't noticed.

Newander bent to examine the man. "We'll get no answers from this one," he announced.

"We are running out of places to look," Cadderly replied.

"Let us get back to the girl," said the druid. "No good in staying here, and I am afraid for Danica with the drunken mob roaming the halls."

They were relieved to find no sign of the drunken men as they exited the headmasters' area, and their return trip through the quiet and empty hallways was uneventful.

Their sighs of relief upon entering Danica's room would have been lessened considerably if either of them had noticed the dark figure lurking in the shadows, eyeing Cadderly with utter hatred.

* * * * *

Danica was awake but unblinking when the two men returned to her. Newander started toward her, concerned and thinking that she had fallen into the same catatonic state as the dean, but Cadderly recognized the difference.

"She is meditating," Cadderly explained, and even as he spoke the words, he realized what Danica had in mind. "She is fighting whatever it is that compels her."

"You cannot know that," reasoned Newander.

Cadderly refused to yield his assumptions. "Look at her closely," he observed, "at her concentration. She is fighting, I say."

The claim was beyond Newander's experience, either to agree or refute, so he accepted Cadderly's logic without further argument.

"You said you know of others who might have escaped?" he said, wanting to get back to the business at hand.

"The dwarven cooks," replied Cadderly, "Ivan and Pikel Bouldershoulder. They have been acting strangely, I admit, but each time I have been able to bring them to reason."

Newander thought for a few minutes, chuckling quietly when he remembered Pikel, the green-bearded dwarf that so badly wanted to join the druidical order. The notion was absurd, of course, but Pikel was an appealing chap—for a dwarf.

Newander snapped his fingers and allowed himself a smile of hope as he found a clue in Cadderly's report. "Magical," he said, looking back to Cadderly. "It is said by all who know that dwarves are a tough lot against magical enchantments. Might it be that the cooks can resist where men cannot?"

Cadderly nodded and looked to the vine-covered bed. "And Danica will resist in time, I know," he said and turned back to Newander immediately. "But what about us? Why have we been spared?"

"As I told you," replied Newander, "it might well be that I have not been spared. I was gone all of yesterday, out walking in the sunshine and feeling the mountain breezes. I found Arcite and Cleo, bear and tortoise, upon my return, but since I came back, I must admit that I, too, have felt compulsions."

"But you have resisted them," said Cadderly.

"Perhaps," Newander corrected. "I cannot be sure. My

heart of late has not been for the animals, as seemingly were the hearts of my druid kin."

"And so you doubt your calling," Cadderly remarked.

Newander nodded. "It is a difficult thing. I so badly wish to join Arcite and Cleo, to join the search they have begun for the natural order, but I want, too . . ."

"Go on," Cadderly prompted as though he believed the revelations were vital.

"I want to learn of Deneir and the other gods," Newander admitted. "I want to watch the progress of the world, the rise of cities. I want to . . . I want," Newander shook his head suddenly. "I do not know what I want!"

Cadderly's gray eyes lit up. "Even in your own heart you do not know what is in your own heart," he said. "That is a rare thing, and it has saved you, unless I miss my guess. That, and the fact that you have not been here for very long since this all began."

"What do you know?" Newander asked, a sharp edge on his voice. He softened quickly, though, wondering how much truth was in the young scholar's words.

Cadderly only shrugged in response. "It is only a theory."

"What of you?" Newander asked. "Why are you not affected?"

Cadderly nearly laughed for lack of a suitable answer. "I cannot say," he honestly admitted. He looked to Danica again. "But I know now how I might find out."

Newander followed the young scholar's gaze to the meditating woman. "Are you going back to sleep?"

Cadderly gave him a sly wink. "Sort of."

Newander did not argue. He wanted the time alone anyway to consider his own predicament. He could not accept Cadderly's reasoning concerning his exclusion from whatever was cursing the library, though he hoped it was as simple as that.

Newander suspected that something else was going on, something he could not begin to understand, something wonderful or terrible—he could not be sure. For all of his thinking, though, the druid could not rid himself of the image of Arcite and Cleo, contented and natural, and could not dismiss his fears that his ambivalence had caused him to fail Silvanus in a time of dire need.

* * * * *

Cadderly sat crosslegged with his eyes closed for a long time, relaxing each part of his body in turn, causing his mind to sink within his physical self. He had learned these techniques from Danica—one of the few things she had revealed about her religion—and had found them quite useful, restful, and enjoyable.

Now, though, the meditation had taken on a more important role.

Cadderly opened his eyes slowly and viewed the room, seeing it in surreal tones. He focused first on the block of stone, stained with his dear Danica's blood. It sat between the downed sawhorses, and then it was gone, removed to blackness. Behind it was Danica's cabinet and wardrobe, and then they, too, were gone.

He glanced left, to the door and Newander keeping a watchful guard. The druid watched him curiously, but Cadderly hardly noticed. A moment later, both druid and door were holes of blackness.

His visual sweep eliminated the rest of the room: Danica's desk and her weapons, two crystalline daggers, in their boot sheaths against the wall; the window, bright with late morning light; and, lastly, Danica herself, still deep in her own meditation on the vine-wrapped bed.

"Dear Danica," Cadderly muttered, though even he didn't hear the words. Then Danica, too, and everything else, was out of his thoughts.

Again he returned to relaxation—toes, then feet, then legs; fingers, then hands, then arms—until he had achieved a sedated state. His breathing came slowly and easily. His eyes were open, but they saw nothing.

There was only quiet blackness, calm.

Cadderly could not summon thoughts in this state. He had to hope that answers would flow to him, that his subconscious would give him images and clues. He had no concept of time passing, but it seemed a long while of emptiness, of simple, uncluttered existence.

The walking dead were alongside him then in the blackness.

Unlike his dreams, he saw the skeletal figures as no threat now, as though he were an unattached observer instead of an active participant. They scuffled along on his mental journey, falling behind him, leaving him in a hallway. There was the familiar door, cracked and showing lines of light, always the ending image of his nightmare.

The picture faded, as if some unseen force were trying to stop him from proceeding, a mental barrier that he now, for some reason unknown to him, believed to be a magical spell.

The images became a gray blur for just a moment, then focused again, and he was at the door, then through the door.

The altar room!

Cadderly watched, hopeful and afraid, as the room darkened, leaving only a single, red-glowing object, a bottle, visible before him. He saw the bottle up close then, and he saw hands, his own hands, twisting off the stopper.

Red smoke exploded all about him, stole every other image.

Cadderly looked again on Danica's room, the image identical to the one he had blocked out—even Newander remained at his position near the door—except that now there hung in the air an almost imperceptible pink haze.

Cadderly felt his heart quicken as the purpose of that haze became all too clear. His gaze fell over Danica, still deep in her own meditation. Cadderly's thoughts reached out to Danica and were answered. She was battling, as he had suspected, fighting back against that permeating pink haze, trying to recover her sensibilities against its debilitating effects.

"Fight, Danica!" he heard himself say, and the words broke his trance. He looked over to Newander, his expression desperate.

"I was the cause," he said, holding up his hands as though they were covered in blood. "I opened it!"

Newander rushed over and knelt beside Cadderly, trying to calm him. "Opened?"

"The bottle," Cadderly stammered. "The bottle! The red glowing bottle. The mist—do you see the mist?"

Newander glanced around, then shook his head.

"It is there . . . here," Cadderly said, grabbing the druid's arm and using it to help him to his feet. "We have to close that bottle!"

"Where?" the druid asked.

Cadderly stopped suddenly, considering the question. He remembered the skeletons, the dusty smell, the corridors lined with alcoves. "There really was a door in the wine cellar," he said at length, "a door to the lowest catacombs, those dungeons no longer used in the library."

"We must go there?" asked Newander, rising beside Cadderly.

"No," Cadderly cautioned, "not yet. The catacombs are not empty. We have to prepare." He looked to Danica again, seeing her in a new light now that he understood her mental struggles.

"Will she be fighting beside us?" Newander asked, noticing Cadderly's focus.

"Danica is fighting now," Cadderly assured him, "but the mist hangs all about us, and it is insistent." He gave Newander a confused look. "I still do not know why I have been spared its effects."

"If you were indeed the cause, as you believe," replied the druid, who had lengthy experience with magical practices, "then that fact alone might have spared you."

Cadderly considered the words for a moment, but they

hardly seemed to matter. "Whatever the reason" he said determinedly, "we—I—have to close that bottle." He spent a few minutes trying to recall the obstacles before him and imagining even more frightening monsters that might be lurking just outside his nightmarish visions. Cadderly knew that he would need allies in this fight, powerful allies to help him get back to the altar room.

"Ivan and Pikel," he said to Newander. "The dwarves are more resistant, as you said. They will help us."

"Go to them," Newander bade him.

"You stay with Danica," Cadderly replied. "Let no one, except for me and the dwarven brothers, into the room."

"I have ways of keeping the world out," Newander assured him.

As soon as he entered the hallway, Cadderly heard the druid chanting softly. Danica's wooden door, suddenly brought to life by Newander's spell, warped and expanded, wedging tightly, immovably, into its frame.

* * * * *

Ivan and Pikel were not fighting when Cadderly entered the kitchen this time, but neither were they cooking. They sat quietly, somberly, at the room's main table opposite each other.

As soon as he noticed Cadderly, Ivan absently handed him the one-handed crossbow, finished to perfection. "Had an urge," the dwarf explained, not giving the magnificent item a second look.

Cadderly was not surprised. It seemed that many people in the Edificant Library were having "urges" these days.

"What's it about?" Ivan asked suddenly.

Cadderly did not understand. Pikel, a grim expression on his normally carefree features, pointed to the door leading into the dining room. Cadderly crossed the kitchen tentatively and when he looked into the adjoining room, he came to realize the reason for the dwarves' somber mood. Half the gluttonous priests, Avery included, remained at the table, hardly able to move. The other half were worse yet, lying on the floor in their own vomit. Cadderly knew without going to them that several were dead, and his face, too, was ashen when he turned back into the kitchen.

"So what's it about?" Ivan asked again.

Cadderly looked at him long and hard, unsure of how he could begin to explain the bottle and his own, still unclear actions. Finally, he said only, "I am not certain what has happened, but I believe I know now how to stop it."

He thought his proclamation would excite the dwarves, but they hardly stirred at the news.

"Will you help me?" Cadderly asked. "I cannot do it alone."

"What do ye need?" Ivan asked offhandedly.

"You," Cadderly replied, "and your brother. The curse—and it is a curse—comes from below the cellars. I have to go down there to end it, but I fear that the place is guarded."

"Guarded?" Ivan balked. "How can ye guess that?"

"Just trust me, I beg," replied Cadderly. "I am not so skilled with weapons, but I have witnessed you two at your fighting and could use your strong arms. Will you come with me?"

The dwarves exchanged bored looks and shrugs. "I'd rather be cooking," Ivan remarked. "Gave up me adventuring pack long ago. Pikel'd rather be . . ." He stopped and eyed his brother intently.

Pikel fixed a smug look on his face, reached up, and waggled one side of his green beard.

"A druid!" Ivan yelled, hopping to his feet and grabbing a nearby pan. "Ye stupid bird-loving, oak-kissin' . . .!"

"Oo oi!" Pikel exclaimed, arming himself with a rolling pin.

Cadderly was between them in an instant. "It is all part of the curse!" he cried. "Can you not see that? It makes you argue and fight!"

Both dwarves jumped back a step and lowered their utensil weapons.

"Oo," muttered Pikel curiously.

"If you want to fight a true enemy," Cadderly began, "then come to my room and help me prepare. There is something below the cellars, something horrible and evil. If we do not stop it, then all the library is doomed."

Ivan leaned to the side and looked around the young scholar to his similarly leaning brother. They shared a shrug and simultaneously heaved their cookware weapons across to the other side of the room.

"Let us go to the gluttons first," Cadderly instructed. "We should leave them as comfortable as we may."

The dwarves nodded. "Then I'll get me axe," Ivan declared, "and me brother'll get his tree!"

"Tree?" Cadderly echoed quietly at the departing dwarves' backs. One look at Pikel's green-dyed braid bouncing halfway down the dwarfs back and his huge, gnarly, and smelly feet flopping out every which way from his delicate sandals told Cadderly not even to bother pressing the question.

Fifteen

Blood on His Hands

Cadderly sorted through the many leather straps hanging in his wardrobe, finally pulling out a belt with a strangely shaped, wide and shallow leather sheath on one side. The fit of the small crossbow was perfect—there was even a place for the loading pin. As usual, Ivan and Pikel had crafted the metal to exact specifications.

Cadderly drew the crossbow out again as soon as he had put it in. He tested the pin next, cranking the bow and firing several times. The action was smooth and easy; Cadderly even managed, without too much difficulty, to manipulate the weapon enough to crank it with one hand.

Next Cadderly took out a bandoleer and slung it over his shoulder, carefully lining up the sixteen loaded darts in front of him, within easy reach. He winced when he wondered what damage a blow to his chest might cause, but he held faith that the darts and the bandoleer had been properly constructed. He felt better when he saw himself in the mirror, as if wearing his latest inventions had returned to him some control over his surroundings. Any smile he felt welling was quickly sublimated, though, when he remembered the dangerous task ahead. This was no game, he reminded himself. Already, and because of his own actions, several men had died and all the library was threatened.

Cadderly moved across the room, behind the door, to a closed and sealed iron box. He fitted a key into the lock, then paused for a long moment, considering carefully the precise steps he had to follow once the box was opened. He had practiced this maneuver many times, but never before had he believed he would need it.

As soon as the box lid was opened, all the area around Cadderly fell into a globe of absolute darkness. It was not a surprise to the young scholar; Cadderly had paid Histra handsomely for placing this reversed form of her light spell within the box. It was inconvenient—and Cadderly did not enjoy dealing with Histra—but necessary to protect one of Cadderly's most prized possessions. In an ancient tome, Cadderly had stumbled upon the formula for the very potent sleep poison used by the drow elves. The exotic ingredients had not been found easily—one fungus in particular could only be gained in deep tunnels far below Toril's surface—and the arrangements to mix them—which the alchemist, Belago, had done deep underground also—had been even more difficult to secure, but Cadderly had persevered. With the blessings and backing of Dean Thobicus, his efforts had produced five tiny vials of the poison.

At least, Cadderly hoped it was the poison—one does not often find the opportunity to test such things.

Even with the apparent success of the brewing, though, there remained one severe limitation. The potion was a drow mix, brewed in the strange magical emanations found only in the Underdark, the lightless world beneath Toril's surface. It was a well-known fact that if drow poison was exposed to the sun, even for a moment, it would become useless in a very short while. The open air alone could destroy the expensive mixture, so Cadderly had taken great steps, like the spell of darkness, to protect his investment.

He closed his eyes and worked from memory. First he unscrewed the tiny compartment of his feathered ring and laid the top in a predetermined place to the side, then he removed one of the vials from the box, carefully popping its cork. He poured the gooey contents into his opened ring, then found and replaced the feathered top.

Cadderly breathed easier. If he had slipped at all, he would have wasted perhaps a thousand gold pieces' worth of ingredients and many weeks of labor. Also, if he had spilled even a drop of the poison onto his hand, and if it had found its way into a tiny scratch or nick, he no doubt would be snoozing soundly right beside the box.

None of that had happened. Cadderly was precise and disciplined when he needed to be, and his many practice sessions with vials of water had paid off.

The darkness disappeared within the confines of the sealed box when Cadderly closed the lid. Ivan and Pikel were already in the room, surrounding the young scholar, weapons ready and faces grim at the sight of the unexpected darkness.

"Just yourself, then," Ivan grumbled, relaxing his grip on his heavy, two-headed axe.

Cadderly could not immediately find his breath to reply. He just sat and stared at the dwarven brothers. Both wore armor of interlocking rings, dusty from decades of idleness and rusted in several spots. Ivan wore a helm fashioned with deer antlers—an eight-pointer—while Pikel wore a cooking pot! For all his precautionary armor, Pikel still wore his open-toed sandals.

Most amazing of all, though, was Pikel's weapon. Looking upon it, Cadderly understood Ivan's earlier reference. It was indeed a "tree," the polished trunk of some black and smooth-barked variety that Cadderly did not recognize. The club was fully four feet long, nearly as tall as Pikel, a foot in diameter on the wide end, and less than half that on the narrow, gripping end. Looped leather hand-grips were spiked on at various intervals to aid the wielder, but still it seemed an awkward and cumbersome thing.

As if he sensed Cadderly's private doubts, Pikel whipped the club about through several attack and defense routines with obvious ease.

Cadderly nodded his appreciation, sincerely relieved that he had not been on the receiving end of any of Pikel's mock strikes.

"Are ye set to go?" Ivan asked, adjusting his armor.

"Almost," Cadderly answered. "I have just a few more minor preparations, and I want to look in on Danica before we go."

"How can we help ye?" offered Ivan.

Cadderly could see that the dwarves were both anxious to get on with it. He knew that it had been many years since the Bouldershoulder brothers had walked into adventure, many years spent cooking meals in the haven that was the Edificant Library. It wasn't a bad life by anyone's measure, but the thought of imminent danger and adventure obviously had worked an enchantment over the dwarves. There was an unmistakable luster to their dark eyes and their movements were agitated and nervous.

"Go to Belago's alchemy shop," Cadderly replied, thinking it best to keep the dwarves busy. He described the distillation equipment and the potion that Belago was brewing for him. "If he has any more for me, bring it back," Cadderly instructed, thinking the task simple enough.

The dwarves already had hopped off down the hallway when Cadderly realized that he hadn't seen Belago about lately, not since before the curse had taken hold of the library. What had happened to the alchemist? Cadderly wondered. Was the shop still operational? Were the proper mixtures for blending his *Oil of Impact* still slipping in the precise amounts through the hoppers? Cadderly shrugged away his worries, trusting in Ivan and Pikel to use their best judgment.

Percival was at the window again, chittering with his

customary excitement. Cadderly went over and leaned on the sill, bending to put his face close to his little friend's and listening intently. Cadderly could not understand the squirrel's talk, of course, no more than a child could understand a pet dog's, but he and Percival had developed quite an emotive rapport, and he knew well enough that Percival comprehended some simple words or phrases, mostly those pertaining to food.

"I will be gone for a while," Cadderly said. The squirrel probably wouldn't understand so complex a message, he realized, but talking to Percival often helped Cadderly sort through his own confusion. Percival never really provided any answers, but Cadderly often found them hidden within his own words.

Percival sat up on his hind legs, licking his forepaws and running them quickly over his face.

"Something bad has happened," Cadderly tried to explain, "something that I caused. Now I am going to fix it."

His somber tone, if not his words, had a calming effect on the rodent. Percival stopped licking and sat very still.

"So I will be gone," Cadderly continued, "down below the library, in the deep tunnels that are no longer used."

Something he had said apparently struck the squirrel profoundly. Percival ran in tight circles, chattering and clicking, and it was a very long while before Cadderly could calm the beast down. He knew that Percival had something important— by Percival's standards—to tell him, but he had no time for the squirrel's distractions.

"Do not worry," Cadderly said, as much to himself as to Percival. "I will return soon, and then all will be as it was."

The words sounded hollow to him. Things would not be as they had been. Even if he managed to close the smoking bottle, and even if that simple act removed the curse, it wouldn't bring back the priests of Ilmater or the dead gluttons in the dining room.

Cadderly shook those dark thoughts away. He could not

hope to succeed if he began his quest in despair.

"Do not worry!" he said again, firmly.

Again the squirrel went crazy, and this time, Cadderly realized, from the direction of Percival's gaze, the source of the excitement. Cadderly looked back over his shoulder, expecting to see that Ivan and Pikel had returned.

He saw instead Kierkan Rufo, and more pointedly, the dagger in Rufo's hand.

"What is it?" Cadderly asked weakly, but he needed no verbal answer to decipher the man's intent. Rufo's left eye was still bruised and closed, and his nose pointed as much toward his cheek as straight ahead. His ugly wounds only accentuated the look of sheer hatred in his cold, dark eyes.

"Where is your light now?" the tall man sneered. "But then, it would not do you much good, would it?" He limped noticeably, but his approach was steady.

"What are you doing?" Cadderly asked him.

"Is not the mighty Cadderly smart enough to figure that out?" Rufo mocked him.

"You do not want to do this," Cadderly said as calmly as he could. "There are consequences . . ."

"Want?" Rufo cried wildly. "Oh, but I do indeed want to do this. I want to hold your heart in my hands. I want to bring it to your dear Danica and show her who was the stronger."

Cadderly looked for some retort. He thought of mentioning the obvious weakness in Rufo's plan—if he did bring Cadderly's heart to Danica, she would kill him—but even that, Cadderly guessed, would not stop Kierkan Rufo. Rufo was under the curse fully, following its devious call with no regard for consequences. Reluctantly, but with no apparent options, Cadderly slipped one finger inside the loop of his spindle-disk cord and moved right up against the side of his bed.

Rufo came straight in, dagger leading, and Cadderly rolled sideways across the bed, just getting out of the angular man's long reach.

Rufo jumped back quickly, faster than Cadderly expected

he could move, to cut off Cadderly's angle for the door. He rushed around the bottom of the bed, launching a wide, arcing swing at Cadderly's belly.

Cadderly easily kept back beyond the dagger, then he retaliated, snapping his spindle-disks above Rufo's swinging arm.

Rufo's already broken nose crackled under the impact and a new stream of blood flowed thickly over the dried stains on his lip. Rufo, obsessed with utter hatred, shook away the minor hit and came on.

Though the blow had not been very solid, it still had almost broken the rhythm of Cadderly's working wrist. He managed to coax the disks back to his hand, but the cord was now loosely wound and he couldn't immediately strike again effectively.

Rufo seemed to sense his weakness. He grinned wickedly and came in again.

Percival saved Cadderly's life, leaping from the window to land squarely on Rufo's face. With a single swipe, Rufo sent the squirrel flying across the room, and Percival had done no real damage, but Cadderly had not wasted the time.

With Rufo distracted, he had snapped the spindle-disks straight down and back up several times to realign and tighten the cord.

Rufo seemed not to even notice the twin lines of blood running down his face from his newest wound, a small bite on his cheek from Percival. "I will hold your heart in my hands!" he promised again, laughing insanely.

Cadderly jerked his arm once, and then again, feigning a throw to keep Rufo off guard. Between dodges, Rufo managed a few weak thrusts that did not come near to hitting the mark.

Cadderly launched the disks finally, in a long and wide throw that brought them to the very end of their reach. He flicked his wrist, bringing the disks back to his grasp, but not with the usual suddenness.

Rufo measured the pace of the throws and bided his time.

The disks came on again, and Rufo leaned back, then rushed toward Cadderly right behind them as they retracted.

Cadderly's bait had worked. On this throw, he had shortened up on the cord, bringing the spindle-disks smacking back into his palm much more quickly than Rufo had anticipated.

Rufo had barely taken his first step when the young scholar's weapon shot out again, deliberately low. Rufo squealed in shock and pain and grasped at his smashed kneecap, his leg nearly buckling. He was under the influences of the chaos curse, though, and nearly impervious to pain. His squeal became a growl and he plowed ahead, slashing wildly.

Again Cadderly had to dive across the bed to avoid the blade, but when he came up this time, Kierkan Rufo had already circled the bottom of the bed and stood facing him. Cadderly knew that he was in trouble. He could not trade hits, dagger against spindle-disks. Normally, the disks might have proven effective, but in Rufo's state of mind, nothing short of a perfect and powerful strike would slow him. That type of attack would be risky indeed for Cadderly, and he doubted that he could even get one through his wild opponent's defenses.

They traded feints and teasing lunges for a few moments, Rufo grinning and Cadderly wondering if he had a better chance by diving out the window.

Then the whole building shook suddenly as if it had been hit by lightning. The explosion roiled on for several seconds and Cadderly understood its source when he heard a single word from the corridor. "Oo!"

Rufo hesitated and glanced over his shoulder, toward the open door. Cadderly realized that his sudden advantage wasn't really fair, but decided immediately to worry about that later. He cocked his arm and let go with all his strength. Rufo turned back just in time to catch the soaring disks right between the eyes.

Rufo's head snapped straight back, and when he righted himself again, he was no longer grinning. A startled, stupefied look came over him and his eyes crossed, as if they were both straining to see the newest bruise.

Cadderly, too transfixed to take his gaze from Rufo's contorted features, heard the dagger hit the floor. A moment later, Rufo followed it down with a crash. Still Cadderly did not react. He just stood there, his spindle-disks hanging by his side at the end of their cord, spinning end-around-end.

When Cadderly finally reached down to wind his weapon, his stomach turned over. The spindle-disks were covered in blood and one had a piece of Rufo's eyebrow glued onto it by the thick, drying red fluid. Cadderly slipped down to the bed and let the disks fall to the floor. He felt betrayed, by himself and by his toy.

All priests of the library were required to train with some weapon, usually a more conventional instrument of destruction, such as the quarterstaff, mace, or club. Cadderly had begun with the staff, and could use his ram-headed walking stick fairly well if the occasion arose, but he was never really comfortable with carrying any weapon. He lived in a dangerous world, so he was told, but he had spent the majority of his life in the secure confines of the Edificant Library. He had never even seen a goblin, except for a dead one once, that being one of the library's most wretched servants, who was said to be a half-breed. The headmasters had not allowed him to bend the rule of preparedness, though; every priest was required to train.

Cadderly had come across the spindle-disks in an archaic halfling treatise, and had quickly constructed his own. Some of the headmasters balked at his new choice, calling it more a toy than a weapon, but it fit all of the requirements set out in the ethical codes of Deneir. The vocal opposition, particularly Headmaster Avery's, only strengthened Cadderly's resolve to use the ancient weapon.

For Cadderly, the spindle-disks had replaced hours of

savage fighting with hours of enjoyable playing. He learned
a dozen tricks, tests of skill that didn't hurt anybody, with
his new toy, for a toy he, too, secretly considered it. Now,
though, covered in Rufo's blood, the spindle-disks did not
seem so amusing.

Rufo groaned and shifted slightly, and Cadderly was glad
that he was still alive. He took a deep breath and reached
down for the disks, determinedly reminding himself of the
gravity of the task ahead, and that he would have to be brave
and thick-skinned to see it through.

Percival was on the bed at his side, lending further support.

Cadderly rubbed a finger down the white squirrel's
smooth coat, then nodded gravely and rewound his weapon.

"He dead?" asked Ivan, entering the room with a smoldering Pikel at his heels. Percival darted out the open window,
and Cadderly, when he looked upon the brothers, nearly
joined him. Ivan's antlers, face, and beard, which stuck out
wildly in several directions, were blackened with soot, and
one of his heavy boots was now as open-toed as his brother's
sandals.

Pikel wasn't much better off. Flecks of ceramics dotted his
sooty face, his smile showed a missing tooth, and a shard of
glass had actually embedded itself right into his iron pot
helmet.

"Belago was not in?" Cadderly asked evenly.

Ivan shrugged. "Not a sight of that one," he replied, "but
me brother found yer potion—what little there was of it."

He held up the small catch basin. "We figured ye'd be wanting more, so we . . ."

"Turned up the spigot," Cadderly finished for him.

"Boom!" added Pikel.

"He dead?" Ivan asked again, and the casual tone of the
question sent a shudder through Cadderly.

Both dwarves noted the young scholar's discomfort. They
glanced at each other and shook their heads. "Ye'd best get

the belly for it," Ivan said. "If ye mean to go adventuring, ye'd best get the belly for things that are likely to be falling yer way." He led Cadderly's gaze back to Kierkan Rufo. "Or at yer feet!"

"I never meant to go adventuring," Cadderly replied, somewhat sourly.

"And I never meant to be a cook," retorted Ivan, "but that's what I got, ain't it? Ye said we got a job to do, and so we do. Let's get doing what needs doing, and if some try to get in our way, well . . ."

"He is not dead," Cadderly interjected. "Put him on the bed and tie him there."

Again Ivan and Pikel exchanged glances, but this time, they nodded in favor of Cadderly's determined tone.

"Oo," remarked Pikel, obviously impressed.

Cadderly wiped his spindle-disks clean, picked up his ram-headed walking stick and a waterskin, and headed down the hall. He was relieved to see Danica's door still warped and tightly wedged, and even more relieved to hear Newander's calm voice answering his knock.

"How is she?" Cadderly asked immediately.

"She is still deep within her meditation," Newander replied, "but she appears comfortable enough."

Cadderly conjured his meditative image of Danica, fighting back the insidious red haze.

"I can reverse the spell and let you in," the druid offered.

"No," Cadderly replied, though he truly wanted to see Danica again. His last image of Danica was a comforting one; he could not take the chance that something she did now would worry him and steal his heart from his coming trials. On a more practical level, Cadderly thought it best to let Newander preserve his magical energies. "When I return, perhaps your spell will no longer be needed," he said.

"Then you want me to stay with Danica?"

"I have the dwarves with me," Cadderly explained. "They are better suited to the underground tunnels than a druid would be. Stay with her and keep her safe."

Ivan and Pikel came up then, and by the eager gleam in their eyes, Cadderly knew that the time had come to set off. Cadderly glanced back at Danica's door several times as they walked away, emotionally torn. A large part of him argued against his journey, reasoned that his best course would be to go with his armed friends, sit by Danica's side, and ride this whole nightmare to its conclusion.

Cadderly did not find it difficult to argue against that irrational notion. Men were dying all around him. How many more Kierkan Rufos lurked in the shadows, murder in their hearts?

"Dear Cadderly," came a purring voice that only reinforced the young scholar's determination. Histra stood behind her chamber's door, opened just a crack, but that was enough to show Cadderly and the dwarves that she wore no more than a filmy, transparent negligee. "Do come in and sit with me."

"Oo!" said Pikel.

"She's wanting more than sitting, boy," chuckled Ivan.

Cadderly ignored them all and ran right by the door. He felt Histra grab at him as he passed and heard her door creak open wider.

"Come back here!" the priestess of Sune screamed, jumping into the middle of the hall.

"Oo!" an admiring Pikel remarked again.

Histra concentrated deeply, meaning to utter a magical command for her would-be lover to "Return!" But Pikel, for all his obvious enchantment, kept a pragmatic attitude about the situation. As Histra began her spell, he clamped a sooty hand onto her rump and casually tossed her back into her room.

"Oo," Pikel uttered a third time when he moved into the room to close the door, and Ivan, standing right behind his brother, whole-heartedly agreed. A dozen young men lay sprawled about the room, exhausted by their exploits.

"Are you so certain that you want to leave?" Histra purred

at the dirty brothers.

By the time the blushing dwarves caught up to Cadderly, he was down to the first floor, dipping his waterskin into a font in the great hall.

"Wretched stuff," Ivan whispered to Pikel. "Oils and water. Tried drinking it once." He hung his floppy tongue out in disgust.

Cadderly smiled at the dwarf's remarks. He had better uses than drinking in mind for the holy water. When the skin was full, he took out a narrow tube, fitted on one end with a rubbery ball of some gooey substance. He popped this onto the open tip of his water skin and capped it with a smaller ball of the same goo.

"You will understand in time," was all the explanation he offered to the curious dwarves.

The Bouldershoulder brothers grew alarmed when the group entered the kitchen and found the place full of priests.

Headmaster Avery led the impromptu chefs, though their progress was limited since each of them spent more time stuffing food into his mouth than actually cooking anything.

More alarming to Cadderly than the eating frenzy was his companions' reactions. Both seemed on the verge of abandoning the quest, as though some greater compulsions now pulled at them.

"Fight it," Cadderly said to them, recognizing their growing desires as curse-induced. Ivan and Pikel were protective of their kitchen, and both took extreme satisfaction in keeping the hungriest priests of the library fed to contentment.

They looked around at the messy kitchen and the gluttonous priests, and for a moment, Cadderly feared that he would be traveling down to the lower catacombs alone. But Newander's claims of dwarven resistance to magical enchantment held true this time, for the Bouldershoulders shrugged unhappily at the disaster that had befallen their space, then pushed Cadderly on, prodding him toward the door to the wine cellar.

The musty stairs were dark and quiet; the torches lining the wall had not been tended. Cadderly opened his light tube and moved down a few steps, waiting there for the brothers to strike torches. Ivan came in last and closed and bolted the iron-bound door, even taking the trouble to slide an iron locking bar into place.

"We've as much trouble behind as ahead," the dwarf explained to Cadderly's questioning look. "If that group gets as thirsty as they are hungry, they'll only bring trouble along with them!"

The reasoning seemed sound enough, so Cadderly turned and started down. Pikel grabbed him, though, and took up the lead, tapping his heavy club to his pot helmet.

"Keep yerself between us," Ivan explained. "We've been on this road before!"

His confidence comforted Cadderly, but the clamor as the bulky dwarves thumped and rattled down the stairs did not.

Their lights intruded into absolute darkness as they came down, but all three sensed that they were not alone. Beside the first wine rack, they found their first clues that someone else had come this way. Broken glass covered the floor and many bottles—bottles that Cadderly had inventoried only a few days before—were missing. The trail led to yet another dead priest. His stomach grossly distended, he lay curled on the floor, surrounded by emptied bottles.

They heard a shuffle to the side and Cadderly put a narrow beam of light down between the wine racks. Another priest was in there, trying futilely to stand. He was too drunk to even notice the light, and his stomach, too, bulged and sloshed. Despite his stupor, he still held a bottle to his lips, stubbornly forcing more liquid down his throat.

Cadderly started toward the drunk, but Ivan held him back.

"Show me yer door," Ivan said to him, then the dwarf nodded to Pikel. As Cadderly and Ivan headed deeper into the cellar, Pikel moved the other way, between the racks. Cadderly soon heard a thump, a groan, and a bottle breaking on the stone floor.

"For his own good," Ivan explained.

They came to the casks where Cadderly had been found and, once again, the young scholar grew confused and frustrated that there was no door to be found. Ivan and Pikel shoved all the casks far away, and the three of them searched every inch of the wall.

Cadderly stuttered an apology; perhaps his entire theory was misguided. Ivan and Pikel stubbornly continued their search, though, keeping faith in their friend. They found their answers not on the unremarkable wall, but on a series of scratches in the floor.

"The casks were dragged," Ivan asserted. He bent low to study the dust, the absence of dust, in the marks. "Not too long ago."

Cadderly's focused beam made the tracking easy and as they moved across the room, he began to get more excited.

"How could I have missed this?" he said. He turned the light back to the wine racks. "We—Rufo and I—came from over there, so the door could not have been back where we found the piled casks. It was a purposeful deception. I should have known."

"Ye took a hit on the head," Ivan reminded him. "And it's a clever trick."

The trail led to yet another cask, tight up against the wall.

The companions knew before Ivan even kicked it aside that the mysterious door would indeed be found behind it. Ivan nodding and smiling, moved right up to the door and pulled it, but it did not budge.

"Locked," the dwarf grunted, examining a keyhole above the pull ring. He looked to his brother, who nodded eagerly.

"Pikel's one for unlocking doors," Ivan explained to Cadderly, and Cadderly got the point when Pikel leveled his tree trunk like a battering ram and lined himself up with the door.

"Hold!" Cadderly said. "I have a better way."

"Ye're a lockpick, too?" Ivan asked.

"Oh," groaned a disappointed Pikel.

"You could say that," Cadderly replied smugly, but instead of instruments for picking locks, he produced the hand-held crossbow. Cadderly had been hoping that he would get to try out his newest invention, and he was hardly able to keep from shaking as he cranked the bow and loaded a dart.

"Stand back," he warned, taking aim at the keyhole. The crossbow clicked and the dart plunked in. A split second later, the momentum of the dart collapsed its weak middle section, crushing the vial of *Oil of Impact*, and the ensuing explosion left a blackened and blasted hole where the lock had been. The door creaked open only an inch but hung there loosely.

"Oh, I'm wanting one of those!" Ivan cried happily.

"Oo oi!" agreed Pikel.

Their glee was short-lived, for behind the open door they found, not the top of the broken stairway, as Cadderly had predicted, but a brick wall.

"New work," Ivan muttered after a quick inspection. He cast a sly glance Cadderly's way. "Ye got a dart for this one, boy?"

Ivan didn't wait to hear an answer. He ran his hands over the wall, pushing at certain points as though he was testing its strength. "Pikel's got the key," he declared and he moved out of the way.

Cadderly started to protest, but Pikel paid him no heed. The dwarf began a curious whining sound and his stubby legs churned up and down, running in place, as though he were winding himself up like a spring. Then, with a grunt, Pikel charged, his battering ram tight against his side.

Bricks and mortar flew wildly. Several fiery explosions indicated that warding glyphs had been placed on the other side of the wall, but Pikel's furious charge was not slowed, by either the flimsy wall or the magical wards. Neither was Pikel able to halt his momentum. As Cadderly had told them before, and as he had tried to warn them again, the stairway beyond the short landing was down.

"Ooooooooo!" came Pikel's diminishing wail, followed by a dull *thump*.

"Me brother!" Ivan cried, and before Cadderly could stop him, he, too, charged through the opening. His torch flared in the dust cloud for just a moment, then both the light and the dwarf dropped from sight.

Cadderly winced and shuddered at Ivan's final words: "I can see the grou—!"

Sixteen

The Walking Dead

Cadderly came down the rope slowly and in control, using a technique he had seen illustrated in a manuscript. He held the rope both in front of and behind him, looping it under one thigh and using his legs to control his descent. He had heard the dwarven brothers grumbling while he was tying off the rope, so he knew that they had survived the fall. That fact offered some comfort, at least. As he neared the stone floor, within the area of torchlight, he saw Pikel running about in circles, with Ivan close on his heels, smacking out the last wisps of smoke from his brother's smoldering behind.

"Oo, oo, oo, oo!" Pikel cried, slapping at his own rump whenever he got the chance.

"Hold still, ye stinking oak kisser!" Ivan bellowed, whacking wildly.

"Quiet," Cadderly cautioned them as he dropped down to the tunnel.

"Oo," Pikel replied, giving one last brisk rub. The dwarf then noticed the stonework in the walls and forgot all about the sting. He wandered off happily to investigate.

"Somebody wanted to keep us outa here," Ivan reasoned. "His fire-wards got me brother good, right on the backside!"

Cadderly agreed with the dwarf's conclusion and sensed that he should know who had set out the glyphs, that he had seen someone in the same room as the bottle. . . .

He couldn't remember, though, and he had no time now to meditate and explore his suspicions. More importantly, neither dwarf had suffered any real damage; Ivan's antler-topped helmet had even been cleaned a bit by the jolt.

"How far to yer cursed flask?" Ivan asked. "Do ye think we'll be seeing more of the magical barriers?" Ivan's face lit up at the notion. "You gotta let a dwarf walk first if you think so, ye know." He pounded a fist onto his breastplate. "A dwarf can take it. A dwarf can eat it up and spit it back at the one who set it! Do ye think we'll be meeting that one? The one who put the fire-ward up there? I've a word to speak with that one. He burned me brother! No, I'm not for letting one go and burn me brother!"

The look in Ivan's eyes grew ever more distant as he spoke, and Cadderly realized that the dwarf was walking a tentative line of control. Off to the side, Pikel, too, had become overly consumed. He was down on his hands and knees, sniffing at the cracks in the wall and uttering an excited "Oo!" every so often. A dozen frantic spiders scurried to get free of their own webs, hopelessly entangled in Pikel's tough beard.

Cadderly set his rock crystal spindle-disks spinning end-around-end in front of Ivan's face and used his light tube to focus a narrow beam on them. The dwarf's talking faded away as he fell more and more into the mesmerizing dance of the light on the disks' many facets.

"Remember why we are here," Cadderly prompted the dwarf. "Concentrate, Ivan Bouldershoulder. If we do not remove the curse, then all the library, the Edificant Library, will be lost." Cadderly couldn't be certain whether his words or the dancing light on thc disks had reminded Ivan to resist the stubborn curse, but whatever the cause, the dwarf's eyes popped wide, as if he had just come from a deep slumber, and he shook his head so wildly that he had to lean on his doublebladed axe to keep from falling over.

"Which way, lad?" the now lucid dwarf asked.

"That's more to the point," Cadderly remarked under his breath. He glanced over at Pikel and wondered if the same technique would be needed on him. It didn't matter, Cadderly decided at once. Pikel wasn't really wide awake even when he was wide awake.

Cadderly looked down at the floor, searching for some sign of his previous passing, but found nothing. He sent his light down to either side of the bricked corridor, but both ways seemed identical and jogged no memories for him.

"This way," he decided simply to get them moving, and he stepped past Ivan. "Do bring your brother." Cadderly heard a clang over his shoulder—axe on cooking pot, he supposed—and Ivan and Pikel came hustling up to his side a moment later.

After many dead ends and many circular treks that brought them right back to where they had started, they came to an ancient storage area of wide corridors lined with rotted crates.

"I was here," Cadderly insisted, speaking the words aloud in an attempt to jog his memory.

Ivan dropped to the floor, seeking to confirm Cadderly's declaration. As with all the corridors, though, no clear tracks were discernable. Clearly the dust had been recently disturbed, but either someone had deliberately brushed away any sure signs or simply too many had passed by this point for the dwarf to track.

Cadderly closed his eyes and tried to envision his previous passage. Many images of his wanderings in the tunnels flooded through him, scenes of skeletons and corridors lined with sinister-looking alcoves, but they wouldn't connect in any logical pattern. They had no focal point, no starting ground where Cadderly could begin to sort them out.

Then he heard the heartbeat.

Somewhere in the unseen distance, water was dripping, steadily, rhythmically. That sound had been here with him, Cadderly knew. It came from no particular direction, and he had not used it as any sort of a guiding beacon his first time through, but now, he realized, it could guide his memory. For, though its interval was constant, its volume became louder and more insistent at some bends in the passages, softer and more distant at others. Too engaged with other pressing problems his first time through, Cadderly had only noticed it on a subconscious level, but that had left an imprint on his memory.

Now Cadderly trusted his instincts. Instead of cluttering his consciousness with futile worries, he moved along and let his subconscious memories guide his steps.

Ivan and Pikel didn't question him; they had nothing better to suggest. It wasn't until they came to a three-way arch, and Cadderly's face brightened noticeably, that even Cadderly really believed he knew where he was going.

"To the left," Cadderly insisted, and indeed, the left archway was less thick with cobwebs than the right, as if someone had passed through there. Cadderly turned back to the dwarves just as he started under the archway, a look of trepidation, even outright dread, on his face.

"What've ye seen?" Ivan demanded, and he pushed his way past Cadderly, under the arches.

"The skeletons," Cadderly started to explain.

Pikel hopped to his guard, and Ivan held his torch far out in front, peering into the dusty gloom. "I see no skeletons!" Ivan remarked after a short pause.

The encounter with the walking dead remained a nightmarish blur for Cadderly. He couldn't quite remember where he had encountered the skeletons, and he didn't know why the thought had suddenly come to him now. "They might be in this area," he offered in a whisper. "Something makes me believe they are nearby."

Ivan and Pikel relaxed visibly and leaned to the side in unison to glance at each other around the young scholar. "Come on, then," Ivan huffed, following his torch's clearing fire into the left passage.

"The skeletons," Cadderly announced again as soon as he came through the archway. He knew this place, a crate-lined corridor wide enough for ten to walk abreast. A bit farther, alcoves lined the corridor's walls on both sides.

"Ye going to start that again?" asked Ivan.

Cadderly waved his light beam in the direction of the alcoves. "In there," he explained.

His warning seemed ominous, at least to him, but the dwarves reacted to it as though it was an invitation. Rather than dim the lights and creep along, they both leaped out in front and strode defiantly down the center of the corridor, stopping in front of the first alcove.

"Oo oi," remarked Pikel.

"Ye're right, lad," agreed Ivan. "It's a skeleton." He propped his axe up on one shoulder, put his other hand on his hip, and walked right up to the alcove.

"Well?" he cried at the bones. "Are ye going to just sit there and rot, or are you going to come out and block me way?"

Cadderly came up tentatively, despite the dwarves' bravado.

"Just as ye said," Ivan said to him when he arrived, "but not moving about much, as I see it."

"They were moving," Cadderly insisted, "chasing me."

The brothers leaned to the side—they were getting used to this maneuver—and glanced at each other around Cadderly.

"I did not dream it!" Cadderly snarled at them, taking a step to the side to block their exchanged stares. "Look!" He started for the skeleton, then had second thoughts about that course and put his light beam into the alcove instead. "See the cobwebs hanging freely in there? And the bits of web on the bones? They were attached, but now the webs hang free.

Either this skeleton has been out of the alcove recently, or someone came down here and cut the strands from it, to make it look as though it has been out of the alcove."

"Yerself was the only one down here," Ivan blurted before he even realized the accusatory connotations of his statement.

"Do you believe I cut the strands?" Cadderly cried. "I would not want to go near the thing. Why would I waste the time and effort to do that?"

Again came the dwarven lean-and-look maneuver, but when Ivan came up straight this time, his expression was less doubting. "Then why are they sitting tight?" he asked. "If they want a fight, why . . .?"

"Because we did not attack them!" Cadderly interrupted suddenly. "Of course," he continued, the revelation coming clearer. "The skeletons did not rise against me until I attacked one of them."

"Why'd ye hit a pile of bones?" Ivan had to ask.

"I did not," Cadderly stuttered. "I mean . . . I thought I saw it move."

"Aha!" cried Pikel.

Ivan elaborated on his excited brother's conclusion. "Then the skeleton moved before ye hit it, and ye're wrong now in yer thinking."

"No, it did not move!" Cadderly shot back. "I thought it had, but it was only a rat or a mouse, or something like that."

"Mouses don't look like bones," Ivan said dryly. Cadderly expected the remark.

Pikel squeaked and crinkled his nose, putting on his best rodent face.

"If we just leave them alone, they might let us pass," Cadderly reasoned. "Whoever animated them probably gave them instructions to defend themselves."

Ivan thought about it for a moment, then nodded. The reasoning seemed sound enough. He motioned to his brother, and Pikel understood the silent request. The green-bearded dwarf pushed Cadderly out of the way, lowered his club like a battering ram, and, before the startled young scholar could move to stop him, charged full speed into the alcove. The ter-rific impact reduced the skull to a pile of flecks and dust and Pikel's continuing momentum scattered the rest of the bones in every direction.

"That one won't be getting up to fight us," remarked a sat-isfied Ivan, brushing a rib off his brother's shoulder as Pikel came back out.

Cadderly stood perfectly still, his mouth hanging open in absolute disbelief.

"We had to check it," Ivan insisted. "Ye want to be leaving walking skeletons behind us?"

"Uh oh," groaned Pikel. Cadderly and Ivan turned at the call, Cadderly's light beam showing the source of Pikel's dismay. This skeleton would not rise to fight them, as Ivan had said, but dozens of others were already up and moving.

Ivan clapped Cadderly hard on the back. "Good thinking, lad!" the dwarf congratulated him. "Ye were right! It took a hit to rouse them!"

"That is a good thing?" Cadderly asked. Images of his last trip through here came rushing back to him, particularly when he had backed away from the first skeleton he had struck, into the waiting grasp of another. Cadderly spun to the side. The skeleton from across the corridor was nearly upon him.

Pikel had seen it, too. Undaunted, the dwarf grasped his club with both hands down low on the handle and stepped in with a mighty roundhouse swing, catching the monster on the side of the head and sending the skull soaring down the cor-ridor behind them. The remaining bones just stood shakily for the moment it took Pikel to smash them down.

Cadderly watched the batted skull until it disappeared into the darkness, then he shouted, "Run!"

"Run!" Ivan echoed, dropping his torch, and he and Pikel charged down the corridor, straight at the advancing host.

That wasn't exactly what Cadderly had in mind, but when

he realized that there was no way he was going to turn the wild brothers around, he shrugged his shoulders, took out his spindle-disks, and followed, seriously pondering the value of friendship when weighed against the burdens.

The closest skeletons did not react quickly enough to the dwarven charge. Ivan sliced one cleanly in half with a great cut of his axe, but then, on his back swing, snagged the weapon's other head in the rib cage of his next intended victim. Never one to quibble over finesse, the dwarf heaved mightily, pulling his weapon and the entangled skeleton into the air around him and then slamming the whole jumble into the next nearest monster. The two skeletons were hopelessly hooked together, but so was Ivan's axe.

"I need ye, me brother!" Ivan cried as yet another skeleton moved in on him, reaching for his face with dirty, sharp finger bones.

Pikel had fared better initially, plowing into the first ranks like a boulder bouncing down a mountainside, breaking three skeletons apart and pushing the rest back several feet. The rush had not been without consequences, though, for Pikel stumbled down to one knee before he could halt his momentum. The fearless undead came in all around the dwarf, advancing from every angle. Pikel grasped his club down low, held it out to arm's length, and began turning fast circles.

The skeletons were mindless creatures, not thinking fighters. Their outstretched arms leading, they came right in fearlessly, stupidly, and Pikel's whirling club whittled them down, fingers, hands, and arms. The dwarf laughed wildly as each bone went humming away, thinking he could keep this up forever.

Then Pikel heard his brother's call. He stopped his spin and tried to discern the right direction, then sent his stubby legs pumping in place, building momentum.

"Oooo!" the dwarf roared, and off he sprang, bursting out the side of the skeletal ring. Unfortunately, his dizziness had deceived him, and as soon as he broke clear of the ring, he slammed headfirst into the corridor's brick wall.

"Oo," came a hollow echo from under the pot helmet of the now seated Pikel.

Only a single skeleton had slipped between the dwarves to face Cadderly, odds that the young scholar thought he could handle. He danced about, up on the balls of his feet as Danica once had shown him, flicking out a few warning shots with his spindle-disks.

The skeleton paid no heed to his dancing feints, or the harmless throws, and continued straight in for Cadderly's mass.

The spindle-disks smacked into its cheekbone and spun its head right around so that is was looking behind itself. Still the skeleton came on, and Cadderly fired again, this time trying to break the thing's body. As soon as he threw, he realized his error.

The disks slipped through the skeleton's rib cage, but got tangled when Cadderly tried to retract them. To make matters worse, the sudden tug of the snag tightened the loop on Cadderly's finger, binding him to the skeleton.

Blindly, the monster swiped out at him. Cadderly dove straight for the floor, took up his walking stick, and shoved it through the rib cage, hoping to dislodge his spindle-disks. As soon as the tip of the stick wedged into the skeleton's backbone, the crafty young scholar changed his tactics. An image of a fulcrum and lever popped into his mind and he let go of his walking stick, then slammed its head with all his might.

The rib fulcrum held firm and the shock of Cadderly's downward blow shot up along the skeleton's backbone and sent its head straight into the air, where it ricocheted off the corridor ceiling. The shattering jolt broke apart the rest of the undead thing.

Cadderly congratulated himself many times as he worked both his weapons free, but his relief lasted only until he looked farther down the corridor, into the flickering light of Ivan's dropped torch. Both dwarves were down, Ivan unarmed and trying to keep out of one skeleton's reach, and Pikel, sitting near the other wall, his pot down to his shoulders, with a whole host of skeletons advancing on him.

* * * * *

Druzil peered suspiciously from between his folded bat wings at the dark and quiet altar room. The brazier fire was down to embers now—Barjin would not leave an interplanar gate burning while he slept—and there was no other light source. That hardly hindered the imp, who had spent eons wandering about the swirling gray mists of the lower planes.

All seemed as it should. To the side of the room, Barjin slept peacefully, confident that his victory was at hand. Mullivy and Khalif flanked the doorway, as still as death and instructed not to move unless one of the conditions set by Barjin had been met.

To Druzil's uneasy relief, none of those conditions apparently had. No intruders had entered the room, the door remained shut fast, and Druzil sensed no probing wizard eyes nor any distant call from Aballister.

The altar room's serenity did not diminish the imp's sense that something was amiss, though. Something had disturbed Druzil's slumber; he had thought it another call from that persistent Aballister. Druzil tightened his wings and sank within himself, turning from his physical senses to the more subtle inner feelings, empathic sensations, that served an imp as well as eyes might serve a human. He pictured the area beyond the closed door, mentally probing the maze of twisting corridors.

The imp's bat wings popped open suddenly. The skeletons were up!

Druzil reached into his magical energies and faded to invisibility. A single flap of his wings carried him between Mullivy and the mummy, and he quickly uttered the key word to prevent Barjin's series of warding glyphs from exploding as he slipped out of the room. Then he was off, flying sometimes, creeping on clawed toes at others, picking his way carefully toward the outermost burial chambers. Already his physical hearing had confirmed what he had sensed, for a battle was in full swing.

The imp paused and considered the options before him. The skeletons were fighting, there could be no doubt, and that could only mean that intruders had come down to this level.

Perhaps they had simply wandered down here in their curse-induced stupor, vagabond priests soon to be dispatched by the undead force, but Druzil could not dismiss the possibility that whoever it was had come with a more definite purpose in mind.

Druzil glanced over his shoulder, down the corridors that would take him back to Barjin. He was torn. If he sent his thoughts to Barjin, established that personal familiar-master telepathic link, he would be bringing his relationship with the priest to a level of which Aballister certainly would not approve. If the wizard back at Castle Trinity ever found out, he might well banish Druzil back to his home plane—a fate that the imp, with the chaos curse finally unleashed on the world, certainly did not desire.

Yet it was Barjin, the imp reminded himself, not Aballister, who had taken the forefront in this battle. Resourceful Barjin, the powerful priest, was the one who had struck boldly and effectively against the heart of law in the Snowflake region.

Druzil sent his thoughts careening down the corridors, into the altar room, and into the sleeping priest's mind. Barjin was awake in a second, and a moment later, he understood that danger had come to his domain.

I will divert them if they get past the skeletons, Druzil assured the priest, *but prepare your defenses!*

* * * * *

Ivan knew he was running out of room. One hand raked at his shoulder, and all that he got for his retaliatory punch was a torn fingernail. The experienced dwarf decided to use his head. He tucked his powerful little legs under him, and the next time the pursuing skeleton lunged for him, he sprang forward.

Ivan's helmet was fitted with the antlers of an eight-point deer, a trophy Ivan had bagged with a "dwarven bow"—that being a hammer balanced for long-range throwing—in a challenge hunt against a visiting elf from Shilmista Forest. In mounting the horns on his helmet, clever Ivan had used an old lacquering trick involving several different metals, and he only prayed that they would prove strong enough now.

He drove into the skeleton's chest, knowing that his horns would likely be entangled, then he stood up and straightened his neck, hoisting the skeleton overhead. Ivan wasn't certain how much his maneuver had gained him, though, for the skeleton, suspended perpendicularly across the dwarf's shoulders, continued its raking attacks.

Ivan whipped his head back and forth, but the skeleton's sharp fingers found a hold on the side of his neck and dug a deep cut. Others were advancing.

Ivan found his answer along the side of the corridor, in an alcove. He could slip in there easily enough, but could the skeleton fit through, laid out sideways? Ivan lowered his head and charged, nearly bursting with laughter. The impact as the skeleton's head and legs connected with the arch surrounding the alcove slowed the dwarf only a step. Bones, dust, and webs flew, and Ivan's helmet nearly tore free of his head as the dwarf tumbled in headlong. He came back out into the corridor a moment later with half a rib cage and several web strands hanging loosely from his horns. He had defeated the immediate threat, but a whole corridor of enemies still remained.

Cadderly saved Pikel. The dazed dwarf sat near the wall, with a ringing in his ears that would last for a long time, and with a host of skeletons swiftly closing.

"Druid, Pikel!" Cadderly yelled, trying to find something

that would shake the dwarf back to reality. "Think like a druid. Envision the animals! Become an animal!"

Pikel lifted the front of his pot helmet and glanced absently toward Cadderly. "Eh?"

"Animals!" Cadderly screamed. "Druids and animals. An animal could get up and away! Spring . . . snake, Pikel. Spring like a coiled snake!"

The pot helmet went back down over the dwarf's eyes, but Cadderly was not dismayed, for he heard a hissing sound coming from under it and he noticed the slight movement as Pikel tensed the muscles in his arms and legs.

A dozen skeletons reached for him.

And the coiled snake snapped.

Pikel came up in a wild rush, batting with both arms, kicking with both legs, even gnawing on one skeleton's forearm. As soon as he regained his footing, the dwarf scooped up his club and began the most vicious and frantic assault Cadderly had ever witnessed. He took a dozen hits but didn't care. Only one thought, the memory that his brother had called for him, rang clear in the would-be druid's mind.

He saw Ivan coming out of the alcove and spotted Ivan's axe, caught fast in the tangle of two skeletons making their unsteady way toward Ivan. Pikel caught up to them long before they reached his brother.

The tree trunk club smashed again and again, beating the skeletons, punishing them for stealing Ivan's weapon.

"That'll be enough, brother," Ivan cried happily, scooping his axe from the bone pile. "There are walking foes still to smash!"

Cadderly outmaneuvered the slow-moving skeletons to rejoin the dwarves. "Which way?" he gasped.

"Forward," Ivan replied without hesitation.

"Oo oi!" Pikel agreed.

"Just get between us," growled Ivan, blasting the skull from a skeleton who had ventured too near.

As they worked their way down the corridor, Cadderly's

tactics improved. He kept his spindle-disks flying for skulls only—less chance of getting them hooked that way—and used his walking stick to ward off the reaching monsters.

Much more devastating to the skeletons were the two fighters flanking the young scholar. Pikel growled like a bear, barked like a dog, hooted like an owl, and hissed like a snake, but whatever sound came from his mouth did not alter his crushing attack routines with his tree trunk club.

Ivan was no less furious. The dwarf accepted a hit for every hit he gave out, but while the skeletons managed to inflict sometimes painful scratches, each of Ivan's strikes shattered another of their ranks into scattered and useless bones.

The trio worked its way through one archway, around several sharp corners, and through yet another archway. Soon more of the skeletal host was behind them than in front, and the gap only widened as less and less resistance stood to hinder their way. The dwarves seemed to enjoy the now lopsided fight and Cadderly had to continually remind them of their more important mission in order to prevent them from turning back to find more skeletons to whack.

Finally they came clear of the threat and Cadderly had a moment to pause and try to get his bearings. He knew that the door, the critical door with the light shining through, could not be too far from here, but the crisscrossing corridors offered few landmarks to jog his memory.

* * * * *

Druzil concluded from the sheer quantity of smashed skeletons that these invaders were not stupefied victims of the chaos curse. He quickly closed in behind the fleeing intruders, taking care, even though he was invisible, to keep to the safety of sheltered shadows. Never allowing Cadderly and the dwarves to get out of his sight, the imp used his telepathy to contact Barjin again, and this time he asked the cleric for direct help.

Give me the commands for the skeletons, Druzil demanded.

Barjin hesitated, his own evil methods forcing him to consider if the imp might be attempting to wrest control.

Give the words to me or prepare to face a formidable band, Druzil warned. *I can serve you well now, my master, but only if you choose wisely.*

Barjin had come out of his sleep to find danger suddenly close, and he meant to take no chances of losing what he had so painstakingly achieved. He still didn't trust the imp—no wise master ever would—but he figured that he could handle Druzil if it came down to that. Besides, if the imp tried to turn the skeletons against him, he could merely exert his own will and wrest back control of them.

Destroy the intruders! came Barjin's telepathic command, and he followed it with a careful recounting of all the command words and phrases recognizable by his skeletal force.

Druzil needed no prodding from Barjin; protecting the flask of his precious chaos curse was more important to him than it ever could be to the priest. He memorized all the proper phrases and inflections for handling the skeletons, then, seeing that Cadderly and the dwarves had stopped to rest in an out-of-the-way and empty passage, went back to retrieve the remaining undead forces.

The next time the intruders met them, the skeletons would not be a disorganized and directionless band. "We will surround and strike in unison," Druzil vowed to the skeletons, though the words meant nothing to the unthinking monsters.

Druzil had to hear them, though. "We will tear apart the dwarves and the human," the imp went on, growing more excited. The chaotic imp couldn't immediately contain his hopes there, pondering the possibilities of taking the skeletal host against Barjin. Druzil dismissed the absurd notion as soon as he had thought of it. Barjin served him well for now, as Aballister had done.

But who could guess what the future might hold?

Seventeen

Danica's Battle

She found herself in the throes of repeated urges, build-ing to overwhelming crescendos and then dying away to be replaced by other insistent impulses. Surely this was Danica's definition of Hell, the discipline and strict codes of her beloved religion swept away by waves of sheer chaos. She tried to staunch those waves, to beat back the images of Iron Skull, the urges she had felt when Cadderly had touched her, and the many others, but she found no secure footholds in her violently shifting thoughts.

Danica touched upon something that even the chaos could not disrupt. To fight the battle of the present, the young woman sent her thoughts into the simpler past.

She saw her father, Pavel, again, his small but powerful frame and blond hair turning to white on the temples. Mostly, Danica saw his gray eyes, always tender when they looked upon his little girl. There, too, was her mother and namesake, solid, immov-able, and wildly in love with her father. Danica was the exact image of that woman, except that her mother's hair was raven black, not blond, showing closer resemblance to the woman's partially eastern background. She was petite and fair like her daughter, with the same clear brown, almond eyes, not dark but almost tan, that could sparkle with innocence or turn fast to unbreakable determination.

Danica's images of her parents faded and were replaced by the wrinkled, wizened image of mysterious Master Turkel.

His skin was thick, leathery, from uncounted hours spent sitting in the sun and meditating atop a mountain, high above the lines of shading trees. Truly he was a man of extremes, of explosive fighting abilities buried under seemingly limitless serenity. His ferocity during sparring matches often scared Danica, made her think the man was out of control.

But Danica had learned better than to believe that; Master Turkel was never out of control. Discipline was at the core of his, their, religion, the same discipline that Danica needed now.

She had labored beside her dear master for six years, until that day when Turkel honestly admitted that he could give no more to her. Despite her anticipation at studying the actual works of Penpahg D'Ahn, it had been a sad day for Danica when she left Westgate and started down the long road to the Edificant Library.

Then she had found Cadderly.

Cadderly! She had loved him from the first moment she had ever seen him, chasing a white squirrel along the groves lining the winding road to the library's front door. Cadderly hadn't noticed Danica right away, not until he tumbled headlong into a bush of clinging burrs. That first look struck Danica profoundly both then and now, as she battled to reclaim her identity. Cadderly had been embarrassed, to be sure, but the sudden flash of light in his eyes, eyes even purer gray than Danica's father's, and the way his mouth dropped open just a hint, then widened in a sheepish, boyish smile, had sent a curious warm sensation through Danica's whole body.

The courtship had been equally thrilling and unpredictable; Danica never knew what ingenious event Cadderly would spring on her next. But entrenched beside Cadderly's unpredictability was a rock-solid foundation that Danica could depend upon. Cadderly gave her friendship, an ear for her problems and excitement alike, and, most of all, respect for her and her studies, never competing against Grandmaster Penpahg D'Ahn for her time.

Cadderly?

Danica heard an echo deep in her mind, a soothing but determined call from Cadderly, urging her to "fight."

Fight?

Danica looked inward, to those overwhelming urges and deeper, to their source, then she saw the manifestation, as had Cadderly. It was within her and not in the open room around her. She envisioned a red mist permeating her thoughts, an ungraspable force compelling her to its will and not her own. It was a fleeting vision, gone an instant after she glimpsed it, but Danica had always been a stubborn one. She summoned back the vision with all her will and this time she held onto it. Now she had an identified enemy, something tangible to battle.

"Fight, Danica," Cadderly had said. She knew that; she heard the echoes. Danica formulated her thoughts in direct opposition to the mist's urging. She denied whatever her impulses told her to do and to think. If her heart told her that something was correct, she called her heart a liar.

"Iron Skull," compelled a voice inside her.

Danica countered with a memory of pain and warm blood running down her face, a memory that revealed to her how stupid she had been in attempting to smash the stone.

* * * * *

It was not a call heard by physical ears; it needed neither the wind nor open air to carry it. The energy emanating from Barjin's necromancer's stone called to a specific group only, to monsters of the negative plane, the land of the dead.

A few short miles from the Edificant Library, where once there had been a small mining town, the call was heard.

A ghoulish hand, withered and filthy, tore up through the sod, reaching into the world of the living. Another followed, and another, just a short distance away. Soon the gruesome pack of ghouls was up out of their holes, drooling tongues hanging between yellow fangs.

Running low, knuckles to the ground, the ghoul pack made for the stone's call, for the Edificant Library.

*   *   *   *   *

Newander could only guess what inner turmoil racked the young woman. Sweat soaked Danica's clothes and she squirmed and groaned under the tightly binding vines. At first, the druid had thought her in pain, and he quickly prepared a sedating spell to calm her. Fortunately, it occurred to Newander that Danica's nightmare might be self-inflicted, that she might have found, as Cadderly had promised, some way to fight back the curse.

Newander sat beside the bed and placed his hands gently but firmly on Danica's arms. While he did not call to her, or do anything else that might hinder her concentration, he watched her closely, fearful lest his guess be wrong.

Danica opened her eyes. "Cadderly?" she asked. Then she saw that the man over her was not Cadderly, and she realized, too, that she was tightly strapped down. She flexed her muscles and twisted as much as the vines would allow, testing their play.

"Calm, dear lass," Newander said softly, sensing her growing distress. "Your Cadderly was here, but he could not stay. He set me to watch over you."

Danica stopped her struggling, recognizing the man's accent. She didn't know his name, but his dialect, and the presence of the vines, told her his profession. "You are one of the druids?" she asked.

"I am Newander," the druid replied, bowing low, "friend of your Cadderly."

Danica accepted his words without question and spent a moment reorienting herself to her surroundings. She was in her own room, she knew, the room she had lived in for a year, but something seemed terribly out of place. It wasn't Newander, or even the vines. Something in this room, in Danica's most secure of places, burned on the edges of the young woman's consciousness, tortured her soul. Danica's gaze settled on the fallen block of stone, stained darkly on one side. The ache in her forehead told her that her dreams had been correct, that her own lifeblood had made that stain.

"How could I have been so foolish?" Danica groaned.

"You were not foolish," Newander assured her. "There has been a curse about this place, a curse that Cadderly has set out to remove."

Again Danica knew instinctively that the druid spoke truthfully. She envisioned her mental struggle against the insinuating red mist, a battle that had been won temporarily but was far from over. Even as she lay there, Danica knew that the red mist continued its assault on her mind.

"Where is he?" Danica asked, near panic.

"He went below," Newander replied, seeing no need to hide the facts from the bound woman. "He spoke of a smoking bottle, deep in the cellars."

"The smoke," Danica echoed mysteriously. "Red mist. It is all about us, Newander."

The druid nodded. "That is what Cadderly claimed. It was he who opened the bottle, and he that means to close it."

"Alone?"

"No, no," Newander assured her. "The two dwarves went with him. They have not been as affected by the curse as the rest."

"The rest?" Danica gasped. Danica knew that her own resistance to such mind-affecting spells was greater than the average person's and she suddenly feared for the other priests.

If she had been driven to slam her head into a block of stone, then what tragedies might have befallen less disciplined priests?

"Aye, the rest," Newander replied grimly. "The curse is general on the library. Few, if any, have escaped it, Cadderly excepted. Dwarves are tougher than most against magic, and the brother cooks seemed in good sorts."

Danica could hardly digest what she was hearing. The last thing she could remember was finding Cadderly unconscious under the casks in the wine cellar. Everything after that seemed just a strange dream to her, fleeting images of irrational moments. Now, in concentrating with all her willpower, she remembered Kierkan Rufo's advances and her punishing him severely for them. Danica remembered even more vividly the block of stone, the exploding flashes of pain, and her own refusal to admit the futility of her attempt.

Danica did not dare to let her imagination conjure images of the state of the library if the druid's words were true, if this same curse was general throughout the place. She focused her thoughts instead on a more personal level, on Cadderly and his quest down in the dusty, dangerous cellars.

"We must go and help him," she declared, renewing her struggles against the stubborn vines.

"No," said Newander. "We are to stay here, by Cadderly's own bidding."

"No," Danica stated flatly, shaking her head. "Of course Cadderly would say that, trying to protect me—and it seems I needed protecting, until a few moments ago. Cadderly and the dwarves might need us, and I'll not lie here under your vines while he walks into danger."

Newander was about to question her on why she thought there might be danger in the cellars, when he recalled Cadderly's own morbid descriptions of the haunted place.

"Have your plants let me go, Newander, I beg," Danica appealed to the druid. "You can remain here if you choose, but I must go to Cadderly's side quickly, before this cursing mist regains its hold on me!"

Her last statement, that the curse might fall back over her, only reinforced Newander's logical conclusion that she should be kept under tight control, that her reprieve from the curse, if that was what this was, might be a temporary thing. But the druid could not ignore the determination in the young woman's voice. He had heard stories of the remarkable Danica from many sources since his arrival at the library and he did not doubt that she would be a powerful ally to Cadderly if she could remain clear-headed. Still, the druid could not underestimate the curse's power—the evidence was too clear all about him, and the choice to release her seemed a great risk.

"What have you to gain by keeping me here?" Danica asked, as though she had read the druid's thoughts. "If Cadderly is not in danger, then he will find and defeat the curse before I . . . we, can get to him. But if he and the dwarves have found danger, then they could surely use our help."

Newander waved his hands and whistled shrilly to the vines.

They jumped to his call, releasing their hold on Danica and the bed, rolling back out the open window.

Danica stretched her arms and legs for many moments before she could bring herself to stand, and even then she got up quite unsteadily, needing Newander's support.

"Are you so certain that you are fit for walking?" the druid asked. "You suffered some serious wounds to the head."

Danica pulled roughly from his grasp and staggered to the middle of the room. There she began an exercise routine, falling more and more easily into the familiar movements. Her arms waved and darted in perfect harmony, each guiding the other to its next maneuver. Every now and again, one of her feet came whistling up in front of her, arcing high over her head.

Newander watched her tentatively at first, then smiled and

nodded his agreement that the young woman had fully regained control of her movements, movements that seemed
ever so graceful and appealing, almost animal-like, to the druid.

"We should be going, then," Newander offered, taking up
his oaken staff and moving to the door.

Renewed sounds from Histra's room greeted them as they
entered the hall. Danica glanced anxiously at Newander, then
started for the priestess's door. Newander's hand clasped her
shoulder and stopped her.

"The curse," the druid explained.

"But we must go to help," Danica started to retort, but she
stopped suddenly as she recognized the connotations of those
cries.

Danica's blush became a deep red, and she giggled in spite
of the seriousness of the situation. Newander tried to hurry her
down the corridor and she did not resist. Indeed, it was Danica
pulling the druid by the time they passed Histra's closed door.

Their first stop was Cadderly's room, and they entered
just as Kierkan Rufo was pulling himself free from the last of
Ivan's stubborn bindings.

Danica's eyes lit up at the sight. Vivid memories of Rufo
prodding her and grabbing at her assaulted her thoughts, and
a wave of sheer hatred, augmented by the red mist, nearly
overwhelmed her.

"Where is Cadderly?" Danica demanded through clenched
teeth.

Newander knew nothing of Rufo, of course, but the druid
recognized immediately that Danica's feelings for the angular
man were not positive.

Rufo twisted his wrist free and tore away from the bed. He
averted his gaze, obviously not wanting to face Danica, or
anyone else at that moment. Thoroughly wretched, the beaten
man wanted only to crawl under his own bed in his own dark
room. He had the misfortune, though, or the poor judgment,
to walk near Danica on his way out of the room.

"Where is Cadderly?" Danica insisted again, stepping in

Rufo's way.

Rufo sneered at her and swung a backhand that never got close. Before Newander could begin to intervene, Danica had caught Rufo's wrist and used its own momentum, with a slight twist, to send the angular man lurching to the side. Newander heard the dull thud, though Danica's next movement had been too subtle to follow. The druid wasn't sure where Danica had hit the man, but from the curious way Rufo squealed and hopped up onto his toes, Newander could make a guess.

"Danica!" the druid cried, wrapping himself around Danica's arms and pulling her back from the tiptoeing man. "Danica," he whispered in Danica's ear. "It is the curse. Remember the curse? You must fight it, girl!"

Danica relaxed immediately and let Rufo slip by. The stubborn man couldn't resist the temptation to turn back as he passed and put one more sneer in Danica's face.

Danica's foot caught him on the side of the head and sent him tumbling out into the hall.

"I meant to do that," Danica assured Newander, making no struggles against his continuing hold, "curse or no curse!"

The druid nodded resignedly; Rufo had asked for that one. He let Danica go as soon as he heard Rufo scramble away down the corridor.

"He is stubborn, that one," Newander remarked.

"Too true," said Danica. "He must have come in on Cadderly and the dwarves."

"Did you notice the bruises on his face?" said the druid. "It would seem that he did not fare too well in that fight."

Danica agreed quietly, thinking it best not to tell Newander that she was the one who had put most of those bruises on Rufo's face. "So Rufo did not slow them," Danica reasoned. "They have made their way to the cellars, and we must be quick to follow."

The druid hesitated.

"What is it?"

"I am afraid for you," Newander admitted, "and of you.

How free are you of the mist? Less than I was believing, by the look on your face when we came upon that one."

"I admit that, for all my efforts, the mist remains," replied Danica, "but your words brought me back under control, I assure you, even against Kierkan Rufo. My argument with him goes beyond this curse. I'll not forget the way he has stared at me, or what he tried to do to me." A suspicious look came into Danica's brown eyes, and she cautiously backed away from Newander. "Why is Newander, the druid, not affected by this thing? And what does Cadderly possess that frees him from the influences of the red mist?"

"As for myself, I know not," Newander replied immediately. "Your Cadderly believes I am free because there are no hidden desires in my heart, and because I came into the library after the curse had started. I knew that something was amiss here as soon as I went to my friends—perhaps that warning has allowed me to fend off the cursing effects."

Danica didn't seem convinced. "I am a disciplined warrior," she replied, "but the curse found its way into my thoughts easily enough, even just now, though I understand the dangers of it."

Newander shrugged, having no explanation. "That was your Cadderly's theory, not my own," he reminded her.

"What does Newander believe?"

Again the druid merely shrugged. "For Cadderly," he said a moment later, "it was he who opened the bottle, and that alone might have saved him. Often in magical curses, the bringer of the curse does not feel its sting."

Danica didn't really appreciate the value of anything the druid had said, but the sincerity in Newander's voice was undeniable. She lowered her guard and walked out beside the man.

The kitchen still belonged to the gluttons. Several more had fallen in an overstuffed stupor, but others continued to wander about, pillaging the dwarves' well-organized cupboards.

Newander and Danica tried to keep their distance as they made their way toward the cellar door, but one fat priest took more than a passing interest in the beautiful young woman.

"Here's a tasty bit still to be tried," he slobbered between several thunderous belches. Rubbing his greasy fingers on his greasier robes, he started straight for Danica.

He had nearly reached her—and Danica thought she would have to clobber the man—when a pudgy hand grabbed him on the shoulder and roughly spun him about.

"Hold!" shouted Headmaster Avery. "What do you think you are about?"

The priest eyed Avery with sincere confusion, as did Danica, standing behind him.

"Danica," Avery explained to the man. "Danica and Cadderly! You keep away from her." Before the man could make any apologies, before Danica could try to calm Avery, the pudgy headmaster swung across with his other arm, holding a hefty leg of mutton, and cracked the offending priest on the side of the head. The man dropped in a heap and did not move.

"But, Headmaster . . ." Danica began.

Avery cut her off. "No need to thank me," he said. "I watch out for my dear friend, Cadderly. And for his friends, too, of course. No need to thank me!" He wandered off without waiting for any reply, gorging on his mutton and searching for new stores to raid.

Danica and Newander started for the fallen man, but the priest awoke with a start and shook his head briskly. He wiped a hand across the mutton-wetted side of his head, smelled his fingers curiously for a moment when he realized the wetness was not his own blood, then began licking them wildly.

The two companions' relief when they reached the heavy, iron-bound cellar door dissipated as soon as they found the portal barred. Danica worked at the jam for a few moments, trying to discover the source of the lock, while the druid prepared a spell.

Newander spoke a few words—they sounded elvish to

Danica—and the door groaned, as if in answer. Wood planks warped and loosened and the whole door rattled to Danica's slightest touch.

When the druid's spell was completed, Danica went at the door more forcefully. It no longer fit neatly on any side, though the locking bar remained firmly in place behind it.

Danica spent a long moment in deep concentration, then lashed out with her open palm. Her blow would have dropped any man, but the door was very old, of ancient oak, and very thick, and the punch had little effect. This portal had been constructed for defense in the earliest days of the library. If a goblin raid ever overpowered the outside defenses, the priests could retreat to the cellars. It had only happened twice in the history of the library, and both times, the oaken door had stopped the intruders. Neither the flames of goblin torches, nor the weight of their crude battering rams had broken through, and now, Danica, for all her power and training, was simply overmatched.

"It appears that Cadderly and the dwarves will have to get the task finished without our help," Newander remarked grimly, though there was a hint of relief in his voice.

Danica was not so willing to surrender. "Outside," she ordered, starting back across the kitchen. "There may be a window, or some other way down."

Newander did not think her hopes likely, but Danica hadn't asked for, or even waited to hear, his opinion. Reluctantly, the druid shrugged and ran to catch up with her.

They split up just outside the double doors, Danica searching along the base of the wall to the south, Newander going north. Danica had gone only a few steps when she was joined by a welcomed friend.

"Percival," the woman said happily, glad for the distraction as the white squirrel peered over the edge of the roof right above her, chattering excitedly. Danica knew immediately that something was bothering the squirrel, but while she could sometimes figure out the connotations of a few of Percival's basic cries, she could not begin to follow his wild stream of chatter.

"Oh, Percival!" she scolded loudly, interrupting the squirrel's banter. "I do not understand."

"Surely I do," said Newander, coming up quickly behind Danica. To the squirrel, he said, "Do continue," and he uttered a series of squeaks and clicks.

Percival began again at once, at such a pace that Newander was hard pressed to keep up.

"We may have found our way in," the druid announced to Danica when Percival had finished. "That is, if we can trust the beast."

Danica studied the squirrel for a brief moment, then vouched for him.

The first place Percival led them was the old work shed to the side of the library. As soon as they entered, they understood the squirrel's noisy introduction to the place, for the chains still hung from the ceiling near to the back wall and droplets of blood had spattered the floor beneath them.

"Mullivy?" Danica asked to no one in particular. Her question set Percival off on a new stream of gossip. Danica waited patiently for the squirrel to finish, then turned to Newander for a translation.

"This Mullivy," the druid asked, looking about with even more concern, "might he be the caretaker?"

Danica nodded. "He has been groundskeeper of the library for decades."

"Percival claims he was brought here by another man," the druid explained, "then they both went off to the hole."

"The hole?"

"Tunnel, he means, as best as I can figure," explained Newander. "All this happened several days ago, perhaps. Percival's grasp of time is weak. Still, it is remarkable that the squirrel can recall the incident at all. They are not known for long memories, you know."

Percival hopped down from the shelf and raced out the

door as though he had taken exception to the druid's last remark.

Danica and Newander rushed to follow, Danica pausing to collect a couple of torches that Mullivy had conveniently stocked in the work shed.

It seemed as if Percival was almost playing a deliberate game with them as they tried to follow his darting movements along the broken ground and rough underbrush south of the library. At last, after many wrong turns, they caught up to the squirrel along a ridge. Below them, under an overhang thick with brush, they saw the ancient tunnel, heading into the mountain in the general direction of the library.

"This might not get us anywhere near the cellars we are seeking," Newander offered.

"How long will it take us to get through the door in the kitchen?" Danica asked, mostly to remind the druid of their lack of options. To accentuate her point, she led Newander's gaze to the west, where the sun was already disappearing behind the high peaks of the Snowflakes.

Newander took a torch from her, uttered a few words, and produced a flame in his open palm. The fire did not burn the druid, but it lit the torch, and then lit Danica's torch, easily enough before Newander extinguished it.

They walked in side by side, taking note that there were indeed prints in the dust on the tunnel floor—boot prints, possibly, though most were scraped away in a manner that neither of them could explain.

Neither of them realized that zombies dragged their feet when they walked.

Eighteen

General Druzil

Ivan wiped a line of blood from his brother's neck.

"Druid?" Ivan asked, and there now remained little sarcasm in his tone. Pikel's wild fighting obviously had impressed Ivan, and the dwarf had no way of knowing how much more there was to being a druid than barking animal noises during a fight. "Maybe that'd not be so bad."

Pikel nodded gratefully, his smile wide under his low hanging helmet.

"Where do we go from here?" Ivan asked Cadderly, who was leaning quietly against the wall.

Cadderly opened his eyes. This passage was new to him and the fight had agitated him. Even concentrating on the dripping water did little to help him get his bearings. "We went mostly west," he offered tentatively. "We have to come back around . . ."

"North," Ivan corrected, then he whispered to Pikel, "Never met a human who could tell his way underground," which brought a chuckle from both dwarves.

"Whatever the direction," Cadderly went on, "wc have to

get back to the original area. We were close to our goal before the attack. I am certain of that."

"The best way back is the way we ran," reasoned Ivan.

"Uh oh," muttered Pikel, peeking around the corner to the passage behind them.

Cadderly and Ivan didn't miss the dwarf's point, and they understood even more clearly a second later, when the now familiar scraping-scuffing sound of approaching bony feet came from beyond the bend.

Ivan and Pikel clasped their weapons and nodded eagerly, too eagerly, by the young scholar's estimation. Cadderly moved quickly to quench the battle-fires burning in their eyes.

"We go the other way," he ordered. "This passage must have another exit, just like all the others, and no doubt it connects to tunnels that will allow us to get behind our pursuers."

"Ye fearing a fight?" balked Ivan, narrowing his eyes with contempt.

The dwarf's suddenly gruff tone alarmed Cadderly. "The bottle," he reminded Ivan. "That is our first and most important target. Once we close it, you can go back after all the skeletons you desire." The answer seemed to appease Ivan, but Cadderly was hoping that once they had closed the bottle and defeated whoever or whatever was behind this whole curse, no further fighting would be necessary.

The corridor went on for a long way with no side passages, and no alcoves, though some areas were lined by rotted crates.

When they at last did see a turn up ahead, a bend that went back the same way as the one they had left behind, they were greeted once again by the scraping-scuffling sound. All three glanced at each other with concern; Ivan's glare at Cadderly was not complimentary.

"We left the others far behind," the dwarf reasoned. "This must be a new group. Now they're on both sides! I told ye we should've fought them when we could!"

"Turn back," Cadderly said, thinking that perhaps the dwarf's reasoning was not correct.

Ivan didn't seem to like the idea. "There are more behind us," he huffed. "Ye want to be fighting both groups at once?"

Cadderly wanted to argue that perhaps there were not skeletons behind them, that perhaps this unseen group in front of them was the same as those they had left behind. He saw clearly that he wouldn't convince the grumbling dwarves, so he didn't waste the time in trying. "We have wood," he said. "Let us at least build some defenses."

The brothers had no problem with that suggestion, and they quickly followed Cadderly a short way back down the passage, to the last grouping of rotted crates. Ivan and Pikel conferred in a private huddle for a moment, then swept into action. Several of the boxes, weakened by the decades, fell apart at the touch, but soon the dwarves had two shoulder-high-to-a-man and fairly solid lines running out from one wall, forming a corridor too narrow for more than one or two skeletons to come through at a time.

"Just get yerself behind me and me brother," Ivan instructed Cadderly. "We're better for smashing walking bones than that toy ye carry!"

By then, the scuffling was quite loud in front of them and Cadderly could detect some movement just at the end of his narrow light beam. The skeletons did not advance any farther, though.

"Have they lost the trail?" Cadderly whispered.

Ivan shook his head. "They know we're here," he insisted.

"Why do they hold back?"

"Uh oh," moaned Pikel.

"Ye're right," Ivan said to his brother. He looked up at Cadderly. "Ye should've left the fighting to us," he said. "Be keeping that thought in yer head in the future. Now they're waiting for the other group, the one we shouldn't have left behind us, to catch up."

Cadderly rocked back on his heels. Skeletons were not

thinking creatures. If Ivan's appraisal was correct, then some-one, or something, else was in the area, directing the attack.

Shuffling noises proved the dwarves' guess right only a few moments later and Cadderly nodded grimly. Perhaps he should have left the fighting decisions to his more seasoned companions. He took up his appointed position behind the dwarven brothers, not sounding his concerns that the undead seemed to have some organization.

The skeletons came at them in a rush, a score from one side and at least that many from the other, and when they found the single opening to get at their living enemies, they banged against each other trying to get in.

A single chop from Ivan's axe dispatched the first one that made its way down. Several more followed in a tight group, and Ivan backed away and nodded to his brother. Pikel lowered his club like a battering ram and started pumping his legs frantically, building momentum. Cadderly grabbed the dwarf's shoulder, hoping to keep their defensive posture intact, and it was Ivan, not Pikel, who knocked his hand away.

"Tactics, boy, tactics," Ivan grumbled, shaking his head in-credulously. "I told ye to leave the fighting to us."

Cadderly nodded again and pulled back.

Pikel sprang away, battering into the advancing skeletons like some animated ballista missile. With the general jumble of bones, it was hard to determine how many skeletons the dwarf actually had destroyed. The important factor was that many more still remained. Pikel wheeled about quickly and came rushing back, one skeleton right behind him.

"Down!" Ivan yelled and Pikel dove to the ground just as Ivan's great axe swiped about, bashing Pikel's pursuer into little pieces.

Cadderly vowed then to let the dwarves handle any future battle arrangements, humbling himself to the fact that the dwarves understood tactics far better than he ever could.

Another small group of skeletons came on, and Ivan and Pikel used alternating attack routines, each playing off his brother's feints and charges, to easily defeat them. Cadderly rested back against the wall in sincere admiration, believing that the brothers could keep this up for a long, long time.

Then, suddenly, the skeletons stopped advancing. They milled about by the entrance to the crate run for a moment, then systematically began dismantling the piles.

"When did those things learn to think?" asked a disbelieving Ivan.

"Something is guiding them," Cadderly replied, shifting his light beam all about the passage in search of the undead leader.

*　*　*　*　*

No light could reveal Druzil's invisibility. The imp watched impatiently and with growing concern. Counting the skeletons back in the earlier passages, these three adventurers had destroyed more than half the undead force.

Druzil was not normally a gambling creature, not when his own safety was concerned, but this was not a normal situation.

If these three were not stopped, they eventually would get into the altar room. Who could guess what kind of damage the two wild dwarves might cause in there?

Yet, it was something about the human that bothered Druzil most of all. His eyes, the imp thought, and the careful and calculating way he swept his light beam, reminded Druzil pointedly of another powerful and dangerous human. Druzil had heard of dwarven resistance to all magic, even potent ones such as the chaos curse, so he could understand how the two had found their way down, but this human seemed even more clear-headed, more focused, than his companions.

There could be only one answer: this one had been Barjin's catalyst in opening the bottle. Barjin had assured Druzil that he had put spells on the catalyst that would keep the man from remembering anything and from posing any threat. Had Barjin, perhaps, underestimated his foe? That possibility only increased Druzil's respect for Cadderly.

Yes, the imp decided, this human was the true threat. Druzil rubbed his hands together eagerly and stretched his wings. It was time to end that threat.

* * * * *

"We've got to charge them before they rip it all down!" Ivan declared, but before he and Pikel could move, there came a sudden rush of wind.

"Oo!" Pikel yelled, instinctively recognizing the sound as an attack. He grabbed the front of Cadderly's tunic and pulled him to the ground. A split second later, Pikel yelped out in pain and grabbed at his neck.

The attacker became visible as it struck, and Cadderly, though he didn't recognize the creature precisely, knew it was a denizen of the lower planes, some sort of imp. The batwinged thing flew off, its barbed tail trailing behind, dripping Pikel's blood.

"Me brother!" shouted Ivan, but, though Pikel seemed a bit dazed, he warded off Ivan's attempts to see to his wound.

"That was an imp," Cadderly explained, keeping the light beam in the direction the creature had flown. "Its sting is—" he stopped when he looked at the concerned brothers "—poisoned," Cadderly said softly.

As if on cue, Pikel began to tremble violently and both Cadderly and Ivan thought he surely would go down. Dwarves, though, were a tough lot, and Pikel was a tough dwarf. A moment later, he growled loudly and threw off the trembling in a sudden violent jolt. Straightening, he smiled at his brother, hoisted his tree trunk, and nodded toward the skeletal host, still at work taking apart the crate defenses.

"So it was poisoned," Ivan explained, looking pointedly at Cadderly. "Might've killed a man."

"My thanks," Cadderly said to Pikel, and he would have

gone on, except that other things demanded his attention at the moment. The imp had targeted him, he realized, and it most probably would be back.

Cadderly released a latch on his walking stick and tilted the ram's head backward on cleverly hidden hinges. He then popped off the stick's bottom cap, leaving him a hollow tube.

"Eh?" asked Pikel, wording Ivan's thoughts exactly.

Cadderly only smiled in reply and continued his preparations. He unscrewed his feathered ring, the one filled with drow-style sleep poison, and showed the dwarves the tiny feather, its other end a cat's claw dripping with the potent black solution. Cadderly winked and fitted the dart into the end of his walking stick, then grabbed a nearby plank and waited.

The fluttering sound of bat wings returned a moment later and both dwarves hoisted their weapons to defend. Cadderly had anticipated that the imp would be invisible again. He determined the general direction of the attack and, when the flapping grew near, tossed out the plank.

The agile imp dodged the heavy board, just nicking it with one wing tip as he passed. While the hit hadn't done any real damage, it did cost Druzil dearly.

With his walking stick blow-gun held to pursed lips, Cadderly registered the sound of the nick, aimed, and puffed. A slight thud told him that the dart had struck home.

"Oo oi!" Pikel squealed in glee as the invisible imp, stuck with a quite visible dart, fluttered overhead. "Oo oi!"

*   *   *   *   *

Druzil wasn't sure if he or the corridor was spinning. Whichever it was, he knew, somewhere in the back of his dreamy thoughts, that it was not a good thing. Normally poisons would not affect an imp, especially on a plane of existence other than its own. But the cat's-claw dart that had struck Druzil was coated in drow sleep poison, which was among the most potent concoctions in all the world.

"My skeletons," the imp whispered, remembering his command, and feeling that he was somehow needed in some distant battle. Druzil couldn't sort it out; all he wanted to do was sleep.

He should have landed first.

He hit the wall before he realized that he was flying, and fell with a heavy groan. The concussion shook a bit of the slumber from him and he remembered suddenly that the battle was not so distant and that he was indeed needed . . . but the thought of sleep felt so much better.

Druzil kept enough of his wits about him to get out of the open corridor. His bones crackled in transformation, leathery skin ripped and reshaped. Soon he was a large centipede, invisible still, and he slipped in through a crack in the wall and let the slumber overtake him.

* * * * *

When Druzil fell, so did any semblance of organization in the skeleton forces. Now the imp's intrusions into the undead creatures' predetermined commands worked against the skeletons, for they were not thinking creatures and their original course had been seriously interrupted.

Some skeletons wandered aimlessly away, others hung their bony arms down by their sides and stood perfectly still, while others continued their methodical dismantling of the crate barricades, though they no longer followed any purpose in their actions. Only one group remained hostile, rushing down the narrow channel at Cadderly and the dwarves, their arms reaching out eagerly.

Ivan and Pikel met them squarely with powerful chops and straightforward thrusts. Even Cadderly managed to get in a few hits. He stood behind Pikel, knowing that Ivan's antlers probably would foul his spindle-disks. Pikel was only about four feet tall, with another few inches added for the pot helmet, and Cadderly, standing at six feet, snapped off shots whenever the dwarf's clubbing maneuvers allowed him an opening.

At Cadderly's suggestion, they worked their way down the channel, leaving piles of bones in their wake. The imp had been controlling the skeletons, Cadderly realized, and with the imp down—Cadderly had heard it hit the wall—Cadderly suspected that the monsters would take little initiative in the fight.

With the one attacking group dispatched, Ivan and Pikel moved cautiously toward those breaking down the barricades.

The skeletons offered no resistance, didn't even look up from their work, as the dwarves smashed them into bits. Similarly, those skeletons still remaining in the area, those standing still and showing no signs that they had even been animated, fell easy prey to the dwarves.

"That's the lot," Ivan announced, blasting the skull from the last standing skeleton, "except for those that are running away. We can catch them!"

"Let them wander," Cadderly offered.

Ivan glared at him.

"We have more important business," Cadderly replied, his words more a suggestion than a command. He moved slowly toward where the imp had crashed, the dwarves at his side, but found no sign of Druzil, not even the feathered dart.

"Which way then?" asked an impatient Ivan.

"Back the way we came," Cadderly replied. "I will have an easier time finding the altar room if we return to tunnels I know. Now that the skeletons have been defeated . . ."

"Oo!" chirped Pikel suddenly. Cadderly and Ivan looked around anxiously, thinking another attack imminent.

"What do ye see?" asked Ivan, staring into the empty distance.

"Oo!" Pikel said again, and when his brother and Cadderly looked back at him, they understood that he was responding to no outside threat.

He was trembling again.

"Oo!" Pikel clutched at his chest and went into a series of short hops.

"Poison!" Cadderly cried to Ivan. "The excitement of battle allowed him to fight it off, but only temporarily!"

"Oo!" Pikel agreed, scratching furiously at his breastplate, as if he were trying to get at his heart.

Ivan ran over and grabbed him to hold him steady. "Ye're a dwarf!" he yowled. "Ye don't go falling to poison!"

Cadderly knew better. In the same book he had found the drow recipe, he had read of many of the Realms' known poisons. Near the top of the potency list, beside the deadly sting of a wyvern's tail and the bite of the dreaded two-headed amphisbaena snake, were listed several poisons of lower plane denizens, among them one from the tail stingers of imps.

Dwarves were as resistant to poison as to magic, but if the imp had hit Pikel solidly . . .

"Oo!" Pikel cried one final time. His trembling mocked Ivan's desperate efforts to hold him steady and, with a sudden burst of power, he threw his brother aside and stood staring blankly ahead for just a moment. Then he fell, and both Ivan and Cadderly knew he was dead before they ever got to him.

Nineteen

Ghouls

They had heard the call of the necromancer's stone; they had sensed the dead walking and knew that a crypt had been disturbed. They were hungry now— they were always hungry—and the promises of carrion, ancient and new, brought them running, hunched low on legs that once had been human. Long tongues wagged between pointy teeth, dripping lines of dirty saliva along chins and necks.

They didn't care; they were hungry.

They came up along the road, darting in and out of the deepening afternoon shadows as they made their way toward the large building. One man, a tall human in long gray robes, was up there milling about the great doors. The lead ghoul bent low over its bowed legs and charged, arms hanging low, knuckles dragging on the ground, and fingers twitching excitedly.

Long and filthy fingernails, as sharp and tough as a wild animal's claws, caught the unsuspecting priest on the shoulder.

His agonized cries only increased the frenzy. He tried to fight back, but the chill of the diseased, ghoulish touch deadened his limbs. His features locked in a horror-filled, paralyzed contortion, and the pack fell over him, tearing him apart in seconds.

One by one, the ghouls drifted away from the devoured corpse, toward the great doors and the promise of more food.

But each of them veered away, shielding its eyes with raised arms as it approached, for the doors were blessed and heavily warded against intrusions by undead creatures. The ghouls wandered about for a moment, hungry and frustrated, then one of them heard the call of the stone again, to the south of the structure, and the pack swept off to find it.

* * * * *

It was a damp place, with pools of muddy water dotting the earthen floor and mossy vines, covered by crawling things, hanging from the evenly spaced support beams. Danica moved cautiously, the torch far out in front of her, and she kept as far from the sinister-looking moss as possible.

Newander was less concerned with the hanging strands, for they were a natural growth, as were the insects crawling over them, and so were within the druid's realm of understanding.

Still, though, Newander seemed even more anxious than Danica. He stopped several times and looked around, as if he was trying to locate something.

Finally his fears infected Danica. She moved beside him, studying him closely in the torchlight.

"What do you seek?" she asked bluntly.

"I sense a wrongness," Newander replied cryptically.

"An evil?"

"Your Cadderly told me of undead monsters walking the crypts," Newander explained. "Now I know he was telling me true. They are the greatest perversion of nature's order, a wrong upon the earth itself."

Danica could understand why a druid, whose entire life was based on natural order, might be sensitive to the presence of undead monsters, but she was amazed that Newander could actually sense they were nearby. "The walking dead have passed this place?" she asked, fully trusting that his answer would be correct.

Newander shrugged and looked around nervously again.

"They are close about," he replied, "too close."

"How can you know?" Danica pressed.

Newander looked at her curiously, confusedly. "I . . . I cannot," he stammered, "and yet I do."

"The curse?" Danica wondered aloud.

"My senses do not lie to me," Newander insisted. He spun about suddenly, back toward the tunnel entrance, as if he had heard something.

Just an instant later, Danica jumped in surprise as a screech sounded from the tunnel entrance, now no more than a gray blur far behind. She recognized the cry as Percival's, but that fact did not calm her, for even then the hunched forms appeared at the entrance, the sound of their hungry slobbers carrying all the way down to the woman and the druid.

"Run, Danica!" Newander cried and turned to go.

Danica did not move, unafraid of any enemy. She saw eight man-sized shapes distinctly, though she had no idea if they were priests from the library or monsters. Either way, Danica saw no advantage in stumbling down the tunnel, perhaps running into a waiting enemy and having to fight both foes at the same time. Also, Danica could not ignore Percival. She would fight for the white squirrel as surely as she would fight for any friend.

"They are undead," the druid tried to explain and, even as he spoke the words, the rotted ghoul stench filled their nostrils. The odor told Newander much about their enemy, and his desire to flee only increased. It was too late, though. "Do

not let them scratch you," Newander advised. "Their touch
will freeze the marrow of your bones."

Danica crouched low, feeling the balance of the torch and
tuning all her senses to her surroundings. Above her, Percival
skittered along a wooden beam; behind her, Newander had
begun a low chant, a spell preparation; and before her, the
pack came on, hissing and sputtering, but slower now, out of
respect for the blazing torch.

The pack came to within a dozen running strides of
Danica and halted. Danica saw their yellow, sickly eyes, but
unlike those of a corpse, these shone with inner, hungry fires.
She heard their breathless gasps and saw their long and
pointy tongues, flicking like a reptile's might. Danica crouched
even lower, sensing their mounting excitement.

As a group, they charged, but it was Newander who struck
first. As the ghouls passed under a crossbeam, the moss came
to life. Like the vines that had held Danica to her bed, the
moss strands grabbed at the passing ghouls. Three of the
creatures were fully entangled; two others scrambled and spat
in horrifying rage, their ankles hooked, but three came right
through.

The lead ghoul bore down on Danica, who stood poised
and unafraid. She held her unthreatening posture until the
very last moment, luring the ghoul right in on her, so close
that even Newander let out an alarmed cry.

Danica was in perfect control of the situation. Her torch
shot out suddenly, its fiery end slamming the ghoul right in
the eye.

The creature recoiled and let out a shriek that sent tingling shivers along Danica's spine.

She popped the ghoul in the other eye for good measure,
but the move put her torch out of line for a continuing defense. A second foe appeared beside the first, its tongue hanging low and its wretched hands reaching for Danica.

Danica moved to punch it but remembered Newander's
warning and knew that her own arm's reach could not match

the taller ghoul's. Danica possessed other weapons. She threw her head backward suddenly, so far that it seemed she would tumble to the ground. Her continued balance caught the still-advancing ghoul by surprise and brought an astounded gasp from Newander behind her, for Danica did not fall. She pivoted her body on one leg, her other leg shooting up before her and her foot catching the charging ghoul right under the chin. The monster's jaw smacked shut, its severed tongue dropped to the floor, and it stopped abruptly, hideous red-green blood and mucus pouring from its mouth.

Danica wasn't nearly finished with it. She dropped her torch and leaped straight up, catching the crossbeam support, and snap-kicked one foot into the ghoul's face, sending gore flying.

Again and again Danica's kicks pounded it.

The third advancing ghoul had met equal punishment.

Newander held his open palm out before him and uttered a few words to produce another ball of magical flame, similar to the one he had used to light the torch back at the tunnel entrance.

As the ghoul came hobbling in, Newander launched the fiery missile. It hit the advancing monster squarely in the chest and suddenly the ghoul was more concerned with patting out the flames than attacking the druid. It had nearly put out the first fire when another ball came in, this one taking it in the shoulder. Then came the third missile, bursting into a shower of sparks as it hit the ghoul in the face.

Danica held her position on the crossbeam and kicked one final time. She knew that she had snapped the ghoul's neck, but the doomed creature managed to get a claw on the side of her leg. As it fell, its dirty nail dug a deep line down Danica's calf. Danica looked upon the wound in horror, feeling the paralyzing touch taking hold of her. "No!" she growled, and she used all her years of training, all her mental discipline, to fight back, to force the chill from her bones.

She dropped from the beam and scooped up the torch,

glad to learn that her leg could still support her. Her anger controlled her now; part of Danica's discipline involved the knowledge of when to let go, of when to let sheer anger guide her actions. The ghoul with the burned eyes spun about wildly, slashing blindly with its claws in its search for something to hit.

Its mouth opened impossibly wide in a hungry, vicious scream.

Danica grasped the torch in both hands and rammed it with an overhead chop down the ghoul's throat. The creature thrashed wildly, scoring several hits on Danica's arms, but the furious woman did not relent. She drove the torch deeper down the ghoul's gullet, twisting and grinding until the ghoul stopped thrashing.

Hardly slowing, Danica tightened one hand and spun about, catching the ghoul battling Newander's fires with a left hook.

The blow lifted the monster from its feet and sent it crashing into the tunnel wall. Newander came on it in an instant, pounding with his oaken staff.

The fight was far from over. Five ghouls remained, though three were still helplessly entangled by the moss strands. The other two had worked their way free and charged, paying no concern to their dead companions.

Danica dropped into a low crouch, pulled her daggers from their boot sheaths, and struck before the monsters ever got close. To the lead ghoul, the coming dagger probably seemed no more than a sliver, flickering as it spun in the dim torchlight.

Then the creature got the point, as the dagger buried itself to the hilt in its eye. The ghoul shrieked and teetered to the side, clutching its face. Danica's second shot followed with equal precision, thudding into the creature's chest, again burying to the hilt, and the ghoul tumbled, writhing in the throes of death.

The second charging ghoul, not a fortunate creature, now

had a clear path at Danica. The monk waited again until the very last moment, then sprang to grab the beam and her deadly foot flashed out. The powerful kick caught the ghoul on the forehead, stopping it cold and snapping its head backward. As the head came back, Danica's foot met it again, then a third and a fourth time.

Danica dropped from the beam, letting the momentum of her fall take her down into a low squat. Like a coiled spring, she came back up, spinning as she rose and letting one foot fly out behind her. The circle-kick maneuver caught the stunned and battered ghoul on the side of the jaw and snapped its head to the side so brutally that the ghoul was sent into an airborne somersault. It landed in a kneeling position, weirdly contorted, with its legs straight out to either side, its lifeless body hunched heavily and its head lolling about, looking over one shoulder.

Danica's rage was not appeased. She charged down the passage, issuing a single-toned scream all the way. She put her right hand in a partial list, extending her index and little fingers rigidly. The closest moss-wrapped ghoul, not Danica's target, managed to free one arm to lash at the woman. Danica easily dove under the awkward attack, went into a roll right past the attacker, and came up a few feet in front of the next ghoul without breaking her momentum in the least. She leaped into the air and struck viciously as she descended. Eagle Talon, this attack was named, according to the scrolls of Grandmaster Penpahg D'Ahn, and Danica worked it to perfection as her extending fingers drove right through the ghoul's eyes, exploding into its rotted brain. It took Danica nearly a minute to extract her hand from the creature's shattered head, but it didn't matter, she knew. This ghoul offered no further threat.

Newander, finished with his ghoul, started toward the young woman. He stopped, though, seeing that Danica had things well under control, and went instead to retrieve the low-burning torch.

Finally free, Danica went back at the ghoul that had swung

at her. Her fist thudded grotesquely against the rotted flesh of the creature's chest; Danica knew that its ribs had collapsed under the blow, but the ghoul, nearly free before the attack, fell clear of the moss with the weight of the punch. It came up screaming horribly, wailing away like a thing gone insane.

Danica matched its intensity, hitting it three times for each hit she suffered. Again she felt the paralyzing chill of a ghoul's touch and again she growled it away. Still, she could not ignore the lines of blood on her arms, and her pain and weariness were mounting. She feigned another straightforward punch, then dropped into a squat under the ghoul's lurching swings.

Her foot flashed straight out, catching the ghoul inside its knee and sending it face-first to the ground. In an instant, Danica was back up. She clutched her hands together in a double fist, reached back over her head and dropped to her knees, using the momentum of her fall to add to the power of her chop. She caught the rising ghoul on the back of the head, slamming it back to the ground. The creature bounced under the terrific impact and then lay very still.

Danica didn't wait to see if it would move again. She grabbed a handful of its scraggly hair, reached under to cup its chin in her other hand, and twisted its head so violently that before the crackling of neck bones had finished, the ghoul's dead eyes were staring straight up over its back.

Danica came up with an enraged scream and advanced steadily on the one remaining ghoul. The moss had lifted this one clear of the ground and it hung there still, barely struggling against the impossible bonds. Danica punched it on the side of the head, sending it into a spin. As the face came around in a full circle, Danica, too, spun a circuit and circle-kicked, reversing the creature's spin. And so it went, punch, kick, around one way and then the other.

"It is dead," Newander started to say, but he didn't bother to press the point, understanding that Danica needed to work through her rage. Still she kicked and punched, and still the limply hanging ghoul spun.

Finally, the exhausted monk dropped to her knees before the latest kill and put her head in her blood-soaked hands.

* * * * *

"Druzil?" Barjin didn't know why he had spoken the word aloud; perhaps he had thought that the sound would help him reestablish the suddenly broken telepathic link with his imp familiar. "Druzil?"

There was no reply, no hint that the imp kept any link at all opened to the cleric. Barjin waited a moment longer, still trying to send his thoughts along the outer passageways, still hoping that Druzil would answer.

Soon, the priest had to admit that his outer eyes had somehow been closed. Perhaps Druzil had been slain, or perhaps an enemy priest had banished the imp back to his own plane. With that uncomfortable thought in mind, Barjin moved to his low-burning brazier. He spoke a few command words, ordering the flames higher and trying to reopen his mysteriously unproductive interplanar gate. He called to midges and manes and lesser denizens; he called to Druzil, hoping that if the imp had been banished, he might bring him back. But the flames crackled unimpeded by any otherworldly presence. Barjin did not know, of course, of the magical powder Druzil had sprinkled to close the gate.

The priest continued his calling for a short while, then realized the futility of it and realized, too, that if Druzil had indeed been defeated, he might have some serious problems brewing. Another thought came to him then, the image of the imp returning to the altar room at the head of the skeletal force with ideas of overthrowing the priest's leadership. Imps had never been known for their undying loyalty.

In either case, Barjin needed to strengthen his own position.

He moved to Mullivy first and spent a long moment

considering how he might further strengthen the zombie. He already had given Mullivy a patchwork armor plating and had magically increased the zombie's strength, but now he had something more devious in mind. He took out a tiny vial and poured a drop of mercury over Mullivy, uttering an arcane chant. The spell completed, Barjin retrieved several flasks of volatile oil and soaked Mullivy's clothes.

Barjin turned to his most powerful ally, Khalif, the mummy.

There was little the priest could do to enhance the already monstrous creation, so he issued a new set of unambiguous commands to it and set it in a more strategic position outside the altar room.

All that remained for Barjin was his personal preparations.

He donned his clerical vestments, enchanted cloth as armored as a knight's suit of mail, and uttered a prayer to enhance this protection even more. He took up the Screaming Maiden, his devilish woman-headed mace, and rechecked the wards at the room's single door. Let his enemies come; whether it was a traitor imp or a host of priests from above, Barjin was confident that the attackers soon would wish they had remained in the outer passages.

* * * * *

Newander moved to comfort Danica, but Percival got there first, dropping from a crossbeam to the woman's shoulder. Danica's smile returned when she looked upon the white squirrel, a reminder of better times, to be sure.

"They sense the raising of the dead," Newander explained, indicating the ghouls. "The meat of their table is the meat of a corpse."

Danica shot him an incredulous look.

"Even if they must create the corpse on their own," Newander replied. "But it is the raising of the dead that brings them." Newander seemed to doubt his own words, but he knew nothing of the necromancer's stone and had no other explanation. "Ghouls will flock to undead from anywhere near, though where these wretches have come from, I cannot guess."

Danica struggled unsteadily to her feet. "It does not matter where they came from," she said. "Only that they are dead and will stay dead this time. Let us go on. Cadderly and the dwarves might have met troubles farther in."

Newander grabbed her arm and held her back. "You cannot go," he insisted.

Danica glared at him.

"My spells are nearly exhausted," the druid explained, "but I have some salves that might help your wounds and a curative spell that can defeat any poison you might have suffered."

"We have no time," Danica argued, pulling free. "Save that poison cure. My wounds are not so serious, but we might need that before this is ended."

"Only a minute for treating your wounds then," Newander argued back, conceding the point concerning the spell but adamant that Danica's scratches at least should be cleaned. He took out a small pouch. "You might be needing me, Lady Danica, but I'll not go in with you if you do not let me tend to your wounds."

Danica wanted no delays, but she didn't doubt the stubborn druid's resolve. She kneeled before Newander and held her torn forearms out to him, and, despite her own stubbornness, she had to admit that the gashes felt much better the instant the druid applied his salves.

They set off again, Newander bearing the torch and his staff, Danica holding her daggers, stained darkly with ghoul gore, and the newest member of the party, Percival, wrapped nervously about Danica's neck and shoulders.

Twenty

Oh, Brother, Me Brother

Me brother!" Ivan wailed, bowing over Pikel's prostrate form. "Oh, me brother!" The dwarf sniffled and wept openly, cradling Pikel's head in his hands.

Cadderly had no words to comfort Ivan. Indeed, the young scholar was nearly as overcome as the dwarf. Pikel had been a dear friend, always ready to listen to Cadderly's latest wild idea, and always adding an emphatic "Oo oi!" just to make Cadderly feel good.

Cadderly had never known the pangs of a friend's death. His mother had died when he was very young, but he didn't remember that. He saw the priests of Ilmater and the dead gluttons in the kitchen, but they were only faces to him, distant and unknown. Now, looking at dear Pikel, he didn't know how he should feel, didn't know what he could do. It seemed a macabre game, and for the very first time in his life, Cadderly understood that some things were beyond his power to control or change, that all his rationale, his intelligence, in the final estimation seemed just a minor thing.

"Ye should've been a druid," Ivan said quietly. "Ye always

were better under the sky than the stone." Ivan let out a great cry and buried his head in Pikel's chest, his shoulders shuddering uncontrollably.

Cadderly could understand the dwarf's pain, but he was shocked nonetheless that Ivan was so openly emotional. The priest wondered if something was wrong with him for not falling over Pikel as Ivan had done, or if Ivan's love for his brother was so much greater than his own feelings for the dwarf. Cadderly kept his wits about him; no matter how agonizing Pikel's death was, if they did not move on and close the bottle, many others would share a similar fate.

"We must go," Cadderly said softly to Ivan.

"Shut yer mouth!" Ivan roared, on the verge of an explosion, never taking his gaze from his brother.

The response caught Cadderly by surprise, but again he did not understand the nature of grief, did not know if it was Ivan who was acting out of sorts or if he was. When the dwarf finally did look back at him, tears streaked his contorted face and Cadderly feared that he knew what was going on.

"The curse," he muttered breathlessly. As far as he could tell, this red mist worked to exaggerate one's emotions. Apparently the curse had found a hold in Ivan's sincere grief, a chink in the tough dwarf's magic-resistant constitution.

Cadderly feared that it was taking hold of Ivan. The dwarf's blubbering increased with each passing moment; he could hardly draw breath, so violent was his weeping.

"Ivan," he said quietly, moving over to put a hand on the dwarf's shoulder. "We can do no more for Pikel. Come away now. We have other business to attend."

Ivan snapped an angry glare on Cadderly and smacked his hands away. "Ye're wanting me to leave him?" the dwarf cried. "Me brother! Me dead brother! No, I'm not going, never going. I'll stay by me brother's side. Stay here and keep me Pikel druid warm!"

"He is dead, Ivan," Cadderly said through his own budding sniffles. "Gone. You cannot keep the warmth in his body.

You cannot do anything for him."

"Shut yer mouth!" Ivan roared again, reaching for his axe.

Cadderly thought the dwarf meant to chop him down, feared that Ivan blamed him for what had happened to Pikel, but Ivan never even found the strength to lift the heavy weapon and instead tumbled back down over Pikel.

Cadderly realized that he would get nowhere reasoning with the grieving dwarf, but Ivan's outburst incited other ideas in the young scholar. There was one emotion that could overrule even grief, and Ivan seemed all too willing to let that emotion take charge.

"You can do nothing," Cadderly said again, "but repay the one who did this to Pikel."

Suddenly Cadderly had Ivan's full attention.

"He is down here, Ivan," Cadderly prodded, though he didn't like leading the dwarf on like this. "Pikel's killer is down here."

"The imp!" Ivan roared, looking around wildly for the creature.

"No," Cadderly replied, "not the imp, but the imp's master."

"The imp's what poisoned me brother!" Ivan protested.

"Yes, but the imp's master brought the imp, and the curse, and all the evil that led to Pikel's demise," replied Cadderly. He knew he was taking license in drawing such conclusions, but if he could get Ivan moving, then it would be worth the deceit. "If we can defeat the master, then the imp and all the evil will follow. The master, Ivan," Cadderly said again, "he who brought the curse."

"Ye brought the curse," Ivan snarled, fingering his two-headed axe again and eyeing Cadderly suspiciously.

"No," Cadderly quickly corrected, seeing his conniving tactics taking an entirely different light. "I played an unfortunate role in its release, but I did not bring it. There is one down here—there must be—who brought the curse and sent the skeletons and the imp down here after us, down here to kill your brother!"

"Where is he?" Ivan cried, springing up from Pikel and clasping his heavy axe in both hands. "Where's me brother's killer?" The dwarf's eyes darted all about wildly, as if he expected some new monster to appear at any moment.

"We must find him," Cadderly prodded. "We can go back the way we came, back into the tunnels I remember."

"Go back?" The idea didn't seem to please Ivan.

"Just until I remember the way, Ivan," Cadderly explained, "then we'll go forward, to the room with the cursed bottle, to where we shall find your brother's killer." He could only hope his words were true and that Ivan would relax by the time they found the room.

"Forward!" Ivan yelled, and he scooped up one of the barely glowing torches, whipped it about frantically to refuel the flame, and stormed off back the way they had come. Cadderly checked to make certain that he had all of his belongings, said a final good-bye to Pikel, and ran to catch up.

They had not gone far when they came upon the first group of skeletons, five monsters wandering down a side passage. The disoriented skeletons, refugees from Druzil's disastrous battle, made no move to attack, but Ivan, blind with rage, turned on them with a fury that Cadderly had never before imagined.

"Ivan, no," Cadderly pleaded, seeing the dwarf's intent. "Let them alone. We have more important . . ."

Ivan never heard him. The dwarf let out a roar and a snarl and rushed at the skeletons. The two closest turned to meet the charge, but Ivan overwhelmed them. He launched a mighty side cut with his axe that cleaved one in half, then shifted the weapon's momentum as it whirled behind him and drove it straight over his head, coming down on top of the second skeleton with enough force to shatter the monster.

Ivan let go of the weapon, entangled once more in bones, and caught the third skeleton with his deer-horned helmet, lifting the monster clear of the ground, shaking it wildly for a moment, then slamming it into the wall. The attack damaged the skeleton, but it also dislodged Ivan's helmet. The clawing fingers of the fourth skeleton found an opening in the dwarf's defenses and dug into the back of his neck.

Cadderly came running down to help, readying his walking stick for a swing at Ivan's newest attacker. Before he could get into the fray, though, Ivan took things into his own hands. He reached around and caught the skeleton by its bony wrist, then pulled and spun for all his life.

Cadderly dove for the ground, nearly sliced by the flying skeleton's legs and feet. Ivan picked up momentum in his twirl and soon had the skeleton spinning straight out at arms' length. He let the momentum build for a moment, then shuffled a step closer to a wall and let the bricks do his work. The skeleton slammed against them and broke apart and Ivan was left holding an unattached bone.

The last of the skeletons was on the dwarf then, and Ivan, dizzy and a bit disoriented, took the monster's first clawing hand squarely in the face. Again Cadderly started to help his friend, but one of the other skeletons was back up and closing, still bearing Ivan's helmet entangled in its ribs.

Ivan slammed a forearm into his attacker's ribs. The dwarf's stubby legs pumped wildly, driving the monster back toward a wall. When it pressed in, Ivan did not stop. His every muscle tensed and then snapped, launching him forward and bringing the only weapon he had available, his forehead, to bear.

He slammed the skeleton in the face, and the creature's skull exploded in the crush between the rock wall and the dwarf's equally tough head. Bits of bone popped out to the sides, other pieces were ground into dust, and Ivan bounced back, his head badly gashed.

Cadderly smacked at the remaining monster with his walking stick and snapped his spindle-disks into its face once and then again. The stubborn creature came on, slashing its bony fingers and forcing Cadderly into retreat. Soon, though, Cadderly felt the wall at his back and had nowhere left to run.

One hand had latched firmly onto Cadderly's shoulder. The other slashed at his face. He got his own hand up to block but found himself helplessly pinned with the bony fingers digging deeper into his flesh. He tried desperately to hook the skeleton's arm under his own, to twist it around and break the monster's grasp, but Cadderly's attack was designed to twist muscles and tendons and inflict such pain on an attacker as to disable him. Skeletons had no muscles or tendons and felt no pain. Cadderly put his one free hand against the skeleton's face and tried to push it away—and got a wicked bite on the wrist for his efforts.

Then the skeleton's head disappeared in an instant, went flying away. Cadderly didn't understand until Ivan's second axe chop, a downward cut, destroyed the skeletal body.

Cadderly leaned back against the wall and clutched at his bloodied wrist. He simply dismissed his own pain a moment later, thinking his wounds minor indeed when he looked upon Ivan.

Pieces of skull bone were embedded in the dwarf's forehead. Blood ran freely down Ivan's face, along the sides of his neck, and from numerous cuts on his gnarly hands. Even more horrifying, a skeleton's broken rib bone stuck out from the side of the dwarf's abdomen. Cadderly could not tell how deeply the bone had gone, but the wound seemed wicked indeed and he was truly amazed that the dwarf was still standing.

He reached for Ivan, meaning to support his friend, fearing that Ivan would topple.

Ivan roughly slapped his hand away. "No time for coddling," the dwarf barked. "Where's the one that killed me brother?"

"You need help," Cadderly replied, horrified by his friend's condition. "Your wounds . . ."

"Forget them," Ivan retorted. "Get me to the one that killed me brother!"

"But Ivan," Cadderly continued to protest. He pointed to

the skeletal rib.

Ivan's eyes did widen when he noticed the ghastly wound, but he only shrugged his shoulders, reached down to grasp the bone, and pulled it free, casually tossing it aside as though he hadn't even noticed the several inches of bloodstains upon it.

Ivan's attitude was similarly uncaring when he tried to put his helmet back on, only to find that the embedded bones blocked him from seating it correctly on his head. He plucked a few chips from his forehead, then, with a grunt, forced the helmet into place.

Cadderly could only assume that the cursing mist had increased the dwarf's rage to a point where Ivan simply did not acknowledge pain. He knew that dwarves were a tough lot, Ivan more than most, but this was beyond belief.

"Ye said ye'd take me to him!" Ivan roared, and his words rang like a threat in Cadderly's ears. "Ye said ye'd find the way!" In a move of concession, Ivan reached up and tore off Cadderly's cloak and used it to quickly tie off his wound.

Cadderly had to be satisfied with that. He knew that the best he could do for everybody, Ivan included, was to find and close the smoking bottle as quickly as he could. Only then would the enraged dwarf allow Cadderly or anyone else to tend to his injuries.

Only then, but Cadderly was not so certain that Ivan would make it that far.

They soon came back to the original areas where they had encountered the undead monsters. All was quiet now, deathly still, giving Cadderly the opportunity to carefully reconstruct his first passage through. He thought that he was making some progress, leading Ivan down several adjoining passages, when he noticed some movement far down one hall, at the very edge of his narrow light beam.

Ivan noticed it, too, and he set off at once, his grief for his dead brother transferred again into uncontrollable battle lust.

Cadderly fumbled with his bandoleer and tried futilely to

keep up with the dwarf, pleading with Ivan to let this enemy go.

It was a single skeleton this time, wandering aimlessly at first, but then coming straight in at the charging dwarf.

Cadderly came to a very important decision at that moment.

He held his light beam in one hand and his loaded crossbow in the other, lining both up between the horns of the dwarf's helmet at the skeletal face beyond. Cadderly had never intended his custom-designed crossbow to be used as a weapon, especially not while firing the exploding darts. He had designed the bow for opening locked doors, or blasting away troublesome tree branches that scraped against his window, or a variety of other nonviolent purposes. Also, he had to admit, he had designed the crossbow and the bolts in part for the simple challenge of designing them. But Cadderly had vowed to himself, as much as an excuse as anything else, never to use the darts or the bow as a weapon, never to unleash the concentrated violence of the explosive darts against a living target.

The arguments in this instance were many, of course. Ivan could ill afford another fight, even against a single skeleton, and the skeleton, after all, was not really a living creature.

Still, Cadderly's guilt hovered over him as he took aim. He knew that he was breaking the spirit of his vow.

He fired. The bolt arced over Ivan's head and crashed into the charging skeleton's face. The initial impact wasn't so great, but then the dart collapsed, setting off the *Oil of Impact*.

When the dust cleared a moment later, the skeleton's head and neck were gone. The headless bones stood a moment longer, then dropped with a rattle.

Ivan, just a few strides away, stopped abruptly and stared in amazement, his jaw hanging open and his dark eyes wide. He turned slowly back to Cadderly, who only shrugged apologetically and looked away.

"It had to be done," Cadderly remarked, more to himself

than to Ivan.

"And ye did it well!" Ivan replied, coming back down the passage. He clapped Cadderly on the back, though Cadderly did not feel heroic in the least.

"Let us go on," Cadderly said quietly, slipping the crossbow back into its wide and shallow sheath.

They crossed under another low archway, Cadderly beginning to believe that they were again on the right path, and then came to a fork in the dusty passage. Two tunnels ran out from the one, parallel and very near together. Cadderly thought for a moment, then started down the right side. He went only a few steps, though, before he recognized his location more clearly. He backtracked, ignoring Ivan's grumbling, and moved at a determined pace down the left passage. This corridor went on for just a short distance, then angled farther to the left and opened into a wider passage.

Standing sarcophagi filled the alcove in this passage, confirmation to Cadderly that he had chosen the right path. A few steps in and beyond a slight bend, he knew beyond doubt. Far in front of them, at the end of the passage, loomed a door, cracked open and with light shining through.

"That the place?" Ivan demanded, though he had already guessed the answer. He started off before Cadderly nodded in reply.

Again Cadderly tried futilely to slow the dwarf's charge, desiring a more cautious approach. He was just a couple of steps behind Ivan when the last sarcophagus swung open and a mummy stepped out to block the way. Too enraged to care, Ivan continued on undaunted, but Cadderly no longer followed. The young scholar was frozen with fear, stricken by the sheer evilness of the powerful undead presence. The skeletons had been terrifying, but they seemed only minor inconveniences next to this monster.

"Irrational," Cadderly tried to tell himself. It was acceptable to be afraid, but ridiculous to let that fear paralyze him in so urgent a situation.

"Outta me way!" Ivan roared, bearing in. He chopped viciously with his axe, scoring a hit, but, unlike the battle against the skeletons, the weapon met stiff resistance this time. The mummy's thick wraps deflected much of the blow's force, and pieces of the linen came unraveled, snarling the axe-head and preventing Ivan from following through.

The hit hardly hindered the mummy. It clubbed with its arm, catching Ivan on the shoulder and sending him spinning into the nearest alcove. He crashed heavily and nearly swooned but stubbornly, unsteadily, forced himself back to his feet.

The mummy was waiting for him. A second hit knocked the dwarf down to his back.

That would have been the end of Ivan Bouldershoulder had it not been for Cadderly. His first attack was almost inadvertent, for the mummy, in going after Ivan, crossed the direct, narrow beam of Cadderly's light tube. A creature of the night, of a dark and lightless world, Khalif was neither accustomed to, nor tolerant of, brightness of any kind.

Seeing the mummy recoil and lift its scabrous arm to block the beam restored a bit of composure in Cadderly. He kept the light focused on the monster, forcing it back from Ivan, while he nimbly loaded another dart with his free hand. Cadderly held no reservations about using his crossbow on this monster; the mummy was simply too hideous for his conscience to argue.

Still shielding its eyes, the mummy advanced on Cadderly, slapping at the beam of light with every sliding step.

The first dart buried itself deeply into the mummy's chest before exploding, and the blast sent the monster back a couple of steps and left scorch marks both front and back on the creature's linen wrappings. If it had suffered any serious damage, though, the mummy didn't show it, for it came on again.

Cadderly scrambled to reload the crossbow. His design had been good, fortunately, and the crank was not difficult to execute. A second dart joined the first, again driving the monster backward.

The mummy came on again, and again after Cadderly had shot it a third time, and each time its stubborn advance brought it a step or two closer to the frantic young man. The fourth shot proved disastrous to Cadderly, for the dart's initial momentum drove it right through the mummy without ever igniting the magical oil. The mummy hardly slowed and Cadderly nearly held the crossbow right against its filthy wrappings when he fired his fifth shot.

This time the dart had more effect, but again it only slowed, and did not stop, the monster. Cadderly had no time to load another dart.

"Coming!" slurred Ivan as he crawled from the alcove.

Cadderly doubted that the dwarf could help him, even if Ivan could reach the monster in time, which he obviously couldn't. The young scholar knew, too, that neither of his conventional weapons, spindle-disks or walking stick, could hurt this monster.

He had just one weapon to use. He stuck the light tube out in front of him, slowing the mummy further, causing it to shield its eyes and half turn away from him, then he dropped his crossbow and reached with his free hand for the waterskin hanging at his side. He grabbed it by the extended nozzle, tucked it tight under his arm, and used his thumb to pop off its gooey cap. Cadderly squeezed with his arm, slowly and steadily sending a stream of the blessed water into his attacker's face.

The holy water sizzled as it struck the evilly enchanted monster and, for the first time in the battle, the mummy revealed its agony. It let out an unearthly, spine-chilling wail that filled Cadderly with fear and even stopped Ivan temporarily. It was the proverbial bark with no bite, for while the mummy continued to advance, it purposely shied away from the man with the light beam and the stinging water. Soon it had passed Cadderly altogether, but it continued down the passage, roaring with pain and frustration, clubbing with its powerful arms against the walls, the sarcophagi, and anything else that got in its way.

Ivan came rushing past Cadderly, intent on resuming the battle.

"The man who killed your brother is behind the door!" Cadderly cried as quickly as he could, desperate to stop the dwarf this time. He couldn't know the truth of his claim, of course, but at that critical moment, he would have said anything to turn Ivan around.

Predictably, Ivan did wheel about. He let out a growl and charged back past Cadderly, forgetting all about the fleeing mummy, his unblinking eyes glued instead on the door at the end of the passage.

Cadderly saw disaster coming. He recalled the newly constructed wall in the wine cellar and the blasts that had followed Pikel's battering-ram charge. He had to believe that this door might also be magically warded, and he saw that the door was heavy, iron-bound. If Ivan didn't get right through, but was held in the area of exploding glyphs . . .

Cadderly dove to the ground, pulling a dart and grabbing for his crossbow. In a single motion, he cocked it, fitted the bolt, and spun about, using his light beam to show him the target.

The dart passed Ivan just a stride from the door. It didn't hit the lock area directly but exploded with enough force to weaken the jam.

Surprised by the sudden blast, but unable to stop even if he chose to, Ivan barreled in.

Twenty-One

A Well-Placed Blow

No!" she heard the druid say at her back, but it was a distant call, as if Newander's voice were no more than a memory of some other time and some other place. All that mattered to Danica was the wall, made of stonework now and not like the natural dirt tunnel that had led them in. The wall, inviting her, enticing her, to emulate her long-dead hero.

That distant voice spoke again, but in clicks and chatter that Danica could not understand.

A furry tail fell down over Danica's eyes, breaking her concentration on the stone. She moved one hand merely by reflex to push aside the distraction.

Following the druid's instructions, Percival promptly bit her.

Danica dipped her shoulder and came across with an instinctive chop that would have killed the squirrel. She recognized Percival before she struck, though, and that led her again out of the red mist and back to reality.

"The wall," she stammered. "I meant to . . ."

"It is not your fault," Newander said to her. "The curse

affected you again. It would seem to be an endless fight."

Danica slumped back against the stone, weary and ashamed. She had put every effort into resisting the intrusive mist, had seen it for what it was and planted deeply in her own thinking the logical conclusion that such destructive impulses must be avoided. Yet here she was, near the heart of danger, abandoning their entire hopes for success for the sake of her curse-enhanced desires.

"Do not accept the guilt," Newander said to her. "You are braving the curse better than any of the priests above us. You have come this far against it, and that alone is more than most others can say."

"The dwarves walk with Cadderly," Danica reminded him.

"Do not hold yourself against that measure," Newander warned. "You are no dwarf. The bearded folk have a natural resistance to magic that no human can match. Theirs is not a question of self-discipline, Lady Danica, but of physical differences."

Danica realized that the druid spoke the truth, but the knowledge that Pikel and Ivan had an advantage over her in resisting the curse did little to diminish her sense of guilt. For all of the druid's talk, Danica considered the intrusive mist a mental challenge, a test of discipline.

"What of Newander?" she asked suddenly, more sarcastically than she had intended. "Does the blood of the bearded folk run in your veins? You are no dwarf. Why, then, are you not affected?"

The druid looked away; it was his turn to feel the weight of guilt. "I do not know," he admitted, "but you must believe that I feel the curse keenly with my every step. "Cadderly guessed that the mist pushes a person to what is in his heart. The gluttons eat themselves to death. The suffering priests cut each other apart in religious frenzy. My own druid brothers revert to animal form, losing themselves in altered states of being. Why, then, is Newander not running with the animals?"

Danica recognized that the druid's last question was a

source of great and sincere anguish. They had discussed this
once before, but Newander had offered little explanation for
himself, focusing his responses on why Cadderly might have
escaped the curse.

"My guess is that the curse has found no hold on my heart,
that my own desires are not known to me," the druid went on.
"Have I failed at my calling?"

Tears rolled openly down Newander's face and he appeared
on the verge of a breakdown, a clear sign to Danica that he was
indeed being affected by the red mist. "Have I no calling?"
Newander wailed. He crumbled to the floor, head in hands, his
shoulders shuddering with heavy sobs.

"You are mistaken," Danica said with enough force to command the druid's attention. "If you have failed in your calling, or
if you have no calling, then why do you retain the magical spells
that are a gift of your god, Silvanus? You brought the vines in
my window, and the moss to life against the ghouls."

Newander composed himself, intrigued by Danica's words.

He found the strength to stand and this time did not look
away from her.

"Perhaps it is the truth in your heart that has led you to
defeat the curse," Danica reasoned. "When did you first feel the
curse acting upon you?"

Newander thought back a couple of days, to when he had
returned to the library to find Arcite and Cleo already in the
throes of their shape change. "I felt it soon after I returned," he
explained. "I had been out in the mountains, watching over an
eagle aerie." Newander recalled that time clearly, remembered
his own insight concerning the su-monsters. "I knew that something was out of sorts as soon as I came back in the library's
doors. I went to find my druid brothers, but, alas, they were
deep into their animal forms by then, and I could not reach
them."

"There is your answer," Danica said after a moment of
thought. "You are a priest of natural order, and this curse is
certainly a perversion of that order. You said that you can sense

the presence of undead—so, I believe, did you sense the presence of the curse."

How had he known that the ghouls were coming? Newander wondered. There were spells to detect the presence of such undead, but he had not enacted any and still knew that they were there, just as he had known that the su-monsters were evil creatures and not just predatory animals. The implications of his insight nearly overwhelmed the druid.

"You give me more credit than I deserve," he said somberly to Danica.

"You are a priest of the natural order," Danica said again. "I do not think you alone have resisted this curse, but you were not, are not, alone. You walk with your faith, and it is that sincere calling that has given you the strength to resist. Arcite and Cleo had no warning. The curse was upon them before they knew anything was wrong, but their failure forewarned you of the danger, and with that warning, you have been able to keep true to your calling."

Newander shook his head, not convinced, not daring to believe that he possessed such inner strength. He had no rebuttals against Danica's reasoning, though, and he would not deny anything where Silvanus, the Oak Father, was concerned. He had given his heart to Silvanus long ago, and there his heart remained, despite any curiosities Newander might hold for the ways of progress and civilization. Was it possible that he was so true a disciple of the Oak Father? Was it possible that what he had perceived as failure, in not transforming into animal form, as Arcite and Cleo had done, might actually reflect strength?

"We lose time in asking questions we cannot answer," he said at length, his voice more steady. "Whatever the cause, both you and I found the way clear."

Danica looked back to the stone wall with concern. "For now at least," she added. "Let us be off again, before my will wanes."

They crossed under several archways, Danica holding the torch far out in front of her to burn the unrelenting cobwebs from their path. Neither of them had much experience with travel underground, or with the common designs of catacombs, and their course was a wandering one; they chose tunnels more or less at random. Danica was thoughtful enough to scratch directional marks at the more confusing turns, in case they had to retrace their steps, but still she feared that she and the druid would become lost in the surprisingly intricate complex.

They saw some signs of previous passage—torn webbing hanging in loose strands, an upset crate in one corner—but whether these had been caused by Cadderly, by other monsters such as the ghouls, or simply by some animal that had made its home in the catacombs, neither could say.

Their torch burned low as they entered one long passage. Several side corridors ran off this one, mostly along the right-hand wall, and Danica and Newander agreed that they would stay the course this time and not continue to wander in circles.

They passed by the first few passages, Danica entering just a few feet with the torch to get a quick glimpse of what lay down each, but stayed in the main tunnel and meant to until they reached its end.

Finally they came to a passage they could not ignore. Danica went in, again for a quick perusal. "They have been here!" she cried out, the realization drawing her farther down the tunnel. The sights there confirmed Danica's suspicions. A battle had been fought here; dozens of bone piles lay strewn about the floor and several skulls, forcibly removed from their skeletal bodies, greeted them with sightless eye sockets. Two lines of piled crates formed a defensive run farther in, a place where Danica soon reasoned that Cadderly and the dwarves had made their stand.

"The bones agree with my sensing of the undead," Newander said grimly, "but we cannot be certain that it was our friends who fought them here."

The confirmation came even as he spoke, as Danica moved her torch slowly about for a wider view of the battle-torn area.

"Pikel!" the woman cried, running to the fallen dwarf. Pikel lay cold and still just as Ivan had left him, his burly arms crossed over his chest and his tree-trunk club lying at his side.

Danica fell to her knees to examine the dwarf but had no doubts that he was dead. She shook her head as she studied his wounds, for none of them seemed serious enough to fell one of Pikel's toughness.

Newander understood her confusion. He knelt beside her and uttered a few words as he waved his hand slowly over the body. "There is a poison in this one," the druid announced grimly. "A wicked brew indeed, gone straight to his heart."

Danica cupped her hands under Pikel's head and gently lifted his face to hers. He had been a dear friend, possibly the most likable person Danica ever had known. It occurred to her, holding him, that he had not been dead for very long. His lips had gone blue, but there was no swelling at all and there remained warmth in his body.

Danica's eyes widened and she turned on Newander. "After we fought the ghouls, you told me that you had a spell to counter any poisons I might have contracted," she said.

"And so I do," Newander replied, understanding her intent, "but the poison has done its work on this one. My spell cannot undo the dwarf's death."

"Use the spell," Danica insisted. She moved quickly, propping Pikel under the neck with one arm and tilting his head backward.

"But it will not—"

"Use it, Newander!" Danica snapped at him. The druid backed off a step, fearing that the mist had again taken hold of his companion.

"Trust me, I beg," Danica continued, softening her tone, for she recognized the druid's sudden caution.

Newander didn't understand what Danica might have in mind, but after all they had been through, he did trust her. He paused a moment to consider the spell, then took an oak leaf from his pocket and crumbled it on top of the dwarf, uttering the proper chant.

Danica opened Pikel's cloak and unbuckled the breastplates

of his heavy armor. She looked to Newander for confirmation
that his spell was complete.

"If there is any poison left in this one, it has been neutralized," the druid assured her.

It was Danica's turn. She closed her eyes and thought of
Grandmaster Penpahg D'Ahn's most prized scroll, the notes of
physical suspension. Penpahg D'Ahn had stopped his breathing, even his heart, for several hours. One day Danica meant to
do the same. She was not yet ready for such a demanding trial,
she knew, but there were aspects of Penpahg D'Ahn's writings,
particularly those involved with coming out of the physical suspension, that she knew would be of help to her now.

Danica thought of the steps required to restart the suspended heart. In the writings, these were internal, of course,
but their principles might be duplicated by an outside force.

Danica laid Pikel back down flat, unbuttoned his vest, and
pulled his nightshirt up high. She could hardly see the details
of his chest through the virtual sweater of hair, but she per-
sisted, feeling his ribs and hoping that a dwarf's anatomy was
not so different from a human's.

She had found the spot—she thought. She looked back to
Newander for support, then, to the druid's obvious surprise,
turned back suddenly and rapped her free hand sharply into
the hollow of the dwarf's breast. She waited just a moment,
then rapped again. Danica's intensity multiplied; all her heart
went into her work on Pikel, and that only encouraged the cursing mist to creep back in.

"Lady Danica!" Newander cried, grabbing the frantic
woman's shoulder. "You should show more respect to the
dead!"

Danica whipped her arm around and back, hooking the
druid behind the knees. A sudden jerk sent Newander to the
floor, then Danica resumed her work, furiously pounding away.
She heard a rib crack but wound up for yet another blow.

Newander was back at her, grabbing her more forcefully
this time and tearing her from the corpse. They wrestled for a

moment, Danica easily gaining an advantage. She put Newander flat on his back and scrambled atop him, her fist coming up dangerously over the druid's face.

"Oo oi!"

The call froze both Danica and Newander.

"What have you done?" Newander gasped.

Danica, as surprised as the druid, shook her head and slowly turned about. There sat Pikel, looking sore and confused but very much alive. He smiled when he gazed upon Danica.

The woman rushed off Newander and tackled the dwarf, wrapping him in a tight hug. Newander came over, too, patting both of them heartily on the shoulders.

"A miracle," the druid muttered.

Danica knew better, knew that reviving Pikel had involved some very logical and well-documented principles in the teachings of Grandmaster Penpahg D'Ahn. Nonetheless, Danica, too amazed by what she had done and too relieved to see Pikel again drawing breath, did not find the resolve to answer.

"This is a fortunate meeting," Danica reasoned after the hugging had ended.

"Oo oi!" Pikel was quick to agree.

"More than for you," Danica started to explain.

Newander cast her a curious look.

"This is our first proof that the tunnel we entered connects to the area that Cadderly went into," said Danica. "Until we found Pikel, we were lost."

"Now we know," added Newander, "and we know, too, that we have crossed Cadderly's path. Perhaps now we shall find a clearer trail to follow." He bent low with the torch, studying the floor for some signs, but came up a moment later shaking his head. "It is a tiny path if it is one at all," he lamented.

A smile widened on Danica's face. "Tiny for us, perhaps," she said. "But maybe clear enough for Percival."

Pikel sat confused, but Newander's smile surpassed Danica's. The druid uttered a few sounds to Percival, asking the squirrel to lead them to Cadderly. Percival hopped about for a few moments, scratching at the ground and searching for some pattern, either in the scuff marks or the scent.

He caught the trail and set off down the passage, Newander right behind. Danica helped Pikel to his feet. He was still unsteady, and still thoroughly confused, but he called upon the two most prominent dwarven traits, toughness and stubbornness, and made his way beside the young woman.

* * * * *

Sleep had been such a pleasant thing, but somewhere deep in his thoughts Druzil realized that he was dangerously vulnerable lying in a crack in the wall of a deserted corridor. The imp pulled himself out of the cubby and shape-changed back to his more customary, batwinged form. Somewhere in his slumber, he had lost the concentration necessary for invisibility and could not sort through the fog that remained in his mind enough to recover it. That sleepy fog was heavy, but the imp kept one thought clear: He must get back to Barjin, back to the safety of his magical gate connection to Castle Trinity. He knew that someone recently had exited this passage and, having no desire to meet any enemies, he took a roundabout, meandering course.

He stopped and held very still a short while later when the crazed mummy came storming by, smashing anything and everything in its path. Druzil realized that something had gone terribly wrong, recognized that the mummy, scorched and blasted in many places, had gone out of control.

The monster was gone then, slamming down a side corridor, growling and bashing things with its heavy arms with every step.

Druzil's wings flapped slowly as he half-walked and half-flew back toward the altar room.

Yes, Barjin would help him, and if not Barjin, then surely Aballister. With that thought in mind, the imp sent out a weak, sleepy message to his master back at Castle Trinity.

Twenty-Two

Face to Face

Ivan hit the loose-swinging door with a terrific impact, jolting it free of one of its hinges. Cadderly's fears were proved true, for several fiery explosions went off in rapid succession as Ivan crossed the threshold. If the door had stopped, or even delayed his charge, he would have been roasted.

As it was, Cadderly was not certain if the dwarf had survived. Ivan skidded into the room on his face, wisps of smoke rising from several points on his body. Cadderly rushed in right behind to get to his friend; he could only hope that no glyphs remained.

The young scholar didn't quite make it to Ivan, though. As soon as he entered the room, squinting in the brightness of the several torches and blazing brazier, he saw that he and Ivan were not alone.

"You have done well to come so far," Barjin said calmly, standing halfway across the room, beside the altar that held the ever-smoking bottle. Torches lined the wall to either side of the priest, but the brighter light came from a brazier along the wall to Cadderly's right, which Cadderly correctly guessed was an interplanar gate.

"I applaud your resilience," Barjin continued, his tone teasing, "futile though it will prove."

Every memory came rushing back to Cadderly in clear order and focus when he saw Barjin. The first thought that crossed his mind was that he would go back up and have a few nasty words with Kierkan Rufo, the man who had, he believed, kicked him down the stairway from the wine cellar in the first place. His resolve to scold Rufo did not take firm hold, though, not when Cadderly considered the dangers before him. His eyes did not linger on the priest, but rather on the man standing next to Barjin.

"Mullivy?" he asked, though he knew by Mullivy's posture and the grotesque bend of his wrecked arm that this was not the groundskeeper he once had known.

The dead man did not reply.

"A friend of yours?" Barjin teased, draping an arm over his zombie. "Now he is my friend, too. I could have him kill you quite easily," Barjin went on.

"But, you see, I believe I shall reserve that pleasure for myself." He removed the obsidian-headed mace from his belt, its sculpted visage that of a pretty young girl. Next, Barjin pulled on the conical hood hanging in back of his clerical robes. This fit over his head as a helmet might, with holes cut for Barjin's eyes. Cadderly had heard about enchanted, protecting vestments and he knew that his nemesis was armored.

"For all your valiant efforts, young priest, you remain a minuscule thorn in my side," Barjin remarked. He took a step toward Cadderly but stopped suddenly when Ivan hopped back to his feet.

The dwarf shook his head vigorously, then looked about, as if seeing the room for the first time. He glanced at Cadderly, then focused on Barjin. "Tell me, lad," Ivan asked, swinging his double-bladed axe up to a ready position on his shoulder, "is he the one who killed me brother?"

*   *   *   *   *

Aballister wiped a cloth over his sweaty brow. He could not bear to continue peering through his magical mirror, but he had not the strength to turn his eyes away. He had felt Barjin's urgency when first he sent his thoughts to the distant altar room, unable to bear his inability to contact his imp. Aballister worried for Druzil and for the cleric, though his fears for and of Barjin were double-sided indeed. For all of his ambiguity, though, for all of his fears of Barjin and the power gains his rival would enjoy, Aballister honestly believed he did not want to see *Tuanta Quiro Miancay*, the Most Fatal Horror, fail.

Then the enemies had revealed themselves—himself, for Aballister hardly took note of the stumbling dwarf. It was the young scholar who held the wizard's thoughts, the tall and straight lad, twenty years old perhaps, with the familiar, inquisitive eyes.

Aballister sensed Barjin's mounting confidence and knew that the evil priest was back in control, that Barjin and *Tuanta Quiro Miancay* would not be defeated.

Somehow that notion seemed even more disturbing to the wizard. He stared hard and long at the young scholar, a boy really, who had come in bravely and foolishly to face his doom.

*   *   *   *   *

Cadderly nodded at Ivan. The dwarf's eyes narrowed dangerously as he glared back at the evil priest. "Ye shouldn't have done that," Ivan growled in a low and death-promising tone. He held his axe high and began a steady advance. "Ye shouldn't have—"

Waves of mental energy stopped Ivan in midsentence and midstep. Barjin's spell broke the dwarf's thought patterns, holding him firmly in place. Ivan struggled with all his mental strength and all the resistance a dwarf could muster, but

Barjin was no minor spellcaster and this was his evilly blessed altar room, where his clerical magic was at its highest. Ivan managed a few indecipherable sounds, then stopped talking and moving altogether.

"Ivan?" Cadderly asked, his voice shaky as he suspected his companion's fate.

"Do keep talking," Barjin taunted. "The dwarf can hear your every word, though I assure you that he'll not respond."

Barjin's ensuing laughter sent shivers through Cadderly's bones. They had come so far and through so much. Pikel had died to get them here, and Ivan had taken a terrible beating.

And now to fail. Looking at this evil priest, with gruesome Mullivy standing obediently at his side, Cadderly knew that he was overmatched.

"You battled through my outer defenses, and for that you deserve my applause," Barjin continued, "but if you believed my true power would be revealed to you out in the empty and meaningless corridors, then know your folly! Look upon me, foolish young priest—" he waved a hand to the ever-smoking bottle "—and look upon the agent of Talona that you yourself brought to life. *Tuanta Quiro Miancay*, the Most Fatal Horror! You should feel blessed, young priest, for your pitiful library is the first to feel the awesome power of the chaos that will dominate the region for centuries to come!"

At that awful moment, the threat did not sound so hollow in Cadderly's ears. Talona—he knew the name: the Lady of Poison, of disease.

"Did you expect to find the bottle unguarded?" Barjin laughed. "Did you think to stroll in here after defeating a few minor monsters and simply close the flask that you yourself—" again the priest emphasized those painful words "—opened?"

Cadderly hardly heard the banter. His attention had gone to the bottle and the steady stream of pinkish mist that issued from it. He thought of loading his crossbow and putting an explosive dart into the bottle. Where would this Talona's agent be then? Cadderly wondered. But Cadderly feared that action, feared that to destroy the bottle would only release the evil agent, or whatever it was, in full.

His attention was stolen from the bottle suddenly, and he realized that the choice, if ever he had one, had passed. The evil priest strode casually toward him, his arm uplifted and holding a curious black mace, its head the image of a pretty young girl, an innocent face so very out of place atop a weapon, a face that strangely reminded Cadderly of Danica.

* * * * *

Aballister did not pause to consider his actions. His thoughts focused on the dwarf, standing rigid a few steps ahead of the young man. The wizard summoned all of his powers, sent a spell into the magic mirror and across the miles, tried to use the scrying device as a magical gate for his focused magical energies.

The mirror's own dweomer, not designed for such uses, resisted the attempt. It could be used to see distant places, to converse with viewed creatures, even to transport Aballister to those places viewed, but Aballister tried to carry that ability farther now, to send not only his thoughts or physical being but his magical energy flowing to the rigid dwarf.

It would have been a difficult enough task, even for a wizard as powerful as Aballister, if the attempt had been made on a human, but Ivan, though fully in the throes of Barjin's paralyzing spell, fought back with typical dwarven stubbornness against the wizard's intrusions.

Aballister gritted his teeth and focused his concentration.

Veins stood out on his forehead; he thought the toll of the attempt would destroy him, but Barjin was close to the young man now—too close!—the awful mace held high.

Aballister put his lips right up against the mirror and whispered, hoping that the dwarf alone would hear, "Let me in, you fool!"

*   *   *   *   *

Barjin came on, smiling wickedly, victoriously. Cadderly gave him every reason for confidence, offering no outward sign of resistance. The young scholar did have his ram's head walking stick in one hand, but he hadn't even lifted it yet.

In truth, Cadderly had decided on another defense, the only one he believed could slow this imposing priest. His free hand clenched and unclenched at his side, tightening the muscles, straightening a single finger for the coming strike. He had seen, and keenly felt, Danica do this a dozen times.

Barjin was only a step away, moving cautiously now for fear that Cadderly would take a swipe at him with the walking stick.

Cadderly kept its butt end firmly to the ground. Barjin maneuvered to the side, away from the weapon, and swung his mace in a teasing cut. Cadderly easily stepped back, though his concentration nearly faltered when he saw the mace's head transform into the leering, open-mouthed visage of some unearthly monster, fanged and hungry.

He kept his wits enough to retaliate, though, and with Barjin expecting him to strike with the walking stick, his hand got through the cleric's defenses.

Cadderly drove his finger powerfully into Barjin's shoulder.

He knew that he had hit the precise spot, just as Danica had so often done to him. A look of sincere confusion crossed the evil priest's face, and Cadderly nearly squealed in glee.

"Withering Touch!" he proclaimed.

While Barjin was indeed confused, his arm, and the cruel mace at the end of it, did not fall limply to his side.

Cadderly was confused as well, and he barely reacted, at the very last instant, as Barjin's mace whipped in with more determination. Cadderly turned and dove, but the weapon clipped his shoulder, the evilly contorted face biting a deep gash. Cadderly had intended to roll back to his feet a short distance away, but the hit put him off balance and he crashed heavily instead into one of the room's many bookcases.

The wound itself was not too severe, but the frozen waves of agony rolling through the young scholar's body most certainly were. Cadderly shuddered and trembled, hardly able to comprehend, hardly able to focus through the dizzy blur. He knew that he was doomed, knew that he could never recover in time to parry or dodge the priest's next attack.

"—killed me brother!" he heard Ivan roar, right where the dwarf had left off, and then he heard Barjin yelp in surprise.

Ivan's axe pounded into the priest's back, a blow that would have felled any man, but Barjin was protected. His magical vestments absorbed the brunt of the hit; the priest didn't even lose his breath. He wheeled about, swiping with his mace in response.

Skilled and seasoned, Ivan Bouldershoulder was ready.

From just his single attack, he realized that the priest was somehow powerfully armored. Barjin's blow cut harmlessly short, and Ivan stepped in behind it, hooked one head of his weapon under Barjin's shoulder, and heaved with all his strength, sending Barjin tumbling head over heels back toward the altar in the center of the room.

Ivan dropped his weapon's head to the ground and clasped his legs about its handle so that he could spit into his hands before continuing. The priest had a wicked weapon and nearly invulnerable armor, but the fiery dwarf had no doubts as to how this fight would end. "You shouldn't have killed me brother," Ivan muttered one more time, then he grabbed his axe and moved in to finish the work.

Barjin had other ideas. He had no time to ponder how the dwarf might have broken free from his binding spell, and it didn't really matter anyway. Barjin understood the fury in this formidable foe, a curse-enhanced rage that more than evened the odds, but Barjin didn't play with even odds.

He scrambled over to the wall behind Mullivy. "Kill the dwarf!" he instructed his zombie, and he pulled a burning torch from its sconce and touched it to Mullivy's shoulder. The zombie's oil-soaked clothing ignited immediately, but

Barjin's protective spell did not fail. While the flames consumed the oil and Mullivy's clothes, the zombie's body was quite unharmed.

Ivan's startled response as the flaming zombie bore down on him would have made Pikel proud: "Oo oi!"

Cadderly started to rise, but the continuing, debilitating chilling bite of his wound sent him spiraling back to the floor. He tried to shake away the pain, tried to find some focus.

He saw Ivan swiping wildly but sorely missing his mark as the dwarf steadily backed away from the fiery zombie. Mullivy's advance showed no concern for the dwarf's meager attacks. Cadderly heard the evil priest laughing, somewhere back by the altar, by the cursing bottle. The priest would get Ivan, even if the flaming zombie did not, Cadderly knew. Then the priest would get him, and then this Most Fatal Horror, this evil agent of an evil goddess, would win over the Edificant Library fully and destroy everything the young scholar valued.

"No!" Cadderly managed to cry, multiplying his concentration tenfold.

The devilish mace had done its work well, even in a glancing blow on Cadderly's shoulder. The mace had a life of its own, an inner and foul energy spawned somewhere in the lowest pits of hell.

Cadderly continued to battle against its stunning touch, tried to realign his physical control with his mental determination, but his body didn't heed to his commands; there remained a long road to travel.

*　*　*　*　*

Nothing rose to hinder the three companions' progress, and Percival appeared quite adept at following Cadderly's trail. They came through several passageways, always slowing to peer into the nearest alcoves and ensure that no monsters waited to spring out.

Pikel grew steadier with each passing step but seemed

distracted, introspective. Danica could appreciate his somber mood; he had just passed through death and returned. What tales might the enlightened dwarf tell? Danica wondered.

When she questioned him about the experience, though, he said only, "Oo," and would not elaborate.

At many places, they could confirm that Percival was leading them correctly. Three-way alcoves, thick with webbing on one side, had been burned clear on the other.

Soon the party came to a fork in the tunnel. Hardly hesitating, Percival scampered off down the right hand side.

Sounds of battle, not far off, echoed in their ears.

The squirrel stopped suddenly and chattered excitedly, but his squeaks and chirps were lost in the sudden commotion.

Pikel, Danica, and Newander heard the fighting, and none of them stopped to listen to the squirrel's banter. The noise came from farther down the tunnel; that was all they needed to know. Off they charged, the dwarf no longer introspective, but head down and running to his brother's aid, and Danica and the druid no less determined to help their friends.

When they came to the altar room wall, they heard Ivan growling about some "flaming hunk of walking kindling," and understood their error. While the words were clear, the path certainly was not. No doors lined this section of the passage, just blank wall.

Percival came up chattering and scolding.

"We have come the wrong way, so says the squirrel!" Newander told them. "The path tracks back to the left!"

Danica nodded. "Run, then!" she cried.

She and Newander started away, but both stopped abruptly to regard Pikel, who was not following.

The agitated dwarf hopped up and down, stubby legs pumping rapidly, his whole body building into a tremendous tremble.

"Me brudder!" Pikel cried, and he lowered both his head and his tree trunk and burst forward into the brick wall.

Twenty-Three

In the Druid's Heart

The wall was made only of brick and mortar and was no match for the rage of Pikel Bouldershoulder. The dwarf battered through into the altar room, sending up a cloud of dust and a shower of bricks.

Pikel stood in the new doorway for a moment, his eyes darting about to take in the scene. Several bricks came straight down, bouncing off his pot helmet with dull clangs, but Pikel seemed not to notice. He was looking for Ivan, his "brudder," and it would take a lot more than a few chunks of stone, however heavy, to deter him.

Then he saw Ivan, far to his left, near the room's original door and backing away from a flaming humanoid creature. Repelled by the intense heat, Ivan's defensive chops were falling short and, fast approaching a corner, Ivan soon would be out of running room.

"Oo oi!" Pikel cried, and he bounded off, pot-covered head and tree trunk leading the way.

Danica started in right behind, but Newander stopped her. She turned and saw a look of sudden revelation on the druid's face, an expression that quickly changed to one of sincere joy.

"You spoke the truth, dear lady," Newander said. "It was not ambivalence, but a sense of order that kept me free of the cursing mist. Now I know how I was spared, why I was spared, and, in truth, it was a power far beyond my own will."

Danica consider the profound changes that had come over the man. No longer did Newander stoop in despair. His back was straight and his visage proud.

"I hear the call of Silvanus himself!" the druid declared. "His own voice, I tell you."

Truly intrigued, Danica would have liked to stay and hear Newander's explanation, but the situation wouldn't allow it.

She nodded quickly and pulled away from the druid's grasp, taking only the split second it took her to come through the wall to survey the room and determine her course. Her heart told her to go to Cadderly, still dazed and struggling by the door, but her warrior instincts told her that the best she could do for her beloved, and for all her friends, was to stop the imposing priest who stood by the altar.

She took two running strides at Barjin, dove into a roll just in case he had some spell or dart aimed her way, then came back to her feet and pounded in. She enacted her moves too quickly for Barjin to block, and she got her fist through his defenses, slamming him solidly on the chest.

Danica bounced back, stunned, her hand sore, as if she had struck an iron wall. Barjin hadn't even moved.

Danica kept her wits enough to dodge Barjin's first attack, and to take note of the contorting, biting movement of the enchanted mace's sculpted head. She circled to the priest's right, away from the altar, wondering if perhaps her daggers would have more effect. By all appearances, the priest wasn't wearing any armor, but Danica trusted her sore hand more than her eyes. She knew that magic could deceive, and she understood already that her tactics against the priest would have to be akin to those she might use against an armored knight.

Barjin waved the Screaming Maiden again easily, attacks designed to keep Danica at bay and to test her reflexes. She realized that again the priest had underestimated her quickness.

She stepped in right behind the swing and snapped off two jabs at her opponent's weapon arm. There, too, the magical vestments repelled the blow.

Her understanding of the extent of the priest's armor growing, Danica realized that she would find few openings for strikes. The priest was covered head to toe, and the kind of power Danica expected she would need to get through the enchanted vestments, a blow that required long concentration, would leave her vulnerable to a preemptive hit. She took a different path then, one designed to get that awful mace away from her adversary.

Danica came in low, feigning a strike at Barjin's groin. The priest whipped the Screaming Maiden straight down at the stooping woman, just as Danica had expected. She brought her forearm up to block the blow. Her next move would have been to reach under with her free hand, grabbing the priest's wrist. Pulling with this hand and pushing with her locked forearm would then tear the mace from his grasp. But, while Danica had correctly anticipated Barjin's overhand strike, she had not foreseen the reaction of his vile, sentient, weapon.

The Screaming Maiden twisted, its maw snapping futilely at the out-of-reach blocking forearm. The ugly visage opened its mouth wide and hissed, loosing a cone of frost over Danica.

Danica began her dodge at the instant the chill emanated from the mouth, but the cone encompassed too wide an area for her to get fully out of harm's way. Chilling ice descended on her, so cold that it burned at her skin and so evil, the chill of death, that it found its way deeper, into Danica's heart and bones. Her lungs ached with her next gasp and it was all she could do to break away from the encounter and stagger back toward the broken wall.

Newander watched it all through a dull haze. He wisely registered the important facts—Barjin's vestment armor and the mace, in particular—but the druid's thoughts were turned primarily inward now, heeding, he believed, the personal summons of Silvanus, the Oak Father. The sight of this room, of the cursing bottle, had put many things into perspective for Newander. Gone now were his fears that he, unlike his transformed druid companions, was somehow not true to his calling. Gone was his fear that he had only avoided the brunt of the curse because of some inner ambivalence. Perhaps that had been the case, but it hardly mattered now to the druid. His gaze locked upon the evil priest, the one who had raised the dead, the bringer of perversion, and he heard the commands of nature's god.

He remembered the su-monsters and how clearly he had sensed the approach of ghouls, and Newander knew his purpose. Druids were dedicated to preserving the natural order, the natural harmony, and his faith demanded that the evil priest be stopped, here and now.

Newander let his thoughts slip to the woodland, to the home of druidic power. He felt the beginning twinges in his body the first time he had ever achieved this level of druidic concentration. Though a bit afraid, he encouraged the engulfing power fully, focusing his own energies to push it along. There was a sensation of distant pain as his bones cracked and reconfigured, a tickle as hair sprouted across his body.

As had Cleo and Arcite, Newander let himself go to his urging, let his body follow his thoughts. Unlike his companions, though, Newander did not relinquish his thinking to the instincts of the animal. His focus did not change with his body.

He saw the evil priest's eyes widen as he pawed toward the altar, past the recoiling Danica.

* * * * *

Ivan saw Pikel's storming approach, but the flaming zombie never turned to witness the attack. At the last moment, Ivan dodged to the side and Pikel slammed in, his tree trunk connecting squarely on Mullivy's rump. His stubby legs pumping wildly, Pikel brutally drove the zombie into the wall. Still Pikel's legs did not stop thrashing; he ignored the intense heat and kept the zombie pinned.

Mullivy swung his good arm about wildly, but his back was to the attacker and he could not reach beyond Pikel's pinning club. He wriggled and squirmed, trying to get out the side of the pin. Every time he made some progress, though, Ivan rushed over and smacked him hard with the axe.

This went on for several moments, then luck turned against the dwarves. Mullivy started out the side; Ivan waded in and hit him. The powerful blow drove deep into Mullivy's arm, but sent a gout of flame flying back in Ivan's direction, instantly igniting the dwarf's beard.

Ivan dove away, slapping at the flames, and Pikel, distracted by his brother's sudden distress, unconsciously loosened his hold.

Mullivy slipped free of his captor and advanced on the rolling Ivan.

Pikel overbalanced and stumbled forward into the wall. He came back up in an instant, but again he saw Ivan in dire need and again the sight sent him on a ferocious charge. This time Pikel held his club perpendicularly in front of him, one hand on either end. Mullivy was just reaching down at Ivan when Pikel hit him. Again the dwarf drove on, pushing the zombie before him. They passed the open door—Pikel thought he saw a batwinged impish form hovering outside—and barreled headlong into an empty bookcase. The ancient wooden shelves fell apart under their weight, and dwarf, zombie, and kindling crashed down in a fiery heap.

* * * * *

Long and pointy teeth bared, the giant wolverine that Newander had become charged the evil priest. The druid had a surprise in mind, an attack that the priest's cloth vestments, however strengthened, might not be able to withstand. Just before he reached the mark, Newander spun over suddenly and loosed a cloud of vile musk.

The disgusting spray rolled over Barjin, stinging his eyes, permeating his clothing, and nearly overwhelming him. He fell back as quickly as he could, trying to escape the cloud, gagging and gasping.

Newander's pursuit was furious. He hooked his claws around the backpeddling priest's knees and bore Barjin to the ground. Barjin kicked and scrambled, but the wolverine was too quick and strong to be easily dislodged. Newander bit into Barjin's thigh, tearing and gnawing. Still the magical vestments repelled the attacks, but they seemed not so invulnerable now. The stinking musk clung to them as would an acid, already wearing at their integrity.

Barjin twisted and screamed. He couldn't see through the burn in his eyes; he couldn't think straight against the suddenness of the attack. He felt the gnawing bites grow sharper and knew that he was in trouble. Very soon, the wolverine would be through his vestments and those wicked teeth would be tearing at his exposed thigh.

The Screaming Maiden reached out empathically to Barjin, calmed him and let him see through its eyes. Barjin stopped his struggling and followed the mace's lead. Newander burrowed in, but the Screaming Maiden bit back.

Barjin hit the wolverine perhaps a dozen times; each strike put more blood and more fur into the hungry mace's gaping mouth. The burrowing stopped, but Barjin kept pounding.

* * * * *

"Ow! Ow! Ow! Ow! Ow!" Pikel grunted, rolling out of the burning pile. His clothes had caught in several places; his beard no longer appeared green, but the thick-skinned dwarf had taken no real damage in his tumble with the flaming zombie, and he rolled about the floor, suffocating the last stubborn embers.

Ivan started toward his brother but changed direction suddenly, seeing that Mullivy, too, had begun to rise. Ivan had seen enough of that one. He crept over, using the crackle of the fire to cover his footsteps, and took up a position just to the side of the rising zombie.

Mullivy was no longer burning. Barjin's protection spell kept the flames from his rotting flesh, and now all the oil and clothing, the fuel for his fires, had been consumed. He came up and inadvertently focused on Pikel, taking no notice of the dwarf winding up just behind his shoulder.

Ivan quickly put a finger across each side of his double-bladed axe, testing to see which edge was the sharper. He shrugged then—both seemed equally capable—and whipped the blade across at his own eye level. It sliced just above the zombie's shoulder, as Ivan had planned, and hit the creature squarely on the side of the neck. More than the weakened flesh of a zombie's thin neck would be needed to slow the blow of an enraged Ivan Bouldershoulder.

Ivan smiled with grim satisfaction as the zombie tumbled to the side, its head spinning through the air far from its body.

"Oo!" remarked an appreciative and admiring Pikel.

"Had it coming," Ivan snorted back, sharing a smile with the brother he had thought dead.

Their mirth was short-lived. Mullivy's corpse stood up between them, deaf and blind but flailing wildly with both arms. One connected on the side of Pikel's head, knocking off his pot helmet.

"Oo!" Pikel squeaked again, and he slipped one step to the side and smacked the headless zombie with his club. He leaned and glanced at Ivan and both brothers understood the proper tactics.

They worked in unison, two dwarves who knew each other's moves as well as his own. They surrounded the zombie, one on either side, and moved synchronously in circles. Ivan prodded Mullivy's shoulder, then jumped back. The zombie shifted and waved its arms futilely at the empty air. Pikel, behind the monster, waded in with a heavy blow.

Mullivy spun to get at the newest attacker, and Ivan came in behind, launching an overhead chop into the zombie's shoulder with enough force to take off one arm.

It went on for a long while, though both dwarves actually would have preferred to make this fun last a bit longer. Finally, though, Mullivy's dismembered corpse fell to the floor and did not try to rise.

* * * * *

Still dazed and disoriented, Cadderly witnessed the horrors at the altar from across the room. He knew that Newander was probably dead, and he knew, too, that the evil priest would advance next toward Danica.

He saw his love, climbing up from the floor, trembling violently from the chilling frost and gasping and squinting on the edges of Newander's musk cloud.

Blood stained one of Barjin's legs, and he limped noticeably as he struggled away from the still wolverine's stubborn clutch, but the priest's expression showed only rage, and he waved his mace with sure and easy swings.

"Newander," Cadderly called hopelessly, desperately, wanting someone to intervene and stop this madness. He knew that the druid, his head and back a bloody pulp, would never answer.

Danica moved next, drawing her crystalline daggers and launching them in rapid succession. The first hit the priest in the shoulder, drawing just a tiny line of blood. The second had even less success. It managed to cut through the priest's conical cap, but the angle of the hat deflected it above Barjin's head, where it hung weirdly and harmlessly.

Barjin rubbed his eyes, stepped over the druid, and bore down on Danica. She fell into a low, defensive posture as though she would spring into him, but then dove straight backward.

Cadderly understood Danica's reaction; she feared another blast from that awful mace. And even as Cadderly watched, the priest brought the weapon in line.

Cadderly watched Danica move back beside the altar, steadily backpedaling from the advancing priest. All of Cadderly's pain, so overwhelming just a moment ago, suddenly seemed insignificant next to Danica's troubles. He shook the dizziness away, denied the weakness in his limbs, and forced himself to his knees, drawing his crossbow and fitting another dart.

He nearly swooned from the permeating cold and bit his lip right through in fighting against it, understanding the price of failure. He leveled the crossbow Barjin's way, had the evil priest in line, and knew that those vestments would not stop the enchanted dart.

He hesitated. A voice screamed in protest inside Cadderly's head, a distant echo of the vow he had made when he had first decided to construct the bow and darts. "Not as a weapon!" he growled under his breath, but as the bow began to slip toward the floor, Cadderly looked back at Danica, growled in defiance, and tightened his grip. Struggling with his conscience through every inch, he stubbornly brought the crossbow up level again.

Cadderly nearly cried out a moment later, believing his hesitation might have cost Danica dearly. Barjin launched a series of mighty blows at the young woman, who somehow managed to stagger out of the biting mace's grasp.

Cadderly saw an out.

"Feel the cold," he heard Barjin snarl, distantly, as though he were viewing it all through a crystal ball. The priest held the cruel mace out in front of him, its mouth opened wide.

Danica, agile despite her wounds, desperately leaped to the side.

"No!" Cadderly cried, and his dart found its way right between the evil weapon's fangs.

There was a sharp crack, and Barjin barely managed to keep his grip on the jolted mace. For an interminable moment, nothing at all seemed to happen, but Cadderly could tell from the priest's shocked expression that something was indeed going on within Barjin's prized weapon.

Without warning, the top of the Screaming Maiden's head blew off. Barjin still held the broken weapon by the handle; he seemed as if he could not let go. Multicolored sparks flared as the magical energy burst forth unbridled, showering the entire center region of the room.

"Oo!" Pikel and Ivan squealed together.

The sparks caught on Barjin's vestments, burning little holes. The priest screamed in agony as a spark slipped through the cap's view hole and sizzled into his eye.

Danica fell away, diving and rolling and shielding her own eyes with a raised arm.

The spark shower went on unabated. Blue sparks erupted right into Barjin's head, catching the side of his conical hood as he desperately lurched. Red sparks flew out in a sudden circular explosion, spinning and rising and then falling over Danica, Barjin, and the evil altar. A small fireball popped straight up from the broken mace, exploding into the ceiling. Lighted specks of dust descended, only to be devoured by the continuing shower.

Across the room, Cadderly squinted and wondered if he had inadvertently set something into motion that would destroy them all.

Then it ended. The base of the Screaming Maiden dropped to the floor and sputtered to a smoldering death.

Off came Barjin's conical hood, and then off, too, came the fast-burning vestments. They fell apart, destroyed by both the wolverine musk and the sparks, as Barjin clawed at them, frantically trying to get the hot embers away from his skin.

He cursed and spat at his own foolishness for putting the spell of fire protection on his zombie instead of on himself. The priest's eyes darted wildly. Cadderly was still kneeling.

To his side, the triumphant dwarves stood over the gruesome remains of the zombie. Then his gaze settled on

Danica, apparently unarmed and unarmored, who seemed the easiest target. Wiping the musk and sparks from her face, she wasn't even looking at him.

Barjin had made many mistakes in his life, but none were more complete than his assumption that Danica would be an easy catch. He reached out for her, meaning to hook her around the neck with his strong arm and bring her in, choking, against his chest.

His arm had almost reached her shoulder when Danica reacted. She spun fully and used her momentum to drive her finger hard against Barjin's shoulder.

"I already tried that!" Cadderly warned, but he fell silent, and Barjin's arm fell dead.

The priest looked down in amazement at his numbed right arm. He started to strike out with his left, but Danica was simply too quick for him. She caught his punch in midswing, hooked her fingers over his hand, and jerked his thumb back so forcefully that, with a crack of bones that sounded as loudly as one of Pikel's tree trunk hits, Barjin's thumbnail touched his wrist.

Danica wasn't finished. With a slight twist, she cupped her fingers around Barjin's, curling her fingertips over the top of the priest's hand. Looking Barjin straight in the eye, Danica squeezed, her grip forcing Barjin's top knuckles back in on themselves and sending waves of excruciating pain rolling up his arm. He tried to resist, mentally telling his arm to pull away, but Danica's assault blocked out his determined call; the unrelenting pain prevented him from taking any actions against her, or any actions at all. Even if his other arm had not been "killed," he could not have responded.

He gurgled indecipherably; all the world became a blur.

Danica sneered and pulled down on the trapped hand, driving Barjin to his knees. She tightened her free hand into a ball and lined up Barjin's face.

"Danica . . ." breathed a horrified Cadderly.

"Here, now, don't we get a piece of him?" came a gruff call from the side. "He's the one who killed me brother."

Pikel turned incredulously on Ivan. "Oh?"

"Well, he tried to kill me brother," Ivan corrected, grinning from ear to ear.

Danica uncurled her fist. Her anger was lost in sadness and concern as she looked at Cadderly. The pitiful image stopped her cold. Cadderly was still kneeling, staring at Danica, his hands outstretched in a silent plea and his gray eyes unconsciously judging her.

Danica twisted Barjin's arm around, cupped her other arm under his shoulder and sent him rolling toward the dwarves.

Ivan scooped him up roughly and half-rolled and half-bounced him to Pikel, crying, "Ye killed me brother!"

"Me brudder!" Pikel echoed, spinning the dizzy priest about and launching him back at Ivan.

Ivan caught him and sent him bounding back.

Cadderly realized that the dwarf's game could easily get out of hand. Both were injured, and angry, and with the cursing bottle spewing smoke so very close, their pain and rage could bring them to new heights of violence.

"Do not kill him!" Cadderly screamed at them. Pikel looked at him incredulously and Ivan caught Barjin, slammed the priest to the ground, and held him by the hair.

"Not kill him?" Ivan asked. "What're ye thinking to do with this one?"

"Do not kill him!" Cadderly demanded again. He suspected that he'd need more than the protests of his own conscience to convince the agitated dwarves, so he played a pragmatic game. "We need to question him, to learn if he has allies and where they might be."

"Yeah!" roared Ivan. "What about it?" He jerked Barjin's head back so violently that Cadderly thought the dwarf had broken the man's neck.

"Not now, Ivan," Cadderly explained. "Later, in the library, where we will find maps and writings to aid us in our interrogation."

"Ye're a lucky one, ye are," Ivan said, putting his considerable nose right against Barjin's, pushing the priest's smaller proboscis flat against his cheek. "I'd get ye talking, don't ye doubt!"

Indeed Barjin didn't doubt Ivan's words, but he hardly felt lucky, especially when Ivan hoisted him back up and bounced him over to Pikel once again.

Cadderly walked over and draped his arm across Danica's shoulders. She stood quietly, looking down at the druid who had sacrificed everything for their cause. Newander's bones continued to crackle, as his body tried to revert to its natural form in death. He got about halfway there. His calm and wise face once more became recognizable, and most of the wolverine hair disappeared, but then the transition stopped. Death had stolen the magic, the energy.

"He was a good friend," Cadderly whispered, but he thought his words incredibly lame. Words could not carry the sense of grief that he felt, both for the druid and for the many others who had perished under the curse—the curse that he had loosed.

That thought inevitably led Cadderly's gaze to the altar and the bottle, still pouring smoke, oblivious to the defeat of its guiding priest.

"It is for me to do," Cadderly surmised, hoping he was right. He took the stopper from the altar and gingerly reached out, his mind rushing through a hundred different scenarios of what would happen if he were unable to close the bottle.

He was not. He placed the stopper over the bottle and patted it down, ending the smoky stream.

Cadderly felt a bump on his shoulder and thought that Danica had put her head on him for support. He turned to acknowledge her apparent relief, but she limply fell past him, face down to the floor.

Back by the door, the others went down, too. Barjin tumbled heavily over Ivan, and for a moment, not a thing moved.

Only Barjin got back up, snarling and cursing.

"You," he said accusingly at Cadderly. The evil priest grabbed Ivan's axe in his one working arm and headed Cadderly's way.

Twenty-Four

The Most Fatal Horror

The shock brought Druzil abruptly from his sleepy state. The bottle had been closed! The chaos curse, which Druzil had waited decades to witness, had been defeated! The imp still could recognize the misty magic in the air, but already it was beginning to diminish.

Druzil reached out with his thoughts toward Barjin but found telepathic communication to the priest blocked by a wall of rage. He didn't really want to go into the altar room; he had seen the formidable dwarves tear apart Barjin's zombie and feared another dart from the young priest. When Druzil glanced around at the empty corridors, he realized that he had no other way to go. He reached down to the small pouch hanging on the base of one wing and pulled it free, clutching it in his taloned hands.

He crept up to the door. Beyond Mullivy's chopped up remains lay the two unconscious dwarves, and farther in, by the altar, a young woman. Druzil's surprise at the unexpected scene lasted only as long as it took the imp to consider what had transpired. The sudden shock of the chaos curse's end, the termination of the magic that had permeated these peoples' thoughts so fully, had overcome them.

Druzil saw Barjin advance on the young priest—and now the imp knew that this young man had been the catalyst, the one who had opened the bottle. Apparently, he also had been the one to close it.

The great evil priest seemed not so powerful in Druzil's eyes anymore. Barjin's vestments and weapon were gone, one arm hung limply at his side, and, most important, he had allowed the bottle to be closed.

There it rested, powerless, atop the altar. Druzil had an impulse to go and get it, to whisk it away through the fire gate back to Castle Trinity. The imp quickly dismissed that notion.

Not only would he have to get within striking distance of the young man who earlier had brought him down, but if he took the bottle and Barjin somehow survived the day, the priest's continuing mission at the library would be futile. And the priest would not be happy.

No, Druzil decided, right now the bottle was not worth the many risks. If Barjin survived, perhaps the priest would find another catalyst to rejuvenate the curse. Druzil could get back here if that came to pass.

The imp opened the small pouch he held and looked away from the impending battle, to the brazier that, fortunately, still burned.

* * * * *

Cadderly started to reach for another dart but realized that the evil priest would get to him before he could load it. Even if he did get his crossbow readied, Cadderly doubted that he could find the courage to use it against a living man.

Barjin sensed his ambivalence. "You should have let the dwarves kill me," he snickered.

"No!" Cadderly replied firmly. He dropped his crossbow and slipped one finger into his pocket, into the loop of his spindle-disks.

"Did you really believe that I would provide information, that keeping me alive would prove beneficial?" Barjin asked.

Cadderly shook his head. Barjin had missed the point. Cadderly had only made that claim to convince Ivan and Pikel not to kill him. His true motives in keeping Barjin alive had nothing to do with information, but with his own desire not to kill a man he did not have to kill. "We had no reason to kill you," he said evenly. "The fight was already won."

"So you believed," snarled Barjin. He skipped across the remaining distance to Cadderly and whipped Ivan's axe across as viciously as his wounded hand would allow.

Anticipating the attack, Cadderly easily dodged aside. He pulled his hand from his pocket and sent his spindle-disks flying out at Barjin. They connected with a thud on Barjin's chest, but the mighty priest was more startled than injured.

He looked at Cadderly—or more pointedly, at Cadderly's coiled weapon hand—for a moment, then laughed aloud.

Cadderly nearly threw himself at the mocking priest, but he realized that was exactly what his opponent wanted him to do. His only chance in this fight was to play defensively, the same way he had defeated Kierkan Rufo back in his room. He grinned widely against the continuing laughter and tried to appear as confident as possible.

Barjin was not Kierkan Rufo. The evil priest had seen countless battles, had defeated seasoned warriors in single combat, and had directed armies marching across the Vaasan plains.

After just a single viewing, this veteran's confident smile revealed that he had surmised the limitations of Cadderly's strange weapon, and he knew as well as Cadderly that he would have to make a huge mistake if the young priest was to have any chance.

"You should not have returned to this place," Barjin said, calmly. "You should have left the Edificant Library altogether and given up what was already lost."

Cadderly paused to consider the unexpected words, and the

even more unexpected, almost resigned, tone. "I erred," he replied, "when first I came down here. I returned only to correct the wrong." He glanced over at the bottle to emphasize his point. "And now I have done that."

"Have you?" Barjin teased. "Your friends are down, young fool. All those in the library are down, I would guess. When you closed the bottle, you weakened your allies more than your enemies."

Cadderly could not deny the priest's taunt, but he still believed that he had done the right thing in closing the bottle. He would find a way to revive his friends, and all the others. Perhaps they were only sleeping.

"Do you truly believe that, once loosed, *Tuanta Quiro Miancay*, the Most Fatal Horror, could be defeated simply by placing the stopper back in the flask?" Barjin smiled widely. "Look," he said, pointing over at the altar. "Even now the agent of my goddess Talona battles its way back through your pitiful barrier, back into the air it has claimed as Talona's domain."

Cadderly should have seen the trick coming, but his own insecurity concerning the unknown bottle and curse caused him to glance to the side again. Still, he was not caught completely off his guard when Barjin waded straight in, growling and swinging.

Cadderly ducked under one cut, then rolled to the side as Barjin reversed his swing and came with a wicked overhead chop. Cadderly tried to scramble back to his feet, but Barjin was too quick. Before he could rise, he was rolling again, back the other way, to avoid another dipping slice.

Cadderly knew that he couldn't keep this up for long, nor could he launch any effective counters from a position on the floor. Barjin, relentless with the taste of victory on his drooling lips, kept the two-headed axe under perfect control and readied yet another strike. The issue seemed decided.

It became an eerie, almost slow-motion sequence for Cadderly as he watched Barjin maneuvering into position. Was this the moment of his death? What then of Danica and Ivan and Pikel?

The flap of wings sounded by the door. Cadderly, too engrossed with his own dilemma, hardly took note, but Barjin did
glance around.

Seeing his opening, Cadderly rolled away as fast as he could.

Barjin easily could have caught up to him, but the priest
seemed more concerned with the unexpected appearance of his
missing imp.

"Where have you been?" Barjin demanded. Stripped of his
vestments and weapon, ragged and beaten, the priest's words
did not carry much authority.

Druzil didn't even answer. He floated across to the brazier,
pausing only to scoop up Barjin's necromancer's stone.

"Put it back!" Barjin roared. "You play a dangerous game,
imp."

Druzil considered the stone, then the priest, then moved to
the brazier. His gaze again drifted back to the closed bottle, but
if he was considering a try for it, he quickly thought better of it.
The enraged Barjin, if not the young priest, surely would strike
him down if he went within reach.

"I will protect it," Druzil offered, holding up the stone. "And
the bottle?"

"You will run and hide!" Barjin retorted sharply. "You think
me beaten?"

Druzil shrugged, his wings nearly burying his head with the
action.

"Stay and watch, cowardly imp," Barjin proclaimed. "Watch
as I regain my victory and finish off this pitiful library."

Druzil hesitated for a long moment, considering the offer. "I
prefer a safer haven," he announced. "I will return when things
are under your control."

"Leave the stone!" Barjin commanded.

Druzil's smile revealed much to the priest. The imp clutched
the powerful necromancer's stone all the tighter and dropped
his powder into the burning brazier. The magical fire flashed and
burned with a bluish hue, and Druzil casually stepped through
the reopened gate.

"Coward!" Barjin cried. "I will win this day. I will loose *Tuanta Quiro Miancay* again, and you, cowardly imp, will no longer be treated as an ally!"

His threats were lost in the crackle of the brazier's flames.

Barjin spun back on Cadderly, now standing around on the other side of the altar, opposite the priest. "You can still save yourself and your friends," Barjin purred, suddenly friendly. "Join me. Open the bottle once more. The power you will realize . . ."

Cadderly saw through the lie and cut the priest short, though Barjin's sudden charm was effective enough to be shocking. "You need me to open it because you cannot, because it must be opened by one who is not allied with your god," he reasoned.

Barjin's coercive smile did not diminish.

"How can I agree, then? Cadderly asked him. "To do so would be to join with you, but would that not ally me with your designs and with your god? Would that not break the conditions?" Cadderly thought himself quite clever, thought that his logic had cornered the priest, as Barjin mulled the words over.

When Barjin looked back at him, his eyes shining fiercely, Cadderly knew that he had thought wrong.

"Not if you open the bottle for a better reason," Barjin said, turning to view Danica and the dwarves, "to save the woman perhaps." Barjin took a step away.

All fear flew from Cadderly at that moment. He jumped out from behind the altar, meaning to intercept Barjin, determined to stop the priest at any cost. He stopped suddenly, eyes widening in horror.

Another being had entered the room, one that Cadderly had seen before.

Barjin's reaction was just the opposite of Cadderly's. He swung the axe high above his head victoriously, feeling that his base of power was returning, that his fortunes had turned back for the better. "I had thought you destroyed," he said to the scorched mummy.

Khalif, the less than complete spirit, savaged and removed

from all sense of sanity, did not respond.

"What are you doing?" the evil priest demanded as the mummy stalked in. Barjin swiped with the axe, hoping to keep the monster at bay, but the mummy simply slapped the weapon from his hand.

"Halt!" Barjin cried. "You must obey me!"

Khalif had other ideas. Before Barjin could say anything else, a heavy arm slammed into the side of his head and sent him tumbling to the wall by the brazier.

Barjin knew his doom. The mummy was out of control, crazed with pain and rage. It hated all life, hated Barjin for bringing it back from its rest. With all that had happened, both to Barjin and to the mummy, the priest's domination was no more.

Barjin looked desperately to the table where he had left the necromancer's stone, the one item that might aid him now against this undead foe. Then he remembered, and he cursed Druzil's abrupt departure.

He propped himself up against the wall and looked about desperately. To his right loomed the burning brazier, the gate reopened but not an escape route for a being of the material plane. To Barjin's left, though, was Pikel's impromptu doorway, an exit to the tunnels beyond the room.

He tried to rise, but a throbbing pain in his head dropped him back to his knees. Undaunted, Barjin began to crawl. Before he could get to the hole, though, the mummy cut him off and slammed him again into the wall. Barjin had no defense against the ensuing onslaught. He raised his one functioning arm, but the mummy's heavy blows snapped it aside.

Cadderly stood very still beside the altar, consciously telling himself to take some action. The fear gripped him, but he at last overcame it by conjuring an image of the mummy's next move after finishing off Barjin. Danica was the next closest target.

He took his crossbow in hand and loaded it, seeking some way to get the monster off the priest. Cadderly had no love for the man, and he held no hopes that helping Barjin might bring some mutually beneficial compromise, but despite the fact that

Barjin was his enemy, he could not let the human be killed by this undead monster.

Another problem presented itself as Cadderly leveled his bow for a shot. The imp's passage had reopened the interplanar gate, and now some lower plane denizen had found its way in. A hideous face appeared in the flames, obscure, but huge, and growing more tangible with each passing second.

Cadderly instinctively lined his crossbow up with this newest intruder, but then swung it back at the mummy, realizing that it was his most pressing problem.

Another scorch mark appeared on the mummy's rotted linen; another jolt shook the monster, but the scabrous thing did not turn away from Barjin. The priest managed once to stand up, only to be immediately pounded back to the floor.

A huge black wing tip came out the side of the brazier fire.

Cadderly nearly lost his breath; the creature forming in the flames was monstrous, much larger than the imp.

Cadderly loaded and fired again at the mummy. Another hit, and now, with Barjin offering no resistance, the mummy wheeled about.

Cadderly felt that paralyzing fear welling in him again, but he did not let it slow his practiced movements. He had used more than half his darts and had no idea if he had enough remaining to finally defeat this undead thing, had no idea if his attacks were even causing any real damage to the monster.

Again, he refused to let his fears slow him. Another dart whistled out at the mummy. This one did not explode, but dove through a hole created by a previous dart and cut right through the tattered linen bindings.

At first Cadderly was more concerned with getting another dart fitted; he knew that his miss would allow the monster to close, but then he heard Barjin grunt.

The dart thudded into the chest of the sitting priest. The next interminable second ended with the noise that Cadderly now dreaded, for the dart had enough remaining momentum to collapse and explode.

The mummy took a step out, giving Cadderly a view of the priest. Barjin lay nearly flat. Only his head and shoulders remained propped against the wall. He gasped and clutched the hole in his chest, his eyes unblinking, though he seemed not to see anything, not to be aware of anything beyond his own demise. He gasped again, a gout of blood bursting from his mouth, and then he lay still.

Cadderly did not even think of his movements. His mind seemed to disengage from his body, to give way to his own instincts for survival and his own boiling rage at what he had done. He took up his waterskin under his free arm, popped off the cap, and drove the mummy back toward the wall with a steady stream of blessed water.

The liquid hissed as it struck the evilly enchanted linen, etching blackened scars. The mummy issued a loud, outraged roar and tried to cover up, but it had no way to block the small but painful stream.

In the brazier, a hideous face was clear now, leering hungrily at Cadderly. Cadderly thought to defeat both foes with a single attack. He angled his waterskin, seeking to drive the mummy into the flames, perhaps to topple the brazier and close the gate.

The mummy did indeed recoil from the spray, but if it feared the blessed water, it feared the open flames even more. Try as he might, Cadderly could not force it too near the burning gate.

He apparently was doing some damage, but Cadderly could not afford this stalemate. He was running out of water; then what might he use to finish off the mummy? And if that monster came through the gate . . .

Helplessly, Cadderly fumbled to keep up the stream and to load another dart. He lifted his crossbow toward the mummy, trying to find a vital area beyond its blocking arms. What area, he wondered helplessly, might be the most vulnerable? The eyes? The heart?

The waterskin was empty. The mummy stood straight.

"Last shot," Cadderly muttered resignedly. He started to pull on the trigger, then, as he had with Barjin earlier in the fight, he noticed another possibility.

Pikel's charge through the wall had caused tremendous structural damage. The hole in the brickwork was fully four feet wide and half that again high, nearly reaching the beamed ceiling. One crossbeam, directly above the hole, balanced precariously on a cracked support. Cadderly moved his arm in that direction and fired.

The dart smacked into the wood at the joint between crossbeam and support, exploding into a small fireball, sending splinters everywhere. The crossbeam slipped, but, still attached at its other end, it swung down like a pendulum.

The mummy took only one short step from the wall before the beam slammed into it, driving it sidelong. It pitched into the brazier, taking the fiery tripod and bowl right over with it.

The hideous image of the otherworldly denizen disappeared in a huge fireball. Flames engulfed the mummy, eagerly devouring its layered cloth wrappings. It managed to stagger to its feet—Cadderly wondered with horror if it might survive even this—but then it crumpled and was consumed.

Without the enchanted brazier, the gate was closed, and gone, too, was Barjin's greatest undead monster. The flames flared a couple of times, then burned very low, leaving the room smoky in the dimness of low-burning torches.

Cadderly understood that victory was within his grasp, but he hardly felt in the mood for rejoicing. Newander lay dead at his feet, others had died upstairs, and, perhaps most disconcerting of all to the young scholar, no longer an innocent, he had killed a man.

Barjin remained propped against the wall, his lifeless eyes staring out at Cadderly, holding the defenseless young priest in an accusing gaze.

Cadderly's arm drooped to his side and the crossbow fell to the floor.

Twenty-Five

Out of the Mist

Cadderly so desperately wanted to close those eyes! He willed himself to go over to the dead priest and turn his head away, get that accusing stare off him, but it was an impotent command, and Cadderly knew it. He had not the strength to go anywhere near Barjin. He moved a few short steps to the side, to get to Danica, but looked back and imagined that the dead priest's eyes followed him still.

Cadderly wondered if they would forever.

He slammed his fist on the floor, trying to shake free of the guilt, to accept the priest's stare as a necessary price that he must pay. Events had dictated his actions, he reminded himself, and he determinedly told himself to foster no regrets.

He jumped defensively when a small form suddenly darted in through the opening beside the priest, then managed a weak smile as Percival climbed up him and sat atop his shoulder, chittering and complaining as always. Cadderly patted the squirrel between the ears with a single finger—he needed to do that—then went to his friends.

Danica seemed to be sleeping quite peacefully. She would

not wake, though, to Cadderly's call or shake. He found both dwarves in similar states, their thunderous snores complimenting each other in strange, rock-grating harmony. Pikel's snores, in particular, sounded contented.

Cadderly grew worried. He had believed the battle won finally—but why couldn't he wake his friends? How long would they sleep? Cadderly had heard of curses that caused slumber for a thousand years, or until certain conditions had been met, however long that might take.

Perhaps the battle wasn't yet won. He went back to the altar and examined the bottle. It seemed harmless enough now, to the naked eye, so Cadderly decided to look deeper. He moved his thoughts through a series of relaxation exercises that slipped him into a semimeditative trance. The mist was fast dissipating, that much he could tell, and no more was emanating from the stoppered bottle. That gave Cadderly hope; perhaps the slumber would last until the mist was gone.

The bottle itself, though, did not appear completely neutralized. Cadderly sensed a life, an energy, within it, a pulsating evil, contained but not destroyed. It might have been only his imagination, or perhaps what he thought was a life-force was merely a manifestation of his own fears. Cadderly honestly wondered if the remaining flickers within that bottle were playing some role in the lingering mist. The evil priest had called the mist the Most Fatal Horror, an agent of Talona. Cadderly recognized the name of the vile goddess, and the title, normally reserved for Talona's highest-ranking clerics. If this mist was indeed some sort of god-stuff, a simple stopper would not suffice.

Cadderly came out of his trance and sat down to consider the situation. The key, he decided, was to accept the evil priest's description of the bottle and not think of it simply as some secular, though potent, magic.

"Battle gods with gods," Cadderly mumbled a moment later. He stood again before the altar, studying not the bottle, but the reflective, gem-studded bowl in front of it. Cadderly feared what magic this item might contain, but he chanced it without delay, tipping the bowl to the side and dumping out the water stained by the evil priest's foul hands.

He retrieved a piece of cloth, a piece of Barjin's own vestments, and wiped the bowl thoroughly, then found Newander's waterskin, full as usual, out in the hallway beyond Pikel's impromptu door. Cadderly consciously avoided looking at Newander as he reentered the room, meaning to go straight to the altar, but Percival delayed him. The squirrel sat atop the dead druid, still in his semitransformed state.

"Get away from there," Cadderly scolded, but Percival only sat up higher, clicking excitedly and displaying some small item.

"What have you got?" Cadderly asked, moving slowly back so as not to startle the excitable squirrel.

Percival displayed an oak leaf pendant, the holy symbol of Silvanus, dangling from a fine leather thong.

"Do not take that!" Cadderly started to scold, but then he realized that Percival had something in mind.

Cadderly bent low, studying Percival more closely and seeking guidance in the wise druid's face. Newander's visage, so peaceful and accepting of his fate, held him fully.

Percival shrieked in Cadderly's ear, demanding his attention. The squirrel held out the pendant and seemed to motion toward the altar.

Confusion twisted Cadderly's face. "Percival?" he asked.

The squirrel danced an agitated circle, then shook his little head briskly. Cadderly blanched.

"Newander?" he asked meekly.

The squirrel held out the holy symbol.

Cadderly considered it for a moment, then, remembering the druids' creed concerning death as a natural extension of life, he accepted the oak leaf and started back toward the altar.

The squirrel shook suddenly, then leaped back up to Cadderly's shoulder.

"Newander?" Cadderly asked again. The squirrel did not

answer. "Percival?" The squirrel perked up its ears.

Cadderly paused and wondered what had just transpired.

His instincts told him that Newander's departing spirit somehow had used Percival's body to get a message to him, but his stubborn sense of reality told him that he probably had imagined the whole episode. Whatever it was, he now had the druid's holy symbol in his hand and he knew that the aid of Silvanus could be only a good thing.

Cadderly wished he had been more attentive in his mundane duties, the simple ceremonies required of the lesser priests of the Edificant Library. His hands trembling, he poured the water from Newander's waterskin into the gem-studded bowl, and added to it, with a silent call to Newander's god, the holy symbol.

Cadderly figured that two gods would be better than one in containing this evil, and also that Newander's god, dedicated to natural order, might be the most effective in battling the curse. He closed his eyes and recited the ceremony to purify the water, stumbling a few times over the words he had not spoken very often.

Then it was completed and Cadderly was left with only his hopes. He lifted the evil bottle and gently immersed it in the bowl. The water went cold and took on the same red hue as that within the bottle, and Cadderly feared that he had not accomplished anything positive.

A moment later, though, the red hue disappeared altogether, from the water and the bottle. Cadderly studied it closely, somehow sensing that the pulsating evil was no more.

Behind him, Pikel's snore was replaced by a questioning, "Oo oi?"

Cadderly scooped up the bowl carefully and looked around.

Danica and both dwarves were stirring, though they were not yet coherent. Cadderly moved across the room to a small cabinet and placed the bowl inside, closing the door as he turned away.

Danica groaned and sat up, holding her head in both hands.

"Me head," Ivan said in a sluggish voice. "Me head."

They exited the tunnel to the south side of the great library half an hour later, Ivan and Pikel bearing Newander's rigid body and both dwarves and Danica sporting tremendous headaches. The dawn, just breaking, looked so good to Cadderly that he considered it a sign that all had been put right and that the nightmare had ended. His three companions groaned loudly and shielded their eyes when they came out into the brightness.

Cadderly would have laughed at them, but when he turned, the sight of Newander stole his mirth.

* * * * *

"Ah, there you are, Rufo," Headmaster Avery said upon entering the angular man's room. Kierkan Rufo lay on his bed and groaned weakly, pained by the many wounds he had received in the last couple of days and by a pounding headache that would not relent.

Avery waddled over toward him, pausing to belch several times. Avery's head ached, too, but it was nothing compared to the agony in his bloated stomach. "Get up, then," the headmaster said, reaching for Rufo's limp wrist. "Where is Cadderly?"

Rufo did not reply, did not even allow himself to blink. The curse was no more, but Rufo had not forgotten all that he had suffered in the past couple of days, at the hands of both Cadderly and the monk, Danica. He had not forgotten his own actions, either, and he feared the accusations that might be brought against him in the coming days.

"We have so very much to do," Avery went on, "so very much. I do not know what has befallen our library, but it is a very wicked business indeed. There are dead, Rufo, many dead, and many more are wandering confused."

Rufo at last forced himself to a sitting position. His face

was bruised and caked in several places with dried blood, and his wrists and ankles were still sore from the dwarves' bindings.

He hardly thought of the pain at that moment, however. What had happened to him? What had caused him to so foolishly go after Danica? What had caused him to reveal his jealousy, in the form of outright hostility, so clearly to Cadderly?

"Cadderly," he breathed quietly. He had almost killed Cadderly; he feared that memory nearly as much as the potential consequences. His memories came to him as if from a dark mirror in his heart, and Rufo was not certain that he liked what he saw.

* * * * *

"We have been five days with no further incidents," Dean Thobicus said to the gathering in his audience hall a few days later. All the surviving headmasters, of both the Oghman and Deneiran sects, were present, as well as Cadderly, Kierkan Rufo, and the two remaining druids.

Thobicus shuffled through a pile of reports, then declared, "The Edificant Library will recover."

There was a chorus of somewhat subdued cheers and nods.

The future might have looked bright again, but the recent past, particularly the wholesale slaughter of the visiting Ilmater sect and the death of the heroic druid, Newander, could not be so easily dismissed.

"We have you to thank for it," Thobicus said to Cadderly.

"You and your nonsectarian friends—" he nodded an acknowledgment to the druids "—displayed great bravery and ingenuity in defeating the evil infection that came into our midst."

Kierkan Rufo subtly nudged Headmaster Avery.

"Yes?" Dean Thobicus inquired.

"I have been requested to remind us all that Cadderly,

brave though he was, is not without responsibility for this catastrophe," Avery began. He cast a look at Cadderly that
showed he was not angered by the young scholar, but that he
indeed held Cadderly's actions against the invading priest in
high regard.

Cadderly took no offense; after seeing the headmaster
under the influences of the curse, he suspected he knew how
Avery really felt about him. He almost wished that he could
get the headmaster back under the influence of the curse and
talking again about Cadderly's father and the young scholar's
first days at the library.

It was an absurd notion, but one that Cadderly enjoyed
imagining nonetheless. He looked past Avery to the tall and
angular man leering over the headmaster's shoulder. Cadderly could point a finger at Rufo, concerning the man's actions against Danica and himself, and including Cadderly's
firm belief that Rufo was the one who had knocked him into
the catacombs in the first place, but many of Rufo's actions
already had been reported and it was unlikely that, given the
extraordinary circumstances, any action would be taken
against him, or against any of the others caught in the curse.
Cadderly, still not fully understanding what the cursing mist
had done, was not sure if any reprimands would be appropriate.

As to the most serious charge, Cadderly believed that Rufo
had kicked him down the stairs, but he really hadn't seen the
blow. Perhaps the evil priest had been in the wine cellar with
him and Rufo. Perhaps the priest had immobilized Rufo, as he
had Ivan later on, then crept up past the man to knock Cadderly down.

Cadderly shook his head and nearly laughed aloud. It
didn't matter, he believed. Now was a time of forgiveness,
when all the remaining priests must band together to restore
the library.

"Do you find something amusing?" Dean Thobicus asked,
somewhat sternly. Cadderly remembered the accusation

against him then and realized that his introspection might not have been so timely.

"If I may speak," Arcite interjected.

Thobicus nodded.

"The lad cannot be blamed for opening the bottle," the druid explained. "He is a brave one just for admitting such a thing. Let us all remember the foe he battled, one who beat us all, except for a handful. Were it not for Cadderly, and for my friend and god, the evil one would have proved strong enough to win the day."

"True enough," admitted Dean Thobicus, "and true enough, too, that Cadderly must bear some responsibility for what has transpired. Therefore, I declare that young Cadderly's duties in this incident are not at an end. Who would be better than he to study the works we possess concerning such curses, to learn more of the origin of both the priest and this Most Fatal Horror that he described as an agent of Talona?"

"A year quest?" Cadderly dared to ask, though it was not his place to speak.

"A year quest," Dean Thobicus echoed. "At the end of which you are to deliver a full report to this office. Do not take this responsibility lightly, as you seem to take so many of your responsibilities." He went on with his warnings, reminders of the gravity of the situation, but Cadderly didn't even hear him.

He had been given a year quest, an honor normally bestowed exclusively upon the top-ranking Deneiran priests, and one most often given only to the headmasters themselves!

When Cadderly glanced back to Avery, and to Rufo behind him, he saw that they, too, understood the honor he had been given. Avery tried unsuccessfully to hide his widening smile, and Rufo, even more unsuccessfully, to hide his frustration. Indeed, Rufo, surely out of order and surely to be punished for it, turned about and stormed out of the audience chamber.

The meeting was adjourned soon after that, and Cadderly came out flanked by the two druids.

"I thank you," Cadderly said to Arcite.

"It is we who should be grateful," Arcite reminded him. "When the curse befell us all, it was Arcite and Cleo who could not fight against it and who would have been beaten."

Cadderly couldn't hide a chuckle. The druids, and Danica and the dwarves, who had come over to join the group, looked at him curiously.

"It is ironic indeed," Cadderly explained. "Newander thought he had failed because he could not find it in his heart to become as you had, to revert to an animal form in mind and body."

"Newander did not fail," Arcite declared.

"Silvanus held him close," Cleo added.

Cadderly nodded and smiled again, remembering the sincere peace on the departed druid's face. He looked up at Arcite suddenly and thought about the squirrel incident, and whether the druids would know if Newander's departing spirit had communicated through Percival's body. He stopped himself, though, before the question was asked. Maybe some things were better left to the imagination.

"I'll be needing that crossbow of yours, and a dart or two," Ivan said after the druids took their leave. "Figuring to make one for meself!"

Cadderly instinctively reached for the weapon belted on his hip, then recoiled suddenly and shook his head. "No more," he said gravely.

"It's a fine weapon," Ivan protested.

"Too fine," Cadderly replied. He had heard recently of smoke powder, of cannons hurling huge projectiles at opposing armies, elsewhere in the Realms. Avery's scolding, calling Cadderly a "Gondsman," echoed in the young scholar's mind, for rumors claimed it was the Gondish priests who had loosed this new and terrible weapon on the world.

For all that it had aided him, Cadderly did not look upon his crossbow with admiration. The thought of copies being constructed horrified him. Truly, the crossbow's power was meager compared to a wizard's fireball or the summoned lightning of a druid, but it was a power that could fall into the hands of the untrained. Warriors and magic-users alike spent years training both their minds and their bodies to attain such proficiency. Weapons such as smoke powder, and Cadderly's crossbow-and-dart design, circumvented that need of any sacrifice or self-discipline. Cadderly understood that it was that very discipline that held the powers in check.

Ivan started to protest again, but Danica reached around him and covered his mouth with her hand. Ivan pulled away and grumbled a few curses, but he let the matter drop.

Cadderly looked over to Danica, knowing that she understood. For the same reasons that Danica would not show him the Withering Touch, he could not let his design become commonplace.

* * * * *

Druzil waited for a very long time in the smoking stench of the lower planes. He knew that Barjin's gate had been closed again shortly after he left, though he had no way of knowing if the priest had done it intentionally or not. Had Barjin survived? If so, had he found another victim to reopen the cursing flask?

The questions nagged at the imp. Even if Barjin had not succeeded or survived, even if the precious bottle had been destroyed, he knew now the potential for his recipe and vowed that one day the chaos curse would again descend on the Realms.

"Do hurry, Aballister," the imp groaned nervously. The wizard had not summoned him back to the material plane, a fact that the nervous imp could not ignore, particularly since the wizard still possessed the recipe. If Aballister somehow had learned of Druzil's mental connection with Barjin, the wizard might never trust Druzil enough to bring him back.

The imp knew not how many days had passed—time was

measured differently in the lower planes—but finally he heard a distant call, a familiar voice. He saw the distant flicker of a fiery gate and heard the call again, more demanding this time.

Off he soared, through the planar tunnel, and soon he crawled out of Aballister's brazier to stand in a familiar room in Castle Trinity.

"Too long," the imp snorted derisively, trying to gain an upper hand. "Why did you delay?"

Aballister cast a foul look at him. "I did not know that you had returned to the lower planes. My contact with Barjin was broken."

Druzil's long and pointy ears perked up at the mention of the priest, a fact that brought a sneer to Aballister's lips. Across the room, the magical mirror sat broken, a wide crack running its length.

"What happened?" Druzil asked, leading Aballister's gaze to the mirror.

"I overextended its powers," the wizard replied. "Trying to aid Barjin."

"And?"

"Barjin is dead," Aballister said. "He has failed utterly."

Druzil ran a clawed hand along the wall and snarled in distress.

Aballister was more pragmatic. "The priest was too reckless," he declared. "He should have taken more care, should have set his goals on a more vulnerable target. The Edificant Library! It is the most defended structure in all the region, a fortress teeming with mighty priests who would seek our destruction if they learned of our plans! Barjin was a fool, do you hear? A fool!"

Druzil, ever the practical familiar, thought it prudent not to disagree. Besides, Aballister's observations apparently were correct.

"But fear not, my leathery friend," Aballister went on, his attitude becoming more friendly toward his imp. "It is but a minor setback to our cause."

Druzil thought Aballister might be enjoying this just a bit too much. Barjin may have been a potential rival, but he was also, after all, an ally.

"Ragnor and his charges march for Shilmista," Aballister went on. "The ogrillon will win against the elves and sweep south around the mountains. The region will fall to more conventional methods."

Druzil allowed himself a bit of optimism, though he preferred a more insidious attack method, like the chaos curse. "But he was so close, my master," the imp whined. "Barjin had brought the library to its knees. It was his to finish, and then the cornerstone of any resistance we might face would have been gone before the rest of the region even knew the danger in its midst." Druzil clenched a clawed hand before him. "He had victory in his grasp!"

"His grasp was not as strong as he believed," Aballister sharply pointed out.

"Perhaps," Druzil conceded, "but it was that one human, the young man who had first opened the bottle, who came back to defeat him. Barjin should have killed that one right away."

Aballister nodded, remembering the last image he had seen of Barjin's altar room, and could not help but smile.

"Surprisingly resourceful, that one," Druzil sputtered.

"Not so surprising," Aballister replied casually. "He is my son."

Epilogue

He huddled between towering piles of huge tornes, immersed in his important year quest. The security of the Edificant Library was at stake, Cadderly believed, and his ability to discern the source of the chaos curse and the background of the powerful priest would be a critical factor in re-establishing that security.

Cadderly knew that the implications of what had happened might go far beyond the library itself. Carradoon, on the lake to the east, was not a large and well-fortified town, and the elves of Shilmista were neither numerous nor particularly interested in affairs beyond their own borders. If the appearance of the evil priest foreshadowed things to come, then Cadderly's headmasters desperately needed information.

The young scholar alternated his time researching known curses and known symbols. He pored through dozens of tornes and ancient, yellowed scrolls, and interviewed every scholar, host or visitor, who had any knowledge of either field.

The evil priest had proclaimed Talona as his goddess, and the trident symbol was somewhat similar to the Lady of Poison's triangle-and-teardrop insignia, but what particular organization that trident represented, Cadderly could not discover.

Danica watched Cadderly from a distance, not wanting to disturb his vital work. She understood the discipline that Cadderly now needed, the focused determination that excluded everything else, including her, from his days. The young woman was not concerned; she knew that as soon as time permitted, she and Cadderly would continue their relationship.

For Ivan and Pikel, the days passed with wonderful boredom. Both dwarves had been beaten badly in the catacombs, but both were soon well on the way to recovery. Pikel held fast to his resolve to become a druid, and Ivan, after witnessing Newander's heroics, no longer chided him about his choice.

"I'm not thinking a dwarf would make a druid," Ivan huffed whenever anyone asked him about it, "but it's me brother's choice to be making."

So life gradually returned to normal at the proud and ancient library. Summer came on in full and the sunshine seemed like deliverance from the nightmare. Those who came to the library's front doors that season often noticed, basking high in the branches of a tree along the road, a plump white squirrel, usually licking casasa-nut and butter from its paws.

* * * * *

To the elf prince Elbereth, the sun did not seem so marvelous. Rather, it revealed him, leaving him open and vulnerable.

It was a strange feeling for the skilled warrior, who could put four arrows in the air before the first ever hit its mark, and who could cut down an enraged giant with his finely crafted sword.

It was that same warrior training that told Elbereth to be afraid now. A week before, he had led a contingent of elves against a small party of huge and hairy bugbears. His troops had won the encounter quickly, but, unlike the expected rabble filtering down from the wild mountains, these bugbears were well disciplined and well armed, and each wore a glove bearing a similar insignia.

Elbereth had fought in several wars. He knew an advance scouting party when he encountered one.

The determined elf plodded on through the broken mountain passes, leading his weary horse. The multitude of bells on the shining white steed did not ring cheerily in Elbereth's ears, nor did the sun seem so warm. The magic of Shilmista had long been on the wane; Elbereth's proud people were not so numerous anymore. If a major attack did come, Shilmista would be sorely pressed.

Elbereth had left the forest, bearing one of the gloves, to discover what his people might be up against, to the only place in the region where he might learn of his enemies: the Edificant Library.

He looked again at the curious trident-and-bottle design on the glove, then high and far in the distance, to the ivy-strewn structure just coming into view.